THE STAR PRINCE

"Another glorious tale of interstellar romance!"
—PNR Romance Reviews

"An out of this world story you don't want to miss!"
—Scribes World

"A strong take-charge kind of hero, an intelligent, feisty heroine, strange new worlds, adventure, and an eclectic cast of characters . . . I was sorry to see the story end."
—The Best Reviews

THE STAR PRINCESS

"[A] beautiful addition to Ms. Grant's fabulous Star series. The talented Susan Grant has penned another keeper that will have her audience anxiously awaiting their next ride to her fabulous world."
—A Romance Review

"*The Star Princess* is an excellent romance, the relationship between the hero and heroine a delightful sparring match . . ."
—All About Romance

A Royal Dare

"Cole assumed I stayed overnight with you."

Ilana propped her hands on her hips. "Didn't you?"

"In your bed," Ché corrected.

She pulled a bathing towel out of a small closet, waving it in a circle as she tipped her head. "All you had to do was ask." Ché reared back. The inability to form an urbane comeback unbalanced him. This woman was completely outside his experience. The females in his life who weren't family either performed a service, like a courtesan or maid, or were those with whom he was required by etiquette to entertain with charming and safe banter at royal functions: elderly widows, or women married and promised to other men. Ilana unaccountably blurred the lines between peer and object of lust, making her unlike any woman he'd met.

Smiling, she breezed past him, headed for her bedroom. He watched her sweet bottom swaying, and the muscles in her legs flex. He wondered if she knew what pleasure those strong thighs could afford her while making love. He wanted to take her to bed, just to show her.

"Perhaps I *should* have asked, Ilana," he called after her. "But I am Vash, through and through, as you say. As the guest in your home, I would naturally expect any hospitality offered to come from you."

She appeared in the doorway of her bedroom. She'd stripped off her clothing and now held only the towel around her. Pressing it loosely to her breasts, she stepped aside. "The bed's right here. Come on in."

Susan Grant

The Star Princess

LOVE SPELL NEW YORK CITY

For Frank Burrows, Captain, USN, ret.
A fighter pilot to the end. We miss you.

LOVE SPELL®

May 2010

Published by

Dorchester Publishing Co., Inc.
200 Madison Avenue
New York, NY 10016

Copyright © 2003 by Susan Grant

ISBN 10: 0-505-52852-5
ISBN 13: 978-0-505-52852-0
E-ISBN: 978-1-4285-0455-4

The name "Love Spell" and its logo are trademarks of Dorchester Publishing Co., Inc.

Printed in the United States of America.

10 9 8 7 6 5 4 3 2 1

Visit us online at www.dorchesterpub.com.

ACKNOWLEDGMENTS

A writer cannot make the journey alone. My deepest gratitude goes to those who have accompanied me on this wonderful, winding road so far. Special thanks to: my agent Amy Rennert, my editor Christopher Keeslar, and my publisher—for believing in me; Charles De Cuir, for reminding this jet pilot what "buttons to press" in a private plane; Theresa Ragan, friend and B.P.; Jesse Crowder for his filmmaking expertise; Laurie Gold, Pat Holt, Tanzey Cutter, and Jean Marie Ward for their guts in taking up my cause; Emily Cotler and Waxcreative for my gorgeous Web site; my readers for enjoying my stories; my parents Dave and Isabel for cheering me on when I needed it most; and my children, Connor and Courtney, for being the two best kids in the whole world.

The Star
Princess

Chapter One

Prince Ché Vedla woke in his royal bedchamber with last night's courtesan curled against his back. Bedsheets of Nandan silk draped his body from the waist down. A delicate, long-fingered hand rested atop his left hip.

Skilled hands those, Ché acknowledged with a resurgence of heat in his loins. The woman was a pleasure server, and she plied her trade quite well. The trade of pleasuring unmarried males of the royal family was one to which she'd been born, and one which she had subsequently chosen of her own free will as her life's work. But this woman, holding him so possessively, she should know better. Courtesans were to bestow pleasure with skill and passion, but were never to mistake a man's midnight ardor for feelings of greater depth.

His bedmate seemed to have forgotten the latter. It would serve them both well were he not to choose her for a time.

1

Ché rolled onto his back, stretching his arms behind his head. Sighing in her sleep, the pleasure server nestled her cheek into his chest and hugged him tighter, as if he belonged to her.

Did she not know? He belonged to no one. No one but his people. Although, of late, he questioned even that.

Yet he respected women; his upbringing demanded it. His culture protected women, revered them. It didn't matter if a woman was a palace worker or a *Vash* queen, Ché would not treat her with cruelty.

He tapped his bedmate awake. "It is morning, Kajha."

Her eyes shot open. Only for a moment did her elegant face reveal embarrassment at finding herself clinging to his body. Then, quite adeptly, a look of sultry hunger replaced her shock. Ché watched with amused interest as she scratched her fingernails down his chest and over the muscles of his abdomen. "Good morning to you, my lord." A flick of her wrist, and the sheet covering his hips was gone.

He was almost fully erect. Of course, his state of arousal was more a consequence of just having woken than the woman in his bed, but royal courtesans were schooled in every idiosyncrasy of the male body, biological and otherwise. She would have expected to find him hard and ready.

Just as he expected her to take immediate advantage of the circumstance by pleasuring him into forgetting her amateurish little gaffe.

Exhaling, he slid his palms up the woman's smooth, slender arms as she caressed him with her lips and hands. Kajha was no different to him from a fine meal, a rare liqueur, or exquisitely tailored clothing. With her body trained in the art of lovemaking,

2

she was simply another delicacy in a life filled with luxury, a life befitting his family's sacrifices to the realm over the years.

Befitting, indeed. In the distant past, when warlords enslaved most populated worlds, Ché's ancestor was one of eight legendary warriors who led an uprising against their oppressors. When those Dark Years ended, the Eight, made weary by the massive destruction and the horrors they had seen, laid down their arms and declared peace for all time. They founded what was now known as the *Vash Nadah*, a modern form of an ancient monarchy that predated the war. But now there were eight kings—one from Ché's family and each of the other seven clans—and the *Vash Nadah* formed the leadership and moral core of the Trade Federation, a vast league of worlds devoted to profit and peace.

Ché was proud to share the blood of heroes. He didn't feel guilt over the privileges his family had gained as a result, privileges such as Kajha and her clever fingers.

Sprawled on his back, Ché relished the pleasure server's ministrations. Her shoulders rose, and her hair spilled over his stomach, cool and silken, a delightful counterpoint to the sensation of her taking him into her hot, wet mouth.

The courtesan's conscientious attention brought an aching, sweet heat to his loins, and a need for completion that intensified with each stroke of her tongue and gentle scrape of her teeth. He lifted his hips and inhaled in a hiss. He needed no words to articulate his desire. In one graceful move, she straddled his hips and lowered herself onto him.

Nothing equaled the feel of being inside a woman. And what this sensual little creature could do with her inner muscles put her incredible mouth to shame.

He'd certainly had many others with whom to compare her, too. He'd received classroom instruction in the art of lovemaking from his toddler years, although no physical contact had occurred until he turned fourteen. Before a *Vash Nadah* man married, he was allowed as many women as he pleased in order to gain skills designed to bring a partner pleasure, ultimately to strengthen a marriage. *The foundation of society is family. Sexuality enhances spirituality.* That teaching was written in the Treatise of Trade: part social and moral edict and part economic law, an eleven-thousand-year-old document that was an integral part of Ché's culture and his faith.

He sank his fingers into the flesh of the courtesan's hips, arching upward, eliciting from her a cry of pleasure. Her thighs opened wider, an invitation, and his fingers found where she was most sensitive.

A prince of the Vash Nadah does not meet his own needs before those of others.

No, he did not. In bed or otherwise. And Ché was a *Vash* prince, the firstborn son of the Vedlas. Bone-deep ran his sense of duty to his people.

All his people. Even Kajha. He watched her as she rose to her peak and reached it. A telltale pulsing within her body heralded her climax. She gasped and then wailed, her entire body trembling. Then her hair spilled over his chest as her head sagged forward.

An unwanted thought invaded. Was her ecstasy staged, modified by what she perceived he wanted to see and feel, or was it genuine?

He frowned. Bah! Why should he care? Take what she offered, take it all. He rolled her over and threw his head back, his spine arching as he again sank into her. His eyes closed, not engaging her as he tried to

4

lose himself in the pleasure, tried to use her body for what it was designed to do: keeping him satisfied.

He drove hard into her wet, yielding flesh, building toward his release, controlling the pace, the pressure. Controlling it all. *You might as well be doing this to yourself.*

Ah, no. His release burst through him.

He bit back a groan, thrusting into the pleasure server until the last shudders passed. Then, vaguely unsatisfied, he withdrew and rolled onto his back.

Had he just compared lovemaking to masturbation?

The idea was against everything he'd been raised to believe. He knew he'd been out of sorts lately, but his reaction to this round of sex proved it.

Frowning, Ché stared at the ceiling, an ever-changing three-dimensional holographic image of clouds drifting across a windswept sky. It struck him that his own, normally staid and stable life seemed just as changeable of late. The future he'd expected and accepted for so many years had suddenly changed.

Changed, yes. But for the worse or better?

Hell if he knew. He was still trying to figure it out. He wasn't a big fan of introspection, but anything that kept him from fully enjoying life's pleasures was worthy of examination.

Mentally, he sorted the possibilities. For one, he'd lost his betrothed to another man. Princess Tee'ah Dar had broken their vows only months ago. She and Ché had been promised to each other since childhood, but losing her had been more a bruising of the ego than the heart.

No, he hadn't loved the princess. Marriages amongst *Vash Nadah* royalty were arranged as part of a complicated, ongoing stabilizing of power shared by the ruling families. They were political alliances, not love matches—although the *Vash* culture emphasized the importance of good, monogamous marital relations. In fact, *Vash* society was built around such.

Ché should consider himself lucky that he'd been jilted. Yes, indeed. In her rebelliousness, Tee'ah had rescued him from months of tedious wedding preparations. Moreover, who besides an Earth-dweller would want such a wild, undisciplined woman as a wife? Certainly not him.

Absently, he slid his fingers up and down the resting Kajha's arm. If the problem was not that he was suddenly unattached, then what ate at him?

The answer came in his father's voice: *You were robbed twice—the princess, and now your title as crown prince.*

Yes, the demotion from crown prince to standard prince had been somewhat hard to get used to. But he'd gotten over the change in rank. How could he in good conscience lament losing something that was never supposed to be his in the first place? The title of crown prince didn't belong to any son of the Vedlas; it never had.

There were eight royal families. Eight kings. One king held the title of "king of kings," the leader of them all, ruler of the conservative, staunchly pacifistic *Vash Nadah*, a responsibility inherited by first-born sons of the B'kah family—not the Vedlas. It was both tradition and law. Only during those years when it appeared as if the B'kah king would not produce an heir had the Great Council chosen Ché to ascend to the throne.

But now there was a B'kah heir.

Romlijhian B'kah, the "king of kings" had married—a non-*Vash* woman, at that. The queen hailed from

Earth, that newly discovered frontier world which was the latest addition to the Federation.

The event had shocked the clannish *Vash Nadah* to the core. But Rom B'kah was a hero, and not even his tradition-defying, seven-year-old marriage had diminished him in his people's eyes. What the Vedlas and others *had* objected to, however, was the king of kings' new, genetically unqualified heir. If marrying Jasmine Hamilton hadn't been heretical enough, Rom B'kah gained two grown stepchildren in doing so: male-and-female twins. The man was Ian Hamilton, the man who was now crown prince—and the man for whom Princess Tee'ah had broken her promise vows to Ché.

They'd met but once, as children, Ché and Tee'ah. Twice, if he counted their recent brief encounter in the Earth city Los Angeles, where he'd journeyed to keep his brother Klark—who had interfered on his behalf—from getting arrested.

Interfered? Ché's lips quirked in an almost-smile. That was a very *Vash Nadah* way of saying that his brother had tried to assassinate Rom B'kah's Earthborn stepson to reinstate Ché as heir. Klark was lucky Ian hadn't chosen to execute him.

But Earth-dwellers were notoriously tolerant. Ché had learned that. Hotheaded Klark should be grateful that he was now living under the Vedla roof, restricted under palace arrest, rather than weaving rain clouds with the Great Mother in the Ever After.

Ché swung his legs off the bed and sat up, scrubbing one hand over his stubbly jaw. He'd lost the princess to an Earth-dweller and his future to the same man. But feel sorry for himself? Never. He didn't indulge in self-pity, and he didn't tolerate it in others.

Kajha's soft breath fell on his back as she knelt behind him on the mattress. Her strong fingers found the knotted muscles in his neck and shoulders. Silent, she began kneading them with her thumbs and the heels of her palms. The kiss on the side of his throat was an obvious invitation for more sex play, but when he didn't respond, she interpreted his lack of interest correctly and spent her energy on his massage.

Eyes closed, he leaned into the pleasure server's hands and pondered Ian Hamilton.

To his surprise, Ché had found that he actually liked the Earth-dweller. Ché was the first of the *Vash* princes to vow allegiance to the new crown prince, and the two men in fact spoke quite frequently of late. It was the beginning of a friendship, one that transcended their vastly different backgrounds. Which was why Ché believed Ian when the man confessed that he hadn't known Tee'ah was *Princess* Tee'ah when they'd first met on a godforsaken planet in the frontier.

As for Ian Hamilton's twin sister Ilana . . . that was different. Ché wasn't sure what he thought of her— only that he had, on and off for months now. Atop that roof in Los Angeles, they hadn't exchanged a single word; Ché had been too busy trying to keep his brother and hers from killing each other.

However, he did recall several details: how she'd alternately amused and bemused him; how her eyes were the precise color of Earth's odd-colored sky; how the wind had tangled her thick, shoulder-length hair.

Ché frowned. Never mind the wind; he'd wager Ilana preferred her hair in perpetual disarray. At her scalp, the strands were as dark as her twin brother's— brown, a shade rare amongst the fair-headed *Vash*. But the rest of what resembled an old-fashioned cleaning mop ranged from dark blond to platinum, falling in twists and snarls around her face and over her shoulders.

What would those tangled strands feel like, he wondered, passing between his fingers . . . ?

His fingers twitched; then Ché pushed aside the thought. An uncultured frontierswoman, she was. Totally unsuitable. Yes. Undisciplined and willful. In fact, in his urbane and educated opinion, Ilana Hamilton stood as the shining example of the *opposite* of everything he'd ever want in a woman.

Yes. That had to be the reason. Why else would thoughts of her have clung to his mind all these months like a convulsed sand tick?

"Lord Ché?"

He turned his head. Nude, kneeling behind him, her thighs pressed together, her hands clasped, Kajha appeared unsure, as if she thought she'd disappointed him in some way. She had, but it was not her fault.

He smoothed her silken hair, cupped her young face. "I thank you for the blessed gift of your body," he said kindly, falling back on traditional words, safe words, recitations from the Treatise of Trade.

Does not your life feel like a script, as well? Ché shook off the thought.

"Would you like me to take my leave now, Lord Ché?"

"Yes. Please."

The courtesan smiled with shyness. Another practiced skill, he thought. No pleasure servant with such a repertoire of sexual acrobatics could be shy.

Kajha gathered her robes around her. When she had ducked out of the chamber, Ché walked to the bathing pool, prepared for him by an unseen silent-footed servant. As he sank deep into the scented water, steam rose, obscuring not only the trappings of luxury all around him but his life from his own fruit-less rumination.

Afterward, dressed in the traditional way, a soft shirt and trousers tucked into gleaming, knee-high boots, Ché took his solitary morning meal on the spacious balcony that jutted out two hundred feet above the shoreline. Only for evening meals did his large family gather. Their dinners were elaborate affairs that lasted often late into the night. This morn, however, he preferred solitude.

Below, the sea appeared endless—and it nearly was, covering roughly eighty percent of the planet Eireya's surface. After an evening of rain, the water shimmered under a fair-weather lavender sky. On the horizon, palace craft trolled for various deep-sea delicacies.

Ché sat at a large round table. Servants laid out a variety of covered bowls containing numerous hot and cold foods. Sipping a cup of steaming tock, he unfurled a flexible computer screen and began reading the Federation news.

Hoe, his advisor, strode across the balcony. "Good day, my lord," the man called cheerily. "How are you this fine morning?"

Ché thought about that. He'd had a good night's sleep framed by good sex, and yet. . . . "I feel quite, ah, acceptable."

Hoe took a seat next to him at the table. The man had worked for him since Ché was a boy. They were almost like family. He could take such liberties.

Ché sat back to listen to the man's morning report. One item seemed rather out of place: "Word has reached us that the invitations have gone out, my lord, announcing Ian Hamilton-B'kah's wedding to

Tee'ah Dar. This was done earlier than what etiquette normally dictates."

Ché swallowed more tock and set down his cup. "It is not that surprising. There will be thousands of guests in attendance, and much to prepare." And he was glad he wasn't part of it. He returned his attention to his news screen. "Now . . . where are the Bajha championship scores?" he muttered, scrolling downward.

"It is said that the B'kahs have invited Earth royalty to the event, my lord, as well as high-ranking members of their government."

"Entertain my sisters with these social tidbits, Hoe," Ché snapped. "And my mother, the queen, and her staff, as well. They will love nothing more than to chat with you about the B'kah arrangements. Not me." He turned his attention back to the Bajha scores.

"I thought you would find it of interest, my lord."

The man spoke as if he disapproved of Ché's reaction. "By the heavens, Hoe. Can I not enjoy a few moments of peace at breakfast without mentions of the B'kah wedding intruding?"

Hoe deflated. For unfathomable reasons, Ché's reaction troubled him.

Lifting his tock cup back to his lips, Ché contemplated his advisor through a cloud of fragrant steam. With the king away on government business, Ché was the ranking male of the household. His days were filled with details and duties related to that responsibility. The B'kah wedding was a subject bordering on frivolity—frivolity for which he did not have the time or the interest. Yet, his reluctance to discuss the matter seemed to leave Hoe in such despair that Ché felt compelled to say something to cheer the man.

"So," he amended pleasantly. "The invitations to the wedding of the year have gone out. Good, good.

I am pleased for the happy couple. Truly. Now, shall we see which of last night's teams were victorious?" He turned back to his screen.

He heard Hoe's comm beep. The man took the call and a moment later said, "Four councilmen are waiting to speak with you, my lord."

Ché took his personal computer out of his pocket and checked its agenda. "I know nothing of a visit from any councilmen."

"Nothing was scheduled, my lord. They arrived during the night. What they wish to discuss, they say, is a matter of utmost importance to the realm. But I had them wait until morning. I did not wish to wake you."

You might as well have, Ché thought. He certainly hadn't left his bed this morning rested or satisfied.

In the foyer off the balcony, four tall shadows milled about. Ché asked: "The Council is in full session. Don't they have duties? In addition, my father is at the Wheel." That five-thousand-year-old space station was the seat of the Federation government, and where the Great Council convened. It was many light-years away.

"They say that there are no matters so important to the Vedlas as this one."

"What one?" Ché asked.

Hoe cleared his throat. The man was transparent; his odd and irritating behavior revealed his discomfort with whatever issue the council members had come to discuss. "Well . . . ah," the advisor stammered. "It seems it may be something to do with the . . . B'kah wedding ceremony."

Ché gave him a withering look. "I hope you're joking."

Hoe replied with a weak laugh. "Shall I summon them?"

12

Ché waved his hand. "Please."

Hoe gave a curt nod and strode across the balcony.

Ché couldn't fathom the reason behind this absurd turn of events, but he couldn't shake the unsettling feeling that he wasn't going to like it.

Hoe returned with the four visitors. Each of the eight families sent forty representatives to the Great Council. Those representing Ché's family were considered the most traditionalist and conservative of the group, and had been for eons. Of all those who had protested the appointment of an Earth-dweller as crown prince, the Vedlas had protested the loudest. Defeat had not gone down easy.

They stopped a respectful distance away. With practiced grace, each went down on one knee. Heads bent, the four men brought their right fists to their chests, their eyes downcast.

"Rise," Ché told them.

They did as he asked, shaking out their travel cloaks. Lavender morning sunlight fell across the black fabric.

An austere gentleman stepped forward. It was said he'd been a handsome man when he was younger, the talk of the ladies at court, but age had thinned his bronzed skin, sharpened his features, and his golden brows grew long and curling. He reminded Ché of a goth-hawk.

"Greetings, Lord Ché."

"Councilman Toren," Ché replied. Everyone knew Toren. Many even liked him. He was a virulent traditionalist. Ché supposed he could find no fault with that. Someone had to uphold the old ways. "What business brings you here when the council is in session?"

Ché detected the barest of stiffening in Toren's shoulders. "It is not an official visit, my lord."

Ah. Ché glanced at Hoe, who stared pointedly at the toes of his boots. "Am I to take that to mean my father, the king, does not know that you've come?"

"This is a matter of utmost importance to the Ved-las, and to the realm," Toren countered.

A non-answer. In other words, his father did not know the men had come.

Toren's fingers tugged at the cape falling over his shoulders. "Lord Ché, we come to you with the Fed-eration's best interests at heart."

"My brother Klark thought he had the Federation's interests at heart when he sought to murder Ian Ham-ilton."

Toren glanced back uneasily at his associates.

Calmly Ché brought his cup of tock to his lips and leaned back in his chair, blowing gently on the steam-ing beverage.

"You are considered by many to be one of the most promising young princes of your generation, Lord Ché. It is important that you continue to build upon that reputation."

"I certainly am not trying to do otherwise, Toren," he returned dryly.

"You are single, an unmarried man."

"Yes, I am." Ché thought of the courtesan . . . and her mouth. "And I enjoy my bachelorhood."

"As you know, the B'kah wedding will take place at the end of the year. The invitations have gone out. Two, perhaps three thousand guests are expected, from all over the galaxy."

Ché sat up straight, his hands flat on the table. "Great Mother, Toren," he growled, though in the back of his mind he suspected that calling on a fe-male deity wasn't going to offer him much help. "What happened to the days when males of our spe-cies gathered to discuss political machinations, trade

14

issues, and sporting events? All I've heard this morning is talk of a wedding. Will we chat about couture next? Or the presentation of cuisine?"

He sagged back in his chair and rubbed his forehead. "Or perhaps I'm to be asked to help choose which morsels the cooks should add to tonight's petit fours," he muttered irritably.

Toren puffed himself up. He was a formidable man. Thus, it followed that his puffing would be formidable, as well. Ché was not impressed.

"My lord, the princess is marrying an Earth-dweller!"

"For the love of heaven, I wouldn't care if she were marrying a morning fly, Toren. In fact, in all honesty I'm grateful she found someone other than me. At least I won't be the one saddled with an undisciplined princess for a wife."

Toren's feathery brows only half hid the disgust in his eyes. "Hamilton is a man who not long ago was considered a barbarian. He still is, in some circles."

"Which circles, Toren?" Ché brought his hand down hard on the table. The saucers there bounced. The tinkle of silverware echoed on the silent balcony, far above the hiss of the sea.

Toren shifted his weight from one foot to the other. "I exaggerated, my lord. My apologies."

"We are trying to rebuild trust in our family, Councilman. It has not been an easy task. We can't afford more Vedla interference in lawful politics." He held Toren's gaze. "Or marriages. The decision to allow Hamilton to marry the princess was made months ago. Rom B'kah himself approved it. The entire Federation supports it. It would not be wise for us, the Vedlas, to question it. Do not forget that my brother is under palace arrest for attempted assassination. We are lucky to have him still alive. You can thank 'the barbarian' for that, for interceding on our behalf, as Rom B'kah certainly might have been harder on Klark. We owe Hamilton our gratitude."

"Yes, my lord."

"Prince Ian Hamilton will marry Princess Tee'ah Dar, and we, the Vedlas, will not interfere. That is our official family stand on the matter. If you hear opinions to the contrary from your circles," Ché said with disdain, "you will inform me. Is that clear? And I will see that the subversives in question never hold political office again."

Toren swallowed. "Yes, my lord."

Ché took his gaze from the council members' only after a long moment. Then he laced his fingers over his stomach and let himself relax somewhat. "Now, what is it that you require of me?"

"To marry, my lord."

Ché winced, rubbing his temples. The morning's dissatisfying sexual encounter must have been an omen. "Of course I intend to marry." Then he twisted one corner of his mouth into a conspiratorial, man-to-man grin. "Sooner or later. Later is far preferable to sooner."

Toren didn't appear to share Ché's enthusiasm for the single life. "We in the Great Council are actively searching out your queen."

"You and my mother both," Ché agreed. He spoke in a pleasant tone to blunt the sarcasm that begged to boil forth.

"Fear not that we will find you a mate suitable for your position and status."

"I have the fullest confidence that your hunt will prove fruitful," Ché replied, lifting his cup of tock to his mouth. "But, please, take your time. No need to rush matters. I am quite content with my status as it is."

"But you see, Lord Ché, you *must* marry. And you must marry now."

Ché almost inhaled his swallow. He started coughing. Hoe ran over and started thumping him on the back. "Now?" Ché croaked.

"As soon as possible," Toren clarified. "Your nuptials must take place before that of the crown prince. Then it will look less as if you, a pure-blooded *Vash Nadah*, lost out to an outsider."

Hoe tried to dab at Ché's mouth with a napkin. Ché ripped the cloth out of his advisor's hand and tossed it onto the table. "You want me to race Ian Hamilton to the altar? The idea is ludicrous. How can it be seen as anything but a crude display of *Vash Nadah* one-upmanship?"

Toren began pacing in a small circle, his hand curled under his square, cleft chin. Then he halted, lifting an inquisitive golden brow. "You like Ian Hamilton, yes?"

Ché paused to consider his answer before verbalizing it. The council member's gaze was calculating. Toren had served more than twice the number of years in the Great Council than Ché had been alive. Ché would have liked to answer in the unhesitating affirmative regarding his opinion of Ian Hamilton, but it wasn't that simple. In preparation for the day that his father retired from hands-on rule of the Vedla kingdom and assumed Treatise-directed duties as an elder of the Great Council, Ché had to continue to build trust and support in the men who would ultimately serve him—Toren included. Above all, he must never appear to take Vedla family values lightly.

"I've sworn *allegiance* to Hamilton," Ché clarified. "Upon that vow I base my actions. It is he who will rule the Federation, along with the other princes and me. It is he we will work with when we ascend to our respective thrones with the intent to preserve peace and stability." He warned, "Personal feelings one way or the other have nothing to do with it."

"Then marry quickly," Hoe interjected, almost pleading. "That way you can arrive at the B'kah wedding with a lovely, pedigreed *Vash Nadah* bride on your arm, a princess, of course, perhaps even by then pregnant with your—"

"*Pregnant!*"

"Your marrying will allow the *Vash Nadah* to save face without appearing to counter the king's decree," Toren explained. "It will alleviate much of the resentment now focused on Ian Hamilton."

Ché's outrage at his advisor's brazen, ill-mannered presumption faded like a lit cigar in a sudden downpour. He fell back in his chair, his anger fizzling as he considered Councilman Toren's observation: *It will alleviate much of the resentment focused on Ian Hamilton.*

Truer words had never been spoken. Many old-school, conservative *Vash Nadah* saw Princess Tee'ah's breach of promise as an insult to the royal bloodlines that ran all the way back to the godlike warriors of their distant past. If Ché married first, as the council member had so audaciously suggested, it would send the signal that *Vash* superiority remained intact. After all, Ché had been slated to marry before the B'kah heir from the beginning, before there ever was a B'kah heir. By doing as the councilmen suggested, marrying before Ian, things would remain as they were supposed to be—would they not?

The *Vash Nadah* liked things as they were supposed to be. Ché had to admit he did, too.

Most of the time.

"The blood of the Eight flows through your veins, my lord. This brings responsibilities, obligations, cir-

18

cumstances you might not have chosen on your own," Toren said with sudden gravity, clearly misinterpreting Ché's brooding for refusal. "The Treatise of Trade tells us: 'The eight royal families lead through sacrifice and example.' "

The condescension in the man's tone stunned Ché.

He narrowed his eyes. His voice was low and deadly. "I am quite familiar with my obligations, Councilman." He might not have guessed how quelling his glare was if Toren hadn't blanched.

"Did you truly think otherwise, Councilman?" Ché continued. "Did you think me weak of will because I was the first of the princes to ally myself with Ian Hamilton?"

"No, my lord!" The older man's expression was one of sincere dismay. He knew that he'd stepped over a line.

Good. In time, Toren and the others must learn to think of him as a man of power rather than the boy he once was. To succeed at that goal, Ché would never let them forget the king he would someday become.

"Klark had nothing to do with this plan, did he?" he wondered aloud after a moment.

"No. Your brother knows nothing of this. He has been left out of all communication since the incident on Earth—as you ordered."

Ché could usually tell if someone was lying to him. The ability served him well in the often-treacherous arena of *Vash* politics, which he'd navigated since his late-teen years. His gut told him that Toren was telling the truth: Klark was not an instigator in this marriage race.

At least the Vedla family's core of idealistic traditionalists was adhering to the rules of Klark's house arrest. His brother was to stay at home and out of all

19

politics until such time it was determined that he was suitably rehabilitated—a goal for which Ché held himself personally accountable. "Reparation, atonement—those are the words we Vedlas must live by. No more disruption, or we will find ourselves the pariahs of the *Vash Nadah*." He directed a hard and searching stare at each council member in turn. "I swear it—I will not allow my family to be left behind while the rest of the Federation moves toward a future that demands flexibility. If we cling to our old ways while everyone else moves forward, we will become artifacts. Instead of building influence, we will gather dust. Is that clear?"

A chorus of "Yes, my lord," met his question.

"I will do my part. I will marry, as you have asked, before the crown prince says his vows. I will not fail my people." Ché brought his fist to his chest and bowed his head in the traditional *Vash* show of steadfastness. "You have my word as a descendant of the Eight."

A ripple of hushed sounds of relief went between the councilmen. The loss of his bachelorhood was a small price to pay for continued galactic stability, Ché reasoned.

Heaven help him.

"How long do I have?" Ché asked the councilmen, as if he were inquiring about the date of his execution.

"A wife should be chosen and a promise officially announced within three standard months," Toren replied. "That will give us time to rush through an arrangement and draw up the paperwork before the B'kah wedding takes place in seven months."

"A four-month betrothal period." Ché folded his arms over his stomach. "Engagements, by law, are supposed to run for one full standard year."

"We have found a way around that. Princess Tee'ah breached her promise with you several weeks *before* you were to have signed the marriage contract—which is what would have set the one-year clock ticking." Toren's eyes glinted. "Since that year was never legally commenced, as soon as we find your wife we'll backdate the new marriage contract to allow for a year's time."

Many late nights had gone into dreaming up this scheme. On the surface it looked simple. But it was not. More rules had to be broken than just what related to timing. Taking into account the intricacies of tradition, Ché couldn't help admiring the creativity and thoroughness with which these council members had devised a plan. Obviously, while he had been indulging in courtesans, these men were masterminding his future.

Ché combed his fingers through his close-cropped hair and sighed. There was a problem: "Aside from the current pack of four-year-olds"—royal *Vash* offspring were matched up at five—"all the eligible women are already promised."

"We have ways around that, as well," Toren assured him.

Ché's mouth twisted ruefully. "We Vedlas certainly have our ways of getting things done," he said. He shook his head. "I can see it now—young princesses across the galaxy dreading that they will be the chosen one, the unfortunate girl sobbing as she is brought to me, a virgin sacrifice to the spurned Vedla prince."

Toren didn't share his smile.

Ché ran his fingers through his hair again. "Is there anything else?" he asked Toren.

The councilmen all shook their heads.

Ché stood, muttering to his hovering, openly sympathetic advisor, "I cannot believe I have been sitting here arranging my own marriage over tock and pastries."

The whole business was rather depressing.

He walked to the edge of the balcony. There, he clasped his hands behind his back and gazed out to sea as the council members conferred in hushed voices behind him, working out the finer details of his future.

He tried to conjure recollections of the eligible women, princesses, and ladies—virgins all—that he'd met at court on his world and abroad over the years. None came to mind. All were lost in a blur of stilted conversations made while sipping expensive liqueurs and wearing stiff ceremonial uniforms. Not one woman had conjured in him more than a passing interest.

But, then, he'd been promised. He hadn't been looking at the women as marriage candidates, or perhaps he would have viewed them differently, considered each as the possible mate to whom he'd be faithful for the rest of his life, the woman who would share his bed, her body, their children. His heirs.

He wondered offhandedly if he'd come to love the woman Toren and his cronies chose for him. His parents, while not demonstrative of affection as some couples were outside their private chambers, appeared to have come to respect and love each other after many years together.

And what did they, his parents, think of this plan? Toren said he'd come here without the knowledge of Ché's father, the Vedla king, but Ché suspected otherwise. The king was a Vedla in the truest sense of the word; he'd want the historical superiority of the family to remain intact. He would not disapprove of this meddling.

Meddling? Rather, it was planning. That was the better term, yes. Ché's life had always been predetermined by others, mapped out from start to finish, even before his birth. He operated on the principle of duty over personal desires. *The good of the people outweighs that of the individual.* It said so in the Treatise of Trade. He followed that document to the letter, lived the prescribed life, pleased his elders, all with the amelioration of an opulent lifestyle.

An opulent lifestyle that had become curiously bland.

The sea glimmered in soft tones under a muted pale purple sky. Eireya was an endless, wide-open panorama, and yet he felt so very penned in.

Ché turned his attention back to the councilmen huddled together with his advisor. The scene typified his life's perpetual condition, the constant coddling and others' desire to please him, their relentless scrutiny. He wouldn't mind escaping it all for a time before he surrendered to it for the remainder of his very public life.

His pulse jumped. This was perfect timing for a get-away, actually. His father would soon be home and would take over responsibility for the household. Palace security would continue to monitor Klark. Ché's presence at the palace would not be needed for weeks, likely months.

Yes, this wife-hunting would take the councilmen far longer than they thought, what with the intricate promises and alliances binding the eight families together, and the fact that all of their maneuvering would have to be done under the cloak of utmost secrecy. It would not do to have it appear to the entire *Vash Nadah* that the rejected Vedla prince had to beg for a bride. Their predicament would give Ché plenty of time to take one last swing around the galaxy before he found himself tied down for good with a woman he may not like but was required by law to worship and protect.

And yet, where could he go? A *Vash* resort didn't hold appeal. He sought a reprieve from this pampered lifestyle he'd come to find tedious. He also didn't want something too remote or primitive. He enjoyed an escape, yes, but appreciated a hot bath and a fine meal at the end of it.

He lifted his hand, tapping one finger against his lips. And then it came to him—a world that wasn't at the edge of civilization, but close enough to have a view of it:

Earth.

A quick triumphant laugh escaped him. Earth was the last place his staff would dream of finding him, living amongst its "barbarians." And plaguing him from the day he'd returned to Eireya was the sense he'd left Earth without exploring or experiencing all he might have wanted.

An image he held of Earth's blue sky coalesced into a pair of eyes of an equally unusual, arresting hue. Ilana Hamilton, the crown prince's sister, lived on Earth. The world rather fascinated him, its brashness, its novelty, its spirit.

Does Earth fascinate you, or does the woman?

Ché's mouth compressed. They'd met but once! Or, more correctly, they'd *seen* each other once. They were strangers, connected by a highly irregular string of events. Oddly, the same events now led him back to her. Certainly, she'd remember him. She'd remember Klark.

A shadow passed briefly over Ché's good cheer. Perhaps he should ask Ian to intercede on his behalf, to notify Ilana of his visit. Decorum demanded it, in fact. But surely the woman would be amenable to showing him to a suitable temporary habitat without her brother's intervention. Ché didn't want to tip his hand or cause a huge political situation.

He'd have to give the matter some thought. Either way, he knew where and how to find Ilana. She dwelled in the Earth city of Los Angeles, and Vedla intelligence would know the precise location of her abode. It would be in the controlled-access database, and Ché would be able to find the information without arousing curiosity.

There, on the most godforsaken world he knew, he would lose the persona of prince without sacrificing too many comforts, and sort out his life in a blessedly anonymous fashion. Then, when he returned to Eireya, he'd be ready to good-naturedly beat Ian Hamilton-the-Earth-dweller-crown-prince to the altar in the name of *Vash* superiority.

Chapter Two

Ilana Hamilton sat in her car clutching a hand-delivered, surprisingly old-fashioned, gilt-edged wedding invitation. She'd finally gotten brave. Or was it desperate? Either way, she'd pulled the letter from her purse—the letter that had languished unopened on her kitchen counter all week, while a small, silly, irrationally optimistic part of her had hoped that denying its presence would cause the letter to vanish without a trace. Instead, it had loomed over her personal happiness like an executioner's axe.

She swallowed, her skin tingling. It wasn't the wedding that was the problem; she'd love to see her twin brother tie the knot. It was the getting-there part she couldn't deal with. Attending the wedding meant—she squeezed her eyes shut—*flying to another planet.* Yet another freaky moment in a life that read like front-page, tabloid news in the *National Enquirer.*

It hadn't always been this way.

When extraterrestrials made contact with Earth, life

26

changed forever for everyone on the planet—but Ilana's life had to have changed more than anyone else's. Her divorced mother had married one of the aliens, Romlijhian B'kah, who'd turned out to be a king—the ruler of the entire galaxy. Even seven years after the fact, it still sounded bizarre. It probably always would. But Jas was happy, happier that Ilana had ever seen her, and Ilana loved her stepfather for that. Rom had no children, but treated Ilana and her twin brother Ian as his own, even going as far as choosing Ian as his heir. Which meant Ian would take Rom's place someday. Her dorky hunk of a brother: ruler of the galaxy. Fact, not fiction.

Ilana's lips thinned. She stared at the sealed envelope in her hands. Now another extraterrestrial was joining the family.

Ian's fiancée was a head-to-toe rebel who'd knocked the stuffing out of his shirt—a lot of it, anyway—and had showed the guy how to *live*, something Ilana had never been able to do for her dear, way-too-serious, four-minutes-older big brother . . . though not for lack of trying.

Ilana's stomach clenched. Her brother's marriage would take place in the same palace on Sienna where her mother had exchanged vows with Rom. Ilana hadn't returned there in all the years since. When she'd landed back on Earth, she could have kissed the ground. That the "ground" was the greasy, sun-baked tarmac at LAX said it all. Barfing for a week each way while stoned on valium and seasickness patches had been a singularly horrific experience that she didn't care to repeat. Ever.

Fortunately, politics brought Jas and sometimes Rom to Earth and Los Angeles at least once a year. From those visits and conversations using the three-dimensional image-phone installed in her condo, Ilana kept in touch with the family she missed . . . the family who thought that her budding career didn't allow the time off that a trip to Sienna required. The family that thought she was a workaholic and didn't know the pitiful truth. The family that didn't know Ilana Hamilton was a fear-of-flying school dropout.

She tipped her head back, digging her fingers into her hair and holding it away from her face. She had to get over this; she had to. She wasn't a sissy about anything else in her life. She was in control, even daring. But not when it came to boarding a spaceship. She'd tried hypno-therapy, clinics, and classes—even "Fly Without Fear For Dummies." What fearful flyer could resist a sixteen-week class with a name like that?

It was with high hopes and a dry mouth that she'd gone to that first meeting. All was fine until the instructors began to describe the end-of-course field trip, a flight out of LAX, gushing on and on about how much fun the class would have celebrating their new-found guaranteed-in-writing ability to survive airplane flying. Ilana was close to hyperventilating.

Flying the friendly skies of United was a completely different ball game from launching her puny, candy-ass, five-foot-seven body into space in something that looked like a triangular, stainless-steel Frisbee. But she didn't see the point in hanging around to explain, so she left.

Er, fled, actually. Dashed to her car, where she'd huddled until she'd calmed down enough to drive home. The memory alone made Ilana's breathing shallow and fast. Pride kept her from admitting that to anyone.

She slid her hand onto the passenger seat, searching for a bag of nacho-cheese-flavored Corn Nuts like a chain-smoker groping for a pack of cigarettes. The salty snacks looked and tasted like fossilized corn, but they were healthier than other vices she could name and lower in calories than a container of Ben and Jerry's New York Super Fudge Chunk ice cream.

Eating them soothed her nerves. Nerves, she knew, that were going to be further frayed once she opened the wedding invitation.

It was time.

She opened the car door and swung her legs out, sitting there for a moment until the butterflies in her stomach settled. Then, glumly, she stood and climbed an iron staircase that scaled the outside of a renovated warehouse, her backless, red patent leather shoes clanging as she did.

On the second floor, she flung open the main door to SILF Filmworks—the film company she owned with three friends: Slavica, Leslie, and Flash—and walked inside. The scene that met her was typical, everyone busy with post-production tasks related to the short film they'd recently wrapped. Ilana had a pile of possible future projects waiting on her desk, but she'd get to that later.

After her private pity-party.

Her shoes click-clacked over a polished, high-gloss concrete floor that screamed the truth of the studio's warehouse origins and yet made it trendy. But it also made it very hard to walk in flat, slippery-soled mules without mincing like a geisha.

Ilana clutched the envelope and bag of Corn Nuts to her chest, her eyes focused on the quiet corner where she planned to indulge her bad mood. She wasn't about to feel guilty about it, either. She was entitled to a little moping. It wasn't as if she did it very often. She was impulsive, volatile, and fickle, according to a now ex-boyfriend, but not moody.

She climbed onto a tall seat that had been a bar stool in another life. A stool in a biker bar. In the bad part of town. When they'd first rented this studio, all she and his friends could afford were garage-sale and bankruptcy-liquidation furnishings. No one felt they'd made enough profit yet to justify giving up the original furniture, although they'd probably keep most of it for sentimental reasons once they moved on to a bigger and better space. "Never forget your roots," Slavica always said.

Roots. Ilana frowned. Hers had been ripped out and transplanted. Her father lived in Las Vegas, her mother and brother in space.

Space, she thought, glowering at the envelope. With the back of her hand, she shoved her hair out of her eyes, blowing away any stragglers with pursed lips. Her earrings swayed as she shook her head, fluffing out the rest of her hair. Then, taking a deep breath, she tore open the envelope. The ornate gold-engraved invitation lay open in her lap like a cracked oyster with no pearl:

His Majesty King Romlijhian B'kah
and
Her Royal Highness Queen Jasmine Boswell
Hamilton B'kah
request the honor of your presence at the
Marriage
of
Ian Hamilton B'kah, Crown Prince of Sienna
with
The Princess Tee'ah Dar

Ilana read through the entire invitation, from the gorgeous royal seal on top to the last of the events on the bottom of the second page that she'd be required to attend as sister to the groom, days before and after the actual ceremony. But those events weren't what upset her; she'd been through them before. She could deal with the receptions and the receiving lines, the constant changing of outfits and the hobnobbing with galactic royalty and diplomats, some of whom even spoke English. It was the getting there that she didn't want to think about.

She sagged in her seat. The wedding was in early December. It was already July. The clock, as they say, was ticking.

Her stomach did a somersault. Quickly she tossed a Corn Nut into her mouth, careful to suck off the salt before chewing. Repositioning her backside on the stool, she crossed her left leg over her right. Her foot bobbed. Her backless shoe wobbled, clinging to her big toe. When she was anxious, she fidgeted. It drove some people crazy. But that went both ways: anyone that easily irritated drove her crazy, too.

She lifted her gaze and studied the others in the big room. These were people who knew her better than most, but even they didn't realize how thwarted she was by the idea of traveling to her brother's wedding, because pride kept her from revealing it. Ilana's friends knew her as someone who wasn't afraid of risk. They thought of her as a gutsy, take-charge chick. And that's the way she wanted it to stay.

She'd known Slavica, Leslie, and their male partner Flash since being freshmen at UCLA's renowned film school. In the five years since graduation, they'd all worked for others, but now they worked for themselves. It was something of which they were all proud.

The Holt film was a step up for them, too. Until now, their projects had been much smaller. Going big meant bucks. They could have done it sooner, but maxing out their credit cards, taking second mortgages, and begging friends and family for cash—like so many of the struggling independents they knew had done—wasn't the route they'd wanted to take. The lure was strong; it wasn't easy finding investors who'd throw tens or even hundreds of thousands of dollars into an independent film. Sure, they could occasionally cut sweetheart deals for crew and equipment, but there were certain costs associated with filmmaking that you just couldn't get around: production insurance, transportation, meals, sound mixing, a lab to process the movie. And they hadn't wanted to cut those corners or sacrifice quality.

Then they'd lucked out: the Holt camp had wanted this documentary made, and had agreed to support it financially without stealing the freedom to explore the actor's imperfections.

There had been a lot of pressure, making the leap to the big time, but Ilana's friendship with Slavica, Leslie, and Flash translated well into their relationship as business partners. Everything had worked out fine. So far. They'd created *Dust*, a documentary following the movie star and former drug addict Hunter Holt's laborious road to recovery. The film had done well at the regional festivals, and if it gained buzz at Sundance, the most prestigious of them all, it would win them notice on the national level. Everyone in the business knew that more notice meant more money. Money meant the ability to hire better actors, and access to better projects.

Things didn't always work out, Ilana had seen. Business ventures broke up friendships. And marriages. Not that she had her eye on *that* particular gamble anytime soon. Unlike her brother.

Brother. Wedding. Space. Flying. Nightmare.

Ah! Ilana's fingers closed convulsively around her bag of Corn Nuts, crushing it. She pressed her knuckles to her thigh. "I really don't want to do this," she said. "I don't want to go."

Leslie spoke without taking her eyes off a publicity trailer she'd created for *Dust*. "Do what?"

"Ian's wedding," Ilana said.

"You have to go. He's your brother."

"I know," Ilana wailed.

All that her juvenile whining won her was a moment of long-suffering silence.

When it came to her fabulously rich stepfamily, from which she stubbornly accepted no financial backing, Ilana didn't expect much pity from her friends. She had access to any party, any club. If she wanted, she could socialize with anyone from the King of England to rock stars, all because of who her stepfather was. But the idea of hanging out with people who opened their doors to her only to gain influence with her family was so obnoxious that it was a struggle to come up with words sleazy enough to describe it. Still . . .

"A little sympathy would be nice," she complained.

Leslie observed her with perceptive green eyes ringed in smoky gray pencil. "I don't see why you're stressing about it now. It's not like you didn't know it was coming."

"Yes, I did." Ilana agreed. "But now every detail is embedded in my brain." She dusted salt off her tight, dark-blue jeans, sucking on another Corn Nut. "It amazes me. Supposedly sane people calling me to debate the merits of old lace versus new, hot appetizers versus cold"—she counted off the most recent crimes on her fingers—"whether Uncle Frank will mind sitting across from his ex-wife's godchild, and if having yellow tulips in the centerpieces will clash with white wine. And then acting as if every single person in the free world cares!"

Slavica laughed and put in, "It's called wedding fever, baby. And you'd better watch out." She lifted up her left hand. A ring twinkled in the overhead halogen lighting. "It's contagious."

Ilana snorted. "I have a natural immunity." Her parents' failed relationship would have turned even Cupid into a cynic on the subject of commitment. "That's not the issue, though. Getting to the wedding is."

"I thought they had a private jet," Slavica said.

"They have a *spaceship*." Sweat prickled between her breasts. "A fleet of them."

Flash regarded her from where he relaxed in a chair on the opposite side of the room. His hair was jet black and his eyes were blue—a killer combination. It was probably why she'd fallen into bed with him their sophomore year at UCLA. It hadn't taken much more in those days to charm the pants off her. She was a little more circumspect now—by her standards, which never seemed to match anyone else's— but one thing she had with Flash Giordano that she didn't with any of her other former flings was a lasting friendship.

"I thought you went to a class last week," he said. His legs were propped on a sad little ottoman, one foot crossed over the other. He'd been reading a script and only now gave any indication that he'd paid attention to their conversation.

She cleared her throat. "Class?"

"*Ilana* . . ." His tone conveyed everything; he didn't need to say anything more. Ilana remembered that, growing up, her father had possessed the same knack. When he'd been around.

"You must mean Fly Without Fear for Dummies."

34

Flash regarded her as he flicked a pencil against his stomach. "How'd it go?"

Ilana let her hair fall over her eyes as she rummaged in the bag for another Corn Nut. "I stayed for the intro." She could fudge facts with the best of them, but lying . . . well, she had never been very good at it.

"How long?"

"Ten, fifteen minutes. Or maybe five."

Leslie and Slavica gave her the kind of pitying stares that only long-term friends and co-workers could.

"Okay, I don't know how long I was there," Ilana finally blurted. "It felt like an eternity."

"So, the 'dummies' stayed and you left."

"Shut up, Flash." She glared at him as she switched leg positions, dangling the shoe on her other foot. She spilled the remains of the bag of Corn Nuts into her hand. Salt sprinkled everywhere.

"But . . . both your parents are pilots." Slavica spread her hands and waited, as if expecting enlightenment.

"Ladies and gentlemen," Ilana said in a nasal voice, pretending to report a breaking news story. "In a horrible mishap of genetics, the 'flying' gene was found to be missing from every single strand of Ilana Hamilton's DNA."

Slavica nodded sympathetically. "That's sad."

"Sad? No. Inconvenient, yes. But I'm working on it." She was the creative twin, she reasoned. Ian had inherited the flying gene and a host of other traits Ilana lacked, such as self-sacrifice and duty, honor, country—all that. At first, Ilana had seen her brother's eagerness to devote his life to the greater good to be as pointless and boring as dating only one guy at a time. But she'd come to respect him for it. As long as

35

he and the rest of her family didn't expect the same from her.

No, the *Vash* life was not for Ilana. Those royals overprotected their women, while giving the single men unlimited freedom. The men got live-in courtesans, who weren't prostitutes but members of a glorified, respected guild that had existed for almost eleven thousand years. Royal women were expected to remain cloistered virgins until they married.

Ugh. Hypocrisy in action and enough double standards to make her blood boil. True, her family was busy trying to initiate changes in the patriarchal *Vash* society, but it would be a slow, careful process, taking years if not generations. As it stood now, only Rom's home world of Sienna didn't require royal women to live by the old rules. There, Ilana's mother was an active pilot, commander of the space wing. But everywhere else, Jas put up with the *Vash* games out of love for her husband. Ian, too, respected his adopted culture. But then, he was an outsider preparing to take over Rom's role as king—he couldn't afford to appear too eager to dismantle the system.

Although her family reassured her that the *Vash* supported Ian, privately Ilana still worried, even feared for his life.

She frowned. The *Vash Nadah* reminded her of a pack of snarling dogs. That jerk Klark had been the worst of them. Lucky for him, the dude was locked up light-years away from where she could get her hands on him.

Ilana hopped down from her stool and walked to a wide window overlooking a sun-drenched parking lot in downtown Burbank. Even after five months, memories of the day her brother was attacked still unsettled her. Klark Vedla's arrogance had made her skin crawl. And yet, it was an image of Klark's older

36

brother Ché that remained stuck in her mind all these months. Stuck, like a splinter in her foot.

Eons of arranged marriages—powerful warrior-princes joining with beautiful women—had given Ché high cheekbones, a long straight nose, and hair and skin in a striking warm bronze that made it look as if he'd overdosed on sunless tanning cream. But unlike what Ilana had seen of Klark, a self-aware, almost tolerant quality mellowed Ché's supreme confidence. And curiosity, too. About her. She'd seen it when she'd met his piercing pale gold eyes.

The curiosity went both ways. What girl wouldn't wonder what such a tall, athletic, broad-shouldered body looked like without all those silly capes?

Hell. Ché was just another tight-assed pretty-boy prince. Ilana wanted nothing to do with him, or with any of the spoiled rich of the galaxy's royalty; their rampant snobbery and class awareness, their grating, suffocating attitudes on the subject of monogamy and commitment, which she'd learned long ago was a dangerous proposition for any sane woman.

That's right.

She hunched her shoulders and shoved her fingers into the pockets of her jeans. Her mother would disagree with her attitude, of course. Tee'ah would, too. And now, apparently, so would Slavica, if that engagement ring was anything to judge by. But Ilana was happy with her life the way it was, and she intended to keep it that way—where *she* held the reins of control, not a man.

Someone had to wear the title of black sheep of the family. It might as well be her.

Chapter Three

Ché rubbed his hands together. Ilana Hamilton had appeared to be clever, from what he could remember, her reputed unruly spirit aside. Surely, understanding his rank and position in her adopted culture, she would assist him once he arrived on Earth. If not, he supposed, he would find his own way.

He turned around, triumphant at the idea of traveling to Earth. The council members and Hoe stopped speaking to stare at him, hopeful smiles forming on their startled faces. His sudden change of mood must have unbalanced them.

Inhaling deeply, he strode across the balcony. "I must be off to other duties. Good day, gentlemen."

He walked through his bedchamber where a lone maid attended his rumpled bed. Passing his clothing repository, he snatched a clean Bajha suit, shoes, and a case containing his sens-sword, then continued on into the morning hush of the palace corridors.

Before he reached his destination, footsteps

sounded behind him. *Hoe.* "I'm going to see Klark," he told the advisor, who fell in step beside him. "He owes me a round of Bajha." During which Ché would determine what his brother knew of this sudden mad shove to the altar, if anything.

"The council's proposal caught you off guard." Hoe's concern for Ché's welfare shone in his seamed face.

"It was not the subject I thought I'd be facing over my morning tock."

"But it's good—a good plan."

"Speak for yourself, Hoe."

"Look at the positives, my lord. Now you won't have to attend the B'kah wedding, looking . . . so alone. You'll arrive with your new queen on your arm, the most eligible of all the available princesses, and the B'kah wedding will be a much happier occasion for all."

"And our Vedla family pride will remain intact."

Hoe beamed. "Precisely."

Ché stopped by a set of heavy double doors and punched in the code to enter Klark's living area—a large suite of rooms with access to a vast locked and guarded garden and exercise arena. Klark certainly wasn't suffering during his imprisonment, but he was alone, kept from communicating with his political cronies. With a nanocomputer implanted in his neck, he could not leave the palace without setting off an alarm.

After his code was accepted, Ché glanced into the retinal scanner. It beeped in recognition, allowing him past. Hoe did the same and followed him into a softly lit foyer. A black polished stone floor gleamed under their boots.

Klark met them, dressed in white from head to toe in an as-yet-unfastened Bajha suit, serenely sipping

from a cup in his hand. His hair was wet and slicked
back from his face. He shared Ché's features—the
high cheekbones, long straight nose, and cleft chin
of their clan—but he was harder, leaner in appearance.

Klark waved his hand at a grouping of large white
pillows on a like-hued rug. "Join me while I finish my
tock."

Ché glanced down with longing. The carpet was
plush, the pillows soft. He fought the almost overwhelming desire to lie down there, close his eyes and
fall asleep, if only so he could awaken and find out
that the news of his impending marriage was a bad
dream.

Klark cocked a golden brow. "You look tired." His
eyes twinkled, indicating that he assumed correctly
what Ché had spent the hours before dawn doing. He
was right, to a degree, but that wasn't what had truly
wearied him.

"I will change into my suit," Ché replied curtly and
ducked into the dressing room. His white one-piece
outfit was stiff, coated with a protective rubbery sub-
stance on the outside. Grimly he closed a series of
fastenings from each ankle to the neck, and lastly
pulled on flexible white boots that were as comfortable as his choicest slippers.

Clearly and understandably curious about Ché's
black mood, Klark followed as Ché exited the dressing room and entered the arena. The doors slammed
behind them, leaving the white-walled, featureless
chamber silent—except for the pitter-pat of Hoe's
boots as the advisor climbed the stairs to spectator
seats above the padded playing floor. Ché and his
brother began their twice-weekly practice session
with a merciless series of stretches and lunges.

"My plans for the next few months have changed,

Klark," Ché said, breathless. "I would like to discuss them with you." He then lifted his clublike sens-sword. "Lights," he called, plunging the arena into darkness.

Bajha was an ancient game based on intuition and instinct. Those skills, when honed, made a man a superior warrior, an exceptional pilot, and, some said, a better lover. But Ché also practiced Bajha to reach a higher state of consciousness, which he found particularly useful when he needed to think, like now.

"I am to marry within the next few months," he explained.

"Marry!"

Ché swerved at the sound of Klark's voice. Muscles tense, his combat instincts vibrating in readiness, he held his sens-sword in front of him in a sure, two-handed grip. "Councilman Toren visited me this morning and unveiled his master plan." His voice echoed hollowly in the cavernous room. " 'Beat the crown prince to the altar,' he told me. And in doing so, preserve Vedla pride."

Ché paused to listen. He was certain he'd heard a muffled laugh. "You find it funny, dear brother?"

"It was a chuckle of commiseration. Only the other day you were waxing poetic about the rewards of bachelorhood—and before you had even finished your second ale."

Klark's voice had come from a different direction than Ché expected. But even as that thought registered, he sensed that Klark had moved again.

Slowing his breaths, Ché stared wide-eyed into a wall of complete blackness. "You make it easy when I can hear you, Klark."

But not with his ears. It was completely dark, but he did not need his eyes. The neurons in his body hummed, pointing to his prey. Sharpened from years of training in Bajha, Ché's senses guided him. Following their ancient, mysterious direction, he inched closer.

The goal of the game was to find his opponent without the aid of the usual five senses. To target Klark, Ché relied on the blood coursing through his veins, his tingling pores, and the prickle of tiny hairs on his body, while he clutched his blunt sens-sword in his fists.

Of course, it made it all very difficult when playing Bajha to try to have a conversation at the same time. On an unspoken signal, he and his brother both went silent, giving in to the game.

Klark attacked, and Ché evaded him expertly. Then Ché whirled and swung in a return strike. But Klark was ready for him. His sens-sword whipped so close to Ché's torso that Ché could feel the rounded blade disturb the air as it whooshed past. But Klark never knew when to stop, it seemed. It was his weakness, and Ché knew it. When Klark came at him again, silently howling a battle cry that Ché could feel in the marrow of his bones, Ché swung his weapon in a brutal arc from above his head and down, then sharply to the left.

The impact of Klark's parry shocked him, took his breath. Ché had not expected to find Klark's sword there. An answering grunt of surprise came from Klark as their swords collided. Shocked or no, they pushed forward at the same time, blades slithering down to lock hilts. A fountain of brilliant violet light erupted at the point of contact, and then both sens-swords vibrated, signaling a hit.

As the purple light faded, Ché saw his own astonishment clearly reflected in his brother's eyes.

"Lights," Ché gasped. The illumination came up,

revealing him practically nose to nose with Klark. "Give?" his younger brother inquired, breathless.

"To hell I'll give!" Ché gasped. "It's a draw."

Hoe, who had been watching the match through an infrared enhancer, called down from the stands, "I have never seen a draw in Bajha, myself. But this was a draw if there ever was one." He glanced apologetically at Ché. "My lord."

Klark lowered his sens-sword and offered Ché his hand. "Good match," he said. "And interesting."

"To say the least." Gripping each other's wrists, the brothers inclined their heads, formally ending the match.

After stripping off their Bajha suits and changing into robes, the two refreshed themselves with a cold ionic beverage back in Klark's main chamber. Lounging amongst the floor cushions, Ché brought his sibling up to date with the council's secret plans. Hoe listened quietly in the background, as he had in nearly every significant conversation Ché had made in his life that concerned political matters or important affairs of the family. Ché trusted him implicitly. It was his brother that he still doubted from time to time.

"Great Mother. I must say I'm impressed by the councilman's cleverness," Klark murmured with approval.

Ché's mouth twisted. "I thought you would be."

"I knew nothing of it, by the way," Klark admitted without anyone having to ask.

"Nothing at all? Preliminary plans? Hints?"

"Tedious as it is, I am enduring my isolation as sentenced. I don't ask, and no one tells." A corner of Klark's wide mouth twitched, telling Ché that his cynicism and biting wit had survived his captivity.

Ché rubbed his chin. "Then the wedding scheme

43

is truly the doing of an concerned Vedla council. I suppose I should feel relieved. Grateful. Our family cannot afford another scandal. Our father no doubt feels the same."

"But you said Father didn't tell you of the plans himself."

"Correct." Ché glanced at Hoe. "He let Toren do the dirty work for him." Then he shrugged. "Perhaps he feared that his feelings for me as a son would interfere with the necessary politics." While his father was often distant and distracted, Ché and the rest of his siblings—a brother and two sisters—had never doubted the man's love.

A servant glided in with a plate of tock and sweet cakes, a bowl of boiled eggs, and a tray of paper-thin strips of crunchy smoked sea serpent. When the food was dispensed, Ché draped his arm over one bended knee and watched his brother eat. "I'm going to take myself a holiday, Klark," he said after a moment.

"A holiday, eh?" Klark nibbled on a strip of fried serpent. "A bachelor's last hurrah?"

Ché grinned. "You might say that."

"My lord," Hoe interrupted. "I was not advised of this, er, vacation."

"I have just now decided upon it."

The picture of efficiency, Hoe took out his palm-top. His hand hovered over the screen. "When and where are we to go?"

"Not *we*. I will travel alone. Nothing personal, mind you," Ché added.

"As you wish." Hoe typed furiously. "I will organize a small security detail. No more than six or seven for bodyguards and general security. Then, your personal chef and valet will accompany you—"

"No staff. No guards. No one from the palace. I wish

to travel alone in anonymous fashion. An entourage will only call attention to my identity."

Hoe's dismay was obvious. "It will never be approved."

Ché lifted a brow. "Approved by whom, Hoe?"

Ché himself approved all palace comings and goings, but Hoe was undeterred. "Leave the entourage at the palace, but take the bodyguards. Traveling without protection simply isn't safe."

"I am trained in the deadliest form of unarmed combat in the galaxy," Ché replied coolly. "I can well handle myself without a legion of babysitters."

Seeking support, Hoe turned to Klark, who in turn studied Ché, his expression reflecting not disapproval but concern. Ché knew his brother would do anything for him, die in his place if it came to that. "Have you decided on a destination?" Klark asked.

"Yes, yes," Hoe piped up. "Where?"

Ché took a breath. "Earth."

"*Earth!*" Hoe practically shouted, and Klark's tock cup hit his saucer with a crisp clink. "Does the king know of this?"

Ché shook his head. "No. No one knows but the two of you. Tell no one, either, please. Otherwise too much will be read into my visit there when all I desire is an escape. It is a place where I can exist anonymously and in relative comfort until my wife is chosen and a wedding date set."

Though Ché had delivered his explanation calmly, and it was one that clearly made sense, Hoe's mouth hung open and his hand remained frozen over his palmtop screen. Ché couldn't remember ever seeing his advisor in such a state of shock.

But Klark's eyes twinkled, and his tone reflected amusement. "I can't imagine you living amongst those barbarians, Brother."

"Given the choice of hiding in the frontier or stay-ing here to endure the tedious trivialities generated by the search for a wife, which would you choose?"

Klark's mouth twitched. "I see your point."

But Hoe was still sputtering. "It's dangerous on Earth. Unstable."

Ché stretched, flexing the finely honed muscles of his back. He worked hard to keep a fit, warrior's body. Too bad his lifelong advisor thought him in-capable of using it. "The political climate there has calmed considerably since Ian Hamilton's engage-ment to the princess."

"But many Earth-dwellers don't like the idea of be-longing to the Trade Federation."

"And some never will, Hoe. That will change, grad-ually, with upcoming generations. But with no recent anti-*Vash* protests marring the current climate of goodwill, it is safe to say that relations are better than they've ever been. Not that I have any intention of visiting in full *Vash Nadah* regalia, or in any official capacity at all. I will disguise myself." *As an Earth-dweller.* He would summon the Vedla chief tailor that very afternoon, in fact.

The more Ché thought of the idea of traveling in-cognito to the frontier world, the more it appealed to him.

Hoe typed furiously. "What of the language barrier, my lord? Most there don't speak Basic."

"I know their language."

Basic would always remain the official language of the Federation, as it facilitated trade between the Fed-eration and far-flung worlds that used individual di-alects. Highborn *Vash* also learned Siennan, but that rich and ancient language was reserved for special and ceremonial purposes. Vedlas learned Eireyan, too, the much-loved tongue of their homeworld.

46

But Ché had made a point to learn English several standard years ago, because it was the birth language of Rom B'kah's queen, and now of the crown prince. He figured that if he were at a party or anywhere else where English might be spoken in dark corners, he wanted to be able to interpret what was said.

Born and raised in the midst of court intrigues, such a desire was second nature. But because he didn't have a natural ability with languages—or the interest, previously—he'd struggled to learn the strange and alien tongue "English." Luckily, recent frequent interactions with Ian Hamilton had improved his skill, and he had no doubts that when on Earth he would be able to make his wishes known.

"I will contact the crown prince's sister once there," he admitted.

"Ilana Hamilton?" Klark regarded him with interest.

"I am growing weary of this constant second-guessing," Ché snapped. "From my staff and the council, I expect it. But from you, I take exception. Don't draw conclusions requiring knowledge to which you are not privy, Brother. This is the precise reason I am taking this trip. I am weary of my every move being examined, dissected, and analyzed, when my behavior has been nothing short of by-the-book—the Vedla book."

Klark pursed his lips. "My, my. Quite an explosive reaction."

Ché shook his head and sighed. "A few months' pleasure before I return to complete my wedding arrangements—is that too much to ask before my freedom ends?"

Klark's gaze remained speculative. "Hamilton's sister may be a B'kah, but like the crown prince she is a commoner."

"Great Mother. Who cares? You speak of her blood-lines as if they were contagious."

"They can be."

Ché ignored the insinuation. "You speak as if I plan to bed Ilana Hamilton and get her with child."

Klark raised his eyebrows. "That would be a triumph for us Vedlas, would it not?" he proposed.

Ché growled. "No Vedla would be that irresponsible, impregnating a woman he did not plan to marry. I cannot believe you would even suggest it, Klark. It must be my willingness to associate with the Hamilton twins that offends your racialist sensibilities. Shall I remind you that seven of the original Eight were of ordinary blood? Including Romjha, the Great One himself."

"But not the Vedlas. Ours is the blood of kings. In the Dark Years, they thought they had slaughtered us all. But we survived. When all who wanted to eradicate us from the galaxy thought they'd been successful, Queen Vedla, the youngest prince, and an unborn princess escaped the massacre and in secret continued our bloodline."

"Under the protection of the Dar family, who were commoners," Ché pointed out. "Our families have intermarried for thousands of years. Commoner blood runs in *all* our veins now."

"*Vash Nadah* commoner blood."

Ché scrubbed one hand over his face. "Why are we arguing history? Why are we arguing this issue at all?"

"Because," Klark replied, "if one looks no deeper than the obvious, then yes, the crown prince's sister's value can be easily dismissed. However, one cannot ignore her lofty rank within the Federation. Her status as an unpromised woman will affect the balance of power. It warrants discussion."

"Enough!" Rigid with displeasure, Ché stood.

Klark remained on his pillows, reclining languidly in their silken nest as he no doubt continued to ponder Ilana Hamilton and the threat he said she posed. Had his plot to assassinate Ian arisen just as casually? Ché wondered.

Ché tried to tell himself that Klark was going through a bad period, that time and maturity would eventually put all this behind them. He loved his brother and knew Klark felt the same. If only Klark would find better ways to express it!

Ché turned to Hoe, who regarded Klark with acute interest. The advisor was an intense fellow, cheerful in his outlook and wholly loyal to Ché. Hoe's greatest value lay in his ability to remain a vigilant observer from outside the maelstrom of Vedla in-house politics, assuring Ché a reliable channel of unbiased information and guidance. There was no better reason to leave Hoe behind at the palace. If nothing else, he'd ensure that Klark's potentially divisive musings about Ilana Hamilton and her detrimental effect on the balance of power in the Federation would not spread farther than this room.

Ché spoke, his jaw tight. "I will now inform Ian Hamilton of my plans. Here on Eireya, I've entrusted only you two with the knowledge of my destination. No one else is to know. Is that clear?"

Hoe and Klark nodded.

"Then, when I have recuperated from this wife-hunt business, I will return and marry." Ché turned on his heel and left his brother's chambers, his steps growing lighter as he went.

He had weeks, hopefully months, in which to see to his pleasure and relaxation away from this scrutiny he'd known all his life. No advisors, no councilmen, no guards. No wedding arrangements to listen to or the exasperating schemes of a bored brother. He'd be free of it all.

He inhaled deeply. His cape slapped against his boots with each long stride. The farther he strode from Klark's quarters, the lighter he felt. His last days as a bachelor would be spent well, that he vowed. While he'd do nothing to put his family's reputation in jeopardy, his options were wide open.

Ché smiled. He could hardly wait to discover what primitive pleasures awaited him on Earth.

Chapter Four

Decadence, Ilana mused as she left a reception at the Beverly Hills agency that represented movie star Hunter Holt. She could almost smell it on the man, the reckless, blasé hedonism embraced by only the very rich and truly powerful. Living to excess—Ilana found it part fascinating, part repulsive; it was so foreign to what she was, and what she wanted to be. "Would you consider Holt decadent?" she asked Linda, her personal assistant.

The woman followed her into an elevator and they rode it down to street level. "The chocolate cheesecake certainly was. But Holt? He tries. I don't know if he's 'quality' enough, though."

"True. He's self-made. He didn't inherit anything he has. Or had, before he blew it all on drugs."

"He's more . . . used. Like an old Lamborghini. Sexy, luxurious, still a status symbol—but if you look too closely, you can see that the leather fittings are worn."

Linda's eyes crinkled behind her narrow, black, rectangular glasses. "I don't think I want to know about Holt's fittings—what they look like or where they've been."

"Debauchery isn't very hygienic," Ilana agreed. Then she laughed and snapped her fingers. "That's the word I'm looking for. Debauched. One step below decadent." Holt exuded it like bad aftershave: late nights, hard partying, and too much money. "But he's got talent, and it's bankable."

"If he can keep straight long enough to finish a film."

"If he led a boring life, no one would have financed our documentary."

Linda studied her. "I wouldn't think Holt was your type, Ilana."

"Are you crazy? I don't have a type. But I do know that I don't do decadent, and I don't do debauched."

The elevator let them out in a marble-floored foyer manned by a bored security guard. Outside, the July evening was tinted orange. It was nearly nine and still twilight. Glass doors swooshed open, and Ilana strode outside, high heels tapping out a staccato beat on the cement.

Linda had no trouble keeping up. Ilana wouldn't have kept an assistant who did. Besides, Linda didn't walk; she bounced along, as full of fire as her short, spiky orange hair. Ilana needed Linda. The woman was indispensable during the chaotic days of filming and the post-production that followed. But now that Ilana was sifting through possible projects, so far unable to decide on any, Linda would retreat on vacation to her Torrance condo and her three schnauzers until Ilana called her back to duty.

"Don't tell me you don't know the type of man who attracts you."

"Available is nice. Not being possessive helps, too."
Linda sighed.

"Don't shake your head at my social life."

"I'm not shaking my head. Did you see me shaking
my head? I'm only stating the facts. Available isn't a
type."

Ilana fluffed out her hair. "It works for me."

"Because you've never stayed with Mr. Right-Now
long enough to figure out if he's Mr. Right."

"Explain to me why when a man says he's a confirmed bachelor, no one minds, but when a woman
says the same thing, everyone has a problem with it."

"I'm not talking about *any* woman—I'm talking
about you, Ilana. I don't see you alone for the rest of
your life, and I don't think you do, either."

"That's right. I don't." She gave Linda a sideways
smile. "I have a social life. I attract men."

"You attract them. But you never let them get
close."

Ilana's chest tightened strangely. Maybe she did
crave closeness. But she wasn't sure it was worth the
risk. Monogamy, commitment—it all might work for
women like Linda, but Ilana had seen the flip side of
the coin, the hurt her mother had suffered when she
found out how long her first husband, Ilana's father
Jock, had been cheating on her.

From a young age, Ilana had suspected that
"Daddy was seeing other ladies." With a child's hyper-
awareness, she could smell the faint perfume when
he'd open his suitcase after returning home from his
trips as an airline pilot, could tell that he'd been with
a stranger, things her mother never seemed to notice.
That innocence—or blindness—had angered Ilana.

She'd directed that fury at her mother, for not seeing, for letting herself love Jock despite what he was
doing behind her back. If he was with other women,

it meant he was bored with his family, tired of them. Assigning that blame had made Ilana a sullen teenager with her mother, and a needy girl with her father, showering him with love and attention so that he wouldn't leave. Her brother Ian had reacted the opposite way, becoming the perfect, devoted son. Only in the last few years of college had Ilana grown closer to her mother. But the deep-down kernel of anger, of resentment, of fear, had never really gone away. "Giving someone that much opportunity to hurt you is crazy."

"I think if you ever opened up, Ilana, let a man inside that stubborn, smart-assed head of yours, you might be surprised and like it."

Ilana groaned. "I know there are decent men out there. I know many relationships truly work. But I *like* my life the way it is. If I didn't like it, I would have changed it. I'm in charge. I'm in control. That's more than I can say about most of the married women I know. If a guy loves you, he loves you. He doesn't have to give you a wedding ring to prove it."

"Bullcrap, Ilana. If a man really loves you, he'll want you to be his. He won't want to share you with other men."

Ilana let out a heavy sigh. She'd had enough psychoanalysis for the day. Probing her mind was like peeking under the bed when you didn't want to find dust bunnies. All it did was remind you that you needed to clean.

Her cell phone rang. "It's Cole," she muttered, reading the caller ID.

"I thought you weren't seeing him anymore."

"I'm not." She'd broken it off with the cameraman the week before, just after her disastrous visit to Fly Without Fear for Dummies. True, he'd been a casualty of her shame over failing at that venture, but he was due to take a hike anyway. She'd been with him for a month, hadn't yet met anyone new, but she'd grown bored. "I admire persistence in a man," she told Linda, setting the phone to pick up the call automatically. "Only not after I'm done with them."

"Ms. Hamilton!"

Ilana's head jerked up. That's when she noticed the white news van with the satellite dish on top.

"Hell. What do *they* want?"

"Probably a few questions answered about Holt," Linda assured her. "Tell them how decadent you think he is."

"Yeah, right." Ilana lowered her voice. "I didn't think there would be that much interest in him. Not enough to warrant a van and a news crew. A phone call, maybe." She was an independent filmmaker. She made films on impossibly small budgets. She operated on the fringes of Hollywood, her chief purpose being to get her movies made the way she wanted to make them. The press didn't follow that type around.

A woman in a mint-green Tahari suit, a killer manicure, and a microphone in her hand waited in front of Ilana's car. *Oh, no*. It was Rose Brungard. She hosted "*Rose Knows*," a small-scale version of *Entertainment Tonight*, focusing on hot celebrities and the parties they attended.

Ilana made sure her eyes remained mostly hidden behind a tangled curtain of curls. Whatever her opinion of Holt, she wasn't going to feed a gossip's curiosity. The man deserved his privacy, she thought, aiming her remote at the silver Lura she'd parked at the curb.

Rose's perky voice startled Ilana. "With official word reaching Earth today that Prince Ian Hamilton has chosen a wedding date, Ilana Hamilton, twin sister to the man who will become ruler of the entire galaxy, remains the last of Earth's newest royal family to remain unclaimed."

"Un-what?" Ilana blurted.

The woman thrust her microphone in Ilana's face. "Who might Earth's Cinderella-heiress choose?"

Linda mercifully wedged herself between them, but the reporter leaned sideways, and pressed her attack. "The word on the street is that you'll soon announce your engagement, Ms. Hamilton. Who is your lucky guy? Or should I say, your lucky prince?"

"I'm not going to marry a pr—"

Linda reached behind her back and pinched Ilana's thigh. "Ms. Hamilton has been instructed by her family not to comment on the subject at this time."

To Ilana's dismay, the reporter appeared charmed by her silence, forced as it was, and not at all put out by Linda's intervention.

"This is such a Cinderella tale! Would you be willing to appear on the show? We'll do an interview, tour your home." Rose turned to her cameraman. "We'll need a shot of her in the kitchen, cooking a romantic, alien dinner for two," she suggested.

Ilana's vision blurred, either from hunger or from shock. Linda was inching her toward her car door.

"We look forward to having you on the show, Ms. Hamilton," Rose called. She winked. "And to finding out who your lucky guy is."

"But there is no—"

Before Ilana could finish, Linda shoved her into the Lura, locking her in and scurrying around to the other side. Linda leaped into the passenger seat.

Ilana looked at her. "Aren't you going to buckle my seatbelt, too?"

"Drive," Linda ordered. "Before you talk yourself into trouble."

"With you or them?"

"Drive."

Ilana started the engine. As she pulled into the street, she tried to smile at Rose, though she suspected it looked more like a grimace.

"Why did you have to say that, Linda—that I've been instructed on what to say? No one has instructed me in anything. That's only going to whet their curiosity."

"It's already whetted, Ilana. It has been for months. Only now that the guests have been invited to your brother's wedding, the pressure from the press is going to heat up. You're the only one in your family who lives on Earth. And the only one who's single. You're a natural target."

Ilana felt the unfairness of it all overwhelm her. "I don't want to be a target. I just want to live my life. And you didn't let me tell them that."

"You're whining."

Ilana gripped the steering wheel. "Damn right, I'm whining. I deserve to whine." The flying clinic, the invitation, and now this? All she wanted to do was crawl home and hide, order Chinese and listen to the surf. "Besides, I've always been able to whine to you," she added with a pleading smile.

Linda pushed aside Ilana's hair so she could see her face. "And you always can," she agreed. A second later she added, "I'm sorry about the whetting. I just said the first thing that popped into my mind. I'm a book reviewer and your personal assistant. A retired teacher. I never said I was a press agent."

Keeping her eyes on the road, Ilana shook her head. Then she reached across the seat and squeezed the woman's hand. "I'll drive around a bit, give the news folks a chance to clear out. Then I'll take you back to your car."

"Whatever it takes. I'm in no hurry."

Ilana gave Linda's hand one last squeeze. "Thanks."

They drove up and down the backstreets. She merged onto the freeway, heading back in the opposite direction, blankly, as if she were driving on autopilot.

Her heart skipped a beat. Autopilot. Airplanes. Spaceships.

Stop!

The beginnings of a headache pressed behind her eyes. Cheesecake and a glass of Chardonnay were hell on an empty stomach. The last thing she needed was a carb overdose when she was stressing.

Her thoughts swung back to the news people. "She called me Earth's Cinderella-heiress."

"Well, you are, technically, an heiress, Ilana. To the galaxy's richest family."

Ilana frowned. She'd never thought of herself as an heiress. It wasn't denial, exactly; she just hadn't made that mental leap with regard to her identity. Heiresses were people whose names ended in Woolworth or Rockefeller, not women who bought supermarket shampoo and used those dryer sheets to save on dry cleaning bills.

She drummed her fingers on the steering wheel. "Word on the street. The reporter said that, too. What the heck did she mean? I haven't heard anything."

"Neither have I, if it makes you feel better."

Ilana had been combing newspapers, magazines, TV, and the Web, looking for inspiration for a new film, but nothing had yet sparked her interest. She'd felt so . . . uninspired. Scriptwriters suffered writer's block. This must be filmmaker's block. But if there had been gossip about her, she would have seen it.

She hoped tonight's incident didn't mean that her privacy had come to an end. Other than an unlisted number and an assumed name on her mailbox, she hadn't needed to do much to stay anonymous, despite her family's high profile. Had that now changed?

A strange suffocating sensation enveloped her.

"Are you okay?" Linda asked.

Ilana huffed, "If they think they're going to discover any gossip-column tidbits about my social life over the next six months, they're going to be very disappointed."

And if they expected to see her hanging on some *alien* prince's arm, they were dreaming.

It was after eleven when Ilana finally pulled into the carport below her building, across the street from the beach in Santa Monica. Twenty condominiums had been salvaged from what used to be an old office complex. Although the building had a chronological age of seventy years, remodeling had made its age feel closer to five. Ilana had lived in her condo for three.

It was early for a Friday night. Most of the other tenants' spaces were empty. Ilana gathered her purse, slipped her shoes back on. Then she noticed an unfamiliar car parked by the curb.

Its engine was off. Its interior lights were on. A lone man sat inside, watching her.

Darkness shadowed his features. Cole? No. Cole didn't drive a black Porsche. Neither did any of the other men she'd dated recently . . . that she knew of. She had no idea who this dude was, only that his unwavering attention was doing a bang-up job of giving her the creeps.

She shoved her hair out of her eyes. Great, just great. A stalker would be the perfect ending to a perfect day.

Keeping an eye on the Porsche, Ilana slipped her hand into her purse and closed her fingers over a cold, metallic tube. With the can of pepper spray armed and ready, she opened the car door and stepped out.

The stranger's car door opened, too.

Shit. He was dressed from head to toe in black. The self-important way he carried himself spoke volumes about his confidence in his strength and purpose. And he was tall and solid enough to assure her that he could kick some butt if he wanted to.

Stop it. She was letting her thoughts run away from her. She did that when she was nervous. Nervous, yes. Not scared. She wasn't scared.

She slammed her car door behind her, locked it, and strode toward her front door as if she meant business. A salty sea breeze caught her hair and blew it around her face.

Her condo was two flights up. She reached the alcove where the stairs began, paused to see if the man had followed her.

He had.

Her heart lurched, dumping a bucketful of adrenaline into her bloodstream. Yet her mounting fear didn't come close to what she'd experienced in Flying Without Fear for Dummies. While flying was a no-go, stalkers she could handle.

Yes, she acknowledged silently—stalker. As far as she was concerned, this guy was a threat. Anyone who dressed in black and followed women in the middle of the night qualified.

Adding to her heebie-jeebies were the sunglasses she could now see that he wore.

Shades? At night? Worse, they were mirrored wraparounds. But he hadn't tripped over the trashcan; nor had he stepped on any of the dog mines littering the wide swath of grass that separated the sidewalk from the building. He was obviously able to see.

Smooth. He was definitely smooth. He reminded her of a highly paid hit man—not that she'd ever seen one, but she had a good imagination. Too good, and it was freaking the daylights out of her. Not that anyone she knew could afford a professional—they'd have hired some guy named Eddie, a down-on-his-luck ex-con with a potbelly and type-II diabetes.

But what if someone she didn't know wished her harm?

Her thoughts sped off in a new direction. She was an heiress now. If the reporter saw her that way, others did, too. Heiresses got kidnapped and held for ransom. Her address was private, but it wouldn't be too hard to figure out.

Enough! She dropped a roadblock in front of her racing thoughts and hurried up the stairs. Halfway to the landing she whirled around, dismayed to find that in only a few, long, determined strides the man had reached the bottom of the staircase and was now half-hidden in the shadow of her building.

Her grip on the can of pepper spray didn't relax.

"Ilana Hamilton," the stranger called.

His voice was accented, almost monotone. It was Arnold Schwarzenegger in *The Terminator*, to a tee. A robotic assassin from the future, the Terminator had hunted down all the Sarah Connors in the Los Angeles phone book, each time asking, "Sarah Connor?" as confirmation before he blew their brains out. In Ilana's opinion, the similarities to this situation were not funny.

"This is a joke, isn't it?" she replied.

The stranger looked confused. Ah, he was good, really good—probably an actor, making some weekend money while he looked for work.

"Come on," she guessed. "This is Flash's idea, right?" Her friend had a habit of practical jokes, most that only he thought were funny. The year she moved in, he'd paid a Mexican trio from a local restaurant to sing cheesy love songs—she wasn't fluent in Spanish and took his word regarding the lyrics—under her balcony. One birthday, he'd sent a male stripper who'd peeled off his clothes right down to the cluster of prettily curled ribbons he'd tied on his—

She gave her head a shake. The neighbors had loved it.

But, delivering a dark stranger to scare her late at night when he knew she was alone? Flash wouldn't do that.

"Flash . . . ?" The stranger brought his hand to his chin.

It was a suave, almost aristocratic-looking gesture. There was something vaguely familiar about it. Maybe she *had* dated this guy. No, he exuded sophistication, confidence. And sex. She would have remembered him.

He dropped his hand slowly. His mirrored glasses glinted. "My apologies. I don't have all my English yet."

"Well, good luck in finding it," she called cheerily and clicked the digital keypad on her keychain. Her front door unlocked with a sharp click. Her escape route was ready.

"Wait. Please."

Breathless, she turned back to the man who stood too few steps below her. She'd bolt into her condo if he made any attempt to charge up the stairs, but he didn't.

A porchlight made a circle of brighter illumination near the base of the stairs, and the stranger stepped slowly into it. Ilana squinted at him, trying to discern features, scars, tattoos—any identifying characteristics that she could pass along to the police when they asked.

He had an angular jaw and sculpted cheekbones. His smooth skin reminded her of the color one turned when one overdid sunless tanning cream. But there were no streaks. His was the real thing. In contrast to his bronzed skin, his hair was blond, but warm and dark like cinnamon sticks.

Exactly the color of her stepfather Rom's hair.

Her heart rate picked up. With those glasses covering his eyes, he could pass for a *Vash Nadah*.

She almost snorted. Right. *Vash Nadah* didn't bebop around Santa Monica on a Friday night. Or any night.

Despite the ridiculousness of the idea, Ilana took a closer look at him.

He was dressed expensively and well—Armani, if she wasn't mistaken—in a black, conservatively cut suit. But it was more than the clothing that unnerved her; the stranger carried himself with the aloof arrogance characteristic of galactic royal men.

Or rich sheiks from Arabia. *Hmm. Good point.* That he was a wealthy foreigner was more likely, though no less bizarre. No *Vash Nadah* would chase her down at night, alone, unless his intent was to assassinate her—a theory too far-fetched for even her worst-case-scenario mind to consider. She wasn't a threat to the *Vash Nadah*; she wasn't even a blip on their xenophobic radar. Unlike the rest of her family, she stayed out of politics and galactic affairs. She lived anonymously on Earth, and intended to continue doing so. The *Vash* would have figured that out by now.

Oblivious to the fact that she'd just processed five hours of mental information in 3.0 seconds—

"thought warp," her brother Ian called it—the rich sheik/highly paid assassin/garden-variety creep wrapped his hand around the banister.

Ilana aimed her pepper spray. "Talk to me from down there."

He obeyed with the utmost deference. "Ilana Hamilton." He sounded less sure now. "She lives here, yes?"

"Why?"

"She is to assist me."

I am? "You have fifteen seconds to tell me why you're here and what you want, and then I'm shutting the door."

He hesitated long enough to worry her. "You are Ilana. Ian did not tell you?"

"Tell me what?" She gripped the pepper spray so tightly that she briefly wondered if she'd explode the can. Women had been known to lift cars off injured children. It could happen.

The man rubbed his face as if he were exhausted. Well, that made two of them. If it weren't for him, she'd be in bed by now.

"Ah. I see this problem now," he said.

"What freaking problem?" Her patience was shot.

"You did not expect me. My apologies."

Off came the glasses, revealing a pair of startlingly pale gold eyes. She wanted to suck in a breath, but her diaphragm didn't seem to be working.

Pressing one fist over his chest, the man bowed his head. "Ché, firstborn prince of the Vedlas," he introduced himself.

Ché? Ilana's finger convulsed over the can of pepper spray. A burst of orange-red gas hissed out.

"Oh—!" She released the button, dropping the can,

but too late. The cylinder bounced down the stairs toward Ché, a gust of wind pushing the small, rapidly dispersing cloud of mist in precisely the same direction.

Chapter Five

"Move away! *That* way!" Her eyes wide with alarm, Ilana Hamilton ran down the stairs. "It's . . ."

She continued speaking English so rapidly that Ché lost the meaning of her words. But he knew enough to turn his head and close his mouth as the mist passed by.

Ilana shoved him away from the staircase and onto the turf. "I'm so sorry," she cried, throwing her weight into him.

He inhaled when she thumped into his ribcage. A whiff of her scent—subtle, sweet—came to him, chased by a bitter odor that burned its way down his throat.

A prickling sensation in his throat made him cough. His eyes began to burn as well, and tears clouded his vision. The heel of his shoe sank into the damp ground, sucking loudly as he pulled it free. He stumbled, then caught Ilana by the forearms and steadied them both.

His fingers touched smooth bare skin, warm and soft. Trained in proper social etiquette from birth, he released the Earth princess like a hot coal, a reaction that undoubtedly startled her—but then she might not realize that in her short sleeveless shift, she revealed more skin than most *Vash* women did in their lingerie.

This was the way Earthwomen dressed, he reminded himself, coughing. It was a different culture, if it could be termed "culture," and not as conservative as his. Yet he had to admit that seeing the crown prince's sister in such a state of undress was, though unsettling, not at all unpleasant.

Now, if he could only see anything else.

He wiped his eyes with the back of his hand. "What is the vapor?" he rasped.

"Pepper spray." Ilana sneezed twice, sniffling. Her eyes watered and undoubtedly stung as his did.

She switched to Basic, the language of the Federation. Her dossier said that she read Basic fluently. Speaking it, she was less proficient. He imagined she didn't get much practice on Earth.

"I spray very small," she tried explaining in Basic. "Wind strong." She pinched her thumb and index finger together. "Only little we breathe."

"Pepper spray. A deterrent chemical?"

"Yes. Was accident." Holding on to his bicep, she dabbed at his tears with the heel of her palm.

Ché's loins tightened. Here was a very pretty woman, scantily clad, standing so close to him that he felt the heat radiating off her body. Yet her intentions were not sexual—he could sense that concern was her motivation. Her sheer proximity, her scent, her curves, her mouth—it was all overwhelming, to say the least. A *Vash* princess in his world would never have touched him with such casual intimacy. But Ilana was not of his world.

"Here. Use this." She shoved a small white sheet of soft paper into his hand, dabbing at her eyes with another. She blinked rapidly, wiping the moisture from her cheeks. "This spray very bad."

"It is quite effective," he agreed in a husky voice.

She gazed up at him with huge blue eyes that were more brilliant than he remembered. Perhaps the tears filling them made them so.

"You surprise me," she accused in Basic, an angry edge to her voice. "Why you come here?"

"I took a holiday. A vacation." He wasn't ready to explain the rest yet. "When I informed Ian, he assured me you would know of my arrival."

"Ian not call." She opened and closed her mouth several times. Finally, she clenched her fists. "I can't argue in Basic," she snapped, switching to English. "Ian didn't call. But I was at work all day. How did you find me? When did you get here? How long were you waiting?"

She went so long without taking a breath that he was almost ready to suggest she inhale. Then she sighed and asked, "What in the world are you doing here, Ché? Maybe you weren't the last person in the universe I expected to see tonight, but pretty damn close."

"Slow . . ." He held up one hand. "Fast words I cannot follow."

"I'll try." She blew her nose. "This has been a horrible day."

"Ian told me the approximate time of your arrival home," he explained. "When you did not answer your door, I returned to the ground car. I waited for many standard hours. I was nearly ready to seek temporary quarters on my own when you arrived."

She peered into the darkness. "So, where's your entourage?"

It pricked his pride to see that even the crown prince's independent sister assumed he needed handlers to make his way. "I left them behind," he answered crisply. "I'm here alone, on my own."

"Is that your Porsche?"

"It belongs to Hollywood Luxury Auto Leasing." He stumbled over the pronunciation, but assumed he got it right when she nodded. "While still home, I studied the procedures with which I'd need to . . . hire—yes, hire a vehicle."

She appeared impressed by the feat. "Rom doesn't know how to drive, so I didn't expect you to. I thought you guys flew everywhere."

"We do." He puzzled over the brief tightening of her mouth. Wouldn't she prefer to fly everywhere, as well? "But the ground cars we use to maintain our gardens are not all that different from yours here on Earth."

"You. In the garden." She looked him up and down. "Somehow I can't picture you weeding."

"I did not perform garden chores. But"—a corner of his mouth edged up with a surge of memories—"the vehicles were irresistible to a young boy and were easily commandeered." He shrugged.

Delight lit Ilana's face. "So, you were a hell-raiser as a kid. A troublemaker."

He gazed down at her. Light from above illuminated her face. *Tell me more,* her eyes pleaded, as if she were more interested in the man inside than his face or imminent crown. That searching gaze jolted Ché's senses like a bracing dive into cold seawater.

Past or present, he couldn't recall a woman who'd observed him so brashly. The others hadn't dared to,

or hadn't cared to, he supposed. It was clear that Ilana fit neither category.

"My childhood years were happy," he revealed,
spurred on by her curiosity. In his new English, he
tried not to mangle the explanation. "But strictly su-
pervised, as I had to be prepared to take my father's
place on the throne. The Treatise of Trade dictated
everything my family did, that I did or did not do. But
no matter how thorough the supervision, no matter
how loving, a child will always find ways to outwit
it."

He would have chuckled, had the situation been
appropriate. Instead, he allowed himself a small
smile. "I will say only that my siblings and I were
creative in seeking out mischievous diversions."

Ilana tipped her head to the side. "Are you still as
creative?"

He opened his mouth to deny it—roguery wasn't
a trait the Vedla clan cultivated—but he'd come to
Earth, had he not? What did that say about the rebel
in him?

He clamped his mouth shut. By the heavens, what
was he thinking, telling Ilana Hamilton about his boy-
hood exploits? No one outside his immediate family
and the palace staff knew of those escapades, which
had earned him many a scolding. The Vedlas were a
disciplined breed. It would not do to have Ilana Hamilton think otherwise. He must act with dignity befitting his class.

His tone turned formal. "On the matter of my driving the Porsche—the markings, the language, and the
mechanisms with which one controls the car are
primitive, but not difficult to learn."

Ilana drew back, as if his abrupt change in manner
chilled her. "Primitive," she muttered. "Not difficult

to learn. Give me a break. It was all those garden carts you hijacked."

He swallowed a groan.

She walked to where her can of pepper spray lay on the pavement. She retrieved it, then brandished it as a wand as she spoke. "You're pretty humble. When my stepfather's people came here for the first time, they had trouble."

He shrugged. "They were B'kahs."

That won him another laugh.

Did all his opinions entertain her? It seemed so. For the life of him, Ché couldn't determine what she found so funny. Could he not maintain his dignity around this woman? "I require your advice with which to choose temporary lodging for my holiday."

"It's too late to find a room. You can stay in my place tonight. We'll worry about the rest tomorrow."

She walked to the staircase. He remained rooted where he was. "You employ a chaperone?" He would have thought she'd have to summon one.

"A chaperone?" She clearly struggled not to laugh.

"We cannot stay alone together. It's a breach of propriety. It will cause a scandal."

"Who'll know? Unless you're planning to call home and confess."

He stuttered. Great Mother, he'd never stuttered in his life! "-I-I I will do no such thing."

Ilana's eyes twinkled delightedly. "I won't say anything, either. I don't have a chaperone. Or a cook, or a chauffer. No plants, no pets, no roommate. But I do have a guest room. That's where you'll sleep, nice and safe. If you're that worried about me assaulting you, you can lock the—oh, damn!" She froze, her eyes widening as she peered over his shoulder at the street.

"Paparazzi!" she hissed.

His body tensed, ready to do battle. A figure crouched behind a ground car, aiming what Ché recognized as a camera.

Ilana grabbed his chin and wrenched his head around. "Don't let him get a shot of your face. Where are your sunglasses?" She yanked them from his coat pocket and slid them over his eyes. "Don't talk."

He opened his mouth to speak, and she pressed her finger to his lips. "If I were on a foreign planet," she said past gritted teeth, "and a representative of the indigenous species had just given me critical instructions, I wouldn't argue!"

She stood so close, clothed only in that distracting, insubstantial tiny shift. His senses soared to full alert, as in Bajha swordplay when he fell within striking range of his opponent. Her warm finger pressed against his lips.

When her awareness of him flared in her eyes, he saw it. Holding himself very still, he watched her react to the feel of his mouth on her finger, the prick of his barely surfaced whiskers, the feel of his breath, the intensity of his stare.

She dropped her hand with satisfying swiftness.

Pleased, he smiled. In this particular arena, at least—man and woman—he'd been able to maintain his advantage.

"This has never happened before," she growled.

It took him a moment to process that she meant the man wielding the camera. "The press usually ignores me," she continued explaining under her breath. "I'm not as colorful as the rest of my family."

"I beg to differ," Ché muttered in Basic.

"It has to be because of the invitations. They've gone out, you know. For Ian and Tee'ah's wedding."

"I well know the wedding," he whispered back dryly.

She winced. "Oops. I guess you would. Sorry."

"I am not."

She smoothed her bangs away from her forehead and stared up at him. Her unruly bleached-blond hair looked soft to the touch. Her eyes were wide, without guile. "Heartbroken?" she asked.

He reared back. "No."

"Bitter?"

"Indeed not."

She smiled kindly as if she didn't believe him.

To make matters worse, a tear crawled down his cheek. With the heel of his palm he rubbed moisture from his stinging eyes. Blasted spray. He was many things right now: weary, annoyed, exasperated, disorganized, dissatisfied, and unfocused, to name a few. But lovesick he was not. If not for propriety, he'd grab Ilana's arm, haul her close, and make her see how wrong she was.

But he could manage courtesy for one night, could he not? Particularly toward the crown prince's sister, who was generous enough to offer him hospitality, though she clearly hadn't expected him, and didn't appear to have any great love for the *Vash Nadah*, family ties notwithstanding. Tomorrow, however, he'd be on his vacation, and away from this disconcerting woman's scrutiny.

"Wait here," he ordered. "I will chase him away." With one hand spread wide and shielding his face, he strode toward the bad-mannered intruder.

Lights from the camera flashed as the man backed toward another vehicle. Smirking, Ché amplified the menacing nature of his advance.

"No!" Ilana caught up to Ché and tugged on his arm.

"But he troubles you."

"I know, but—"

"I will make him go."

"It's only a few photos. If we turn it into an incident, they'll have a whole story."

The flashes began anew. Ilana tugged on Ché's free arm, the one that didn't shield his face. "Please?"

He made a noise in the back of his throat and reluctantly turned, dropping his hand once his back was to the cameraman. "At home this would not happen," he grumbled. "We have palace guards to prevent it."

"I don't live in a palace."

For that, he was grateful. "Palaces can become tedious," he admitted.

She threw him a curious glance. Then she swore. "Walk faster. He's following us. What a jerk. He's on the grass, there in the dark." She scowled. "I hope he steps in dog poop."

"Dog . . . poop?"

"Canine excrement."

"Ah." So, it was true: Earth-dwellers permitted their captive creatures to defecate in public places. It would take some getting used to, this wild-and-woolly planet Earth.

They ducked up the stairs. "Then I, too, will hope that he steps in dog poop," he said magnanimously.

Ilana choked out an unexpected laugh. As they rounded the top of the second flight, a man jogged down from an upper floor. He wore typical Earth attire—jeans and what Ché recognized as a "sweatshirt." On his head was a brimmed cap labeled "Angels."

The man almost tripped over his own feet, slowing to stare at Ché—because of the mirrored eye-shaders, Ché supposed. But if he removed them, his pale *Vash* eyes would give the curious Earth-dweller even more to gawk at.

"Hey, Ilana. What's up?"

"Hi, Sam." Ilana dabbed at her reddened nose. "This is my upstairs neighbor," she explained to Ché. "Sam, this is . . . this is my friend, Ché."

Sam stuck out his hand, and Ché grasped it, an Earth-dweller gesture of greeting with which he was fortunately familiar. "What's up, Frenchie?" Sam asked.

"Not—," Ilana began to correct.

Ché stopped her with a touch of his hand on her arm. He hadn't given it much forethought, but an assumed name would not hurt.

Simultaneously, they sneezed.

"Aw," Sam said, grinning. "Matching colds. Love sucks, doesn't it?"

Ilana wiped her nose with a tissue. "I sprayed us with pepper spray."

Sam's mouth twisted. "Different strokes—"

"Accidentally."

"Right." Hands shoved in his jeans pockets, Sam grinned, then skipped the rest of the way down the stairs. There he turned and called up to them, "Try Reddi-Wip next time. It doesn't have as many side effects."

Ilana groaned and shoved open her door.

"Ready whip?" Ché queried. Colloquial speech baffled him.

"Never mind," Ilana said. She pulled him through her front door and slammed it closed behind them.

Chapter Six

Ilana expelled a breath of relief. Closing her eyes briefly, she leaned back against the closed door, her hands flat against the cool white wood, and inhaled the sweet scent of her living room. She'd bought fresh lilacs the day before in the flower market by the pier. Good thing. The scent calmed her. A little. And it eased the effects of the pepper spray, which thankfully had been mild due to the smallness of the burst, bonehead that she was, and the wind. Here she thought she'd stepped into *The Terminator*. Instead, the last few minutes had played out like a bad romantic comedy.

She opened her heavy eyes and massaged her temples. A few curling strands of hair fell over her face. With the inbred insolence so characteristic of royal *Vash Nadah* men, Ché clasped his hands behind his back and took in the details of her small living room. Her couch was yellow, the two chairs sea-blue, and the walls white. The floor was whitewashed wood covered with groups of pillows, area rugs, and nautical bric-a-brac she'd acquired here and there. Nothing matched. She found the disarray appealing. In her home, there was only one rule: no plants, pets, or anything she had to water, trim, feed, or walk.

She liked her place. It was bright and happy, so she could feel that way, too. Even when she wasn't.

Sniffling, she pressed the tissue in her hand to her burning nose. Ché sneezed. Removing his glasses, he wiped his eyes, muttering something that didn't sound like language Mama Vedla would likely use.

Ilana hid her smirk by blowing her nose. "We're a mess, aren't we?"

It looked as if he'd smile. Then he appeared to catch himself. "Quite." He pocketed his sunglasses. "It is safe to remove my eyeshaders now that we are inside, yes? I would not want to further anger the indigenous species."

Startled, she laughed. He looked pleased. "You have a sense of humor," she told him.

"You think I am joking?"

Touché.

She shook her head. "Prince Ché What-the-hell-are-you-doing-here Vedla, I've already convinced myself not to like you. Don't make me change my mind."

He gave her that you-are-an-alien-creature look she'd come to expect. "Actually, Ilana, you do not know as much as you think you do about *Vash* men."

"I know enough. All I ever want to. Believe me."

His golden eyes sparked with challenge, an almost playful look that made Ilana wonder if Ché knew was sexy as hell. "We shall see," was all he said.

"I guess we will, won't we?" she shot back.

The air crackled with this unexpected verbal sparring; She found it exhilarating.

Smoothly, Ché moved on to the photos on her

walls, Ilana's UCLA diploma, and the filmmaking awards she'd won. He stood there, handsome and poised, at the top of his game; he exuded power and wealth, the kind of confidence born into a man. If ever there was a surreal scene, this was it: Ché Vedla, the man who personified everything Ilana wanted to avoid, standing in the middle of her living room. She was tempted to grab the Canon in her bedroom so she could record the event for all posterity.

"You create entertainment," he said.

She liked the way he said that. He'd expressed what she did for a living perfectly. "Yeah. I'm a film-maker. My partners and I run a production company that makes movies. We've only made three so far, just finished the last. That was what I was working on when I met you the first time." *When your idiot brother singlehandedly almost tore apart the Federation.*

. . . Before Ché stepped in and along with Ian helped save the day, she reminded herself. "We each have our specialties, and even then we share tasks. Mostly, I'm the DP—the director of photography. That means I'm the person responsible for the lighting and cinematography of a film. I decide how a scene should look, taking into account things like contrast and depth of field. But when I can, I enjoy just being the camera operator." She added Basic words and hand motions to her English to help him grasp her explanation. Strangely, she wanted him to understand what she did for a living. She wanted his respect. And yet, she wasn't sure why. Why was it so important that this man, this uppity *Vash* prince, acknowledge that a woman could do more than produce babies, or act as a decorative fixture on his arm? She had a snowball's chance in hell of changing his views, just as he'd never get her to see why the *Vash* liked their royal women held back and hidden away.

"But now we're in between projects. We're hoping to find a great script, or an idea we love. Then we'll have to find investors, or get a grant. And if that doesn't work out, we'll probably have to find work as a crew for other people's projects to make money." She cracked a smile. "If it gets really bad, I'll find a part-time gig at a restaurant, or the video store across the street so I can eat."

At that, Ché glanced up sharply. Had he assumed she lived off the limitless B'kah wealth? Had he ever socialized with anyone who lived as simply as she did? *Welcome to the real word, Mr. Prince.*

"But that's the nature of the business," she finished with a shrug. "It's unpredictable at first—and even later on, everyone tells me."

He nodded, his classic features reserved. "You love your work."

She jerked her gaze up to his. Pale, intense eyes glowed in his shadowed face. And yet, she couldn't read his expression, couldn't make out what he thought of her passion for her art. "Yes. I love it. I love making movies. I can put the pictures I see in my head out there for others so they can enjoy them, too. I love tweaking a scene until it gives the exact feeling I'm looking for, the shot that evokes the right mood. I never want to give it up."

She felt suddenly awkward. It was that morning-after feeling where, now that the rush of lust had passed, you realized that you'd been physically very intimate with someone you weren't sure you wanted to know that well—or know at all. It felt like that now with Ché, only she'd been intimate emotionally, not physically, revealing hopes and dreams she'd never intended to bare.

He rewarded her with interest and maybe even admiration; she could see it in his expression as he took a closer look at her trophies, accolades, and memorabilia. Or was it wishful thinking on her part? One thing was for sure: *enigma* described Ché Vedla perfectly.

On her kitchen counter, her answering machine was blinking. She strode across the room to get a closer look. There were fifteen messages waiting. Since her friends and associates used her cell, this could only mean one thing.

Dread filling her, she touched the Play button. "Ms. Hamilton, this is Paul Friedman from the Wall Street Journal—" She skipped to the next message. "Hello, I'm Marjorie Stevens with the Los Angeles Ti—" Ilana winced. "This is Newsweek magazine calling for—"

"Ah!" She punched the Off button. "First the reporter, then the jerk with the camera, and now this."

Ché waved at the front door, which she'd bolted. "At least the beasts are locked outside for the night."

She snorted. "*You're* still here, aren't you?"

Ché appeared unsure whether he should laugh or act insulted. "You consider me a beast?"

She dropped her hands to her hips and gave him a slow, very thorough once-over. Big hands. Big feet. She supposed it would be too crude to admit that she hoped so. "Too early to tell," she said.

With something between indignation and awe, Ché regarded her. She strode across the living room and extended her hands. "Since you're staying, let me put away your coat."

Slowly, he unbuttoned his Armani suit. His shoulders and biceps flexed as he shrugged off the jacket.

"Thank you." He draped the coat across her outstretched arms. The fabric smelled like him, a masculine scent of clean, warm skin, and something exotic and different, reminding her that he was anything but the guy next door.

He tugged on his shirt sleeves, smoothing out the wrinkles. The white linen was so fine that the *Vash*-bronze skin of his upper body showed through. The palms of Ilana's imagination slid over the cool shirt, her fingers slipping under the fabric to explore firm, hot skin.

"I'll put away your coat," she said quickly. "Sit down, make yourself at home." *Take off the rest of your clothes; I won't mind.*

She spun away to hang the jacket in the closet. An umbrella fell out. She righted it. Then her vacuum cleaner tried to lunge forward. With her knee, Ilana shoved it back inside, slammed the door, then paused to compose herself before she turned around.

Did Tee'ah have any idea what she'd given up to marry Ian?

Ilana cut off the thought. Her brother was an Earth guy at heart, and that's what Tee'ah wanted. Someone without pretense, someone who wasn't spoiled, who would let her have the freedom she wanted. Not someone like Ché. Sure, with the sex lessons he'd had and a genetically perfect bod, Ché would be the ideal fling. But what woman in her right mind would want to be his wife? His queen?

A *Vash* woman, she guessed with a shudder. The thought of losing herself, everything she was, everything she'd worked for, in the black hole of Ché's patriarchal society scared Ilana in a deep, almost irrational way that was almost as bad as flying. Marrying a *Vash* would be the ultimate loss of identity. Of control.

Her mother hadn't lost herself, Ilana thought.

Yeah, but Jas had a husband who supported her independence. Ché was everything Rom wasn't. He was a Vedla, a family of stuck-up, narrow-minded, chauvinistic pigs. He didn't appear that way now be-

81

cause he was in her home and wisely on his best behavior. But scratch the surface and she'd find the real Ché: a wealthy prince who kept a legion of concubines on call, a man who thought a wife's only role was to make heirs, and who deep down felt that anyone from Earth was a barbarian.

He begged for redirection.

She turned around. Ché stood in front of the window that overlooked the street and the ocean beyond. At this hour, the light-dotted blackness of the Pacific was almost indistinguishable from the starry sky, soon to be swallowed up by midnight fog.

His hands were clasped behind his back, one placed neatly inside the other, and his back was ramrod straight, as if to stand another way had been forever forbidden. But his legs were set apart, a relaxed confident stance, as if watching the ocean were soothing.

Well, they had that in common at least. She couldn't imagine ever moving away from the shore. For someone who'd grown up in Tempe, Arizona, it was a strange sentiment. Ian loved the desert. So did her mother. But not Ilana. She needed to be near water. As soon as she could afford it, she'd live *on* the beach, not across the street from it. But even here, she could hear the waves if she listened hard enough above the Friday-night summer beach traffic.

There were the smells, too—salt, dampness, dead kelp fermenting on the sand—carried in with the breeze billowing past her gauzy white-and-yellow striped curtains. The air ruffled Ché's elegant white shirt, but he remained so very aristocratic, dignified, and confident with his broad shoulders, perfect posture, and lean athletic build. He'd look just as noble standing around in his underwear.

Now, there was an interesting thought: Ché Vedla—boxers or briefs?

"So," she said. "Feeling better now?"

"Quite." His tone had turned formal again, she noticed. "I traveled here by private courier. The journey was rather long." Stiffly he kept his hands behind his back. "My sleep period is not yet aligned with yours on Earth."

"We call it jet lag."

"Jet lag, yes," he replied courteously, his attention drawn back to the window.

Drawing-room conversation, she thought. It must be his way of keeping distance between them, dampening the palpable intimacy of the two of them alone.

He radiated confidence, sexual confidence, and yet she could unnerve him with a casual touch. A bizarre blend of puritanical values and sexual abandon, he was the consummate product of his society, a people who adhered to laws set down by an eleven-thousand-year-old book.

She'd been studying the Treatise of Trade. Five years, and she still hadn't made it all the way through. But she kept at it doggedly, partly out of intellectual curiosity and partly out of a desire to understand the strange culture into which her family had married. When it came to societal guidance, the Treatise was one-stop shopping. It was the *Declaration of Independence* crossed with the *Kama Sutra* and the *Old Testament*. Where else could you find detailed information on lovemaking—with illustrations!—alongside passages on family values that gave new meaning to the words moralistic, stuffy, and old-fashioned?

"Here it reminds me of my home," Ché said, gazing outside.

She thought of the gorgeous images she'd brought

up on the computer months ago. A world of water. It had spawned both the man who'd tried to ruin her brother, and the man who'd smoothed it all over. Ché was also the first of the princes to give Ian his support, which had proved crucial for Ian's acceptance amongst the *Vash Nadah*. "Eireya," she said.

He turned around. "Yes."

"Ocean covers eighty percent of the surface. You have one continent. The rest is broken into small islands."

Scattered across blue-purple water as if a giant had flung a handful of emeralds from the lavender sky, she thought.

Ché reacted with genuine pleasure. "You've studied my world."

"It sounded pretty, so I looked it up once." She shrugged it off. "So—homesick already?"

He looked startled by her sudden change in subject, or maybe by her directness, but he recovered instantly. Oh, how she appreciated a man who resisted intimidation! Of the many words she could use to describe Ché Vedla, wimp wasn't one of them.

Ché shook his head. "If I had to go many days without the sea nearby, perhaps. But it is near, and so I am not."

Something ate at him, though. There was a little muscle in his jaw that made a dimple when he concentrated; she'd noticed. Now it looked like the Grand Canyon.

She leaned one shoulder against the wall. "Tell me why you're here, Ché. Why did you come to Earth?"

"For a holiday." He hesitated. "Of a sort."

He was hiding something. "Of a sort? What's that supposed to mean? Spare me the mystery, please." Anger thickened her voice. Ian maintained that Ché knew nothing of the attempts on his life, but that the incidents occurred at all tainted her interaction with Ché with risk and danger. "Neither of us has forgotten that your brother tried to murder mine. And here you are, showing up without warning—"

"I notified Ian," he corrected.

"But he didn't notify me!"

They glared at each other. Her heart hammered in her chest. How quickly the atmosphere had chilled. "I want the truth, Ché."

His face turned hard. He wore the veneer of good manners very well, but she saw how formidable he could be if he ever loosed the outrage he checked so well. "I am *not* lying to you."

He told the truth. She heard it in his voice. She saw it in his eyes.

She pushed loose hair off her face. "Ian told me that you had nothing to do with Klark's plot. I believed him. I believe you, too," she added grudgingly.

His hackles went down somewhat, but a powerful heartbeat pulsed in his throat.

"Still, this 'of a sort' crap won't fly, Ché. If your visit is some kind of palace plot, I don't want any part of it."

"Neither do I, Princess."

She bristled. "Don't call me that."

Ché appeared stumped. "Call you what?"

"Princess." Her chin came up.

"But it is what you are. A princess."

"Technically, yes. But I have my own life. I have a career. Here, no one thinks of me as a princess." She jerked a finger at the window behind him. "That's why I didn't expect that photographer, and all those reporters, calling. That's why I didn't expect *you*!"

She pressed her fingertips to her temples. The stress of the last few weeks had caught up to her. Burning the candle at both ends, that's what she'd been doing. Sometimes she wondered where it would all lead, and if working like a dog was worth the effort. She needed a break, a rest. A vacation. Ché had the right idea. But with her brother's wedding looming and thoughts of traveling to Sienna eating at her, how would she be able to relax?

She felt suddenly tired and drained, creatively if not physically. For the first time in memory, she couldn't bear the thought of searching for new material for SILF. She wanted to lurch into her bedroom, slam the door, and shut out the world.

At least for the rest of the weekend.

Oh, that sounded too good. She'd take off all her makeup, slip on her grungiest sweats, order in food when she was awake, which wouldn't be very often. Mascara, hairbrushes, and shoes would not enter her reality. She'd be a slug, a total, worthless slug.

She almost sighed out loud.

Ché crossed his muscular arms over his chest. Silent, he regarded her. Was that commiseration she saw in his eyes? Quietly he said, "It is not easy to escape the influence of our families."

"No," she agreed softly. "It's not."

Whatever tension lingered seemed to drain away. She remembered his remark about palaces being tedious. "That's why you're here, isn't it? To escape from them."

His relief at her statement was obvious. "Yes."

"No plots."

"No."

"No quests for vengeance."

"None," he insisted. "Escape is my only goal."

"Good. I have no stomach for intrigue. That's why I'm a filmmaker and not a spy." She lifted her chin. "And why I don't go around calling myself a princess."

He bowed gallantly. "The word will not cross my lips again."

"Thank you."

"If," he continued, "during my stay on your world you do not remind me that I am a prince." A hint of rebelliousness flared in his eyes.

That unexpected spark of defiance only added to Ilana's curiosity about him. "Okay. You've got a deal."

A car door slammed outside. "Is that him?" she asked. She'd memorized the photographer's vehicle; if he ever came sniffing around again, she'd know who he was. He'd driven an old, non-electric Toyota pickup. You had to either love the old trucks to still drive them, or be well off, because the yearly penalty charged by the state of California for driving fossil-fueled cars made them a luxury.

Ché leaned over the windowsill, scanning the front lawn with narrowed eyes. "No. The . . . jerk with the camera is gone."

She laughed in surprise. The slang humanized Ché, made him somehow less forbidding. "Fifteen minutes with me, and look what's happened to your language."

Ché's eyes warmed. "Earth colloquial speech is essential to my fluency."

"Yeah. And by tomorrow, you'll be talking like a truck driver." She translated, using a nasal tone. "A barbarian driver of large ground cars. I vowed I'd never use the b-word, but after driving to Bakersfield last week, I'll have to make an exception for truck drivers."

"Slow. I do not know all your words," Ché pleaded.

"Too much local lingo—sorry. And I'm probably talking too fast. I'm trying to slow down, really I am." But hell if she was going to repeat it all again.

She sighed cheerily. "Amazing how much better I

feel now that I know no one's trying to kill me." She walked over, grabbed Ché by the wrist, and pulled him away from the window. "I'll find us a couple of cold beers," she explained as she positioned him in front of the couch. "Which—even if you don't—I need. But first you need to relax."

She reached up and pushed on his shoulders. Ché went down hard, almost taking her with him. She almost wished he were badly behaved enough to do it; she would have liked to know how he kissed.

He had a great mouth, just the way she liked them: wide with a friendly tilt at each end, with lips thin enough to be masculine, yet luscious enough for long, deep, wet kisses. Of course, she was assuming he knew how to use that mouth. If not, she'd be happy to show him—in the name of galactic understanding and peace, an exchange of culture, so to speak. Who said she wouldn't do her part for intergalactic diplomacy?

She grinned. "Are you hungry?"

"I do not wish to impose."

"Okay. You're hungry. So am I. I'll make us something to eat."

"Considering the circumstances of my arrival, you are an impeccable hostess," he said, resting one hand on his thigh.

"I'll tell my mother you said that." Ilana found the remote on the coffee table and turned on ESPN. "Soccer," she said. "Live from Europe, too. That's one advantage of being up in the middle of the night."

She thrust the remote at Ché. He took it. Her hands on her hips, she gazed down at him with pride. "Look at you now. On the couch, sports on the tube, the remote in your hand. Once I get you a beer, you'll be Earth-dwelling like a pro."

Again it looked like he missed half of what she'd

said. Oh, well. Body language would fill in the blanks.

Feeling his eyes on her, she sashayed from the living room to the kitchen, threw open the refrigerator door—and faced the reality of her lack of grocery shopping the last week.

Her shoulders sagged. The refrigerator was empty but for a quart of milk, four bottles of beer, an apple, a stick of butter, something that looked like leftover lasagna from Tony's, and three white cardboard takeout containers from Ming's.

"Gah, what a bonehead," she mumbled. Who bought flowers and no food? But then, she hadn't been expecting any guests.

"We'll have Chinese food." Microwaved, leftover Chinese food.

Welcome to Earth, bud.

She carried the containers to the microwave. "Beef chow fun and Kung Po chicken," she called. "And rice. Watch out for dried red peppers. But *Vash* like spicy food, right? Or at least on Sienna they do. Some of the dishes there about burned a hole in my tongue."

She found her serving spoons and matching bowls, then her best dishes. Cloth napkins, too, which was as formal as she ever got. Crisscrossing several times to the café table with its four mismatched antique chairs, she made two place settings.

The microwave beeped. She reached in, stirred the food. Then she sagged against the island to wipe her hands on a kitchen towel. Blowing her hair out of her eyes, she found Ché watching her with a mix of amusement and amazement. "What?" she demanded.

"I have never seen anyone who can do so much at once."

He appeared so fascinated that it made her blush.

Her hands twisted the dishtowel. She realized what she was doing, threw the towel on the counter, and smoothed her dress, just to have something to do with her empty hands. Rarely was she awkward. More rarely still was she awkward around men.

Men like Ché Vedla are out of your area of expertise, though. Yeah? Maybe. But hell would freeze before she'd admit that he flustered her.

"I'm multi-tasking," she explained. Let him figure that one out.

"Multi-tasking." He sounded out the phrase. "Doing many things at once. Why, are the cooks not on duty? The serving staff?"

She almost collided with the island in the center of the kitchen. "Serving staff?" Then she saw the mischief lighting up his gaze.

He was teasing her. She narrowed her eyes. "God, you are a beast."

"Perhaps." He smiled lazily.

Her stomach did a little flip-flop.

She heard cheers coming from the television. To her relief, the commotion drew Ché's attention. By the time she returned to the living room, a cold bottle of Red Rocket Ale in each hand, the soccer match had engrossed him. "Here you go," she sang out.

Immediately he pushed himself off the couch. He stood, dipping his head in a gesture of respect.

She sighed silently. "Don't do that."

"You are a woman, and thus deserving of such respect, as directed in the warrior's code."

More *Vash* mumbo jumbo. He'd recited it from memory. "Ché." She sighed. "I appreciate a man with manners, but if you're going to jump to attention every time I show up in my own house, I'll go nuts. You're on Earth now. You're not in the palace, not in the spotlight. You don't have to act the way *they* want

90

you to. Sit down and relax. I command you."

He complied, but with reluctance, taking the beer she offered. "I will seek to adapt to the rules of your culture, Ilana."

"The rule in my house is that there are no rules."

Exhaling, he smiled up at her and loosened his tie. Then he unbuttoned his collar, revealing a nice throat. *Vash* men didn't have hair on their chests, or much body hair, period, other than the expected places. Just smooth, firm, bronzed skin. Six feet, three inches of firm bronzed skin.

She pretended she didn't know that.

"So. Who's playing?" she asked.

"Sweden. And Latvia." His accent made the names of the countries sound truly exotic. "The score is"— he rotated his hand—"together."

She smiled. "Tied?"

"Yes. Tied."

An exciting game on TV, and yet he didn't try to peer around her to watch. Wow. A point for the prince, she thought.

She sat on the opposite end of the couch. She wasn't sure if it was to keep her hormones from self-combusting, or out of respect for Ché's fear that they needed a chaperone. "Go on, try the beer. You've tasted it before, right?"

"No, I have not."

"Not on your trip to LA?"

His mouth thinned. "That visit was to bring Klark home. I returned to Eireya immediately afterward."

"You'll have to make up for that on your holiday."

"I plan to, yes." He sniffed the vapor swirling out of the mouth of the bottle. Then he took a swallow, and his eyes lit up. "Beer," he murmured, studying the label before he took another drink. "Ah. It is quite good."

"*Quite* good?" She rolled her eyes. "Admit it, Ché. It's fantastic. You have nothing else like it in the galaxy. The Federation loves it. I know the man who brews Red Rocket Ale. Dan Brady. Purveyor to the king. He can't keep up with demand. I can't believe you missed out."

"I am afraid my family has never ordered beer for the kitchens."

"Why not? Too *Earth* for the Vedlas?"

He tipped his head, putting on that mask of politeness she suspected he used when he didn't want to reveal what he really thought. Royal tact. Like his posture, she'd bet that had been drilled into him from birth.

Of course, that made it more tempting to push his buttons. "If your family ever wants to understand us—and I have the feeling they do—they'll have to get over their fear of our exports."

"To admit that Earth could exert an influence on our culture, however small, would be the same as accepting it. By banning Earth products from Eireya, we can keep ourselves pure."

"Really," she said flatly.

"That was our belief. Then Rom chose your brother as heir to the throne." Smoothly he used his fingers to comb his hair back from his face. "I was one of your brother's first supporters, Ilana. If assuring his acceptance in the realm means importing Earth products, then I will have my family do it." He lifted the bottle. "It would seem that they do not know what they are missing."

She clinked her bottle against his. "Damn right, they don't."

He smiled. "Damn."

"That's another bad word," she warned sheepishly.

"I know. Ian taught it to me."

"My goody-two-shoes brother?" she asked approvingly.

Closing his eyes, Ché appeared to savor the taste of the icy ale before swallowing. His throat moved; the muscles in his jaw flexed. His eyes were heavy-lidded, as if he found the flavor of the ale pleasurable on a sensual level.

Talk about decadence, the *Vash* royal lifestyle defined the word. Ché had probably sampled every extravagance available to the very privileged, and then some. And yet, she'd been able to introduce him to something new. She liked that, considering how much effort the *Vash* put into their cuisine, which also reminded her that she was about to serve him reheated leftovers. Well, he'd deal with it. Her staff was on vacation. *Snort.*

"I like this 'soccer'," he said, his attention back on the game.

"You and the rest of the population. It's the most-watched sport in the world. We have some great local teams. I played a few seasons on one. I can take you to a game, if you want to go." She conjured a picture of wealthy, sophisticated Ché rooting for the home team on the rutted field behind Long's Drugs.

His eyes shifted from the TV to her. "You played with men?"

She'd played with plenty of men, actually, but she had the feeling that was not what he was asking. "It was a women's league."

He grew even more doubtful. "A team of *females*?"

Her chin came up. "Yeah. So?"

Ché's initial disapproval melted into genuine interest. "*Vash Nadah* royal women . . . they do not play sports."

The remark sounded more like a statement of fact than a criticism, a way of coaxing her into telling him more. But it didn't mean he didn't deserve a sassy reply. "Getting down and dirty in the grass and mud—it's the best way to reduce stress. Well, one of the best ways." She smiled slowly, rubbing the cold lip of the bottle against her lips. "Your women ought to try it. I bet it'd do more for your sex lives than those old books of yours."

The sudden heat in his intense, searching gaze made her toes curl. From inside her bedroom, the computer that handled incoming messages from her family chimed. "I bet that's Ian." She jumped off the couch. "I'll let him know you're here."

She lunged for her bedroom and closed the door. She slid around, pressing her back to the wall, and took several deep breaths. Every cell in her body blazed. Especially where it counted the most. Ché was damned lucky she hadn't ripped off his clothes so he could put out that fire.

Desire clutched at her, stealing her breath. The sex would be sweaty and wild, and when it was over, they'd argue, passionately and naked, about his grossly old-fashioned points of view, and why the hell his people overprotected their women over ten centuries after the danger of evil warlords sweeping down from the stars to rape, pillage, and enslave had faded into the archives of history. She wouldn't win that argument, not yet, and neither would he—not that he ever would—and they'd wind up making love all over again.

Aching from temptation, she almost groaned. Her hands curled into fists to counter the sensation as she tried to shake off his effect on her. It was bad enough he'd been on her mind for months now; he was a waste-of-time obsession any way she looked at it.

Again, the comm box beeped shrilly. "Okay, okay," she muttered. Scowling, she crossed the room on stiff legs. She slapped her hand on the answer panel, opening a channel for interstellar communication. If Ian had been able to persuade an empire to come together, he'd sure as hell better be able to convince her why this was her lucky day.

Chapter Seven

A stream of data made its way toward Sienna, a harsh desert world harboring a palace as ancient as it was beautiful: the ancestral home of the B'kahs. Made possible by the ancient technology of a civilization whose origins were lost to history, the data coalesced into a hand-span-high, three-dimensional holographic image of the crown prince's sister.

The miniature appeared on the table in front of the comm, blue-white radiance slithering around its outmost edges. "Yo, Ian!"

A towering man hefted his hulk of a body off a chair in the anteroom of the crown prince's bedchamber. He lumbered across the room to fetch his charge and let him know that the image-call he'd put through several standard hours ago had finally connected.

Officially, he was King Romlijhian B'kah's bodyguard—a position he'd held since he was little more than a lad, over two standard decades now. But just as often of late, he found himself assigned to missions involving Ian Hamilton, Rom's heir. It was difficult to decide which man he enjoyed working for more, the king or the prince.

His adventures with each had nearly gotten him killed several times over, but always there were side benefits: new worlds to see and people to meet. He didn't talk much, but he liked people, though not the ones he had to kill, the ones who tried to hurt the men he loyally served, the men he'd die defending. Still, he tried to concentrate on what he enjoyed about his job. On the last adventure, he'd been there when the crown prince found his bride-to-be, Tee'ah. And he'd got to see more of the galaxy's frontier, the worlds on the outer rim of settled space, than he'd ever wanted. The grimy border towns, the sorry bars, the colorful inhabitants . . . what a time that had been. Dangerous, too, yes, but what was life without a bit of spark? He liked spark in his life—and in his women, too, when he could get them.

He cracked a smile. Earthwomen—now, they had spark. His only regret was that he couldn't have stayed longer on the planet to see how deep that spark went. They might have liked him, those female Earth-dwellers, he thought hopefully. Ilana, Ian's sister, told him that his shoulders were as wide as one of their football player's with full padding, and that was a good thing; and that being six-foot-eight and over three hundred pounds—in Earth measurements—won him a lot of second glances. If his attention hadn't been so focused on protecting Ian Hamilton from the Vedlas, he might have noticed, too.

He scratched his big hand over the stomach he worked at keeping hard. Ilana and her mother, Queen Jasmine, said that on Earth he'd have been called "Conan" or "Thor" or some such thing that meant nothing to him.

Muffin sighed, shaking his head. He always had to explain it, all the time, to English speakers like Ian's family. But they never seemed to understand that on his homeworld his given name personified rugged masculinity, a warrior's unflagging endurance.

Not a "sweet little breakfast cake."

Muffin stopped in front of the comm box. It sensed his proximity. A soft, melodic computer voice said, "Incoming message waiting."

"Acknowledged," he replied. "Stand by."

An afterimage of Ilana Hamilton waited in suspended motion. It would come to life again once the call was answered.

He paused to study the image of the prince's twin sister, and the back of his neck tingled. *Great Mother*. He froze, his hand extended toward the comm. The sensation passed, and he drew his hand back slowly.

He'd felt his neck prickle like that only rarely. But every time, the peculiar sensation preceded his life taking a different direction.

A slow grin spread over his face. Ah, it looked like another adventure awaited him. He hadn't asked the prince why he'd been summoned here this morning—it wasn't his place to do so—but he now knew that he'd come here for a reason.

He gained speed as he lumbered into the prince's private chamber. Not too long ago, Rom had asked if he was ready to consider retirement. That had surprised Muffin. He was still relatively young, thirty-six standard years, and physically he was in top form. But Rom had said that anytime he desired, he would consider Muffin's service to him and to the realm complete.

Yet the idea of returning to his homeworld didn't

appeal. He'd only be coddled by his mother, and expected to drink mugs of hot galag with his father and grandfathers during the long, frigid nights—and that, after having been begged by the village children to tell story after story of his exploits.

Muffin told the king he'd think about it. Maybe in another few decades he'd make a decision.

Ian met him at the door, a steaming cup of the Earth-brew coffee in his hands. The crown prince didn't wear typical *Vash Nadah* capes and boots unless he was meeting with Federation visitors, preferring casual Earth attire when at the palace, including the blue jeans that Earth-dwellers favored.

This morning, Ian also wore the look of contentment he'd had about him lately: a powerful new self-confidence. He'd also put on more muscle, Muffin noted approvingly. It must be the Bajha he played daily. The sport was a vigorous and ancient sword-play game that sharpened the senses and built stamina, both of which were valued highly by the *Vash Nadah*. As pacifistic as their society was, they strived never to forget their roots: the Eight original founding warriors who had long ago restored peace and life to a warring, dying galaxy.

"Your call has arrived, sir," Muffin announced in Siennan. After many head-wracking lessons, he'd finally achieved fluency in English, but he followed Ian's rule, using Basic or Siennan when at the palace, and English when dealing with Earth or Ian's sister.

Ian walked over and sat at the console in front of the comm box. "Please stay here," he told Muffin, then: "Security screens off." The anteroom's monitoring equipment went black.

The prince turned his gaze to Muffin. "Only three other individuals besides me know of what I'm going to tell my sister." There was a flicker of warning in those greenish Earth-dweller eyes. "Rom B'kah isn't one of them."

Muffin held his tongue. He had no interest in politics, nor the experience to understand all its workings; only fierce devotion to the men he served and their families drove him. He went where he was told, and he protected those to whom he'd sworn loyalty. That was all.

"Understood," he replied, taking up a position behind and to the right of Ian, strategically placing himself between the prince and the door, from instinct more than necessity. There had never been danger to the B'kahs within the palace. But complacency killed.

The prince answered the call. "Hey, Ilana," he said in English.

Ilana's image flickered, disappeared for a moment, and then came alive. She leaned forward at the waist. "Well, look who finally showed up."

"I've been calling *you*," Ian corrected.

"So I heard. I'd have gotten back to you sooner if you'd left a message."

"The device doesn't allow for that."

"I know." She sighed, appearing tired to Muffin's trained eye. He had a talent for observation of body language and other subtle characteristics often missed by others. Perhaps that was why Ian had called him here today.

"I meant on the cell phone," Ilana continued. "I had to work late. A reception."

"I couldn't call your cell. I couldn't risk anyone listening in. And I can't now."

Her voice dropped. "What's wrong?"

Ian folded his arms on the table and leaned toward her. "Are you alone?"

"You're scaring me, Ian."

"There's nothing to be scared about."

She walked closer. "The truth?"

"The truth," he reassured her, and repeated his question. "Are you alone?"

"No," she said, smiling as she drew out the word. "But *he's* out of earshot—in the living room, a beer in one hand and a remote in the other." She fisted her hands on her hips. "Now, would you mind telling me what the hell Ché Vedla's doing on my couch?"

Muffin almost keeled over. Ché Vedla was on Earth?

The tension left Ian's shoulders. "So he made it."

"Yep," she said.

Muffin couldn't believe it. He'd encountered the unexpected many times in his years working for the royal family. Nothing much surprised or shocked him. But as hard as he tried, he couldn't wrap his mind around the image of a Vedla making himself at home in an Earth-dweller's household.

Ian looked enormously pleased. He laced his fingers together and placed his hands on his stomach. "He wanted to take a vacation."

"That's what he said, too. But, come on. A Vedla taking a holiday on Earth? What's going on, Ian? What's his family up to this time?"

Muffin concentrated, glancing from Ian to his twin and back again.

"Arranging a wedding," Ian replied. "For him. Ché's getting married in six months."

Muffin pondered the odd expression that flickered across Ilana's features. "But isn't that a little close to yours?" she asked.

"Because of the situation with Tee'ah, we want Ché to marry before I do. It will preserve *Vash* pride and help the Vedlas save face."

"You're kidding."

"I would never joke about matters concerning the Treatise of Trade."

Ilana appeared disgusted. "So who's the lucky woman?"

"His advisors are taking care of it."

"He's letting his future wife be chosen by committee?" She shook her head. "How sad."

"That's the way it's done, Ilana."

"You agree with this? This is okay with you?"

"Yes."

Ian's firm, patient tone broadcast how comfortable he'd become in his leadership role. Only he didn't sound like the Ian that Muffin knew.

Ilana appeared perplexed by the change in Ian, as well. "I still don't understand why he came to Earth."

"Because it was distant, remote, and not expected of him."

"I see."

She did? Muffin didn't.

"Ché wanted out of town, for lack of a better term. He didn't want to be bothered with the details of wedding planning."

Ilana raised her hands like a shield. "Wedding fever."

The ends of Ian's mouth twitched. "I knew you'd understand."

"Yeah. Totally." She tucked loose tendrils of hair behind her ear. "How long is Ché going to be able to escape—er, I mean stay here?"

"As soon as a wife candidate is found, he'll fly home and seal the promise. It might be as early as a few weeks, or as long as a few months."

First, Ilana glowered. Then her face lit up. She shook her finger at Ian. "Ooh, tradition breach," she scolded mockingly. "Royal engagements have to last a year. That means Ché's off the hook until next summer."

"Actually, no. The Vedlas are going to backdate the documents to when Ché should have sealed his promise with Tee'ah. It'll make it all legal."

Her arm dropped slowly. "They're serious about this, aren't they?"

"It's the Vedlas."

"True." She sighed and shook her head. "Poor Ché. He doesn't stand a chance."

"Ilana, he doesn't look at it that way."

"No. He probably doesn't. He's so . . . *Vash. Vash* follow the rules, especially when family pride's involved."

"As it should be," Ian said.

Ilana gave him another strange look. So did Muffin. The crown prince and his sister shared a great love of Rom B'kah, but they differed in their views of the Federation and its eleven-thousand-year-old traditions. Though liberal for a prince, Ian was the more conservative of the two, while his sister seemed to rebel oftentimes for the sheer joy of doing it. While Ian knew to appear as a traditionalist when around the Great Council, to come across this hard-line when talking to his sister seemed . . . well, out of character.

"This is scary, Ian," she said. "You're starting to sound like one of them."

"I am one of them."

Although Ian's face was friendly, and he looked younger than his twenty-seven standard years, his eyes revealed the dogged strength of the man inside. "It's my duty to keep stability and harmony in the realm."

Ilana's eyes were no less intense. But in them, the spark of rebellion glittered. "It my duty to save Ché."

"Save him from what? Marriage?"

"From the great sucking hole of *Vash Nadah* tradition." She pushed her hair away from her face, revealing flushed cheeks and a frown. "You should see him, Ian. He pretends that nothing affects him. But it does. I'm not wearing the blinders that you all are. I can see. He's wound up like a coiled spring. He can't loosen up. I can see why, can't you?"

"I'm sure you'll tell me, Ilana."

Ilana went on as if she hadn't heard him. She probably hadn't, Muffin thought. "Look at the year he's had," she said. "First, he's demoted. Then his fiancée dumps him. Then he has to deal with his idiot brother's shenanigans! He deserves a break. Hell, he needs one. He needs to loosen up." An impish smile began in her bright blue eyes and spread to her mouth. "He needs to have some fun."

"Ilana," Ian warned.

"You'll only encourage her," Muffin cautioned under his breath.

Ian's eyes willed him into silence.

Muffin hunched his bulky shoulders and frowned. Why didn't the prince listen to sense? Admonitions would only goad his twin into defying him.

Ilana screwed up her face. "I despise overbearing, arrogant, controlling men, but Ché's very polite. Almost to a fault." She brightened. "Despite my determination to provoke him."

Muffin made a sound in the back of his throat, imagining the two of them together, unsupervised.

"It's a facade that begs to be cracked, Ian. And I know just the women to do the cracking."

Ian pushed his tongue against the inside of his mouth.

"I'll introduce him to my friends," she offered cheerily. "My single, attractive, eligible girlfriends."

"He has to marry a princess. Or if not a princess, a woman of high rank in the Federation."

"Who says he's going to get hitched? My aim is to provide him with a distraction. A good time. If, after my best efforts, he still caves in and marries"—she placed her hand over her heart—"at least I'll know that he spent his last days as a single man having fun."

"It's not a question of caving in. Ché will marry as instructed. I have no doubt of that. He's a model *Vash Nadah* prince."

Ilana lifted a brow. "Tee'ah didn't cave in to an arranged marriage, or she wouldn't be marrying you. What makes you think Ché will toe the line?"

"He will."

"Overconfidence killed the cat," she retorted.

"That was curiosity."

"Overconfidence got him there. It's irritating, how you assume he'll do what you say."

"He will." Ian's grin broadened, heightening Muffin's puzzlement. It was almost as if he were pushing Ilana to take a stand.

"Wanna bet?" she shot back.

There. Ian had gone and done it. But there was still the chance to repair his tactical blunder with a strategic retreat.

"Ilana, Ilana." Ian shook his head. "When have you ever won a bet we've made?"

Muffin slapped his hand over his face and groaned.

Ilana's smile was sweet. Too sweet. "There's always a first time, bucko. Ché marries on schedule, you win. He doesn't, and I win. We'll work out the terms later."

"You're on." Ian relaxed in his chair.

Muffin scratched his head, trying to figure out what he'd just witnessed.

"Where will Ché be staying?" Ian asked. "Your place?"

"Hell, no. Tomorrow, he's out. A hotel, a resort, whatever he wants. But we'll be in touch. I guarantee that."

Ian leaned forward. This time, his expression was that of the man Muffin knew. His voice had gentled, too. "I know this isn't your thing, Ilana, getting involved with palace affairs. I appreciate it. I appreciate your helping me out."

"I didn't think I was helping."

"You know what I mean."

Her voice softened. "I know."

They exchanged a look of affection. "Ché needs to stay anonymous," Ian warned. "For security reasons. Promise me that."

"I'll promise anything except keeping him out of trouble."

What did Ian expect, Muffin thought peevishly, after encouraging Ilana so?

The image of Ilana lifted its miniature arm. "Give my love to Tee'ah."

"I will."

Ilana's face shimmered. "Love you."

Ian drew his index finger through the projected image with clear affection. "Love you, too."

The image faded. Ian slapped his hands on the console and let out a whoop. "Excellent! This couldn't have gone better in my dreams."

He stretched his arms over his head, his fingers laced together. Releasing a gust of air, he turned to Muffin and sobered. "What's that face for?"

Muffin dipped his head to peer into the prince's eyes. "What's going on, sir?"

"You play poker, right? The Earth card game."

"The king taught me."

"Do you recall the term bluffing?"

"When you make the other player think you have different cards."

Ian nodded.

"You *want* Ilana to corrupt the prince?" Muffin asked, incredulous.

Ian groaned. "No. I want them to fall in love."

Muffin stared at his ward. No words came to him.

"I think they're halfway there already," Ian explained. "I can sense it. She gave him a look that day in Los Angeles that I've never seen before. And Ché—he couldn't keep his eyes off her. We've all heard of love at first sight, but I don't think I even believed it until I watched Ché and my sister. Neither of them would ever admit it, though."

Muffin folded thick arms over his chest and awaited the words that would release him from his confusion.

Ian leaned back in his chair. "What I'm going to tell you is totally off the record. It goes against the spirit of the Treatise of Trade, as well as the wishes of the *Vash* kings. I'm playing matchmaker with Ché and my sister. I want them to get married."

"To each other?"

Ian laughed. "Yes, to each other." He pushed himself to his feet.

Muffin watched him stroll across the room. "But, sir, would you breed a ketta-cat to one of your Earth dogs?"

"Opposites attract. And often make the best matches. Look at Princess Tee'ah and me."

"You two are more alike than not," Muffin pointed out.

Ian's face gentled. "We know that now. We didn't then, when we met. I think Ilana and Ché have even more in common. They just don't see it yet."

Muffin shook his head. "I don't know . . ."

"Have some faith, Muff. Worst case, Ché returns home to marry and my sister stays single. Status quo. Nothing changes." Ian's mouth tipped. "Of course, I'm hoping that won't happen. Looking at Ilana just now, looking in her eyes, I can see he's already growing on her."

Muffin's frown deepened. Had they observed the same woman? All he'd seen in Ilana's eyes was trouble. But it wasn't respectful to disagree with your boss.

Ian withdrew his palmtop from his breast pocket and walked away, pacing slowly as he studied something on the computer. The prince spoke without glancing up from his typing. "How does a trip to Earth sound?"

Muffin's head snapped up. "When?"

Ian grinned. "That's the spirit. I need you to leave as soon as possible."

Muffin rubbed the back of his neck, remembering the tingles he'd felt there, heralding this new adventure. Ah, his neck hadn't led him wrong yet.

"Ché Vedla's there alone," Ian explained. "Without guards, without staff. He's incognito, yes, but it could get sticky. And not only because of my interference. Ché's father doesn't know where he is. Rom doesn't, either. But I do. If anything were to happen, there'd be hell to pay. We don't need that controversy. *I* don't need that controversy."

"No, sir." Muffin shook his head briskly.

"Officially, everyone here will think I'm sending you to Earth on a matter of diplomacy. No one will question it." Ian held his gaze. "On Earth, you'll have to be equally covert. We'll come up with a convenient cover story."

Muffin grinned. "My specialty."

"Also, you'll need to refresh yourself with handling

a car—an automobile. You're going to be driving in L.A."

Muffin's grin wobbled. Downtown Los Angeles. That was where Ian had driven him for his one experience traveling by ground car on Earth. A clear image came back to him, of hanging on to the meager safety harness in the rear seat as Ian crossed lanes thick with other travelers only to accelerate onto a high-speed lane reserved for electric vehicles. He remembered, too, Ian's amused attitude toward his *Vash* passengers' protests. Traveling at such high velocities while so close to other primitive vehicles, all under individual control, seemed to Muffin a suicidal venture. "On an electric speedway," Ian had assured him, "this is perfectly legal, trust me."

Muffin swallowed, buried the memory, and managed a smile. "What's a mission without a little danger, sir?"

"In the meantime, I'll get you the documents you'll need, cash, a bank account, and an apartment and car for Earth—the usual. I don't want you distracted with details when you get there. I need you to be my eyes and ears, to warn me if anything goes wrong."

Muffin understood Ian's concern. Huppnuts don't fall far from the tree, his mother always said. And neither did Vedlas. Ché, after all, was that blasted Klark's brother, scud-sucker that he was.

Muffin drew himself up to his full height, bringing his fist over his chest with a hearty thump. "Never fear, sir. I'll keep your sister safe from the Vedla heir."

"Ilana?" Ian laughed, shaking his head. "You don't know my sister." Holding his stomach, he regarded Muffin with mirth-filled eyes. "If you've got to worry about someone, Muffin, you'd better save it for Ché."

Chapter Eight

Ilana shut the bedroom door quietly. Ché sat on the couch, his back to her. Engrossed in the soccer game, he didn't hear her tread into the kitchen.

He was on a forced march to the altar. A decision that Ilana's own brother supported!

Angrily she punched the reheat button on the microwave. A week ago, she would have saved her pity for Ché's soon-to-be wife. But based on what she'd just learned, her feelings had done a complete one-eighty. She'd put the word out tomorrow that a guy she knew was in town, an incredibly good-looking and rich man who just happened to need a little cheering up after being dumped by his girlfriend.

She stole a glance at Ché. How perfectly at home he looked. He'd draped one arm languidly over the armrest. His long legs were stretched out in front of him, crossed at the ankles. The lamplight turned his hair amber-gold and softened his sculpted features. She liked the way his long, straight nose came that extra, delicious fraction of an inch closer to his upper lip, giving him the look of an ancient Greek statue.

Poor, poor sexy beast. Her mouth tipped. Oh, yeah. There'd be no shortage of volunteers to help out. Ché Vedla had "challenge" stamped right across his forehead.

Too bad she couldn't save him for herself. But, besides the obvious problems, it smacked of a conflict of interest after the bet she'd made with Ian. Not that they'd set any rules as to just how she'd keep Ché off the marriage market, but she liked to think she had principles. Well, one or two, anyway.

She returned to the microwave and pulled out the heated food containers, scooping steaming rice into a bowl, which she then hefted into her arms to carry to the table. It would be better to gather the players, sit back, and watch the games begin.

"The game is over," said an accented man's voice.

The blood drained from her head. She straightened abruptly and spun around. Her knuckles banged into a tall, warm, and very solid body.

Ché grabbed the bowl to keep her from dropping it. She watched his lovely mouth form words of apology. Then he stated, "Latvia won. Three to two."

She exhaled, squeezing her eyes shut. "Oh. That game." He hadn't overheard her conversation with Ian. Or mind-read her newest bad habit: fantasizing about what he looked like naked.

Leaving him looking a bit lost, as usual, she breezed back and forth in front of him until she'd brought the remaining bowls to the table.

He waited until she sat, and then joined her. "Ian told me about your wedding," she said.

Ché kept his expression neutral. "Yes. I assumed he would."

"That explains the timing of your little holiday."

Ché's mouth tightened almost imperceptibly. "I would have been more of a hindrance to their plans than a help."

She spread her hands on the table and leaned toward him. "Hey, you don't have to explain it to me. I understand." She pointed to her left hand. "You don't see any wedding ring here, do you?" She shook her head. "I can't stand it. The planning, the preparation, the anxiety. The minute details people will obsess over! Not how much food, but what shape it needs to be, and what color. Even the drinks. Would you care if the wine didn't match the flowers?"

She could tell by his expression that he understood exactly what she meant—and had suffered through it, too. "Your weddings last only a day," he pointed out. "Imagine ours, lasting six days."

"I don't have to imagine it. I experienced it." Ilana dropped her chin onto her hands, joining with him in misery.

"Ah, yes. When your mother married King Romlijhian B'kah."

"The feasts, the parties, the ceremonies," she began.

"All day, every day," he added.

"Until you can barely drag yourself out of bed for the next round," she finished. "Ugh! And those receiving lines!"

"They last the entire day."

"I felt so sorry for my mother and Rom, having to stand there and smile through the whole thing."

"The worst sort of torture," he agreed. "More thought goes into the order of who passes through those lines than some of the most critical issues our Great Council has had to consider."

She laughed. "I can see why you wait a year to marry after making promise vows. How else would you have time to practice everything, to memorize everything?"

His mouth twisted. "I suppose that's what I should be doing. Practicing. My promise period will be greatly abbreviated."

"No." The word came out more forcefully than she intended. "You're not doing homework while you're here."

"Homework? I do not know the word."

"Practicing, preparation," she explained. "If your family wants to rush you into this, then it's their problem if you're not ready."

His jaw hardened. "I will be ready."

"Oops," she said. "I pushed a button, didn't I? You're *Vash Nadah;* you're better prepared than the Boy Scouts." Her slang likely went over his head, but the feelings behind her words came through loud and clear.

His eyes went dark. "I do as my family commands. It is our way. It is the way it has always been done."

"I know. No matter how many corners your family pushes you into." She shook her head. "These are your last weeks as a single man. You ought to enjoy them. Without guilt."

She herself had had enough guilt to last a lifetime, namely left over from her parents' divorce, and she didn't care to accumulate any more. So she'd simply exorcised the emotion completely. Whatever she did, she refused to feel guilt over it.

She watched steam twirl up from the bowl of rice. "Guilt sucks," she repeated, more softly.

Ché gave her a curious and yet intrigued look, his brow lifting.

Ilana took a long drink from her bottle of beer. Plunking the bottle onto the table, she leveled her gaze at him. " 'The good of the people outweighs that

113

of the individual.' It's the *Vash Nadah* mantra. Hey,
it's worked for eleven thousand years, so who am I
to argue?" She leaned forward. "All I'm saying is that
having fun is not a crime. That's why you came here,
and that's what you're going to do. I've come up with
a few ideas to kick things off. Just let me handle it."

He sat back in his seat, fingers steepled under his
cleft chin as he observed her. She tried to appear as
innocent as possible. Finally, he said, "What is the
word you use—*okay?*"

"Yes. Okay." Her smile returned. "So. It's okay,
then?"

"Yes. I am grateful for your help in this matter."

Her chuckle veered a little close to an evil cackle.
"Ah, Ché. Don't thank me yet. I haven't even started."

Ché wasn't sure what woke him, but the moment he
opened his eyes, he was instantly alert. He was in
Ilana's home, in her spare bedroom. Judging by the
amount of sunlight flooding the small bedchamber,
it was well past dawn, his usual waking hour.

He sat up and swung his legs over the edge of the
bed. Well past dawn? Of course. He hadn't retired
until after sunrise; he'd been too busy conversing—
or rather, arguing—about a dizzying variety of sub-
jects over a meal that finally ended hours after they'd
started, long after the beer and food had run out.

He scrubbed his palm over his stubbly jaw. Responsible for a good deal of his vertigo was Ilana's
reaction to his upcoming wedding. He wasn't quite
sure what he'd expected from her, but outrage overlaid with pity wasn't it. If only on that matter alone,
he'd found an unexpected ally in the Earth princess.

Wedding fever. Yes, that was the derisive term she'd
used to describe those who displayed an over-
abundance of enthusiasm and meticulousness in

planning a wedding ceremony. Ché could think of no better description, and would certainly use the term when he returned home—to amuse himself as his wedding loomed. How would Councilman Toren react upon hearing he suffered from the exasperating malady? Or Hoe?

Chuckling, Ché rose from bed. As he stretched sleep from his limbs, he realized that he couldn't recall the last time he'd risen from bed with a smile. Perhaps Earth agreed with him, and his decision to vacation here wasn't as symptomatic of folly as Hoe had accused.

He glanced about the bedchamber. The room was small, like the rest of Ilana's abode, but colorful and charming—in a disorderly way, much like the woman herself.

But the desk . . . it did not seem to belong amongst the chaos. The surface was polished and clear. Ché's father, the king, tended toward exacting standards of organization, but Ilana's workspace would have put even him to shame. Along the wall were neat and ordered stacks of printed periodicals, data storage discs, and paper of various sizes covered with neatly handwritten notes. A camera Ché recognized as one that created moving images sat to the right of a computer and next to a metal cup containing writing implements of every description. The only frivolity on the entire desk was a cluster of frames containing images of Ilana's family.

The organized desk opened a window to the inner workings of the woman's mind that Ché didn't know, or expect. He stored away the information, wondering what else he'd underestimated about her—like her focus on her career, her creativity, her drive.

Vash women didn't carry on a trade. It would drain time and energy away from their obligations. Not only that; there was the issue of propriety to consider regarding princesses and careers. . . .

Propriety. Bah. Had he not come here to escape such boundaries? Today, he'd not let decorum govern his actions. Here, on Earth, he was far from the watching eyes of his household, far from the requirement for respectability. As long as he didn't look *Vash*, there was no need to act *Vash*.

From outside, he heard shouts and laughter. That was what had woken him, he realized. He slipped on a pair of eyeshaders his jeweler had fashioned for him for the purposes of this trip, combed his fingers through his hair instead of styling it more precisely, and walked to the window, open to let in the sounds of the street and shore.

Three boys played below, not quite children and not yet adults. They rode flat boards with four wheels apiece. He searched his memory for the name of the recreational vehicles. Something . . . boards. Surfboards, perhaps?

The angle of the sun told him it was well past midday, perhaps nearing late afternoon. He'd slept far later than even his late night with Ilana would explain. It was due to his out-of-adjustment body clock: Earth used twenty-four-hour days, and Eireya used closer to twenty-eight, in standard hours. It made for shorter nights than what he was used to.

Cool ocean air whooshed around his torso and thighs, reminding him that these quarters were not private, as were his at the palace. Nor did the averted eyes of palace servers surround him. While the balcony shielded Ché from the waist down, he realized that perhaps he should not be standing there without clothing.

He rummaged through the supplies he had packed and donned faded blue pants over boxers, Earth's version of an undergarment. An emblem decorated a black short-sleeved shirt he pulled over his head: "Harley-Davidson." The T-shirt and blue jeans guaranteed that he'd blend in, according to Ian, who had so kindly sent him the images necessary for the Vedla tailor to fashion the items and a number of other pieces comprising a small wardrobe. The rest Ché would acquire once he was more familiar with the attire of the local inhabitants.

He caught a reflection of himself in a narrow wall mirror, stopped and stared. Great Mother. Look at him—barefoot, trousers hugging his hips, the snug black shirt tucked into the jeans, his short hair finger-combed. And he could use a shave, he thought, rubbing his jaw. But he wasn't bothered in the least. No, indeed. With his vision-enhancing shaders covering his telltale *Vash* eyes, he looked like an Earth-dweller.

At that, he winced at the cries of protest emanating from his conscience. Usually, he had to enter meditation in order to connect with his ancestors, but he could hear their howls of collective dismay without trying, the entire, long traditionalist line of them, Vedlas all, stretching back eons before the Eight Great Warriors joined together and took back the galaxy. *Barbarian!* they accused.

Ché tried to soothe them. *I am here for you, and because of you,* he said silently in the ancient Eireyan tongue that no one outside his family and people knew. *I traveled here only because I would not wish to impede the Great Council's efforts to find me a wife.*

That was mostly true, he thought. But he heard nothing but ominous silence in response.

Ian Hamilton had once laughingly told him that *Vash Nadah* and Catholics shared one indisputable characteristic: guilt. But Ché was not going to let that ubiquitous trait dampen his enjoyment of his visit here.

The main room was empty. The wood floor felt cool beneath his feet. While he didn't expect that a prepared bath awaited him, he hoped that Ilana had set out breakfast. Instead, displayed on the table were last night's dirty dishes and four drained bottles of beer. The only thing that looked fresh was the water in the clear, globular vase holding the flowers.

Ché noted that fact well. Ilana had seen to the flowers, prolonging their freshness, while she let the other chores slide or ignored them altogether. The woman's priorities were intriguing. Perhaps he should take a lesson from her while on Earth: Savor the pleasures of life without the encumbrance of conventional expectations.

He wasn't sure if he knew how.

Ché smelled something fresh and nutty. The Earth beverage, coffee. Ilana was awake. But where was she?

"Ilana?" He flattened his hand on his stomach and glanced around. A radio played music and a man's voice: "Don't forget the sun block if you're headed to the beach. We're looking at sunny skies today, temperatures in the mid eighties . . ."

The exotic and tempting smell led him into the kitchen. He picked up the note he found on the counter. *You're finally up! I went out running*, she'd written. *Take coffee. We'll find us something to eat when I get back.*

Find something, eh? He already knew it would not be in this abode. They would have to find an eating establishment. He had Earth currency. He'd pay for the venture!

He eyed the pot of hot, brewed liquid suspiciously. He recognized the apparatus from the Earth programs he'd studied. He'd tried coffee once, years ago when a Federation merchant had attempted to convince the Vedlas to import the product; Ché hadn't cared for it, giving his family another reason besides a disinclination to stock Earth products to decline the shipment. Coffee tasted bitter to him. Harsh. He preferred tock. Tock had a mellow, sweet-spicy taste that was so much more pleasant than this Earth-dweller brew. But the result was the same—both beverages stimulated the central nervous system, and his needed some stimulating, with his body still insisting that it was the middle of the night.

He poured a cup and took the mug with him, intending to sit outside on the balcony, where he'd spied two simple chairs and a tiny round table.

But the sound of a chime stopped him. Not a moment later, the front door swung open, revealing a tall man with shaggy black hair.

The man stomped in. "Ilana?" He wore battered tan ankle-high boots and shorts of the same fabric of Ché's pants. Jeans. His shirt was flimsy with wide armholes and had no sleeves, revealing muscled arms bronzed from sunlight. His dark eyes grew blacker the more disappointed they became.

How presumptuous, Ché thought, to enter unannounced and expect Ilana to be there, waiting. He took another sip of coffee. "Ilana is not here."

At the sound of Ché's voice, the man froze. His black eyes swerved to the kitchen, where Ché stood. "Who the hell are you?"

Before Ché could reply, the man's gaze dropped to the cup of coffee in Ché's hands, and then to Ché's bare feet. His face crumpled. "Aw, hell." He lowered his head and blew out a few gusts of hair, as if he were trying to compose himself. Then he sized up Ché. "She didn't waste any time, did she?"

Ché lifted a brow. "Waste time?"

"Two weeks ago she was with me. Now she's with you. And she let you stay the night? I tried. She told me no one stayed. Consider yourself lucky, dude."

The man assumed Ché was Ilana's lover. He must have shared such a relationship with Ilana or he wouldn't have jumped to that conclusion. Earth-women could take lovers, Ché reminded himself. But the thought of Ilana making love with this oaf irritated him. Acutely.

But show it he would not. He would not descend to the same level of barbarism as this uncouth intruder. He extended his hand in Earth-dweller fashion. "Greetings. I am"—he caught himself—"French," he said, taking the moniker Sam had given him and making it a bit . . . stronger.

"French." The man made a face. "That explains it."

"Ilana and I, we—"

The man's hand shot up. "That's okay. I don't need details."

Details? Did he expect Ché would share them, had there been any? It would be coarse and crude to do so. Intimate relations between a man and a woman were to be celebrated and kept private out of respect. To do otherwise countered everything his people believed. "Allow me to clarify. Ilana and I, we are not—"

"And you won't be, just in case you're hoping." The man raised his voice to make it sound like Ilana's. " 'An exclusive relationship is so confining. It's more fun being friends'." He shook Ché's hand in a sinewy, callused grip. "Cole Miller. The one she told you about."

Ché covered his distaste for the man's boorish presumption with a polite smile and said nothing.

"I'm a cameraman," Cole explained with increasing gloom. "I worked with SILF on the Holt film." He tried to peer past Ché's eyeshaders. "So, what are you—an actor?"

"Of a sort," Ché replied smoothly.

"Of a sort." Cole rolled his eyes. "The accent may not get you work, buddy, but it'll get you laid—I guarantee that." He stopped himself, his cheeks turning red as if he'd realized what he'd said. Swearing, he handed Ché a thick roll of paper he'd carried wedged between his arm and ribs. "The *Times*."

Shoulders hunched, he marched into the kitchen. "I'll get my dog bowl and go." He grabbed a shapeless blue item off the counter, crushing it in his fist. "She can't stand them, you know. Dogs."

Ché shrugged. "I do not care for the creatures myself."

Cole appeared to search for something else. "And she's commitment-phobic, too. Here's some more advice, French—attachment is futile. Enjoy what you got with her while it lasts, because it won't last long."

Triumphant, Cole stomped away and down the stairs, where another man arrived. They eyed each other suspiciously, walking past each other without saying a word.

Ché shook his head. Was this newcomer yet another disillusioned discard in Ilana's parade of lovers? How many more would he have to endure before she returned?

Exhaling, Ché donned his shoes and walked outside to greet the man. The newcomer was balding and slender, and he appeared to be in better spirits than Cole.

"Hello," the man called out cheerily. He carried a palm computer and a comm—cell phone, as the Earth-dwellers called them—and wore the same eager, slightly furtive look as the jerk-with-the-camera from the night before. "Jim Bohannon. *Coastal Chron-*

icle. Is Ms. Hamilton in? I'd like to ask her a few questions about the wedding."

The wedding. Ché growled silently. This was no rebuffed lover. No, he represented something far more troublesome. "She is not here."

"Do you know when she'll be back?"

"No. I do not."

The man's curiosity homed in on Ché. "And you are . . . ?"

"French."

"That explains the accent."

"French is my name."

"Ah," Bohannon said. "Are you a member of the family, Mr. French?"

"No."

"A friend."

Ché hesitated. "Yes."

The reporter flashed a grin. "Boyfriend?"

Ché felt his jaw stiffen. The man began scribbling something on a pad. Ché averted the potential disaster with a preemptive strike: "I am her advisor."

He could indeed function in that capacity while he was here, he thought wryly. The Earth princess could use his advice on nearly every aspect of her chaotic life. Whether she would heed his counsel was another matter entirely. "I'm advising her on Earth matters."

At that, Bohannon glanced up.

Great Mother. Earth matters? Ché sounded alien, even to his own ears. Bohannon peered at Ché's golden skin and his face, clearly trying to see what color eyes he'd hidden behind the mirrored sunshaders.

"World matters," Ché clarified. "I am from . . . Latvia." *Latvia?* The impetuous alibi burst to the surface like a deep-sea jet-trawler, the small country fresh in his mind after its triumph over Sweden in soccer. Luckily, the information seemed to satisfy the exasperating interloper.

As the journalist scribbled more on his pad, a movement below caught Ché's attention. The street and walkways teemed with pedestrian and vehicle traffic. From behind a hedge, a man stood, aiming a camera at both him and Bohannon.

This was preposterous! The man was walking about freely, taking photos of them? Why did the B'kahs leave Ilana so open and vulnerable? Ché straightened his spine and squared his shoulders. If the B'kahs wouldn't protect her, the Vedlas would.

Ché marched down the stairs.

"Mr. French!"

Would the man's prattle never cease? "I must return to my duties now. You are dismissed," Ché added over his shoulder as he strode across the lawn. The reporter was beginning to remind him of Hoe, his advisor. That thought made him walk all the faster.

The sun angled closer to the ocean now. A dearth of wind allowed the air to hold fast to sea scents and summer heat. But there was no time to enjoy the day. Years of dealing with the many faces of innuendo and the veiled threats of the palace court and Great Council had made him a master of intimidation, and he intended to use the talent to convince the "paparazzi" to give up their relentless hunt of Ilana.

The photographer wore a pencil-thin mustache and a bright yellow tank top far more loose fitting than Cole's had been, exposing his armpits and chest furred with dark hair, and a wealth of body art. It was difficult to determine who wore less clothing in Los Angeles, the men or the women.

Ché slapped the rolled-up newspaper Cole had

given him in his open palm. Not quite a weapon, but wielded properly it could serve as reasonable intimidation. "You there! I wish to speak to you."

But the paparazzo appeared to be in no mood to talk. He shoved items into a black bag and threw it over his shoulder as he jogged into the road.

That was when Ché spied Ilana crossing the street. Passing by the photographer, she showed him the middle finger of her right hand. "Take a picture of this, you jerk."

Ground cars clogged the thoroughfare, preventing Ché from chasing after the fleeing photographer. Gasping, Ilana jogged to a stop in front of him. Hands propped on her thighs, she bent over to catch her breath. Her wild mass of hair, bound at the back of her head, flipped forward. She was barely dressed— or rather dressed barely in very short black pants and a matching shirt that left her abdomen exposed. Half of him wanted to throw a cape around her to provide her with modesty she appeared to have forgotten. The other half, quite a larger half than he would have anticipated, preferred to admire the way her pants molded her rounded bottom. Other females walked by dressed in similar attire, but Ché didn't feel the same need to protect them—or watch.

"Stupid, stupid, stupid," Ilana muttered. "I shouldn't have done that. My family has a tough enough time trying to keep both sides happy, you guys and Earth, without me flipping off paparazzi." She groaned unhappily. "It's like my life's not my own anymore!" She jerked her hands in the air. "You live like this all the time. Don't you resent having to consider the consequences of everything you do?"

If only she knew how much. Ilana's skin looked hot and damp. Where her hair lifted away from her neck, dark tendrils clung to glistening skin. Ché's lips twitched as he thought of pressing them there. "All the time," he said, his gaze dropping to her shirt, if one could call it that. It appeared designed more to support her breasts than to hide them, leaving no doubt as to their luscious curve and shape. One would fit very well cupped in each of his hands, Ché thought with a jolt of heat in his loins. Ilana would be a spirited bedmate. He could easily imagine loving her into sated exhaustion, bringing her to fulfillment again and again until her strong body was warm and yielding beneath his—

Great Mother! He met Ilana's wide-eyed gaze, and she blushed, her lips pursing. Despite the sunshaders covering his eyes, he had the feeling that she was somehow privy to his erotic thoughts.

When she spoke, her voice sounded hoarse. "If those pictures show up in the news, I'm sunk."

"You needn't worry, Ilana." Ché scanned the crowded road. He tracked his quarry to a white vehicle parked by the curb, where traffic blocked the car's escape. "That is his vehicle—there. I am going after him. I want to confiscate the images. But first I intend to give the fellow an introductory lesson in manners."

Ilana lifted a brow, the ends of her mouth curving. "*Vash* manners?"

"Perhaps. But some things are universal, such as discretion and respect." He walked to the curb.

"Ché, don't."

"Do not reveal my name," he whispered loudly.

"Sorry." She rolled her eyes. "Frenchie."

"I will use French."

"It does have a manlier ring to it," she acknowledged sassily.

He refused to allow the woman to think she had a

window into his motivations. "It is the name I gave the reporter before I sent him away."

"What reporter?" she blurted.

"Bohannon. *Coast Chronicle.*"

"I don't freaking believe this. These people need a life."

He thrust the newspaper into her hands. "Await me here."

"I'm not the *awaiting* type."

"I know. Await me anyway."

Traffic cleared. Ché walked into the street. Ilana followed. "You're not doing this alone."

Ché let his displeasure show. She might not want his protection, but, by the heavens, he'd give it to her. "Why will you not mind me when it is so obviously for your own good?" But then, he had the feeling she obeyed no man's command. "I pity the poor fellow you will marry," he muttered.

She burst into laughter. "You're such a dinosaur!"

"I am glad I entertain you," he said with sarcasm.

"You know what a dinosaur is, then."

"An extinct reptilian creature. But you are mistaken. Honor and gallantry are never out of date."

"Then why has every guy I've met expected me to fend for myself?"

"They are not *Vash Nadah.*"

She snorted. "I knew you were going to say that."

They reached the pedestrian path on the other side of the street. "Hold this," Ché commanded. He shoved the newspaper into Ilana's hands. Then, fists flexing, he strode toward the photographer's white car.

The windows were black, making it impossible to see inside. The passenger window was open a hand span or so, though. Through the narrow opening, the lens of a camera protruded.

In a blur of motion, Ché lunged forward and reached for the camera. Yanking it away, he tossed it to Ilana, who somehow managed not to drop it, despite holding the newspaper.

Quick reactions the woman had, Ché thought admiringly and turned back toward the vehicle. The passenger door swung open, revealing a flustered female driver and the empty-handed, clearly furious photographer.

Ché grabbed the man's flimsy shirt. Wrapping his knuckles with scraps of fabric, he yanked him out of the truck. The woman pressed her palms on the horn, shrill and loud. Pedestrians slowed down to watch.

"Get out of his face!" the driver shouted. "Or I'm calling the cops."

Ché swung the photographer around and pressed him belly-first over the hood of the vehicle. "As you wish."

The man's knees thumped against the metal siding. Ché caught his arm and pressed it behind him, pushing it upward in an arm lock. The move would not injure the man, but it would hurt.

But the photographer's yowl was louder than he expected. "Ah, Jesus! It's hot! The hood!"

Great Mother. Ché pulled him away from the hood of the vehicle. He hadn't meant to laminate the fellow to his ground car.

The fellow began swearing and blathering in unintelligible English. With icy efficiency, Ché intimidated him into silence with the infamous Vedla glare used by his family for millennia to quell their foes. "You will not cross my path again," he snarled. "You will not bother this woman."

Ilana appeared at his side. "Gah," she whispered into his ear. "Where'd you get that face?"

127

Ché looked at her askance. "I was born with this face."

"Yeah, well, it's scary as hell. Don't kill him, okay?"

At that, the photographer wriggled in Ché's grip. "I'm just trying to make a buck," he rasped worriedly. "I didn't hurt no one."

Ilana turned on him with unexpected bitterness. "Bull. You'd love it if he hit you. You'd love it if we made a scene. Scenes make news."

"A man of my class does not lose his temper," Ché reminded Ilana.

Ilana's gaze swung back to him. "Klark did."

Ché struggled not to rise to the bait. "Klark thought out every step he made. Only, he chose absolutely the wrong steps to take."

Briefly she squeezed her eyes shut. "I know, I know."

Ché could tell by her expression that she did indeed understand. At times, Ilana seemed to open up to him, giving him a peek, intentionally or otherwise, into the inner workings of her mind. Then, without warning, she would push him away, as she'd tried to do a moment ago. It certainly left a man on insecure footing.

Perhaps that was her objective.

"I just don't want you involved in this," she explained.

Or involved with her.

What was he thinking? He couldn't get involved with her.

Why not? The dissenting opinion came from the rogue in Ché, the same voice that had spurred him into stealing those garden carts as a boy, and had recently urged him to visit Earth. He admitted it to no one, but the moments instigated by the rogue stood out starkly as the times in his life when he felt truly alive.

Speculatively he studied Ilana. If he were to pursue intimacies with her, it would be horribly uncivilized and totally politically incorrect. But it wasn't as if he'd be ruining a virginal princess. That brought his thoughts back to Cole, and he frowned.

"It's my problem," Ilana snapped at him, dragging him from his lust-induced reverie.

He took a breath. "Not so, Ilana. Those photographs are of me, as well. This oaf has invaded our privacy. He has overstepped his bounds."

"Actually, he hasn't. Unfortunately. It's the law."

"Bah! Regardless of what one *can do*, we cannot forget what's honorable." He tightened his grip on the wriggling man.

"Honorable. Sheesh. You make a great knight in shining armor. But you're barking up the wrong tree if you think I'm going to be your damsel-in-distress."

Why did she insist on using such incomprehensible jargon? "Speak English," he demanded.

"I am speaking English!"

The photographer swore. "Do I really need to listen to this? It's bad enough I got my wife in the car."

"Oh, shut up," Ilana yelled.

"Screw you, Ricky," the woman in the car shouted.

At the same time, Ché commanded, "You will speak only when spoken to!"

There was silence for a moment. Then the man spoke. "What do you want—the film? Take it. Eat it, for all I care. Just let me get the hell out of here." He looked peeved, henpecked, and utterly browbeaten.

It took all of Ché's ingrained discipline not to chuckle at the absurdity of the situation. Obviously feeling the same, Ilana compressed her lips.

Ché released the photographer with a small push.

The man fell backward into his vehicle, landing on his rear with a bounce.

Ilana showed him a small plastic rectangle pinched between her index finger and thumb. "I'm keeping your memory stick. This"—she tossed the camera into the photographer's lap—"is yours."

Ché gave the paparazzi couple one last Vedla glare. "Where I come from, you would not have gotten away so easily."

Ilana grabbed his arm and tugged him away. They wove in and out of throngs of pedestrians—tourists and local inhabitants, he surmised.

The day was pleasant, the weather extraordinarily fine, but Ilana did not appear to share his lighthearted frame of mind. "I'll shower up," she said. "And then we'll find you a hotel."

"Yes. Of course." Ché's mood sank like a sea stone in a tide pool. He'd known it from the start—he would seek out his own quarters. It was the only proper course of action. He'd nearly forgotten that fact in the exhilaration of staying afloat in the torrent of energy that was Ilana, forgotten that he'd come to Earth in pursuit of solo adventure, to do as he wished away from Hoe's nagging and the relentless coddling from a swarm of well-meaning staff and servants. He'd best get on his way.

"It will not take me long to pack my things," he replied. But he knew it would take far longer to put this exasperating, engaging, and unexpectedly enchanting Earthwoman out of his mind.

Chapter Nine

On the way back to Ilana's building, yet another car appeared to trail them. It drove off at Ché's glare.

"This sucks," Ilana said. She had a hunted look in her eyes. Ché knew the feeling well. He'd felt the same the day Toren showed up with grand plans for his unwanted betrothal.

He did his best to cheer the both of them. "I think that last fellow will think twice before harassing you again. We make a good team, Ilana. A very good team indeed. Who would have guessed such a thing? Certainly not your brother. I believe Ian was rather concerned about my visit here. Worried, perhaps. He took great pains to facilitate my arrival."

"Really." She appeared to ponder that. "And yet Ian *forgot* to tell me you were coming. He who never forgets anything." Her narrowed eyes broadcast her suspicion. "Did he forget on purpose, so you'd show up no-notice? At night? After it was too late to find you a place to stay? Doesn't that strike you as strange?"

Ché wasn't sure whether her displeasure was aimed at him, her twin, or both of them. But then, much about Ilana remained a mystery. Perhaps he should contact the crown prince and see if she came with a handbook. "Considering the short time in which he had to help me organize my journey, no. It does not. But if it were true, if Ian did want to surprise you, what would be the purpose?"

Ilana looked even more suspicious. "To set us up. To get us together."

"Together . . . ?"

"Yeah, you know—a couple. An item. One plus one. Damn it, Ché—you're single and eligible, by *Vash* standards, and so am I. What if he wants us to get married? Not only Ian—both our families might be in on this!"

"Absurd! My family and my advisors are arranging a marriage as we speak. By the heavens, even the Great Council is in on the plan. The crown prince wouldn't involve himself in such a scheme." Would he?

Of course Ché had confided in Ian as a friend. Else, the man wouldn't have known of Ché's predicament.

Suspicion seeped in where it hadn't been before.

Ilana, on the other hand, appeared inordinately relieved, as if she'd transferred her doubts to him. "You're right," she said. "It doesn't make sense. Ian wouldn't interfere like that."

Was she trying to reassure herself—or him? "This journey was my idea and mine only from the very first. As I told you last night, I wanted to escape involvement in my wedding plans. I thought it was best I do it here." He left out the fact that he'd wanted to see her again, to see why she'd remained in his thoughts all these months when he'd certainly had enough beautiful women to divert him.

"And here we are," Ilana said disgustedly, "talking about weddings and"—she shuddered— "c-commitment. The C-word."

Unlocking her front door, she let them in. "Thanks, by the way. Your help out there . . . I really appreciated it."

"Your gratitude magnifies our cultural differences. You do not need to thank me for what I was raised to do."

Her expression changed, almost imperceptibly, but Ché could detect such subtle cues: She acted as if he'd disappointed her in some way. "Oh, that's right. Playing protector is ingrained in you. You worship and protect women. It's part of your culture."

He folded his arms over his chest and studied her. "Did you expect that I would have run in the opposite direction if not for my upbringing?"

"Maybe."

"Who caused you to be so cynical? Who disappointed you so?" Ian was an Earth-dweller, but Ché knew he wouldn't run, especially if it meant leaving a woman undefended.

A wall fell down over Ilana's eyes. "I'm used to fending for myself, that's all. It's nice for once to have someone do the dirty work for me." Her voice softened fractionally. "Really nice. Even if it was just a knee-jerk reaction because of the way you were raised."

"What I did, I did for *you*. Regardless of my background."

"Well, double thanks, then." Tugging her hair from its band, she shook her tresses free. She breezed past him on the way into the kitchen. There, she filled two glasses with ice and water, offering him one. "I guess

133

I don't make a very good damsel-in-distress."

Her vernacular baffled him. "What is this damsel . . . ?" He circled one hand.

"Damsel in distress. A woman in need of rescue. A knight in shining armor is . . . someone like you. The guy who does the rescuing."

"And this bothers you? Being a distressed damsel?"

She sipped her water. "I'm pretty independent, Ché."

"Is that a warning?"

"I'm not like the women you know."

"Thank the heavens."

Her mouth twisted as if she couldn't decide whether to grin or scowl. He'd flustered her.

"Go on with what you were saying," he coaxed indulgently. "Or do I distract you?"

Her nostrils flared. "Hardly." She took another swallow.

Liar, he thought.

She lowered her glass, searched his face. "You don't believe me?"

"No. I don't." The air between them heated. This flirtation, it was a dangerous game, but it exhilarated him. The end goal was far more tempting than hijacking a garden cart, he thought, running his gaze lazily over Ilana's sweet curves. "But I have met the sort of fellow with whom you keep company: powerless, easily chased away. I, on the other hand, am not. That intrigues you. You argue to keep your distance from me."

"You egotistical pig! I—I thought you were different from the other *Vash*. But you're just as full of yourself as the rest of them. You have no idea what I like in a man."

He exchanged his glass for the newspaper she had

put down and handed it to her. "I know what you do not like."

Warily she took the newspaper.

The urge to bait her proved irresistible. "Cole Miller wanted you to have it," he informed her.

"Tell me he didn't come here for his dog bowl."

"Ah . . ."

"His Acme A-one super-duper foldable doggie water bowl."

"Perhaps it was you he wanted. He left rather quickly after coming to the conclusion that I'd taken his place."

The mild exasperation tightening Ilana's mouth told him that what feelings she'd had for the man, if any, were gone. That should have made Ché feel better. But the more he pondered Cole's appearance, and the man's easy acceptance that Ilana had already let another man into her bed, the more it irritated him. It was becoming clearer by the moment that he simply didn't like the idea of Ilana having a lover. Himself, yes. Others, no. "Cole assumed I had stayed overnight with you."

She propped her hands on her hips. "Didn't you?"

"In your bed," he corrected.

She pulled a bathing towel out of a small closet, waving it in a circle as she tipped her head. "All you had to do was ask."

Ché reared back. The inability to form an urbane comeback unbalanced him. His ensuing befuddlement left him tongue-tied, which was obviously Ilana's intent. If this were a Bajha match, at this point he'd be parrying desperately, his back to the wall, cursing himself for seriously underestimating his opponent.

Ilana was completely outside his experience. The females in his life who weren't family either performed a service, like a courtesan or maid, or were those with whom he was required by etiquette to entertain with charming and safe banter at royal functions: elderly widows, or women married or promised to other men. Ilana fell into none of those categories. She unaccountably blurred the lines between peer and object of lust, making her unlike any woman he'd met.

Smiling, she breezed past him, headed for her bedroom and, he presumed, her cleansing rituals. He watched her sweet bottom swaying and the muscles in her legs flex. He wondered if she knew what additional pleasure those strong thighs could afford her while making love. He wanted to take her to bed, just to show her.

"Perhaps I *should* have asked, Ilana," he called after her. "But I am *Vash*, through and through, as you say. As the guest in your home, I would naturally expect any hospitality offered to come from you."

She appeared in the doorway of her bedroom. She'd stripped off her clothing and now held only the towel around her. Pressing it loosely to her breasts, she stepped aside. "The bed's right here. Come on in," she dared.

He would not let her get away with it. Affecting lazy charm, he allowed his gaze to settle on her mouth before he returned his attention to her eyes. "I refuse to contribute to your moral recklessness when you are doing such a fine job on your own."

Ilana's cheeks turned a deep shade of pink. But when her voice finally emerged, it was husky with fury, not embarrassment. That she was nearly nude and ready for a fight aroused him. How many of his bedmates feigned passion? Most of them, he realized, if not all. Ilana's was real.

"Let me get this straight," she said. "If we slept together, it'd be morally wrong for me but not for you? A man can have sex and remain unattached, but when a woman does the same, her morals come into question? You, with a palace full of courtesans. I can't believe you don't see the hypocrisy in that!"

Ché dismissed her judgment. "Men and women are different."

"Well, duh. I'm not arguing biology here."

He fell back on quoting the Treatise of Trade—the ultimate authority on everything was extraordinarily useful in such circumstances. " 'A woman's body is sacred. It must not be abused, or used without forethought.' "

Her eyes glinted with sudden mirth. "So. Sex with you would be abusive. If that's supposed to scare me away, it's not working."

He wouldn't let her distract him—but by the heavens, it was growing blasted difficult! "I am referring to your body! To Cole's use of it."

"Use. *Use?* At least *I* don't have to hire anyone when I want to get laid."

"You are better than that," he persisted. "You deserve more than casual relationships."

"Ah, yes. My vast scrapheap of boyfriends. The chicken bones of the slutty banquet of my life."

He shook his head at her self-deprecating irony. "You give yourself too easily, Ilana."

"I don't 'give' myself at all." She gathered her towel to her breasts. "Did you ever consider that, Mister Holier-than-thou? That I have the upper hand? That I leave *them*? It's not moral recklessness. It's smart!"

Pain glittered suddenly in her eyes, and he knew not the cause of it. Hurting her was not his intent, and he felt like a boor for doing so. But her distress ran deeper than the argument at hand; he was sure of it.

Before Councilman Toren called him back to Eireya to marry, Ché vowed to find out why.

Ilana clutched her towel and spun away from him. She left the door to her bedchamber ajar, the towel slipping lower as she swayed away. He heard the hiss of water falling as another door farther within the room opened.

She passed into view again. Satisfied that he was watching her—how could he not!—she let the towel fall, dragging it along the floor from the tips of one finger.

Ché's loins tightened, hardened, reacting to the sight of Ilana's nude body, her purposeful disregard of his presence. Her breasts were full and high, and her bottom generous. She was curvaceous, not skinny, her legs sleekly muscled. Her smooth skin was suntanned all over, except for that incredible rear end, pale and silken. He envisioned clutching her bottom as he made love to her, pressing her closer to seat himself deeper inside her.

Great Mother. He was hard, almost painfully so. Though he was already aroused from their arguing, the intensity of his reaction shocked him. But years of discipline and sexual training kept him in control.

Ilana paused before disappearing behind the other door. Steam rose, blurring her features. She glanced over her shoulder at him, through her tangle of streaked hair, as if daring him to follow and feeling secure in the knowledge that he wouldn't. Then she flounced smugly into her bath chamber and shut the door.

Ché stood there, aching, his breath rapid. Sweat prickled his skin. Blast her! She was too confident— and dead wrong, if she thought a Vedla would allow a woman to tantalize him so and then escape un- scathed. Fists clenched, he strode into her private quarters and across the room to where she'd gone. He pushed open the door, releasing a cloud of scented steam, and stepped inside. She had no idea what she'd called upon herself by dangling the invitation of her body in front of him. But she was about to find out—in one unforgettable, exquisitely administered lesson.

Ilana heard the door to her bathroom slam open. Startled, she smoothed her wet hair away from her eyes and peered through the shower enclosure. A dark, hulking form loomed outside. Ché.

He flung open the door. Cooler air hit her skin. Her heart slammed in her chest. Water ran down her face, streamed down her exposed body.

Ché stood still, gripping the door as tendrils of mist drifted all around him. Moisture glittered on his hard, stubbly jaw. Meeting his eyes, molten gold, was a shock. She saw hunger there, raw and determined.

She felt suddenly way too naked.

Fully dressed, he stepped inside the shower. Water gushed down on them, spraying everywhere. Ché slapped his hands onto the shower wall behind her, one broad hand to each side of her head. Then he lowered his face.

"Ché!" She tried to duck. "What the—"

All in one move, he closed his hands around her skull and kissed her. She was too shocked to struggle, too stunned to try. Her aborted objection left her lips parted. Ché took full advantage. His tongue swept into her mouth, not clumsy or thrusting, but with mastery. Desire scorched through her. It was the longest, most luscious kiss she'd experienced in ages. Maybe ever, but she didn't want to go there.

Ché didn't bend down to reach her; he lifted her up to him. The balls of her feet skidded over the slick tile floor of the shower enclosure. She flattened her hands on his soaked T-shirt, stretched tight over hard muscles, and tried to wrest back control of the kiss— of *everything*.

She'd always been the one to call the shots! But Ché held her firmly to his body, angling her head so that he could kiss her how *he* wanted. He was rough enough to take her breath away, gentle enough to let her know he was aware he held a woman in his arms.

Water gushed down over them, beating against her upturned face, running in rivulets past their locked mouths. Ché's clothes were drenched—and he was wearing far too many of them, Ilana thought dazedly, collecting some of the wits she never usually lost. She reached for his jeans to unbutton them. Her knuckles grazed over the huge bulge straining his fly. But he stopped her, trapping her between his hard body and the cool, slick shower wall. His jeans were wet and rough; the denim abraded her skin.

She pulled her mouth from his, breathless. "Ché," she gasped.

He made a sound of smug satisfaction and nuzzled her neck. Water battered them both, hissing and spraying. Her breasts ached for his touch, his mouth; but he didn't touch her there. Instead, he slid his soapy, wet hand between her thighs. He knew exactly what he was searching for—and found it.

Her knees almost gave out. She had to keep control, had to keep from showing him how aroused she was. She would not get weak-kneed in front of this self-professed sexual connoisseur. Ché Vedla was just another guy. No better, no different from the rest. She could prove it. Almost angrily, she guided his mouth back to hers. And the moment he kissed her back, he made her a liar. The pressure of his lips forced her head backward, triggering a flood of desire that pooled low in her belly.

Thick and hot, his fingers rubbed slickly between her folds. She wanted to sag to the floor and pull him down there with her. She wanted him inside her, wild like this; she wanted everything he could give her. Again she tried to unbutton his fly. But he swatted away her hand and slipped two fingers inside her.

He caught her moan with his mouth. She could feel her inner muscles contracting, squeezing his gently thrusting fingers. And, oh, God, the things he could do with his thumb . . .

A pulsing pressure began to build, deep inside her. Her belly contracted and her hips writhed. A low moan began deep in her throat. She arched into his hand, ready to come apart, and so blatantly at his command. But a fraction of a heartbeat before she climaxed, at the very worst possible moment, Ché withdrew his hand.

Quivering and incredulous, she watched him turn his back to her and walk out, leaving her alone under the gushing shower.

Chapter Ten

"Ché, you are so busted," Ilana snarled to herself as she jammed her arms one at a time into her bathrobe.

But deep down, she knew she deserved what she'd got. She'd teased him, tempted him. Flashed him. She'd done everything but give him a handwritten invitation to join her in the shower. Only she never thought he would.

In the first seconds after he'd left, she'd stood there, water pouring on her head. Her body strung tight in frustration, she'd cursed him for giving in to his Stone Age values. But it wasn't prudishness that kept him from finishing what he'd started. *Don't play with me*, his actions said. *Or you'll pay.*

But Ché was no more likely to play anyone's games than she was. In a way, it made them equals. It hit her that she'd never really respected the men she dated, in part because they'd allowed her total control over the relationships. They let her walk away. Oh, some whimpered a bit, like Cole, but no one had ever really fought hard to keep her. Not the way she'd want a man to fight for her.

Wait a second. She and Ché didn't have a relationship. And how could they? Considering the circumstances, the best they could do was a fling.

But if she was smart, and she liked to think that she was, she wouldn't sleep with him at all. Better to hook him up with one of her girlfriends. And knowing what she knew now about Ché's . . . abilities, her friends were going to owe her big time for the favor.

Peering into the fogged mirror, she frowned at herself, her combed hair dripping. Sexual frustration was hell on the complexion.

She knotted the belt on her puffy yellow chenille robe decorated with steaming cups of java and forced herself to walk into the living room. She didn't know what she'd do when she saw him. Call him names? Kick him out of the house? Or drag him to bed, the floor—heck, the shower—and make him finish what he'd started?

She knew the answer: She'd apologize. She owed him that.

He'd helped her out. Rescued her. Okay, so the knight-in-shining-armor routine had nothing to do with her; playing protector was ingrained in him; it was part of his culture. So was his politeness. His courtesy. But did it really matter how he got to be a gentleman? Or only that he was one?

But the living room was empty. Wet footprints cut a straight path to the front door. He'd left.

She ran to the window. The Porsche was still there. She released the breath she'd been holding, not realizing until now how disappointed she'd be if Ché had left.

The sun was lower in the sky. It must be six or seven by now, but the air was still warm. The beach was emptying out. Summer traffic clogged the street. People were coming off the beach in droves, carrying coolers, towels, and fold-up chairs. Somewhere out there was Ché, a fully clothed, soaking-wet, sexually frustrated *Vash* prince in squishy, squeaky shoes.

Would he be all right out there? Of course he would. He'd proved very pointedly in the shower that he could take care of himself.

But she worried about him anyway.

She'd give him forty-five minutes. If he wasn't back by then, she'd go looking for him. Man, she needed a Corn Nut fix. Bad. Frantically she rifled through her purse. Her hand closed over a crinkly foil bag. *Thank God*, she thought shakily, grasping the bag. Beaten down by hunger and exhaustion, she poured a handful of Corn Nuts and salt into her palm. Automatically she flipped through the newspaper, needing to read or talk when she ate.

And there she was—swooning in Ché Vedla's arms on the center of the front page of the "Lifestyle" section. "Bite me," Ilana blurted out, staring down at the blaring headline.

EARTHBOUND CINDERELLA LOOKS FOR PRINCE
B'kah heiress wedding plans reportedly hush-hush

LOS ANGELES—Seen leaving the lavish downtown digs of playboy and star Hunter Holt last night, Princess Ilana Hamilton was photographed in the arms of an unidentified man only hours later. However, when asked about her mystery Prince Charming, Hamilton claims, "There is none." Despite keeping company with Holt and others, the reclusive heiress, also part-owner of SILF Filmworks, has

resisted settling on a match, despite mounting family pressure. "Ms. Hamilton has been instructed by her family not to comment on this subject at this time," said an unidentified royal staffer, leaving only wild speculation as to when Earth's Cinderella will find a glass slipper to fit her fickle foot.

"Fickle foot!" As if it weren't bad enough to have her mother or even Linda worrying about whether she'd ever find her happily-ever-after with "Mr. Right," now the press had gotten in on it, too. They thought Ché was her Prince Charming.

The photo sure made it look like it. She and Ché looked as if they were embracing, when she was really trying to wipe pepper-spray tears from his eyes. How romantic.

Swearing, Ilana dropped three more Corn Nuts into her mouth and read the article again. It was like driving past the scene of an accident—you had to look even though you didn't want to.

The second read changed nothing. It was still tabloid trash. What was it doing in a respectable newspaper? They linked her to Ché—and Hunter Holt, of all people. They thought she was dating one or both of them.

Rose was behind this, that TV gossip-show host. The woman was the only one she'd talked to last night. If this was what the media could concoct when given no information at all, Ilana could only imagine the stories printed if she ever did talk.

Talk about what? Nothing had happened. She hadn't even made it past third base with an über-masculine *Vash* prince in the shower. Butt naked!

Hunched over the table, she dumped her face in her hands, feeling as if she'd been snared by an invisible lasso that stretched across the galaxy and it was pulling her, bucking and kicking, into the sphere of influence of her family.

Speaking of which, just wait until they got wind of this. They were going to be thrilled to think she was dating anyone seriously. But they'd also ask questions. Holt, they'd know was a fabrication. But the photo of her and the "mystery Prince Charming" was more serious. She and Ché would have to put their heads together if they wanted to concoct a bullet-proof cover story.

This was the weekend she was supposed to be revving her creative engine, sorting through some scripts that had come in and musing about some of her own ideas for a film. Unfortunately, the only inspiration she wanted was how to get the press off her back.

She munched more Corn Nuts, counting her blessings that she'd bought a jumbo bag. A shot of tequila would have made a good chaser, but she didn't keep hard liquor in the house and all the beer was gone. Everything was gone. Even Ché.

It had been almost forty-five minutes since he'd left.

Sweat tickled the back of her neck. She'd better go find him. While she hated to admit it, she wouldn't mind his levelheaded advice. But they'd had a fight. He might not be in the mood to help. On the other hand, he was in the paper, too. Like it or not, Ché was knee-deep with her in this mess.

In her bedroom, she zipped on a short, fitted, pale blue cotton dress and dabbed on some makeup. The front door slammed. She jumped, her heart accelerating. It had better be Ché. But if it wasn't . . .

Her pepper spray was in her purse, and her purse was in the living room. Taking a carved Aboriginal walking stick she'd bought in Sydney, she stalked out of her bedroom, holding the stick like a baseball bat.

Ché stood by the front door, soaked, as if he'd been swimming. Confirming the swim, his T-shirt, wrung into a damp, twisted lump, hung from one hand. Like most *Vash*, he had no chest hair, and the lack showed off his golden skin to perfection. *So this is what you've been hiding under that Harley T-shirt.* She gave him a blatant once-over, admiring his six-pack abs and rounded biceps with the eye of an aficionado of the male species. Ché quirked a wary brow at the stick. She lowered it. It reminded her of how he took charge in the shower, then ended the encounter on his terms, leaving her high and dry.

"You're lucky you're you," she said. "If you'd had a camera in your hand, I would have whacked it with my walkabout." She leaned her stick against the wall.

"You should have locked the door after me."

"It took a while to crawl out of the shower."

Smoothing one hand over his hair, he regarded her with inscrutable eyes. Water dripped from the spiky strands, slipping down his neck and over his bare shoulders. Wet, his blond hair was almost brown. She remembered how it felt. The texture was different. Luxurious, like mink.

"So, was the water cold?" she asked saucily.

"Not cold enough."

"Oh. So you were affected, too?"

"Of course I was affected, Ilana. Would you think otherwise?"

His frank question nipped her cheekiness in the bud. A lesser woman would have stuttered. "No matter how I answer that, I can't win."

"I was not aware that this was a competition, Ilana."

"Ouch. Are you always this direct?"

"You are as casual with your sexuality as an unmarried man is in my culture," he went on. "And so my automatic response was to deem your lifestyle shocking and disgraceful."

Here we go. She rolled her eyes. "I'll take that as a yes."

"When you flaunted yourself in front of me, Ilana, I didn't know how to react. I thought to punish you, because I did not want you to have the upper hand. But once I began touching you . . ." He swallowed. "I did not want to stop."

They stared at each other. She felt the heat of sexual arousal from his words alone.

"It was not easy to leave, Ilana."

"Why did you?" she asked hoarsely.

"Because I am a Vedla." He squared his broad shoulders. "Because I have eons of ancestors watching me, judging me. Because I am a man who follows through with decisions. The need to prove that, to them, overrode my need for you."

So it wasn't prudishness that had sent him running. He'd set out to teach her a lesson, and stayed until he had.

She wasn't sure she liked what she'd learned.

"Spoken like a true *Vash*," she said bitingly. "I asked Tee'ah once, what it was like, living your life with generations of dead relatives looking over your shoulder. She told me that you never feel alone. Maybe I should try it. Huh, Ché? Then maybe I wouldn't be so *morally reckless*."

Ché winced. "Ah, that. It was a vulgar remark—and invalid, I realized while swimming. You, Ilana, view the sexual act with casual partners as a physical activity. It is no different from the way I am with a pleasure server. Emotions are not involved. The soul is not engaged. But you are a woman. That you approach your sexuality the same way I do is foreign and, in true Vedla fashion, immediately suspect. I consider myself enlightened, but put to the test I react just as judgmentally as those I scorn for their closed-mindedness." Stiffly he acknowledged, "I have experienced little beyond my own world. It makes me a barbarian on yours."

She pushed curling strands of hair out of her eyes. "Wow. Was that an apology?"

"Yes. And quite an insufficient one if you had to ask."

Surprise and satisfaction filtered through her. Ché's pale eyes glowed.

It was her turn. Clasping her hands, she tried to appear as contrite as she now felt. "I'm sorry I didn't act more appreciative for your help with the paparazzi and the reporter. I was. *I am*. The comment I made about Klark was uncalled for. I don't know why I said it. I guess . . . I guess I got scared."

"Having your privacy threatened by strangers is unsettling. Your fear is justified."

"I meant by your protecting me. Looking out for me."

"Why ever would that scare you?"

Good question. What could she say? That she was afraid of losing what control she'd gained over her life? Or that she had trust issues stemming back to her childhood that made it difficult if not impossible to give her heart to a man? Her father's infidelity and its effect on her mother was no doubt the cause of that. But the subject was still so painful that she'd rather not address it at all. Opening up wasn't her thing. "I don't know," she replied. "Blame it on cultural differences."

Ché regarded her with suspicion. She averted her eyes, hating the way he seemed to be able to tell when she was holding back.

"I've eaten enough humble pie," she told him.

149

"Why don't you get changed and we'll go out."

"What is humble pie?" Ché looked so eager at the prospect of food that she had to laugh.

"You don't eat it. It's slang for putting aside your pride. But, here, you can eat these." She offered him her bag of Corn Nuts. Ché had no clue how tough that was for her. "It's a snack. They're salty." His golden eyes lit up. Elsewhere in the galaxy, salt was expensive to obtain. It was rare for salt to occur as naturally and plentifully as it did on Earth. Salt was expensive, valuable enough to be used as currency in some far-flung places. It was one reason Earth was such a valued trade partner in the Federation.

Ché held a Corn Nut between two fingers, brought it to his sexy lips. He watched her as he chewed and swallowed. Only he could make an erotic show of eating Corn Nuts. Or maybe that was because she knew what else he could do with his hands and mouth.

She practically swallowed in unison with him. "What do you think?"

"They are quite good." He lifted the bag as if toasting her. "May I have another?"

"*One* Corn Nut? You are so freaking polite! Go— eat them all." His charming ways made her want to give him a hug, which helped take the edge off wanting to slug him or jump in bed with him, which was how she felt the rest of the time. "You haven't had a meal since last night. Any other guy would be ripping apart that bag, picking up the phone to order pizza, running across the street to the Thai place, or ransacking my refrigerator."

His tone was sardonic. "An intelligent man would already know that there is nothing of nutritional value in your refrigerator."

"I can't tell if you're insulting my taste in men, or only my ability to shop for groceries."

"Your taste in men," he clarified.

"No fair! You only met Cole."

"It was enough."

She snorted. "Cole's a nice guy."

"I have no doubt of that. But having always left the stocking of food to the kitchen staff, how can I in good conscience criticize your dearth of supplies?"

She couldn't help laughing. Excitement ran high. They were having fun again. When times were good with Ché, they were really good. But when they were bad . . .

Ché set the bag of Corn Nuts on the table. "Great Mother," he muttered.

Ilana followed his gaze down to the open newspaper. For a few blissful moments she'd forgotten all about the article. Reality had returned to slap her in the face.

Chapter Eleven

"Royal advisor?" Ché asked, looking up after reading the text.

"They mean Linda Hurst, my assistant. I share her with my partners, but she mostly works with me. She's on the SILF payroll. Which isn't saying much, it isn't a very impressive payroll. Though as a small studio, we're lucky to have one at all."

"Hmm. And 'fickle foot'?"

"Let me tell you a story. Once upon a time, there was a beautiful and fictional young woman named Cinderella who lived with a stepmother and a couple of evil stepsisters. They made her dress in rags and do all the housework." Ilana wrinkled her nose. "One day the local prince held a ball . . ."

Ché tried his best to follow Ilana's torrent of words. She was standing close enough for him to catch her scent, a light floral perfume, clean skin, and a hint of the smell that was hers alone. The memory of running his lips over her firm, slippery skin brought back the almost constant ache of arousal to his loins. He shifted uncomfortably. Earth clothing was rather restricting in fit, he'd come to find out. To make matters worse, he was afraid his jeans had shrunk after his saltwater swim.

". . . and when the prince saw that the glass slipper fit Cinderella's foot, he knew he'd found his true love."

"Then 'fickle foot' refers to your reluctance to marry."

"Yep. But lack of enthusiasm is more accurate. It's not that I don't want to get married, I just don't want to now. I wish everyone would leave me alone about it. That's something you can relate to, I'm sure."

"Very much so." They exchanged a glance of acute understanding, of sudden solidarity. Unexpectedly, the paparazzi and their own meddling families had made them fighters on the same side of the line.

Ilana crossed the room and fetched him a towel. She offered it to him, and he used it to scrub his hair dry. "You live in the public eye, Ché. You're the expert. What do I do about this? How do I fight back?"

"By living as normal a life as possible."

Tucking strands of hair behind one ear, Ilana searched his face. Her voice broadcast her skepticism. "Do you? Live a normal life?"

"Within my area of the palace, my private residence, I try." He draped the towel over his shoulders, hanging on to each end with his fists as he thought of his future, his arranged marriage, his increasingly important role in the leadership of the Federation. He wondered if he'd ever achieve the level of intimacy, of normalcy in the personal life, he'd only recently begun to admit that he desired. "It has not been easy of late."

His attention fell to the newspaper. "It seems my bad luck has chased me here."

"Or it collided with mine."

Their gloom was mutual. Ché tapped a finger on the photograph. "It makes us appear as lovers, but one cannot see my face. This is what intrigues them. That is why the photographer came here today."

"And they're going to keep coming until they find out who you are."

"Which I do not want any more than you do."

"The interest in me is going to get worse before it gets better."

"I told the reporter that I was your advisor. And that I am from Latvia."

"From the soccer game last night. Good. It'll help explain the accent. And Latvia is a very small country—no one here knows much about it, including me. We'll research what we can, but it gives us room to make mistakes. Plus, saying that you work for me will be a great deterrent for them."

He smiled. "You are eager for my protection now."

"I wouldn't go that far," she retorted. "But I'll say this: If I were rich and you weren't, I'd offer you a job."

"Why not a trade? My abilities as a bodyguard for yours as a tour guide."

Her eyes flashed. "Are you serious? If you are, I'm game."

"I came here for adventure, Ilana. To see and do things as far removed from my life on Eireya as possible. I say posing as your temporary bodyguard qualifies." He rubbed his chin. "But I would have to stay here to be effective," he mused aloud.

Her face came alive. "Perfecto."

Great Mother! What had he proposed? If the palace got wind of this, that he was lodging with Ilana Hamilton, unchaperoned, the scandal would sweep the Federation.

Danger be damned! What harm would come of it? A little impetuosity might be just the thing he needed to come to terms with his recent and frustrating lack of enthusiasm about his life and the obligations that went along with it.

"We'll get you some contact lenses," Ilana offered. "I could bleach the ends of your hair. Maybe an earring. It would have to be the left ear . . . unless you want to pierce both—"

He held up his hands. "I do have to go home at the end of this, Ilana."

"I guess that means a tattoo is out. Body art," she clarified at his obvious puzzlement.

"I already have all the body art I desire."

"Really?" she breathed.

Her sharp curiosity flattered him. "Really."

Her wide blue eyes scanned his exposed chest and stomach, his arms and shoulders, but he knew she would not find anything there. "I didn't know the *Vash*—"

"The Vedlas do."

She swallowed. Then she recovered with a saucy smile. "I don't think your family would be too happy about this plan. Their perfect prince, under the direct and corrupting influence of an Earth-dweller."

"I am sure they would see it differently: a B'kah princess undergoing education and enlightenment under the guidance of a Vedla prince."

Her smirk gave way to a genuine laugh. He found it extraordinarily easy to smile around her. "Then I think we'd better keep this arrangement to ourselves," she suggested.

"I intend to. As planned, I will check in with Hoe every standard week via direct comm call. But I never intended to divulge all the details of my travels."

Now, it seemed, he'd be revealing even less.

Several hours after dinner, Ilana found herself drinking mineral water spiked with a lime at a bar backing up to giant mirrors that periodically transformed into glass boxes displaying nearly naked male and female dirty dancers. In the dance area beyond, above a clear ceiling, more dancers rolled and slithered over each other in highly suggestive acrobatics.

She didn't have to sweet-talk her way into Reach like the people waiting outside in line would have to. The brother of her former roommate Tara was part-owner of the place. Reach was a heavily guarded dance club, and currently considered the "only place to party" in L.A. Ilana didn't care so much for the reputation as she did the exclusivity the club boasted. Actors and other industry types frequented the place. Security was tight. Paparazzi would be shot on the spot—or at least thrown out by bouncers wearing secret-service headsets whose sheer mass made the average World Federation wrestler look like a bulimic leprechaun. It was the perfect place to bring Ché.

She'd offered to be his tour guide, hadn't she? So why not start with total cultural immersion?

Ilana returned from the dance floor, where she'd danced first with a male acquaintance, and then with a few unknowns who'd asked. She was breathless, damp, and having fun. Reuniting with the glass of mineral water she'd left on the bar, she looked around for Ché. Without sunglasses he blended into the crowd, but only as well as a tall, extremely hot-looking guy with confidence oozing out of every pore could. He looked wealthy, in an understated, truly elegant way, and powerful—in bed and out. Dressed in brown pants and a crisp, black, collarless shirt with the top two buttons undone, he wore a replica of an outfit Ilana remembered from a recent *GQ* magazine cover. Hats off to the Vedla tailor.

Languidly Ché leaned his elbow on the bar, sipping from a small glass of something expensive, she'd bet. He liked beer, but instinctively knew where and when to drink it. The guy put the "s" in suave. But he wasn't decadent, she decided. He was sophisticated. She was beginning to understand the difference.

Ilana took her mineral water and squeezed through the crowd milling around the bar until she could find an opening to sidle up to Ché. But his attention was on Barrie, a tall, slender, ultra-hip cinematographer who had fortunately been one of the ones to answer her cell phone when Ilana attempted a last-minute roundup of single women to dangle under Ché's nose.

Ché leaned over and said something in Barrie's ear. Ilana's friend laughed, looking utterly taken. Ché's newly gray eyes were a little bloodshot from his colored contact lenses—an after-dinner purchase—but that didn't stop him from making some very intense eye contact with Barrie.

That was the way it was with Ché: When he spoke to you, you felt like you were his sole focus.

Go for it, girl, Ilana thought, trying to feel smug about matching Ché up on the first night she tried. But then she'd known when she made the bet with Ian that it wouldn't be difficult to drop the prince into someone's bed. She was going to win the wager with time to spare. Only she hoped Ché wouldn't abandon his deal to scare off the paparazzi as easily as Ilana had lured him off the *Vash* path.

She inhaled deeply and smiled at those around her. She had always been a magnet for people, and

here at Reach it was no different. Ilana, the party girl.
Yeah, she supposed she was, sort of. Inside, she felt
too driven for the label, too goal-oriented. For as long
as she could remember, she'd dreamed of crafting
original films for the masses while earning enough
money doing it to live near the beach. Oh, and to be
able to eat, too, if there was any money left over.

Conversation spun all around her. Ilana tried to listen and act interested in what her acquaintances
were saying, but it was Barrie and Ché's voices she
wanted to hear. What were they talking about? Ché
appeared alternately concerned and amused at what
Barrie was telling him.

Oh, well. She couldn't possibly have believed she'd
be the only woman Ché would treat that way. In
twenty-four hours with him, their conversations had
ranged from bitter arguing, to passionate debating, to
sexy banter, and everything else in between. She was
full of life when she talked to him, fully engaged, even
when she wanted to scream and pull her hair out.
Ché was a charmer of the worst kind. He had the
knack, the ability to captivate a woman. Lucky him.
Hell, lucky Barrie.

Ilana poked at the lime in her glass and fought a
baffling surge of possession that made her want to
break up the pair's grating little tête-à-tête.

A big, warm hand landed on the small of her back.
A low, very familiar accented voice tickled her ear.
"I would like to dance with you."

She turned her head. Gray eyes watched her. She
missed the gold. "Dance with Barrie. You were doing
so well with her. What happened?"

Ché appeared puzzled. "Nothing has happened."

Craning her neck, Ilana glanced past Ché. Barrie
smiled at her and gave her a thumbs-up. Encouraging
her to go off with Ché, Ilana thought incredulously,

turning away. This was not the plan. She needed Ché to be with Barrie. Or Chessie, Linnea, or Debra. She had a bet to win.

"I did not think you were shy, Ilana," Ché teased.

"Shy? Hell." She put down her drink. "Let's go."

She had the feeling Ché was smiling behind her back as he followed her through the crowd to the dance floor.

Lights and music pulsed. The press of bodies forced them close together. Ché took her wrists and lifted her hands to his shoulders. She was aware of his scent, and his body heat. "No one else is slow-dancing," she said, smiling slyly when he slid his arms around her waist.

"I know how to hold a woman," he said.

She tipped her chin up. Her mouth was inches from his. It was the only way they could hear each other above the beat. The gentle press of his stomach against hers was . . . distracting. But for now, she'd leave the dirty dancing to the people gyrating on the glass floor above their heads. "Barrie's an amazing dancer. She can teach you all the moves. Ask her. She'll be flattered."

"Barrie suggested that I invite you to dance."

Was Barrie nuts? If it had been Ilana, she'd have kept Ché for herself. What was going on here? Ilana had made it very clear when she'd had the chance to brief each of her friends that Ché was single and not hers.

Oh, well. She leaned closer to Ché. Who was she to complain about holding on to a hard, hot body? "So, what were you guys talking about?"

"Ian's wedding," he said.

"Are you serious?" It was the one topic he wanted to avoid, and Barrie was the last person she'd expect to show interest. "What did she want to know? Did she read something in the news?"

"No. The conversation came about when we discussed your aversion to flying."

Blood rushed to Ilana's face.

"Barrie told me you have struggled with this for many years. And because of it, you are loath to travel into space."

"Loath." She wrinkled her nose. "That's too nice a word." Ché's educated speech and accent made everything sound so . . . pleasant.

"So, it is true?"

"How did this come up? You were supposed to be getting to know Barrie. Not talking about me."

"You are all we wanted to discuss."

Ilana almost growled. That was it. Barrie was out of the running. She'd blown it. Maybe it was time for Chessie to step up to the plate.

"Barrie feels bad knowing you do not care for space travel. She worries you may be 'stressed' about your upcoming journey."

"I am not stressed!"

He gave her a knowing smile.

"Concerned, maybe," she admitted. "Not stressed."

Liar, liar, pants on fire.

Her inner voice was out of line. She fought the childish urge to slap her hands over her ears and sing, "La, la, la."

"Since I am Latvian," Ché continued with a subtle smile, "she thought I might have some words of advice for you. She assumes I am a world-traveler."

"You are. Just not this world."

"All the better. I will help you solve this problem."

Guys. They always wanted to "fix" you. "I don't need a problem solver in my life."

"I am not 'in your life.' "

"Bull! You are, too."

Ché's mouth curved in a sanctimonious twist. "Of course."

She would not react. She *would not*. He'd turned her words on her again, trapping her into admitting the truth. She *was* involved with him. Maybe not in the sexual way she was used to, but she was involved nonetheless.

"It is true, then? You fear flying?"

From the way he watched her with such rapt patience, she knew he wasn't going to let this go. There was no use denying it; he would see the lie in her eyes. "Yeah. So what? There are worse things. I'll deal with it."

"It can be conquered, Ilana. Like all inner demons."

"I made a treaty with my 'demons' a long time ago, Ché. I let them be, and they let me be."

She realized that her stomach muscles had clenched. The conversation had veered into uneasy territory. It had become too personal. Deftly she masked her emotional retreat with a physical advance, which always worked. "This is a dance, not an interrogation."

Faking a smile, she leaned her cheek against his chest. His heart thudded under her ear. And he smelled great. Closing her eyes, she melted against him as he held her close. His body was warm and strong. She felt good with him. Safe. *You could fall for a man like him*.

Maybe if he were from Earth. Maybe if he weren't heir to a family that to her symbolized the polar opposite of everything she'd worked toward all her life. Maybe if he weren't Prince Ché Vedla.

He was starting to seep into her heart, and it was the last thing she wanted.

" 'Hurry, hurry, baby.' " Under her breath, she sang along with the song playing. " 'Baby, hold on tight. Don't let me fly away . . .' "

When the song ended, she blinked, as if waking from a particularly vivid dream. Ché tucked a finger under her chin and moved her back. His brows lifted. He was going to bring up flying again; she could tell by the expression on his face. "Ché, let's just drop it."

Puzzlement washed over his face. "Drop . . . what?"

She fought a smile. He was so fluent in English that it took her by surprise when slang threw him. "The flying issue. I'm never going to like being in an airplane. Nothing you say is going to help."

Ché dropped his hands onto her shoulders. "When you are seated with your hands on the controls, flying will be a different experience entirely."

Her stomach flipped. "What do you mean?"

"I am going to teach you how to fly."

Chapter Twelve

Ilana's first impulse was to flee. Ché wanted to teach her to fly a plane? No one had ever suggested such a thing!

Not her parents, her stepfather Rom, or any of the other pilots in her life. There was a reason for that, Ilana knew.

They wanted to keep the skies safe. They didn't want anyone at the controls of a plane who believed that too many passengers waiting to use the restroom in an airliner might upset the delicate balance of weight and send the jet spinning to the ground.

Only not Ché. He thought she could fly an airplane. Acted as if he hadn't any doubts. She stepped away from him.

He caught her hand and tugged her back. They collided.

She blew strands of hair out of her eyes. "Oh, so now we're doing the tango?"

"The tango . . ."

"A sexy Earth dance."

"Ah." Ché caught her around the waist and pressed her to him, close enough for her to feel the hard contours of his body through the negligible scrap of a dress she wore. He was a veteran of the *Vash* social scene. He'd danced with queens and the beautiful women of the royal court. Now he expected her to bend to his charm like the rest of them, to make her forget through the sheer potency of his masculinity that he hadn't just made the most laughable proposition she'd ever heard.

Ha!

"Is this how the tango is accomplished?" he inquired.

"No."

He pulled her closer. Her physical reaction to him was immediate. Her skin warmed, and she tingled low in her belly. But in that irritating way of his, Ché managed to look cool and composed.

Holding her gaze, he lifted her hand to his lips, pressing them to the heel of her palm, and then the inside of her wrist. Goosebumps prickled her arms. "Is this?"

Her lips compressed. If he kept this up, she was going to have to make an emergency rendezvous with the ice cubes in her mineral water. But if she did, he'd think he'd gotten to her. Quickly she took the offensive. "No. The tango is much more intense. Rougher." Smiling her best sultry smile, she smoothed her hands over and behind his solid hips. "Do you like it rough, Ché?" she asked and gave his rear a firm little push.

His pupils dilated, darkening his gray eyes, and she faced the aroused and hungry male who had come to her in the shower. The familiar dimple in his jaw deepened. "Do you think we Vedlas are so easily distracted?" he challenged.

"If you insult one *Vash Nadah*, you insult them all," she muttered. "I'm not arguing with your entire family, Ché. I'm arguing with you. And you're trying to change the subject, trying to get me to argue about something else. That falls in the same category as distraction. You're guilty of it, too."

"Ilana, I . . ." He stopped. Sighed. "I did not do this on purpose."

She grinned. "You know, you're getting pretty darn good at those almost-apologies."

After a moment of incredulity, Ché laughed; he actually laughed, deep and rich. Even with the contact lenses on, the delight in his eyes shined through. It made her want to laugh, too.

Something fleeting and wonderful flashed in his eyes. "I made a wise choice in tour guides. For this is exactly what I came here to find." He surprised her by taking her in his arms and whirling her around. It was the most spontaneous she'd seen him, the most relaxed. She wanted to kiss him. Badly. But she'd brought him here as bachelorette bait; she couldn't steal the lure.

Still chuckling, he hugged her close, swaying slowly as the music changed to a tune that at long last suited their slow dancing. Ché brought his mouth to her ear so she could hear him. His lips brushed her earlobe; her diamond earring clicked against his teeth. "See? The melody changed for us."

She smiled. "Dream on, Ché." But she guessed that when you were prince of a good chunk of the galaxy, it was easy to believe that fortune bowed to your wants and desires instead of the other way around.

But, just once, wouldn't it be nice to go along with the fantasy? Cinderella, Sleeping Beauty—every fairy tale she'd ever read as a kid, where Prince Charming came and swept you off your feet, protecting you, loving you, forever and ever. Never sleeping around. Never sneaking around with other women behind your back. Yeah, it was a fairy tale, the happily ever after. Then there was real life. No one could say Ilana Hamilton didn't know the difference.

"Excuse me," she told Ché. "I have to go freshen up."

She walked off the dance floor and spent the next twenty minutes locked in a stall in the women's bathroom, wondering what the hell she was going to do about Ché's offer to teach her how to fly a plane.

Ché was waiting for her when she came out, his drink in one hand and a fresh mineral water and lime in the other. She sighed, veering toward a warren of luxurious private vestibules and conversation nooks. Plush walls muffled the music but magnified the odors of sweat, liquor, and perfume.

She found an empty nook. He followed her inside. Shadows fell across his handsome face. "You've said nary a word about flying," he said, and handed her the glass of water.

"Well, duh. It doesn't take a rocket scientist to figure out it's not my favorite topic. How do you think you're going to teach me how to fly anyway? You don't have enough time left here to become an instructor."

"I already am a pilot."

She tipped back her head. "Help! This is some kind of cruel joke."

But Ché as adventurer intrigued her. She took a deep swallow of her fizzy drink. It made her eyes water. "I didn't know you flew."

"I hold ratings in several varieties of sub-atmospheric craft and starfighters. I even docked a starcruiser once. It would not take long to earn clearance to fly your small, private sub-atmospheric Earth craft."

"Airplanes," she corrected automatically. "Coast Muni is near my house. They rent planes." Her heart thumped harder. Why was she giving him this information?

Because if you don't, he'll find out anyway.

"But you'll need ID, Mister French of Latvia. A pilot's license. You don't have either." She pretended to be disappointed for him, for *them*. "I guess your plan won't work. Thanks for offering, though—"

"On the contrary, Ilana. My flying credentials are in the galactic database, and under my real name. They will be able to access the records."

"I thought your visit was secret."

"From most, yes. Only my advisor, my brother, and yours know where I am. The treaty the Federation signed with your world requires me to enter your world using my real name. But without any mention of 'prince,' or the presence of a diplomatic entourage, no one cared." His mouth curved. "It was not until I was linked to you that the paparazzi came after me."

"Don't remind me." She sagged against the plush wall. Without a thumbs-up from Earth System Patrol and Customs—ESPAC—Ché would have been denied entry. As a high-ranking *Vash Nadah* and a member of the Great Council, he would have caused an interstellar incident if he'd been caught sneaking past Earth's border-patrol starships with fake ID.

She drank more water, wishing suddenly it were a margarita—a strong margarita. "I know you princes don't have outside careers. Is flying a hobby? Do you fly much? Lack of practice makes a pilot rusty. I'm warning you, Ché, if I suspect even one rust flake, I'll refuse to listen to another word about you taking me"—she swallowed—"up there."

"I am not forbidden to pursue an outside career. There simply is no time for it. My piloting is a hobby, yes, but more than that. It is a way to empower myself. For the same reason I strive to be fluent in English. The more skills a man has, the less likely he is to find himself helpless in any situation."

She clutched her glass in sweating hands. "How can you not feel helpless flying? You are so not in control when you're in a plane. No sane person could actually like strapping into something resembling a tin can with wings, flying miles and miles above the Earth, which is spinning on its axis at a thousand miles an hour, and whipping around the sun at eighteen-point-five miles a second! A *second*, Ché." Out of breath, she tried to slow down. "They told me that," she said, panting. "In a clinic. They thought it would help me, knowing that even when I'm not flying, I am. Ugh! I left and never went back." From behind a wavy curtain of hair, she peeked at Ché.

"The stars move as well, Ilana." He appeared almost bored by the thought. "Your sun and its solar system circle the center of the galaxy—a path it completes, I believe, approximately every two-hundred-and-twenty-million standard years. In addition, our galaxy is part of a group of galaxies. And that group is part of a massive concentration of galaxies, called the local supercluster—"

"Ché," she almost squealed. She gripped his forearm for balance.

"The supercluster is racing away from the other enormous superclusters of galaxies at an incredible velocity. The universe is expanding, every second of every day, and we are helpless to stop it—"

"But I can stop you!" She laughed and pressed her

finger over his mouth. His lips were firm and warm. That touch brought a zing of attraction. "Do you know what I thought yesterday when you got out of your car? I thought you were a hit man, an assassin. I was right. You are. Your weapon of choice? Death by vertigo."

His eyes lit up with amusement. He drained his drink and set it down on a narrow sidebar. "I have never heard of this method, death by vertigo, but its uniqueness makes it worth mentioning. Alas, killing you is not on my travel agenda, Ilana. Or on any agenda."

Faint beard stubble glinted on his chin, and the amber glow from the walls of the nook filled the hollows of his cheekbones, made round by his grin. "Assassination of a princess . . . the aftermath would be most unpleasant. Vicious accusations between the families, shifting loyalties, volatility in the realm. And should the Great Council choose to keep me alive after the deed, which I doubt, we Vedlas would then have both heirs imprisoned. Klark and me, both. My father would not like that. It would be too damaging to family pride. At that point, he would likely be disgusted enough to dispose of us both—by his own hands."

Ché brought his hand to his chin and studied her. "But if doing away with you were made to look like an accident . . . Hmm. Now, that could work."

"You pig. I don't believe you." Laughing, she pushed at him. "You've given this way too much thought."

"I have not given it any thought at all. But I have spent enough time amidst the intrigues of the royal court to know what works and what does not." He regarded her more soberly. "I did not come here to hurt you."

"You are not your brother any more than I am mine, Ché."

"No," he agreed soberly. With the obvious loyalty and pride of a devoted older brother, he insisted, "I love him."

"And I love mine, too." Ilana put her nearly full glass next to Ché's empty one on the sidebar. Breezily, to lighten the suddenly serious mood, she said, "We have a saying on Earth: 'You can't live with them, and you can't live without them.' I'd say that applies to brothers."

"Perhaps entire families. Our families."

They looked at each other and laughed.

"I'm glad you came, Ché. I'm glad we had the chance to really meet. What can I say? You're fun."

"Fun . . ." He pondered that, his mouth tipping belatedly at one end. "I have been called many things. Never that."

"It doesn't surprise me. Most of the royals wouldn't know 'fun' if it jumped up and bit them on the nose."

"Or doused them with pepper spray."

She pretended to punch him. He caught her fist, holding on to her fingers. She laughed, but her smile faded in the intensity of his gaze, a little too deep for her comfort zone. Instinctively she gave him a mental push away. An emotional push. She had to keep distance between them, keep him from getting to her.

He took her hand, pressed it to his chest. A suave, casual gesture. But the feel of him rocked her. Balanced precariously between banter and body contact, she decided that stealing a kiss didn't scare her as much as his intimate regard.

Ilana leaned toward him, hesitantly, and then with more purpose, rising up on her toes to touch her lips to his.

Their warm breath mingled. Ché's hand squeezed

hers, more of an involuntary movement, she suspected, than a conscious act. She kissed him lightly, tasting him, most definitely intending to entice him, here in the semiprivacy of the nook, where her girlfriends wouldn't know. Then, slowly, she moved back far enough to see the bemused expression on his face. She'd surprised him. "I was curious to see how you kissed when you weren't angry."

He made a soft sound of protest and reached for her hair. "I was not angry. Annoyed, perhaps. And curious . . . curious to see what you would look like." He took a few strands between his fingers, sliding them down to the ends. Her body reacted instantly, awash in tingles. "And what you felt like," he murmured.

A thought intruded. Ché was a man accustomed to courtesans meeting his sexual whims. Was this gentle caress what it seemed? Or was he only inspecting the merchandise as an objective potential consumer? She didn't know.

She wasn't supposed to care.

"And I was curious," he continued in his deep and sexy voice, "to see if you tasted as good as I suspected."

"Did I?" she whispered.

Ché cradled her face in his hands, oh-so-lightly, as if he couldn't choose between studying her upturned face and hauling her close for a kiss. She made the decision for him.

Ché responded to her kiss with a sound low in his throat. Her mouth opened, her tongue searching out his. A shudder coursed through his body, and he pressed her close, one big hand cupping the back of her head.

She ran her hands over his shoulders and back, feeling the hard muscles shifting under the fabric of his shirt. It was a lush, sensual kiss that seemed to go on and on.

His scent filled her nostrils, spicy and exotic. She sensed his arousal on an elemental, almost animal level that was shocking and new. An image of them, sweating and naked, rolling on twisted bedsheets, flared vividly in her mind. He had to feel it, too, the heat blazing between them.

"Let's go home," she said, pulling away slightly. "We'll figure out an excuse. I can have a headache," she suggested. "Or you can." And then she'd take him to bed.

Already she felt better, taking charge and putting on the moves, deciding where and how their relationship—if one could call it that—would advance.

She'd have to be careful, though. She'd already found out how dangerous he was. He was no pushover. He was a worthy challenge, an equal. Keep it light, she warned herself. Keep it casual.

Keep it *physical*.

Ché lazily tasted his way from one corner of her mouth to the other. "You wish to go home?"

"It's time for bed," she mumbled against his mouth.

"Sleep, yes. I suppose we must."

She chuckled huskily. "But you know we won't."

His misunderstanding showed. He did have a problem with slang. "Not *sleep* sleep, silly." She buried her face in the warm hollow of his neck, her arms wrapped over his shoulders. "I want you to make love to me," she whispered, moving her hips against his.

He moved her back. There was something in his eyes that was a little too direct for comfort. He shook his head. "No, Ilana."

Saying those words cost him; she could tell by the reappearance of the dent in his jaw.

"I will not bed you tonight."

172

Stung, she pushed away from him. He'd turned her down. She couldn't believe it. She wasn't sure if she wanted to be embarrassed or disappointed or both. No one had ever rejected her before. Granted, she chose her targets with precision, she wasn't promiscuous or indiscriminate, but Ché . . . she'd assumed he was equally attracted to her, and when men were attracted to her they didn't say no.

But she was wrong. She wasn't sure if she wanted to die of embarrassment, be pissed off, or both.

Somehow she managed an amazingly light, casual tone. "Bummer. And here I was, looking forward to searching for your tattoo. But I guess you're tired out from all that dancing."

"No, Ilana." Emotions played over his face, surprisingly raw and honest. "I am not too tired to make love to you all night. To wake with you in my arms, to stroke you, and kiss you, until you were ready for me once more. If I were to love you tonight, tomorrow not even the longest bath would erase the memory of me between your legs."

She stared at him, wide-eyed. Only pride kept her from whimpering at the sensual picture he painted with those words. Sure, she'd known men who could talk the sexy talk. But no one had ever done it with the carnal certainty that Ché did. His unshakable self-confidence with regard to lovemaking was an aphrodisiac all on its own. She wondered if he knew how close her knees were to giving out.

"You've made your point. You're not tired. But you are curious about me. You said so. So am I, about you. Why not spend the night together and satisfy our curiosity?"

"I am not another Cole," he said with distaste. "A toy that you can bring out when you want to play and then cast aside. When the time comes for you to remember me, it will be as the man who was different from the others." He leveled a steady gaze at her. "Nor are you a plaything to be discarded. I have thought about you since the day I saw you on that rooftop, but I have been with you now for a day. One day. If I were to take you to bed tonight, I would be treating you in the same offhand manner I do the pleasure servers in the palace. An appealing indulgence, but ultimately forgettable."

Her face grew hot. She hugged her arms tighter to her ribs.

"I do not intend to forget you, Ilana Hamilton," he said, gentler.

Ilana swallowed. It was another rout, she thought, only this time one of emotions; she felt psychologically what she'd felt physically after he left her alone in the shower.

She felt wrung out and inside-out. A curious achy feeling swamped her, as if she'd just had a long and draining cry. Leaning her weight on the cushioned wall behind her, she regarded Ché. He hadn't escaped unscathed, either. She'd seen the regret darkening his eyes. The tinge of bitterness. It was plain to see, the duty he felt he owed his family, and what it cost him personally.

Ilana might have a *Vash* stepfather, and a brother who seemed more and more *Vash* as time passed; she might have spent five years trying to figure out the Treatise of Trade, but this was the closest she'd come to understanding what it meant to be a *Vash Nadah.*

Ché was honorable to the core. "Fealty, fidelity, family" was the *Vash* warrior's creed. Like Rom, Ché had been raised on and was devoted to the ancient code of the warrior, one that stressed control and self-discipline. It was seen as an honorable way of life, one that supposedly set an example for the lower classes. As a Vedla, Ché was as *Vash Nadah* as you could get. If he made a promise, he would keep it. When he married, he would be fully committed to that woman, arranged marriage or not, even if he wasn't in love with the woman. Ché stood as the exact opposite of her father, whose cheating and lies had made it difficult for her to form a lasting relationship with a man.

Ilana was at a loss how to reconcile this epiphany with her fear of falling for Ché. They'd just met. But the potential was there; she could feel it. And yet she feared it. Why? If she knew the root cause, why did the thought of commitment, of permanence, scare the stuffing out of her?

Ché lowered his chin. The corners of his mouth looked to be fighting a smile. "Great Mother. Have I actually rendered you speechless?"

At that, she staggered back to something resembling composure. "Dream on."

"Slang," he reminded her.

"It means that you are so, so wrong."

"I had that feeling." He exhaled. "Ilana, I do not know how I can convince you of it, but I have no lack of desire for you. On the contrary." His eyes blazed darkly. "I have had visions of making love to you since we first met, months ago. I want you, Ilana. Surely you can tell. But," he said, "I am loath to squander my fantasies on one impulsive night."

She squeezed her eyes shut for a moment. Took a calming breath. He was going to talk her right into an orgasm if he kept this up. "When I said you were wrong, I meant the speechless part."

He blinked. She almost smiled. "Ah," he said.

To his credit, he acted unruffled. Then again, talking about sex did not embarrass the *Vash*.

She rubbed her hands up and down her bare arms. "If you're worried that I'll see you the same as the other guys, don't. You've already pulled away from the pack. No one's ever turned me down before. You're the first. I don't think I'll be forgetting that— or you—anytime soon."

Again he gave her that helpless look.

"It's a compliment, Ché. And some humble pie, too. I figured you for the predictable one, not me. I . . . don't know what to say. Other than I don't like it—I don't like being predictable. I won't settle for being forgettable, either."

She picked up her glass of water, stepping backward to the nook's entrance. At Ché's raised eyebrow, she waved him forward. "Come on. At least four women are dying for your attention out there. You can't spend all your time with me. We came here to have fun, and that's what we're going to do. Especially you."

"And you?" he asked.

"Hell. Don't worry about me. I always enjoy myself. Fun is my middle name. Now, go. Get out there and have a good time."

He dipped his head in that charming *Vash* way of his. "As you wish."

"That's more like it." *When I make a bet, I don't like to lose.* Smiling wickedly, Ilana sashayed out of the nook.

Chapter Thirteen

Parked across the street from her condo in Ché's Porsche, Ilana killed the ignition. The lovely hush of an upscale automobile surrounded them like a luxury cocoon.

It was late, well after two a.m. They'd closed down Reach. After the nook, she'd avoided Ché, leaving the flirting to her girlfriends—that was why she'd invited them dancing in the first place—but at the end of the night, Ché had bade her friends farewell, leaving without promises for dates, without a single exchange of phone numbers. Maybe, despite her earlier coaching, he didn't "get" how dating was done on Earth. The social scene was completely foreign to him. But she wouldn't give up. She had a bet to win.

Though he appeared unaffected by the alcohol, Ché had knocked back a number of drinks. So when it came time to leave, she'd offered to drive.

She pulled the keys from the ignition and handed them over. "Cool car. Drives like a dream. Makes drinking fizzy water all night worth it. Almost."

Ché peered through the windshield into the misty night. "I will escort you inside, and then I would like to take a walk." He turned to her. "If you don't mind."

"I mind that you'll be out alone. This is L.A., not the palace. It's a fairly safe neighborhood, but it's the middle of the night. The police don't swing by that often."

"I have been trained since childhood in unarmed combat. I possess the martial skills with which to defend myself."

"Still, people have knives, guns. At night the beach is deserted."

He looked startled. "How did you know I will go to the beach?"

"Where else would you go? We both love the ocean."

"Yes, we do." His expression gentled. Ilana shifted in her seat. When he gazed at her like that, a feeling of lightheartedness and lightheadedness bubbled up inside her. It made her feel like a shaken Pepsi bottle with a tight cap. If she opened the lid and released her feelings, would Ché suck the bottle dry before throwing it away?

Yuck. Pepsi bottles and exploding emotions and long-term commitment—whoa. She was getting way ahead of herself, and she was in too good a mood to live anywhere else but in the moment. She drop-kicked the thought out of her mind.

Now Ché had turned pensive, too. Maybe it was contagious. On the plus side, he didn't mention anything else about going off into the night alone. It was really pretty funny, the way she was so protective with him, when his stature and fighting skills screamed *Don't mess with me.*

"My wife will likely be a desert girl," he said. It took

her a second to catch up to him. He was still thinking about the ocean. "Perhaps she will come to love the sea. But most of them do not, the princesses from desert worlds."

"Your homeworlds are pretty forbidding places, but not all of them are desert worlds, right?" There were eight *Vash* homeworlds. To the *Vash* they were symbols of the victory over the warlords of their dark past. Good over evil. They formed the moral fiber and unity of the *Vash Nadah* federation. "Look at Eireya."

The pleasure of good memories softened his features. He loved his home, she saw. "It is the most beautiful of all the worlds."

"It is. And how did you Vedlas pull that one off, by the way? How did you get the best planet?" The climate was temperate and rarely stormy. What wasn't ocean was beach. The landscape reminded Ilana of a warmer Tasmania: green, achingly lovely, unspoiled. Of course, she wouldn't have known anything about Eireya if she hadn't done all that snooping months ago to find out more about the man she couldn't get off her mind. "Connections?" she persisted in a light, teasing tone. "Good real estate agent?"

He shook his head at her confusing implications. "The Vedla ancestral home predates the Federation, you see. My family has always lived on Eireya. We ruled the galaxy from there for so long that our origins are lost in history. Then, after losing the throne and being massacred down to only a few survivors, we helped reunite and stabilize the galaxy after the Great War. The Vedlas have to share power now, but we got to keep Eireya." Ché's triumphant smile made it seem as if the event had happened last week instead of eleven thousand years ago.

"While the other seven warriors had to go looking

for the nastiest real estate in the galaxy," she supplied. In Basic, she quoted from the Treatise of Trade in a pompous voice, " 'The Original Warriors chose the most forbidding worlds, to lead by example, to prove their willingness to sacrifice for the good of the many.' "

She shrugged off Ché's startled delight and said, "I've built up a nice little repertoire of recitations from the Treatise of Trade. I don't know why—I never have the chance to show off. My point is, you don't know where your wife will be from. There are other climates."

"Only two. Eireya and Mistraal, which is covered in grasslands."

Ilana perked up. "Tee'ah's from there."

"Yes," he said dryly. "I know."

"Oops." Ilana sank back in her seat. "I guess it will be a desert girl for you."

"My mother was from a desert world—a Lesok princess. She grew to tolerate the water, to my father's relief, but I suspect it was the sandy beach she enjoyed. She watched us swim, my siblings, my father, and me, but she rarely waded in herself. . . ."

Ilana hung on the images he painted of a loving family, the glimpses of his privileged and sheltered childhood. "Your father was a king, but he still made time for his wife and kids. Count yourself lucky."

With obvious cultural pride, Ché reminded her, "Family binds my society together."

Maybe, she thought. But she suspected that his family's closeness transcended the rules. "My mother pretty much raised us herself, Ian and me. My dad was an airline pilot. He used to pick up extra trips—for the money, he said—but the truth was that he liked flying more than he liked being home. My mom divorced him when I was a teenager." Ilana spread her hands on her bare thighs, pretending to study the pale pink polish covering her short, manicured fingernails. Divorce didn't happen amongst the *Vash*. There wasn't even a word for it in the Basic language. "Since then, he's remarried, had another kid, divorced, and remarried." She glanced up at Ché. "The new wife's pregnant."

"I know about your father, Ilana. Jock Hamilton." A hint of a grimace curved his lips, as if the name itself left a bad taste. "I cannot stomach adultery. In my culture, when a man promises to be a woman's protector, to worship her body, to father her children, he does not stray." The dent in his jaw was back. It was a good barometer for his mood—his bad mood. "Your father left your mother with children."

"Ian and I were practically grown. A year later I was out of the house."

"You make excuses for him."

Anger flooded her. "He's my father. Faults and all, *I love him*."

"And so you justify his behavior. You try to make him look better in the eyes of others."

"I don't support what he did. It was wrong. But he's not completely evil. He's a good man. He just has . . . problems. Your culture tries to see everything as black and white, good or evil, right or wrong. Life's not like that, Ché. It's naïve to think it is."

To her amazement, he agreed. "I know what you try to do for your father, because I do the same for Klark. You have an adulterer father. I have a fanatical, xenophobic brother."

Ilana pushed hair off her forehead and studied him. She'd expected him to preach *Vash* gobbledygook.

"I have lived what you have, Ilana, done what you have done. Many in the palace and Great Council viewed Klark's ambition in my behalf as improper and brash. They frowned on him for it. At the same time, they admired him for his passionate support of me. It put me in a difficult position. It was difficult to disapprove without coming across as unappreciative. I often explained away the worst of his behavior—until he tried to sabotage Ian's ascension to the throne and punish Tee'ah for breaking her promise to me. Then I could no longer make excuses. I had spent years propping up Klark's reputation, even when his behavior appalled me."

"If they don't look so bad," she ventured, "then maybe we don't look so stupid for loving them."

He pulled back, dismay making his features taut. "Great Mother. I hope not."

But she'd given him that doubt, made him question what she often saw in herself. Ché's gaze turned introspective. He opened and closed his hands, his face contorted as if he were disgusted with himself. But he did not speak; he kept his emotions under tight control, a trait drilled into the *Vash* from birth. Yet, after spending time with Ché, Ilana could see that the *Vash* were in fact very emotional people. In private and only with those they trusted, her mother had told her. Now, Ilana understood.

"So you say it is *pride* that drives us to defend them," Ché said finally in an even tone.

"I think so. There's love, too, and that always makes everything more complicated. Nothing is ever black and white."

He gave a short, self-deprecating laugh, then relaxed. "I am beginning to believe it. This past year has introduced me to more shades of gray than I ever knew existed. As you said, I love my brother as you love your father: faults and all."

Then sudden realization flared in his eyes. "It

seems we have more in common than our love of the ocean, Ilana."

She winced, squeezing the steering wheel. She wasn't supposed to have anything in common with him. He was supposed to be all wrong for her. "I don't know, Ché. It sounds very different to me. Klark did what he did to help you. But my father? I wish I could say he had a reason for being unfaithful, a reason for breaking apart the family, but he didn't. He just couldn't keep his pants on."

He gave her that Pepsi-bottle-shaking look again and leaned forward, resting his forearm on his thigh. A shadow fell across his face, muting his penetrating regard. "And you, Ilana? Can you keep your pants on?"

She stiffened. "You're one to talk! You and your harem."

Her outrage didn't faze him. It was clear that he hadn't asked the question to tease her; he very much wanted to hear her answer. And no matter how crazy it seemed, it was important to her, what he thought. It was the only reason she didn't respond with a tart *Screw you.* "If you're asking if I cheat, no, I don't. It's the ultimate act of betrayal. I know; I've lived it vicariously through my mother. I don't do it, Ché. I never have. I just—I just don't stick around very long. And there's no law against that."

"They never gave you reason, your men, to 'stick around.' "

"What's this? Are you making excuses for me now? Don't bother. Klark keeps you busy enough."

Ché leaned forward. "I am saying that you deserve better. You deserve a man who will not let you go." She caught the scent of his warm skin, of faint masculine sweat. His expression was so intense, she wanted to look away. But she couldn't bring herself to do it. The conversation had taken a deeply personal turn, and she didn't like it. It was one thing to talk about her father, quite another to reveal too much about herself.

Don't look under the bed if you don't want to find dust bunnies. That was what she felt like telling him. But Ché was to dust bunnies as an open door was to a stuffy room. Without warning, he'd stomped inside her head. Now he was peering around as if he wanted to move in.

Now, that was a frightening thought. *Frightening but exhilarating,* her inner voice whispered in her ear. *Admit it, Hamilton. Or are you too scared?*

Ché moved closer. One big hand smoothed over her hair, revealing her face to him. Tingles cascaded down her spine, and she trembled at his forthright touch. "If you were mine, I would not let you go."

Suddenly there was no air left in the Porsche to breathe. "But I'm not yours."

"I know." His fingers moved in her hair. Every time they did, she shivered. "We are wrong for each other. We were never supposed to meet. We were never supposed to"—His attention dropped to her mouth—"Kiss."

She swallowed her sigh as he bent his head to brush his lips over hers. A slow and tender exploration. Her tingles became a roaring blaze. Ché was a master; he could charm her even when she was angry, even when she was scared. But was he really that skillful? Or did she happen to be susceptible to him? Neither could be a good thing, she thought before his skill blanked out everything but his incredible mouth.

She slid her arms over his shoulders, her head tipping back. His hard body trembled, muscles shifting. He came up and over her, groaning softly as he kissed her hard and deep, his fingers twisting in her hair.

The surge of rightness inside her and the passion with which she returned the kiss made no sense at all. The righteous warrior and the barbarian princess—it sounded more like the title of a bad novel than any relationship that stood a chance of getting off the ground.

He was the one who ended the kiss, not she. The realization left her dazed and unsettled. It was like waking in the middle of the night and not knowing where you were.

Ché's face hovered over hers, dark and serious. Before he could say anything, she pressed one finger to his lips. "Don't make a bigger deal out of this than it is. I like to kiss and . . . well, you're a great kisser. How would the *Vash* put it? We shared a little pleasure. That's all." She made her voice drop lower. "We could share more, if you want to."

He gazed at her in wonder, as if he'd never seen her before. If she hadn't known better, she'd have said he looked lovestruck, head over heels—or like someone who'd been hit over the head with a two-by-four.

The change in him was unsettling. The hair on the back of her neck prickled. "Ché, let's go inside. I'll make you a drink. I'll have one, too. Maybe three. How about a turkey sandwich? We've got lots of food now." She wriggled out of the embrace—she'd had plenty of experience at that—and opened the car door. Cool, damp air swept into the Porsche, ruffling Ché's dark, copper-gold hair.

"You are a princess," he said.

"And we know what you are. But I thought we weren't going to bring it up while you were here. I'm the tour guide and you're the bodyguard, remember?"

He simply watched her, intently. She felt like a deer

in the sights of a game hunter's rifle. "Ché, are you feeling okay? It's jet lag, right? Or space lag or something."

"Or something," he agreed without changing his absorbed expression. *Hmm,* his face said. He was deep in thought, plotting, picturing something from every angle.

"Let's go, Ché. You're going right to bed." She swung one leg out onto the pavement. Her heel scraped across the blacktop.

He didn't open his door. "We are both unattached," he said.

"Yep. Isn't it grand? Now, come on."

"It could work, Ilana."

She gaped at him. "Are you asking me to marry you?"

He sputtered. "No. Certainly not. I was merely suggesting that a union between us could work." He appeared to catch on to her question, and lifted a brow. "Why? Would you consider marriage? To me? This is all hypothetical, of course."

It felt as if she'd swallowed her heart. She shot out of the sports car and pirouetted around. "Hypothetical, my ass. Let's not even go there. Your family would freak if you brought me home. You know it."

"Hmm. I have no reason to believe my family would object to a B'kah-Vedla union."

"I do."

"You do now."

She ground her palms into her temples. "Okay, so I'm attracted to you. I like your confidence, your intelligence—and, yeah, your butt." That didn't shock him as much as she'd expected or hoped. In fact, he couldn't have acted more pleased, the smug bastard. Maybe he was getting used to her. "But we're from different worlds, Ché. Literally. Marriage is out."

"Not for me. It is inevitable."

"Exactly. You have to get married. I don't."

"But you want to, yes?"

"Yes," she admitted. "Someday."

"Do you want children?"

"Someday after someday."

A look of satisfaction warmed his face. "The B'kahs and the Vedlas . . . I do not know why I never considered a blood alliance between the two."

"Blood alliance? Oh, be still, my heart. If that's the *Vash Nadah* version of romance—"

"You are a B'kah, a member of the most powerful clan in the Federation," he went on, lost in his sick fantasy. "I am a Vedla; my family is influential, a bastion of conservatism. A marriage between the two would strengthen the entire Federation."

"You're drunk."

"On your feeble Earth liquor? I think not."

"You're sober? That's even worse."

His mouth spread into that know-it-all slight smile of his she found so incredibly sexy. His lean, chiseled, noble face glowed in the dome light. If only he weren't so damned good-looking. If only her heart didn't do back flips every time he looked into her eyes.

"Even hypothetically, it's ridiculous." She bent over, sticking her head inside the car. "How would I fit in? Seriously. You have so many rules governing an individual's life that I've only cracked the surface after years of studying the Treatise of Trade."

"The Federation is changing. Philosophies are changing."

"They haven't changed that much."

"The past seven years have seen more change than the past eleven thousand. And all for the good of the people, if not the comfort of the Great Council. A

187

union between us would serve to further that social and cultural evolution." Nervously Ché assured her, "Naturally, this is all hypothetical—"

"Of course it is," she cut him off. She plopped back down in the driver's seat and slammed the door closed. "We're wrong for each other, Ché. Totally wrong, and you know it. Just yesterday you called me a barbarian. What changed? Hypothetically."

"*I* did."

"Quit it." She pushed at him. "You're scaring me."

He exhaled, becoming more serious. That worried her more than his teasing. "Pure theory only, Ilana. Do you think I would force you to give up your creative endeavors?"

"I haven't thought about it."

"Perhaps you should."

"Ché," she said warningly.

"I meant, in the spirit of speculative discussion, naturally."

"Naturally." She rolled her eyes.

"I have wondered," he said. "Do you think the Federation could be a market for Earth popular-culture entertainment?"

His interest startled her. "Well, yeah. Actually, I've given it a lot of thought, the Federation as a market for film. The *Vash* love our jeans, our beer, our coffee. Why not our films? Your society is incredibly high-tech when it comes to entertainment, but you have nothing like Hollywood. What a market, if we could crack it." She tried to keep her speech slow enough for Ché to follow. It wasn't easy. "This subject totally excites me."

Ché's eyes glinted. "I could not tell," he teased.

"But we have to face reality. SILF doesn't have the finances to lobby for inclusion." She felt uncomfortable asking her family for money. Then it hit her. Ché seemed interested. Heck, he'd even brought the subject up in the first place.

Ilana put on the straightforward, competent air she used whenever she met with potential investors for her films. "If SILF were to try something like that, would you be interested in helping fund the venture? As a service to your people. A new form of entertainment for the masses."

"Altruism—the key to a *Vash Nadah*'s heart. Or rather, his money. You have learned well from Rom B'kah and Ian."

She smiled unapologetically.

"But I would like to do more than *help* fund your enterprise, Ilana. I can easily fund it all."

She was shocked, thrilled, but she fought not to show it. Overeager producers had turned off more than one investor at the crucial moment. "It would come back to you in spades, Ché. That's slang for: I doubt you'd lose on the deal."

"Wealth is not the issue. I have all I could ever want. What I have long craved is intellectual stimulation. Excitement. I have found it here on Earth. I do not want to leave it behind when I depart."

"Now you won't have to."

He nodded. "Since you are my tour guide, I must ask you to bring me to a site where I may view some popular films, so that I can better see what I have agreed to do."

"Movies? No problem. I'll take you. Popcorn, peanut M&Ms, the whole experience." When was the last time she'd got excited about going to the movies?

Again his gaze turned contemplative. His appraising stare made her fidget.

She groaned. "You're doing it again."

"Doing what?"

"Looking at me like that. What is with you? No one offered you any drugs at Reach, did they?"

"Pharmaceuticals?" He stumbled over the pronunciation.

"Not medications. Illegal mind-altering substances." She hoped not. Ian would kill her.

"I am not drunk or drugged. Nor am I jet-lagged or mentally broken."

"Mentally ill," she corrected. "Unless you meant a mental breakdown. I might agree with either diagnosis."

Smiling, he ran a finger down her arm, shoulder to wrist, pausing there to circle his thumb over the fleshy connector between her thumb and index finger. The movement was confident, sensual, and aroused her instantly. That tiny little spot on her hand was a hotbed of sensation. What other places did he know? Her heart beat harder, faster. "Have you given any more thought to my offer, Ilana?"

"You mean, what we just talked about?"

"No." He drew out the word as if to tease her.

"Oh, that. No. I thought the wedding stuff was hypothetical—"

"It was," he said, quick enough to make her feel better.

"Thank God."

"I meant my offer to teach you to fly."

"The flying lessons," she whispered with dawning dread. It had been a very long weekend, maybe the longest in her life. And now it had just gotten longer. But at least the whole marriage discussion had sputtered out. Even Ché recognized the impossible when he saw it.

She fell back in her seat to mope, and caught a glimpse of her face in the rearview mirror. Lips pursed in a frown. Blue eyes, almond-shaped and mascara-smudged, brighter than she ever remembered seeing them. Face it, she thought. With Ché, she came alive. Whether it was with anger or happiness, every nerve ending in her body sang when she was around him. She'd felt it the day she laid eyes on him, that surge of . . . something.

Linda would call it love at first sight.

An indentation between her brows deepened with her frown. She had a lot of feelings building inside her—but love? Lust she knew. Infatuation, too. But when it came to falling in love, she hadn't a clue.

"I've tried drugs, clinics, therapists, hypnosis, acupuncture, just about everything," she said.

"Everything except flying the plane with your own hands," he reminded her.

"Right." She let out a breath. "And you think this will work."

"When you become familiar with a pilot's duties, when you learn what a craft can or cannot do, and what the air can or cannot do, you will hold on to much of the sense of control you lose when you climb into a flying craft. As I said, my goal is not to teach you to be a pilot." He paused and looked at her. "Unless you want to—"

Her hand shot up. "No. No thanks."

"Then I seek only to help you gain power over fear."

She sank down in the buttery-soft leather seat. Her reflection stared back at her, but this time she didn't want to look. She'd inherited her mother's curvy figure, but everything from the neck up she owed to her father: the sandy brown hair, the eyes, the freckles on her nose.

And trust issues that affected her life on every level, from feeling comfortable flying to giving away her heart.

She gripped the steering wheel as if she could drive away from her past.

"I need to think." She opened the car door and got out. Hopping on one foot at a time, she removed her heeled sandals and tossed them onto the driver's seat. "Come on, Mister Bodyguard. I need you."

She didn't wait for an answer. The thud of a car door closing told her that he was on the way.

A summertime moon shining through mist frosted the sand and sea. Plastic cups and wrappers lay here and there on the sand, scarred from a busy summer day's worth of foot traffic. In a few hours, at sunrise, county workers would rake the sand clean.

She was surprised to see anyone else out there. Another couple huddled together in sweats walked a black-and-white dog. It was unleashed. Water sprayed behind skinny pumping canine legs as the dog ran across the shallows.

Ilana waited until they passed, then stood where the waves licked the shore. The water was cold, a shock, and her toes curled in the squishy wet sand. A light breeze flipped her hair up and around her face. Her short dress rippled and fluttered.

Ché stood by her, a silent, stalwart companion. She waited for him to transform into the pushy, arrogant *Vash* royal she'd expected, waited for him to push her into making a decision about the flying. She waited for him to launch his campaign to change her, to "fix" her. But he didn't. He simply stood next to her, savoring the quiet of the beach at night.

He'd handed the control of her choice to her. That was all it took for a kernel of trust to sprout a tiny root.

"Okay," she blurted. "I'll do it. I'll try flying."

He dipped his head in the universal *Vash* sign of approval.

Her heart hammered so hard against her chest that she figured Ché had to hear it. "But only with you," she said. "I'm not going to do it with anyone else."

His mouth quirked. "I have no intention of sharing you with another." Then his lips formed a blazingly sexy smile. "Hypothetically, of course."

Her knees had started to weaken before she caught herself melting and snapped back to her senses. "You know what, Vedla? They ought to classify that smile of yours as an assault weapon. It's going to kill a woman one of these days."

Looking amused, he brought his hand to his chest as if to recover some of his noble bearing. *Touché,* she thought. She hoped someone was keeping score. "As for your innuendos, we have an expression for that on Earth." She crossed her arms. "Talk is cheap."

She could tell by his dark gaze that he knew exactly what she meant. Good. He might have his reasons for not wanting to sleep with her, but it didn't mean she couldn't give him a hard time about it. "Now, are you ready for sleep? *Real* sleep? I am. I've got twenty-four more hours until this weekend is over—some of us have to work for a living, you know—and if I don't make up for lost time, I'll be a witch come Monday." With her windblown hair hiding her grin, she grabbed Ché's hand and led him home.

"Ah, at long last—the movies," Ché said on a pleased exhalation, his mirrored sunglasses glinting in the late evening light as he walked with Ilana toward the suburban eighteen-theater multiplex. It was several nights later, and he was as curious about the medium of film and the role of Hollywood as he was her career, though Ilana was sure the latter drove the former. Everything about her was "alien" to him; she embodied a concept of woman he couldn't quite grasp. Grasp? Ha! Since he refused to come to grips with her on the physical level, he damn well would intellectually—she'd make sure of it. One way or the other, Prince Ché Vedla was *not* going home uneducated.

"I'm taking you to Passing Fancies," she informed him. "The reviews have been awesome. Audiences love it, too. I'm pretty sure it'll rack up its share of nominations come Oscar-time. All in all, a good movie." She winked at Ché. "Which makes it the perfect end to your virginity."

Ché lifted an amused brow. "My virginity ended some time ago."

She had no doubt of that. "Your *movie* virginity."

"Ah." The end of his sexy mouth turned up slightly. "It is indeed my first time."

"That's right. The first time is special. I want you to remember it."

His gaze turned so intense that she felt its heat through his glasses. "Have no doubt of that, Ilana. I would not forget our . . . first time."

What was he saying? Or rather, proposing?

Ché was the only man who could make her blush. She tried to pretend she wasn't, and pushed her sunglasses higher on her nose. "Two for Passing Fancies—eight o'clock," Ilana told the ticket taker.

Ché paid for tickets with his cash card and they pushed past glass doors, trading a soft, warm evening for a rush of noise and cold, air-conditioned air thick with the aroma of hot buttered popcorn. It was a typical summer night at the movies; kids and their parents, teenagers and their dates streamed past.

Ché looked to Ilana for guidance. "Now we make our way to the appropriate viewing chamber, yes?"

"We will. But first things first." She took him by the arm and tugged him over to the concession stand.

"There's more to going out to the movies than the movie."

"There is *always* more to whatever activity you introduce me to than what meets the eye." With that, Ché flashed his killer grin.

Don't react. Keep the upper hand. "Are you complaining or commentating, Ché?"

"Congratulating. *Self*-congratulating, actually. No one can argue my taste in tour guides." Smug, he used his flattened hand to rub his chest. The thin fabric of his mostly white T-shirt let his bronzed skin show through. It spurred a memory of the feel of his hard body, his clothes transparent from the gushing water in the shower . . .

"Popcorn, ma'am?" prompted the teenager behind the counter.

Looking Ché up and down, Ilana answered distractedly. "Large . . . buttered . . ." She winced. Unfortunate word choice, considering the direction of her thoughts. She shoved her hair off her forehead, pulled her gaze away from Ché. "And two big *ice-cold* Diet Cokes."

She loaded Ché's arms with their booty. "To the viewing chamber," she said in imitation of his arrogant *Vash* accent.

After they found their seats, Ilana sank down deep into the cranberry crushed velvet cushion. And immediately fell under the spell of the theater: the hush of anticipation, the willingness to be entertained, and, if the movie was any good, an escape from reality for the next couple of hours. No matter how long she worked in the industry, the feeling she got every time she stepped into a movie theater was the same.

She bent her head toward Ché, whispering, "Passing Fancies is what you'd consider a high-profile, big-studio production. But the director is one whose

195

work I respect. She started out as an indie filmmaker."

"Like you," he said, nodding.

"She's A-list now. She proved her value over the years with a quality track record."

Ché held the tub of popcorn in his lap, regarding Ilana who poked through it, looking for the yellow-colored kernels. "As will you, Ilana."

She jerked her gaze up to his. He'd spoken with such certainty. "Hey, thanks. I . . . appreciate the vote of confidence."

He appeared immune to her surprise. Maybe, deep down, he didn't disapprove of her career, exactly; it was simply outside of his experience. It proved just how much outside his envelope of comfort he'd stepped when he'd come to Earth.

It proved just how different he was from her original opinion of him.

She turned her attention to the blank screen. "These are the kinds of movies I hope someday to make. Entertainment. But quality entertainment."

"Fictional stories?" He appeared surprised. "You have made documentaries until this point."

"Because they make us money, and they get us noticed. Believe me—if a fantastic script came our way and we managed to scrape together the financing, we'd be all over it. But that hasn't happened yet. So we do what we can until it does. We inch toward that goal." She wondered if a fabulously wealthy prince could understand the concept of putting aside your dreams until you could afford to make them reality. "I'm actively searching for scripts. But it has to be right. I want a happy ending, like Passing Fancies. My favorite kind of flick."

"Flick." He absorbed slang with the thirst of a de-hydrated sponge. "Chick flick."

Ilana muffled her laugh. "Well, not this one. It's got

trans-gender appeal—mushy stuff *and* action. Guy
stuff. You'll like it."

"No need to reassure me." He waved a hand. He
sank down in his seat as the theater darkened, stretching his long legs out in front of him. "I trust you."

"Do that at your own risk," she retorted in a sassy
whisper.

"I will, Ilana," he assured her in a deep voice that
she felt right down to her toes. "I will."

An Earth week later, Ché was to meet Ilana and her
business partners for the midday meal. Lunch. He'd
become fond of the way the Earth-dwellers gathered
in cafes and eating establishments at the noon hour.

In Burbank, where Ilana's place of work was located, Ché pulled up to a restaurant a little before the
appointed time. Mikuni. Japanese cuisine, he thought
with an eager smile. It most resembled the type of
food he ate on Eireya—fresh fish and other sea delicacies, carefully prepared yet untouched by heat of
any kind.

He tossed his keys to a young man, leaving the
Porsche with "valet parking," as it was called, and
strode into the restaurant. Ilana hurried up the moment he stepped inside. Her scent came to him first,
floral and fresh, followed by the pleasant surge he
always felt upon meeting her. Today she was the
woman he'd come to know as "work Ilana." When at
home, she dressed in simple, loose-fitting clothing—
unless she was off running, in which case she donned
those distractingly tight "Spandex" shorts of hers—
but when in the public eye, like now, she dressed
confidently and well. Her sleek suit was dark, opalescent blue, reminding him of the inside of a rhea
shell, with a skirt so short that it practically disappeared under her long form-fitting jacket. Good

breeding and an even healthier grip on discipline were all that kept his gaze from lingering over much on those long bare legs that ended in low-heeled open-toed backless shoes.

Women on Eireya wore gowns, but that in no way meant Ché disapproved of Ilana's mode of dress. On the contrary—he delighted in the curvaceous body she revealed to him. No one could say he was a closed-minded Vedla, and here was the proof!

"Everyone's waiting to meet you." She squeezed his hands in hers, came up on her toes, and gave him a light kiss on the cheek. She didn't touch him at all when they were alone in her condo—they were both too afraid of the instant conflagration that would likely follow—but in public she was as physical as ever, and he enjoyed it as much as a man could who craved more.

Ilana took him by the hand and led him from the foyer into the restaurant proper, decorated in a very masculine fashion in black granite and dark woods. Huge floor-to-ceiling windows let in a flood of sunshine, keeping shadows at bay. "Here he is," she announced to a table seating three women and a man— Ilana's partners and Linda, the energetic flame-haired assistant whom Ché had met a few days before.

Introductions went around. Leslie and Slavica acted friendly but reserved, while Flash's unabashed, distrustful stare told Ché in no uncertain terms that the man felt protective toward Ilana.

Ché opened his menu and tried not to appear like the sexual predator Flash obviously believed him to be. He wondered if Ilana might have mentioned to Flash what she'd come to term the "shower incident," and shifted his weight on his seat. Nonsense! Of course she wouldn't. But Flash's regard made him uneasy nonetheless.

"Octopus," Ché told the server when she asked. "A triple order. No rice. Also, I would like a dish of seaweed on the side, please."

Ché heard a muffled sound of dismay from Slavica. When the server left, Slavica told him, "The octopus you ordered is raw." She glanced at Ilana, as if asking for help. "He knows that, right?"

Ilana appeared amused by her friend's consternation. "Yep. He doesn't like it cooked. He tried fried calamari the other day and"—she looked at Ché— "What did you call it? The way you put it was so funny."

"The tragic result of overzealous preparation," he replied with a shrug.

Even Flash laughed at that, and the mood eased somewhat. But it would take some time for this group to accept him, if they ever did, he realized. They were Ilana's closest associates and friends, and they obviously cared very much for her, enough to want to protect her heart. It told Ché what he already knew: Ilana Hamilton was more vulnerable than she let on.

Ché sat back in his seat, folding his hands casually over his stomach. "I prefer seafood that is raw. Octopus especially. This particular creature of yours reminds me of Eireyan serpent."

"Serpent." Slavica almost moaned.

"Yes. In its chewy texture, and the rows of small suction cups on the limbs. I am delighted to have found here something so similar to one of my favorite dishes."

Ilana hid her grin by bringing a glass of water to her lips, while Slavica and Leslie stared at Ché, their eyes wide. He could tell that they'd wanted to act worldly around him, sophisticated, and had now resigned themselves to failure. Linda, on the other hand, cheerfully watched him as he explained his preferences. Nothing appeared to shock the woman. And she'd seemed to approve of him from the very start—unlike Flash, Ché thought, returning his attention to the dark-haired, blue-eyed man who continued to examine him. Ché supposed that the motivations of extremely wealthy and powerful men were easily suspect.

After the food arrived, small talk ceased. Ilana opened the work discussion. Ché knew this wasn't only an opportunity for him to meet her business partners, but for them to talk about bringing Hollywood to the *Vash*. "The Federation represents a vast market for all creative ventures, but for film especially," she began. "We already know that. What I don't fully get is why in the seven years since Earth has been part of the Federation, our entertainment hasn't made more inroads into your culture."

"We're used to that, you see," Leslie put in. "At least from our viewpoint as Americans. Our culture is pervasive all over the world. Some say invasive. But it's been the opposite with *Vash* culture. You export yours, and yet we can't seem to do the same. Look at virtual-reality tech, for example. It's consumed us. It's everywhere. It's changed how people see entertainment."

"But it hasn't diminished the demand for *films*," Ilana pointed out. "Which tells us that film as entertainment remains viable and unique."

Slavica joined in. "Then, why haven't we seen our popular culture gain even one small toehold in the Federation?"

"Their entertainment is incredibly high-tech," Leslie said.

Ilana nodded. "True. But I've been out there. The Federation has nothing that compares to Hollywood." She turned to Ché. "You of all people know how excited I am about this." She waved a hand at her partners, who listened raptly. "All of us are. SILF wants to be part of this. We want to get our projects, our ideas, to your market, Ché. Though I admit that we're a little overwhelmed by the magnitude of it all. The potential is there for much more demand than what our one small studio could handle."

Flash spoke finally. "I've met with four different studio heads already. It's amazing how a small independent like me got meetings the same day I called. Know why?" He drank some beer and set down his glass. "They're desperate. The minute they heard that SILF might be a way in for them, they wanted to hitch a ride. And they've tried on their own, believe me. For years now. But you've completely thwarted them."

Ilana came to Ché's defense. "Not Ché, Flash. He's all for this."

"I mean the Federation. The big machine. All the studios have tried to get their requests heard, but none of them were able to, because it gets bogged down in the Great Council every single time."

"As everything does,"—Ché sniffed—"that seeks to proceed without a political patron within the Council."

Flash was suddenly humble. But his question was bold. "Would *you* be our patron?" He glanced at Ilana. "She has her family, but none of us have ever tried to make her use their influence. Yet you, Ché, you come to this from a different place. From what Ilana tells me, you're really interested in this—in what we do."

"In what Ilana does, yes."

It was quiet for a moment as Flash absorbed that distinction. While Ché hadn't actually gone ahead and said that he'd assist Ilana in the SILF venture because of the feelings he'd developed for her, Flash understood as only a man would. Something in the man's gaze changed slightly. Softened, perhaps?

"As well," Ché went on, "I have genuine personal interest in the venture. You see, long ago, before my ancestors became kings, they were traders. Commerce. It is in the blood. I cannot resist the lure of profit any more than Ilana, or the rest of you, could turn your backs on the promise of achieving your life's dreams."

Ilana watched him with a stunned and appreciative expression that made his chest feel tight. How much longer did he have here with her? Not long enough, he knew. Hoe had assured him only the other day that the hunt for a wife was well under way, and that within weeks a woman would be chosen. But the least he could do was lay the groundwork for a way of keeping in contact with her long after he'd gone home to the life planned for him from birth.

"So, you're in?" Flash asked.

Silent for a moment, Ché stabbed at a piece of octopus with grim determination and a certain somber inevitability. "Yes," he said at last, to the relief of those at the table. "I am 'in.' "

Deeper, perhaps, than he'd ever intended.

Chapter Fourteen

Muffin had taken to starting his day in Flew The Coop. The eating establishment was what the Earth-dwellers called a "grunge diner." He liked the sound of the word *grunge*. It felt good in his mouth, like the food they served there. But why the label? He'd been coming here mornings for the better part of two Earth weeks and hadn't seen any grime. If the Earth-dwellers wanted filth, they ought to visit some of the bars he had seen in the frontier. Now *that* was grunge.

The food was good, hearty and filling, the way he liked it. It took a lot to fill him up, and in this establishment, only two breakfasts did the trick. He had a limitless amount of money to finance this mission, though in truth he didn't like to spend it. He'd seen and done more than most men did in a lifetime, but Muffin was a simple farm boy at heart and always would be.

He wasn't sure why the food servers wore pink wigs and legwear that resembled fishing nets, but a smiling young female slid his second plate of breakfast onto the table, an overstuffed concoction called an omelet to go with his steak and eggs. "Heya, cutie," she crooned. "Can I bring you something else?" She popped pink chewing gum between her teeth. It was another staple of the servers here. Muffin had tried it—he was willing to try anything once. Odd confection, gum was. He'd had to swallow it whole.

He shook his head. "In time," he told her.

The girl winked at him and wiggled off to her other duties. Ravenous, Muffin bent his head to the task of cutting and eating. These Earth-dwellers, they used so many utensils, but he had managed to master them all.

Chewing, he watched the scene outside, waiting for his quarry to arrive. Dozens of small aircraft sat parked on the landing pad—or "tarmac." Prince Ché had been on time every morning for the last two Earth weeks, attending an aviation school at the small airport across the street. It was easy work. Ian Hamilton had gotten Muffin hired as an airport groundskeeper and refuse collector. He worked from 8:30 to 1:30, and left early if Ché did. No one seemed to care.

He and Ian felt a bit uncomfortable about the forged identification and falsified records that won him the employment. When they'd lived in the frontier, they'd done far worse, deeds that could have gotten them jailed—and did. But this was different. This was Ian's home planet Earth. Should the boggling number of government agencies with authority over the airport catch their wrongdoings, Ian would find himself with much explaining to do. The crown prince seemed to think his intended purpose was worth the means. Muffin wondered.

Since arriving on Earth almost three weeks ago, he'd trailed Ilana and Ché from Disneyland to Tijuana. Though he wasn't privy to every conversation, they seemed to argue more than they spoke civilly. On the other hand, they laughed as often as they battled each other, and sometimes he thought they *enjoyed* fighting. He'd never seen a friendship quite like it. And friendship it must be, for several times lovely women had come for Ché and left with him for hours, returning to Ilana's home well after dark. Muffin puzzled at that. While Ilana always appeared happy to send the couples away together, as soon as Ché was out of sight, the truth of her feelings showed in her face: She wanted him for herself.

Ché seemed no more enamored of the women who came for him. Muffin knew the *Vash Nadah* almost as well as he knew his own people. When a *Vash* man behaved that cordially, and held himself that stiffly, he was not interested. They were not emotionally demonstrative people, but when a man was taken with a woman, it was obvious. Muffin was an expert in nonverbal cues. He saw interest and feeling in Ché only when he was with Ilana.

Heaven knows, it had to be why he allowed Ilana to film him. Muffin knew she'd made documentaries in her line of work. But now she seemed taken with an impromptu project—filming a *Vash* prince adjusting to life on Earth—with the real theme being one that neither of them appeared to see: polar opposites falling in love. (All this while Ian Hamilton stayed in the background, rubbing his hands in glee.) Muffin hadn't yet decided if Ilana intended to market the completed effort as a comedy or tragic adventure.

He reached for what the menu called a "bottomless" cup of coffee, the Earth drink he'd come to most enjoy, and emptied the mug in two big gulps. Bottomless—bah! He didn't like it when anything ran out early, whether it be food or women.

He left the mug at the table's edge for the pink-haired woman to refill. Thick arms folded on the table, he peered through his custom-made sunshaders and watched pilots ready their craft for takeoff. During his first few visits, Ché had spent hours inside a small concrete building. A classroom. In the afternoons, he would fly with an instructor. Early this week, he'd taken the plane up alone, and had continued to do so all the days since.

Muffin had massacred an entire hedgerow with the hand trimmer while waiting for Ché to land that first day. Ché had previous flying experience, yes, but he was a prince, a valuable asset for his family, and to the Federation. No one could afford for him to throw away his life flying such flimsy little Earth craft.

"They're safe," Ian had assured him. "Ché is methodical and cautious. He knows what he's doing."

Maybe so. But Muffin wished the princes and princesses he knew would take better care of themselves. Ian included, he thought, and shoveled a heaping forkful of omelet into his mouth.

The hair on the back of his neck prickled. He lifted his attention from his plate and scanned the bustling restaurant. A woman watched him from a stool by the booth where many of the airport's employees took their meals. Her brown jumpsuit told him that she worked in aircraft maintenance. Muffin's own was green. Her curves filled the outfit. She was a lushly built woman, sturdy, with arms and legs that looked like they could actually do some labor. He appreciated a good-sized woman. Unfortunately, most of the women he met looked as if they would blow away in the first good breeze. This one's hair was just as lush as the rest of her. It streamed past her shoulders in flaming copper to reach the middle of her back. That was when his eyes finally made it to her round, open face.

The woman jerked away her gaze. Standing quickly, she paid for her breakfast. Frowning over her shoulder, she gave him one last glance before she pushed open the swinging door and left.

Through the large window, Muffin watched her go. She donned a helmet that said "Trouble," boarded a vehicle that looked like a tiny motorcycle, and sped off toward the hangars. Earthwomen came in many different varieties, but he hadn't seen anyone like her before. Maybe she'd come again and he could scare her off a second time, he thought, wiping his mouth with a paper napkin.

It was 8:20. Time to go to work. He left a tip in Earth currency, and then swiped the currency card on the reader on his way out, paying for the meals.

Running his hand through his newly shorn blond hair—Ian had said his shaggy locks would have kept him from being hired—Muffin lumbered off toward the airport. The tarmac gave off a biting petroleum-based odor, which reminded him of the frontier. This *was* the frontier, he reminded himself, even though Earth never thought of itself on the edge of civilization, but at the center of it.

He slung his IDs-on-a-string over his head and swiped it on the scanner. A gate opened, allowing him inside. Cameras watched him until he'd walked out of sight on an access road that ran straight to the gardening shed.

He showed a scanner in the shed a second ID card, logging him in and unlocking a storage room of supplies. As high-tech as some worlds could be, one thing stayed relatively the same: taking care of plants. There was only so much automation one could apply to their care. The rest required a man's touch.

He filled a cart with shears, pruners, fertilizer, weed killer, rake, and shovel and wheeled the tools of his supposed trade outside to await Ché's arrival. Absently repairing the hedge he'd all but ruined the week before, he waited. But when the prince finally arrived, late for the first time, it was with Ilana at his side.

Hell and back! Why was *she* here? Muffin tossed the shears into the cart and pulled his surveillance palmtop computer from his front pocket. It magnified sight and sound.

With one thick finger, Muffin worked a wireless speaker into his ear canal. That would magnify the sound of their voices as long as he aimed the computer in the right direction.

The hedgerow kept him hidden from the flight line. Hangars behind him cast him in shadows, soon to be gone when the sun rose higher. Holding the palmtop close, he watched the couple walk past rows of chocked and tied aircraft, while taking care to hide his face. Both had seen him before—Ché months ago on the rooftop in Los Angeles, and Ilana at her mother's wedding to Rom B'kah, and again on the rooftop. Aside from Muffin's shorn hair, he looked no different from before. Unlike the royal *Vash Nadah*, his physical characteristics didn't stand out as much on Earth. With his light brown eyes and white-blond hair, he blended right in.

To his disbelief, so did Prince Ché, more and more these past weeks. Today the man wore mirrored sun shaders, a T-shirt, and jeans—typical Earth attire. Muffin liked imagining what the conservative Vedlas would think of such an outfit on their prized heir. Ilana had exchanged her usual dress for a tight black shirt that barely covered her midriff and jeans. She'd covered her hair, bound at the back of her head, with a black cap that bore her company's logo—a fairy-like creature holding a camera. Of course, she wore her ever-present Canon slung over one shoulder.

Was she here to fly? Blast it all—he hoped not. Ian had assigned him this mission with minimum instructions: "*Tell me if they spend time together, and how much.*" But in Muffin's mind, his job was to protect Ilana from Ché, and he didn't like the idea of the Vedla prince forcing her up into one of those flimsy flying contraptions. Should he break cover to save her?

Not without earning the wrath of the crown prince. It was a dilemma indeed.

Ilana and Ché stopped at a blue-and-white two-seat airplane. The plug in Muffin's right ear brought the sounds of their voices to him: "We're just going to sit in it today," Ilana confirmed. She sounded nervous, unhappy.

"Yes. You on the left side, me on the right."

"Cool," she said. "The position of power."

"No. I will be on the copilot side."

"I meant me."

Ilana gave Ché a cheeky smile and walked over to the door on the left side of the plane. "I can't believe I'm doing this." She put her foot on the step-up and reiterated. "We're not going anywhere, right? We're not flying?"

Ché groaned. "Ilana, I will not trick you. If you take this plane into the sky, it will be by your own hand, and by your own decision. Did you not say the same to me on the teacup ride in Disneyland?"

"That's different. You weren't scared. You were embarrassed."

"And for good reason."

Muffin heard Ilana giggle. Then there were clanking and shuffling noises as the pair climbed into the craft.

Muffin inched forward, as close to the tarmac as he dared without being in full sight of the plane. But a man his size was hard to hide.

Ilana's voice sounded muffled. "Well. This is . . . okay."

"Then let go of the yoke," Ché told her.

There was some rustling. Then a nervous laugh. "Ouch."

Muffin's neck prickled. He looked over his shoulder, but no one was there. To be safe, he slid the computer into his pocket. In his earpiece, Ché continued to describe the instrumentation and the design of the plane. But when he got to the altitudes and air speeds, Ilana stopped him. "Stop! I'm breaking into a cold sweat. I don't mind the tech stuff—just don't tell me how far I'll fall before I hit the ground."

"You will not fall, Ilana."

"I know that. But the brain doesn't."

There was more conversation. And laughter. Muffin noticed the easy banter between them. There was tension, too, but not the unpleasant kind. It was the anticipation of two people who were attracted to each other but who were not yet sleeping together. He'd add that to his report when he next contacted Ian.

Again Muffin sensed something. The prickling on the back of his neck came with a rush of sweet-scented wind. Before he could turn around, a foot hooked his ankle and threw him off balance. An arm came over his chest and finished the job.

Muffin landed hard on his back. It knocked the air from his lungs. He lay there like a landed fish, eyes watering and gulping for air.

"Don't move!" a woman's voice ordered. "Show me your ID."

Hell and back! A female. He couldn't believe it. In all his missions, no one had ever made such easy work of him. The bright flashes of light in his eyes faded. Blinking, he stayed where he was, taking a moment to ascertain his foe.

A shadow moved over him. His eyes traveled up a pair of sturdy, brown-clad legs. The copper hair he recognized at once.

She appeared as startled as he was.

"Trouble," he muttered. She lived up to her name.

He started to sit up. "Wait!" she yelled. "I need to see your ID first."

"Must I lie down to do that?"

Her eyes narrowed, and he saw that they were green—angry green. "You're not a gardener."

"I am so."

She made a derisive sound that rivaled any of Ilana's. "Tell me another story."

"I can tell *you*, Miss Trouble, that you do not have a weapon, and that you are not a member of this airport security. You give me no reason to believe you are anything but a maintenance worker here."

"You were aiming something at that Cessna. We're taught to challenge any suspicious characters."

"Challenge means"—Great Mother, he couldn't say it; it was blasted embarrassing—"knocking a man to the ground?"

She appeared so chagrined, he couldn't resist adding, "Interfering with a gardener—it is a capital offense."

She recovered. "It is not! But a terrorist act toward a civilian aircraft will get you life in prison."

"I am not a terrorist. Look at my ID. My name is there." His assumed name.

"Take it off your neck and throw it to me." Her work boots crunched past his ear as he lay there, waiting for her to make a mistake and come too close. His hand shot out and snatched her ankle. Before she could utter any sound at all, he had her pinned beneath him on the ground. He caught the back of her head in his open palm to cushion her from the pebbly cement. Then he smiled. "Gotcha."

He'd been dying to use that particular bit of Earth slang he'd learned from Ian.

She squirmed beneath him, trying to get her knee into his groin and her hands free. She didn't have a chance. That he'd overpowered her so easily made it even more humiliating to admit she'd knocked him flat on his back. That, he decided, was not going in the crown prince's report.

He kept one of her hands pressed to the ground above her head, the other pinned between their bodies. Her breasts strained against the bodice of her jumpsuit, and her body beneath him was equally ample and soft. It was nice to have a bit of flesh to lie on rather than what, in his opinion, amounted to a bag of bones. Why thin women were attractive to so many men, he'd never know.

"Let me up," she said.

"Aha. You see? It is no fun lying on the ground."

"Okay! I get the point, big guy." She wriggled. Arousal flared, he felt himself harden. He was not a small man. She'd feel him swell. But he wouldn't intentionally force himself on a woman or intimidate one sexually. His size was usually daunting enough. He released her and pushed away before, he hoped, she realized why.

She sat up and pushed dirt off her jumpsuit. Her skin was pale, dotted with faint coppery freckles. She had a heart-shaped face with the slightest of double chins and lips that tempted a man for a kiss. "You are true to your name," he told her. "Trouble."

Her mouth twisted. "Yeah. I can't seem to escape it lately. I just got this job washing planes. I need the money." She glanced sideways. "You're not going to turn me in, are you?"

"Not when you thought you were defending the airport." That's what he liked—a woman who stood up for what was right.

"Let me see your pass, anyway. I gotta be sure who you are before I let you go."

Let him go? He smiled to himself and showed her his airport pass. He didn't want to cause "Trouble" any trouble, lest she complain to the authorities. He was certain his background could withstand a cursory check, but why invite the risk?

She studied his airport pass. "John Black."

It was strange hearing his assumed name on the woman's lips. Then she stuck out her hand, and he took it. "Copper Kaminski." She took her hand back and waved it over her head. "The hair," she explained in a way that told Muffin she'd been doing it all her life. He'd been explaining "Muffin" to the Earth-dwellers for far less than that, but it still tired.

" 'Bright as a newly minted penny on the day I was born,' my mother said. I don't see why she just didn't name me Penny."

"I like Copper."

She lifted her eyes. "Really?"

Nodding, he smiled. This one was easy to please. And all he was doing was telling the truth.

"Taxi? Ché, I'd love it. Can we?" Ilana's voice.

Muffin jumped to his feet. Whipping the computer out of his pocket, he aimed it at the plane and listened to the princess's voice coming out of his earpiece. Ché spoke next: *"I have a flight plan on file. I need to add your name to it before we move."*

They were going to move the aircraft? With Ilana in it?

Ché hopped down from the craft and strode into the operations building where pilots checked the weather, maps, and completed their flight preparations.

Copper peeked past his arm. "What is that thing for?"

"Solitaire." It was not so much of a lie. He'd become addicted to the Earth game during his long hours alone in his room.

"That's not true. You're using it to listen to that plane."

"Yes, it's a voice amplifier." No use lying about everything. The more you did, the deeper you got, and he was in too deep as it was.

"Is that legal?"

Muffin heaved a great sigh. "As much as I like to look at you, Copper, I wish you would go away."

Her eyes opened wide. If it were possible to appear wounded and flattered at the same time, she'd managed it.

"I have work to do," he explained, weakening somewhat.

"So, you are a spy."

"I'm not a spy."

"Hmm. I guess if you were, you wouldn't have gone down so easily. I never knocked anyone down in my life!"

Muffin winced. If she didn't have such a sweet, innocent face, he'd . . . he'd . . . "I'm the gardener."

"Sure you are." She looked him up and down. "If Dolph Lundgren and Arnold Schwarzenegger had a lovechild, it'd be you."

Muffin shook his head. "I do not know this couple."

214

She gave him a disbelieving look. "The actors. You know. Those old action movies. And, by the way, you have a weird accent. German?"

"Ah . . ."

"And you hardly ever do any real work, except for trying to fix the mess you made of these hedges."

Muffin squared his shoulders. "I have done more than that," he insisted. "I have weeded all the beds." He might only be posing as a groundskeeper, but he tried to do a good job. He came from a family with a good work ethic.

"You're after them, aren't you? That couple. You're one of those reporters who's always bothering celebrities. Paparazzi. There have been a lot of them sneaking around here lately. We've seen them from the wash shed. Photographers, too."

Ché returned to the airplane. *"We will need to make an exterior inspection. Then I'll get us cleared to taxi."* Muffin's hand shot to his ear, cupping it. He stared at the ground, concentrating.

"That's him. He's famous, right?"

Muffin shrugged. "Hollywood."

"I figured. We always ask whenever someone brings us a plane to wash, but no one seems to know, or want to say, but everyone's watching. And you're one of the snoops."

She made no secret of the fact she didn't approve. Muffin almost confessed that he didn't do this for a living, that he used to be proud of his role as bodyguard to the ruler of the galaxy, but here we was, reduced to snooping as she put it.

Now Ché and Ilana both appeared outside the airplane. Muffin went flat against the wall and inched closer to get a better view without going too far past the hedgerow, which was no where near as ragged looking as Copper seemed to think. Shaggy, but not ragged. He'd had haircuts worse than that.

He watched as Ché took Ilana on a walk-around check of the outside of the airplane. Periodically, they'd crouch close together while Ché explained how a piece of equipment worked.

Copper peeked around Muffin's arm. Her breasts brushed his elbow. He tried not to look. All women were petite to him—but if this one were in his arms, at least he'd have something to hold on to.

In no time at all, it seemed, Ché and Ilana had climbed back inside the aircraft. *"Cessna one-four-five-alpha-kilo request taxi."*

A female voice answered over the craft's radio speakers. *"Five-alpha-kilo, cleared to taxi. Hold short runway two-five."*

A drumming roar burst into Muffin's ear as the craft's propeller began to turn, drowning out any further conversation. Muffin yanked out the earpiece. It would be impossible now to hear the voices. The engine was too loud, and soon they'd be too far away.

Muffin watched helplessly as the little airplane taxied away. He could barely see it now. Sunshine reflected off the white paint, and it suddenly looked very small. He couldn't listen and couldn't see. Glumly, he trudged back to his cart and grabbed a pair of pruning shears.

"Wait, John! Don't take it out on the hedge. The people in the Cessna, they'll be okay. I know. I washed their plane this morning."

Muffin jerked his gaze around to Copper. She looked even prettier with the concern for him that she wore on her face. She wasn't a space-hand or a jaded frontierswoman. She reminded him of the women of his homeworld, the homeworld he hadn't wanted to return to because he didn't want to live there alone while drowning in his family's good intentions.

"Washing gives me a close-up look at the airplanes," she explained. "If I think the maintenance isn't being kept up, or if anything's loose or too dirty, I yell at the owner." She swallowed. "I lost my parents and my brother in a crash that shouldn't have happened. I figure it's the least I can do."

A shadow passed over Muffin's mind. It had been a long time since he thought of the war, but Copper's words spurred a memory of that time. "I flew in combat," he said, almost without realizing it. He did have the good sense not to say more, that his last mission was part of the raid to free Queen Jasmine. That they were running to their starfighters on foot when the young pilot he was paired with took a shot in the abdomen. Muffin had got the lad off Brevdah Three, but he'd bled to death during their escape. "I haven't had the heart to pilot a craft since."

Copper waited for him to say more, but that was all there was to tell. "I am not a man of many words," he apologized, opening and closing his fists.

Her gentle smile told him she'd already figured that out. "Do you want to get a Pepsi or something? There's a machine over by the wash shed."

Nodding, Muffin put the shears back in the wheelbarrow.

"I don't think you should be snooping, anyway," she scolded. "No matter how good it pays." Her expression pleaded with him. "If it's not right."

Suddenly he was less motivated to follow Ché and Ilana as carefully as he'd been doing. What was the point? Their relationship was going exactly as Ian wanted. Perhaps Muffin should step back a bit, notifying Ian only if things changed for the worse. Maybe he'd been following the couple so closely because he'd had nothing else to do. But now there was Copper. She might be a better way to fill his time.

He answered her with a broad smile. "Show me the Pepsi. I will buy it for you."

She gave her head a shake as they walked. "Nah. I'm buying this time. It's the least I can do for you after throwing you down on the ground."

Muffin cringed. "And she's such a little thing, too," he muttered.

Copper's mouth fell open. "What did you call me?"

Had he said something to hurt her? Blast the language barrier. He was not swift of tongue in his own language, let alone in a difficult and confusing one like this English. "Little?"

"Bless you. I'm five-eight, and two hundred pounds. No one has ever called me 'little.' Forgive me if I swoon."

As far as Muffin was concerned, she could faint away right into his arms and he wouldn't complain. But she looked too steady on her feet for that. "Where I am from the people are big. Trust me, Copper, you are not." He brought his fist to his chest. It made a solid thump. "We grow large and hardy in the cold crisp air, the bright sunshine, and our bountiful food supply, all of it homegrown and hunted locally."

Copper said, "You can tell me more over a soda."

"If you buy me the beverage, it is only right that I buy you dinner."

Her green eyes swerved his way. "Dinner?" Her cheeks turned pink. "You mean . . . like a date?"

"I think so." He hoped he'd gotten the translation right.

"Okay." She looked happy and stunned. Muffin was delighted he had made her that way, because it was exactly the way he felt. All the more reason to take a little more free time.

But at one p.m., he'd intended to follow Ché and Ilana to their next destination, wherever that might be. But was it necessary? Would Ian have asked it of him? Muffin doubted it. Clearly, Ilana and Ché could get into no worse trouble than taxiing, and there was nothing he could do about that now that they'd taken to wheeling around the tarmac.

No, this afternoon Muffin was free. Work, work, work made him an unhappy boy, Muffin thought, grinning at Copper. "We have arranged for Pepsi, and for dinner. Would you like to share lunch with me?"

"Share? Mmm. No. But I'll eat with you if I can have my own plate."

Muffin laughed, a deep and rich sound, even to his own ears. But ever the dutiful guard, he couldn't enter the wash shed, a metal-sided hangar that smelled like soap, without turning to look toward the runways one more time.

Copper snatched his sleeve and tugged. "They'll be fine."

Sighing, he turned back to her. On a normal day, he'd not have taken his attention away from a woman like Copper for a single moment, but the prickling in his neck wouldn't go away. He knew it had to do with the flying.

Chapter Fifteen

Forty-eight, forty-nine . . .

Klark Vedla hung upside-down from an exercise bar. His arms were crossed over his chest, and his feet were held snug by ankle restraints. With each silent count, he lifted his upper body from the vertical.

Fifty, fifty-one, fifty-two . . .

Sweat dripped onto the mat below his head. An occasional drop entered his eyes and burned. He kept his eyes open, however. Guards watched him around the clock, but one must never become complacent or trust fully the so-called unbreakable security of the palace. His ancestors had made that mistake, and they were slaughtered, nearly all.

That's why it was different for the Vedlas than for the other families. The Vedlas had survived near-extinction. Passed down from generation to generation through the millennia was the need to be vigilant, to always question, to always keep their clout intact, so that no one would ever become powerful enough to harm them again.

There was no question in Klark's mind that Vedla blood was superior to all the rest. It was his goal in life to keep it that way. Because of his purist views, in some circles he was considered a hero. In others, he was a nuisance and even a danger. "It is best to be one or the other," his father told him. "But not both. The disparity will get you killed, Klark," he had warned.

But some things were worth dying for. All true Vedlas felt the same.

Fifty-seven, fifty-eight . . .

His stomach muscles burned. Gritting his teeth, he grunted with each lift of his upper torso. He was stronger than he'd been a standard month ago, and expected to become stronger still. If there was one good thing he could say about incarceration, it was that he'd never been in better shape. Daily now, he put his body through what he would have considered sheer torture in the old days.

Fifty-nine, sixty, sixty-one . . .

Old days? Not even a standard year had passed between now and then, the days of freedom, of decadent pastimes, of women and other sports, and of the glorious game of politics that ultimately saw him imprisoned in his own home.

It was merely a setback.

Seventy-three, seventy-four . . .

There were those who considered him finished— in politics and as a man. Bah! They were sadly mistaken. Klark Vedla, second son of the Vedla king, would rise again. And when he did, glory would be his. He would prove to all that the Vedla name stood above the other seven, by ensuring that Ché Vedla, his beloved brother, won his final victory over the humiliation foisted upon him. When it came time, far in the future, to sing out the names of the heroes, Ché's would be among them.

Eighty-two, eighty-three . . .

Klark kept his eyes focused on the door to his exercise chamber. He took in the burn, the pain, used it to forge his strength, so that it would be there for Ché. Sweat ran in rivulets down his bare chest, over his crossed forearms. It dribbled along his neck and jaw, sprayed by the breaths hissing in and out between his gritted teeth. It was worth it, worth the price.

"One hundred," he gasped out, letting his shoulders fall. He hung upside-down for a moment, arms dangling limply, blood roaring in his head.

Then he saw the guard standing by the entrance to the chamber come suddenly to life. Klark froze, ready to swing upward and release his ankles.

"Good morning," a cheery voice rang out.

It was Hoe, Ché's eternally effervescent and efficient advisor. With a businesslike bounce in his step, the man strode toward him, walking bent over sideways as if that were the only way to communicate with a man hanging by his feet. In his hand was his ever-present computer, and he was waving it. For the first time, Klark saw that Hoe was upset. The man's cheeks were ruddy, and there were shadows under his sharp eyes.

"What is it?" Klark inquired.

Hoe tipped further to the side. "It is terribly important, my lord." He cast a glance over his shoulder at the door guard, somehow without throwing out his neck in the process. "And confidential."

"You heard him," Klark yelled to the guard. "Leave."

Klark knew the guard would not go; they never did.

They merely moved their post to outside the room. "Is it Ché? Is my brother in danger?"

Hoe hesitated just long enough to worry Klark. "He is uninjured, my lord. There is a problem, however. One that could be construed as danger." He was still standing sideways. "Will you be coming down, sir?"

"Oh, I suppose I must." Lifting up, Klark opened the ankle cuffs, holding on to them as the device lowered him gently to the mat below. "I couldn't bear it if you injured your back," he added.

Hoe gave a half-smile as he poured Klark a refreshing drink. The man never seemed completely comfortable around him. It was as if he were afraid of him. Well, Klark supposed he'd earned it. No one could say he didn't deserve his reputation.

He donned a robe, tying the belt around his waist, before taking the glass of icy ion and botanical infused fluid Hoe offered. Without having to be told, the advisor trailed him outside to his balcony. The scent of fresh-cut greens wafted in the breeze; at this early hour, the army of palace gardeners was already busy. The vast ocean sparkled in the sunshine.

An illusion, that freedom, Klark thought, scrutinizing the fair-weather sky. As if the locator surgically implanted in his neck weren't enough, palace security had erected a force shield all around his balcony. One could break through it without injury, but the breach would alert Security within an instant, simultaneously putting out a warning on computers all through the palace. Why bother, Klark reasoned, when there were more efficient ways of escape? He'd figured out nearly all of them by now, and remained within his quarters only to please Ché. He owed his brother that, at least.

Klark sat down at a table of polished tree sap made stone-hard after millennia spent deep underground—

on a planet that no longer existed, reduced to mere molecules after its parent star went supernova five thousand years earlier. When Klark felt like brooding, he'd get drunk on Heart of Taj ale and stare at the bizarre creatures frozen forever within the depths of the amber, until he'd convinced himself of the insignificance of his suffering within the grand scheme of existence.

At times, it even worked.

But there was no need for that on this fine day. "Sit, Hoe," he said magnanimously. "Join me and tell me what you have learned."

Hoe dispatched a servant for a carafe of tock and another pitcher of the beverage Klark drank after exercise. They sat in silence, Hoe awkward and Klark amused, until the servant arranged the beverages on the table and left once more.

Hoe began without preamble. "I have failed, failed in my monitoring of the prince's activities. The images are weeks old. The articles, as well. It will not happen again. I have found the reason for the lag and repaired it." Sighing, he offered Klark his computer. "These were taken from a series of what the Earth-dwellers call newspapers. I've translated them for you. But the images need no translation."

Warily Klark took the computer from Hoe. " 'Earth-bound Cinderella looks for prince?' " he murmured, glancing up. " '*Cinderella*?' "

"An Earth fable of some sort. Involving a cleaning woman as the central character, and a prince as her mate."

"Ah." Klark frowned and read on. *Princess Ilana Hamilton was photographed in the arms of an unidentified man only hours later* . . . He lowered the computer. "Unidentified man, my eye. That's Ché."

Hoe nodded gravely. "I, too, am sure of it."

224

Klark's attention dipped to the screen. He studied the dark, blurry image of Ilana Hamilton with a tall, shadowy form he knew with all certainty was his brother. Then he skipped forward to another article. This one had photos of Ilana only: Ilana at work; Ilana at play; Ilana thrusting out her tongue at whoever had taken the pictures. But other than the first image, no Ilana holding on to Ché. "Great Mother."

"So you saw it," Hoe moaned.

"To be frank, I wish I hadn't." His brother sat in what looked like a giant cup of tock. Klark winced. "Look at him—his knees are nearly touching his ears!"

"It is an amusement ride, apparently. One made for very small children, it would seem. Only he is not riding with a child."

Klark slid the computer across the table. Hoe caught it, clutching it in fidgeting hands. "No, indeed. Ilana Hamilton is very much a woman." In many of the photos, Ilana had held a camera to her eye. The camera was large, resembling the contraption she utilized at work, if it wasn't the same one altogether. She created entertainment for Earth-dwellers. Was she documenting Ché's visit for that purpose? Was he actually agreeable to such a bizarre circumstance? Ché was normally a very private man. Yet here, viewed at the other end of a primitive image-making device, he appeared quite cheerful. "My brother has changed," Klark murmured.

Hoe looked miserable. "I knew this would happen. I knew there would be trouble if he came within a light-year of that girl. If he had taken Princess Ilana to bed, and only that, it would be merely another scandal—a manageable one, at that. But he appears to be with her almost constantly."

"How did you discover this? Do you have a spy in place?"

"I would have sent spies, but the prince made me swear not to. Had he not made me give my word . . ." Hoe sighed. "But I have been watching all available Earth media forms since the day the prince arrived." His face darkened. "I would have caught this sooner, but with some of the more primitive periodicals, there is a lag between dissemination in print and availability in the transmittable format our comm equipment can receive."

Klark studied the images again. Ché and the Earth princess certainly looked cozy—Klark knew his brother well enough to tell. He'd never seen Ché behave in such a way with any female, in court or with any he had picked from the ranks of the courtesans. It was not unusual for a young royal to develop misplaced feelings for a pleasure server, and when it occurred, the family always intervened. But Ché, had always been stronger than that. He did what was best for the family, unfailingly, even to the detriment of his happiness, as it was with the sudden wedding plans foisted upon him.

"My brother is a model Vedla," Klark said thoughtfully. "Never has he given the family any cause for concern. But I wonder . . . in the midst of his holiday, his personal pleasure, if he is of a mind to think of his future, to see the tremendous consequence that a union with the Earth princess would bring to our family."

"He is not 'of a mind!' Look at his face. He is in love with her!"

"Of course he is. There can be no other explanation for his presence in that . . . cup." Klark shook his head. He would never have allowed himself to become that witless with any female, and he would

226

have thought Ché would be immune to such foolishness, as well. Alas, these images proved he was not. Ché might be a Vedla, but in the most basic of ways he was only a man.

That meant it was up to Klark to save the Vedlas from certain humiliation, if Ché's love-boggled mind blocked his common sense.

Klark spread his hands on the table and leaned forward. "Bring him home to us, Hoe. Immediately."

"But the prince gave orders not to summon him until a wife is chosen."

"Then choose one." *Buffoon.*

"I can try to speed it along."

"Do. Tell Toren, as I cannot communicate with him."

Hoe frowned in thought. "Toren and his people have narrowed the field down to two."

"Good, good."

"One is a princess, seemingly agreeable, but her intended has balked. The other is the daughter of a high-ranking noble, but very young. Thirteen, fourteen, I cannot recall. But Toren assures me they will decide very soon, my lord."

Excitement surged through Klark, as it had done a heartbeat before his sens-sword contacted Ché's the day their Bajha match had ended in a draw. That game was an omen of sorts. For the conclusion to the game he played now would prove equally startling to his brother. "I need Ché home. *Now.*"

"Excuse my impertinence, sir, but you saw the way he is with the Earthwoman. He may protest."

"He agreed to return when it was time. He will not do otherwise. He is a Vedla. Now go. Do as I ask of you, if you care at all about Prince Ché and the status of our family." Klark pushed to his feet and left the advisor alone at the table, staring after him. "I don't care how you bring Ché home, only that you do."

Chapter Sixteen

Ilana shouted over the noise of the engine. Her face reflected excitement, to Ché's delight, and not fear. But then, they were only on the ground. "This is a blast. Can I try driving—I mean taxiing?"

She put her feet on the rudder pedals without him having to show her. Wisely, she did nothing else as Ché steered. They traveled straight along the taxiway, needing only slight corrections. "Ready to taxi solo?" he asked.

Her sunglasses hid her eyes, and the headset with its wraparound microphone hid her mouth. "Ready."

He pulled back his feet, and she was steering the craft. She whooped again. He laughed. "You were born to fly, Ilana."

"Hey, that doesn't mean I want to. But this is fun!"

"Like driving a ground car, yes?"

"If it wasn't so damn noisy."

The plane was indeed primitive. The air-conditioning barely compensated for the direct sum-

228

mer heat. The noise from the engine roared through the cockpit, and the vents brought in the scent of fuel and heated electrics. Ché was aware of the smells only because they were absent in the modern craft that he flew. Or perhaps "sanitized" was a better word. This was flying the way it once had been, millennia ago. Back to the basics. Noise and sensation. But Ché flew with one goal: to bring Ilana into the sky, to hand her the control she needed to blunt her fear if not conquer it outright.

And yet each time he took the Cessna into the sky, each time he left the ground behind, he felt like one of the birds that soared above the shore on Eireya. The sea-raptor, the symbol of his family. Sleek and strong and deadly—like a Vedla.

"There," Ché told her. "Intersection Quebec. Make a right turn." He felt Ilana's right foot depress the rudder pedal as she completed the turn. "We will stop there, at that line." A painted yellow line separated the taxiway from the active runway.

Ilana brought the airplane to a jerky stop. She laughed, and he smiled at her delight. Her black top had ridden up. A slice of soft golden skin showed above her jeans. That place on her stomach would be the perfect spot to kiss, he thought, forcing his gaze back outside. "I'll ask tower to clear us to taxi down the runway. We can go a little faster."

"Okay." She seemed game. When it came to the rides at Disneyland, she was a daredevil. It made it even more confusing as to why she was so opposed to flying.

"Tower, Cessna Five-alpha-kilo. Request a high-speed taxi down runway two-two."

"Five-alpha-kilo, cleared for high-speed taxi down two-two."

"Hold on with me, Ilana. Lightly. Not too hard," Ché instructed.

She grabbed hold of the steering yoke with both hands.

"As we gain speed, she'll want to fly, so you'll have to hold down pressure to keep her on the runway."

Ilana swallowed. "And me, too."

He put her hand on the throttle and let her follow his forward movement as he pushed the knob in. The engine noise increased. The propeller spun faster. The tension in the cockpit fairly crackled as they gained speed.

The little plane danced lightly on its wheels. "She wants to fly," Ilana called out.

"Hold her down. Pull back on the throttle, too. We're going a little too fast."

Ilana did neither. "What would it take to fly?"

To fly? "*Now?*" He peered straight ahead. The airplane was loaded so lightly that there was more than sufficient runway left to allow takeoff.

"Yes. Now. I . . . I want to do it. I want to do it before I chicken out. Before I have to think about it."

Swiftly, not wanting to lose the chance, Ché grabbed the radio. "Tower, Cessna Five-alpha-kilo request takeoff."

"Five-alpha-kilo, cleared for takeoff."

He grabbed Ilana's moist hand and together they pushed the throttle full in. He used the rudders to steer. She held on to the yoke. "As we lift off," he said, "I'm using the yoke to keep level, steering, almost like a car."

The noise drowned out all extraneous noise except their shouts. But not Ilana's resounding shriek as the wheels lifted away from the paved surface.

Then they took to the air. "Oh, my God, Ché. Oh, my God."

His heart sank. Holding the yoke, he glanced over at her. She was rigid as a board. Her chest rose and fell rapidly. "Easy, Ilana. I'll get us down on the ground right away. You are doing great. Just great. There is no need to worry. I can fly. We are safe."

"Oh, my God," she whispered.

"Hang in there," he urged, using more of his newly acquired Earth slang.

She said something. He didn't hear what. "Louder, Ilana. I can't hear you."

"Can I hold the yoke with you?"

Stunned, he looked sideways. "You want to continue?"

When she turned, he saw the joy lighting up her face. He felt the answering surge of pleasure in his heart. "This is no worse than any roller coaster, Ché. Noisier, but a whole lot less rocky."

"Fly, then."

"Fly?" He could see her gulp.

His grin broadened. "Take hold of the yoke. Lightly."

He still wasn't sure of her reaction. If she were to panic on the controls, he'd have to hope for the strength to break her free.

But her hands closed around the yoke in a normal grip, if a little tighter than most. Ché received clearance from approach control to fly along the coast. Keeping a watch on the enormous passenger transports not that far below them, lumbering on and off the runways at Los Angeles Interstellar Airport, he urged the little craft higher.

LAX-I had a boggling amount of traffic crawling on its surface, but only one starcraft that he could see. It must have earned its name from occasional space transport that landed there. Despite the free exchange of technology with the rest of the Trade

Federation, it would be a number of years before Earth became a true spacefaring society.

Yet the Earth-dwellers still had the singular pleasure of flying the primitive Cessna, Ché thought. Here, one could still fly in the manner of the earliest aviation pioneers.

Ilana sat to his left, her mouth pulled back in a smile. Her breaths had slowed, but he could still see the pulse throbbing in her throat. The buzz of the engine filled the small cockpit. Radio chatter was almost continuous. But the sky was brilliant blue, as was the sea below. The closest clouds lay far to the west like a folded-back quilt.

"Ilana, what do you think?" He was almost afraid to ask the question lest he break the spell.

She turned to him, her face shining. "It's everything I didn't think it would be."

Together they laughed.

"It's like breaking a barrier. It's like when I thought I couldn't run a marathon and then I did. The barrier itself can psyche you out, but once you're through, once you get past it, you kind of wonder what you found so intimidating."

Her words struck home. He thought of his feelings for Ilana, how badly he wanted her in his life, and how he hadn't dared try to break past the barriers his family had placed in front of him and his personal happiness. But now that he did see a way around that barrier, the thought of crossing it seemed exactly as Ilana had put it. He wondered what in blazes he'd found so intimidating about going against the tide of tradition.

To his shock and Ilana's, he let out a whoop. Grinning broadly, she kept her hands on the yoke, riding his movements as he banked to the right and leveled off at two thousand feet above sea level, just off shore.

The noise lessened with the engine running at a lower speed. "She's yours if you want her."

Her smile wobbled. "Sure." Her hands clamped around the yoke.

"Lighter. So you do not fly rough. Like the tango," he teased.

Her laughter silenced suddenly when he pulled his hands from the yoke and placed them on his thighs, fingers spread in the ready position. Ilana was flying the plane now. And doing a marvelous job of it.

He was ready to take over if necessary. Somehow he didn't think it would come to that.

"I'm flying. I'm really flying." She was nearly whispering again. "Wahoo," she added in a soft little cheer.

"Shout it out, woman! It is possible to yell and fly at the same time. Ask my former instructor." Ché took a breath. "Come on. Let's hear it. A celebratory exclamation worthy of this milestone."

"*Wahoo!*" they shouted together.

Then Ilana quieted. "Ché?"

"Yes."

"Take the plane for a minute."

Worriedly he did as she asked. Ilana reached into her jeans pocket and removed a tissue. Sniffing, she lifted her sunglasses and dabbed at her eyes. "Sorry," she croaked. "Emotional moment here."

His chest filled to bursting. He'd never experienced such feelings before for another, never knew it was possible to feel what he did to this degree.

Slowly, reverentially, he placed his free hand on Ilana's thigh. Her hand settled on his and squeezed. "Thanks for doing what no one else ever bothered to try, Ché. Maybe no one expected that I could. I don't know if . . . if I can transfer this feeling to a larger plane, or a spaceship—"

"You can," he said with confidence.

She smiled softly. "But I did this."

"Yes, you did."

"I did it!" she said, louder.

"*Waa-hoo!*" they whooped together.

Then, hesitantly at first and then with more purpose, Ilana leaned across the seat and pressed a kiss on his lips. He began to follow her as she pulled back, and then remembered where he was: in a light plane with Ilana high over Earth's Pacific Ocean. And without a doubt, the closest to heaven he'd ever been.

When Hoe next appeared in Klark's chambers later that day, he brought with him an official missive. He handed the computer to Klark. "A wife has been chosen."

Klark rose from a nest of luxurious pillows, where he'd been doing his nightly reading from the Treatise of Trade. He cinched the belt on his evening robe and took the computer Hoe offered. "Music off," he told the chamber's computer. The Bonali orchestration ceased. The room was silent save for the beating of his heart in his ears. "Toren has chosen?"

"And your father gave his approval."

"Excellent. So you will be calling our wayward prince home?"

"Yes. Right away."

"Good. It appears destiny is on our side."

Hoe swallowed nervously. "With a few minor complications."

Klark watched him carefully, wondering if the man would come through when it came time to ask it of him. But he would worry about that when the time came.

He opened the missive. "Ah. It will be the Lesok princess, after all." He lowered the computer. "Is

Prince Haj the complication? Is he raising a fuss?"

"More than a fuss. He is on his way to the Wheel. He plans to make a formal protest there to the Great Council."

"And the princess?"

"She seems quite delighted with the prospect of Prince Ché. A biddable sort of woman, she is."

Klark returned the computer. "Speed it along, Hoe."

"My lord?"

"Get Ché back here. Without delay!"

Hoe took a step backward and bowed. Fist pressed over his chest, he turned on his heel and left.

As soon as Hoe left his chambers, Klark began to pace. So . . . Ché was smitten with the crown prince's sister, was he? Well, his older brother would soon be home. And if Klark couldn't convince him to make the choice that was best for the Vedlas, then he would have to make it for him.

Destiny called to him; purpose sang in his veins. He knew that the sole reason he existed was to make the Vedlas the proudest and most respected of the *Vash* families, if not the most powerful. Ché Vedla was the instrument with which to achieve that goal.

Soon, and at his doing, the magnificent Vedla reign would once more be back on track. Klark's senses told him that the time was near. The Earth princess would not ruin it for him. No, she would not.

Klark had honed his body, kept his mind sharp, all so that he could achieve the goal of ensuring that the Vedla name once more reigned supreme. No matter how addled his older brother, Klark would see the fruition of his plans. By the holy blood that ran in his veins, he would not fail again.

Chapter Seventeen

After leaving the airport, Ilana and Ché went for a drive in the Porsche, celebrating with Gatorades and Corn Nuts, and recounting the flight.

Somehow they found their way to Highway 1 and were following the road north. Ilana noticed that neither of them had proposed a destination, and that neither seemed to care. For two fairly ambitious, focused people, it was a little strange, driving around with no goal in mind. But then the entire impulsive, dizzying, unforgettable day had been strange. Why not keep it going?

The Pacific was on their left, shining in the afternoon sun. They had the windows open all the way. Ché's long, athletic body just barely fit the Porsche. He drove with the driver's seat pushed back as far as it would go to make room for his long legs. His attention was on the winding highway, his driving fast and efficient. Confident. Sunlight and shadows played across his wonderfully sculpted profile. His nose was too long to be perfect, but she loved its imperfection.

Ilana was on the phone with Linda, after sharing the news with Leslie and Slavica at SILF. Flash was at home. She'd called him there, and he'd met the news with droll astonishment. Now she grinned as she finished breaking the news to her assistant. "And he let me take it through a few turns while we were over the ocean. Yes, me. Linda, I am not making it up!"

The open window tousled Ché's short hair, a honey-eyed cinnamon in this light. Automatically Ilana reached over and combed it with her fingertips as she recounted the highlights of the flight to Linda. Ché's driving didn't change one iota, but a contented grin transformed his Greek-statue profile, making it warm and real. She thrust the cell phone at Ché. "Tell her, Ché. She doesn't believe me."

He spoke into the phone like into a microphone, keeping both hands on the wheel. One thing about him—he was always careful, whether driving or flying, and kept his attention on the road . . . or on the runway, thank goodness. "Indeed, Ilana spent one-point-four hours in the air, Linda. I have the log in my possession, should you wish to verify the feat."

Ilana pressed the phone back to her ear. "See? Ha!"

"Congratulations. You're a flyer now."

Ilana felt a ripple in her stomach. "Um, I still have a few issues. Starships, mostly—but I did it, Linda. I flew! Ché's done more for my sanity than a decade worth of clinics. Can you believe it?"

"If any man was going to make you fly, I knew it was that one."

Linda meant more than the obvious. And she was right.

Ilana glanced at Ché, her face heating. When was the last time she'd dated anyone since he'd arrived? Hell, when was the last time she *thought* about any other man? Not that she and Ché had really done anything yet, or had even kissed after that night at Reach—by mutual, unspoken consent—a record unbroken until the chaste kiss she'd given him a half mile above the ocean. Despite the lack of physical contact, it was the closest she'd ever come to having a steady guy, the closest in years she'd ever come to having a—she could hardly bring herself to think the word—*relationship*. But then, she'd never dreamed she'd fly a plane, either. "Yeah, well," she told Linda.

"Yeah, well *what*? You'd better make up your mind soon about that boy, or he's going to go home and get married, and you'll kick yourself the rest of your life because you're too darned dense when it comes to men."

"Linda!"

Lifting a brow, Ché glanced her way. Ilana gave him a helpless shrug. He knew Linda, enjoyed her company, but Ilana didn't need him to hear any of this.

"Okay, so then we landed," she said, changing the subject. She could tell that Linda was smirking on the other end of the line. "But I haven't. I'm still flying." She saw a road sign speed past. "Actually, we both are. Where are we, Ché?" She hadn't been paying attention.

"South of Santa Barbara."

"I heard that," Linda said. "Get off the phone and celebrate. Take the day off. Take tomorrow off. Go."

Ilana laughed. "Yes, ma'am." They said their goodbyes, and she hung up.

"Linda thinks we should celebrate."

"Linda is right." He made a sudden turn off the highway.

"Where are we going?"

"It is scenic here."

She wasn't sure exactly where they were. Ché drove down a narrow off ramp that doubled back on itself, and pulled up to a small inn and parked. "Serenity Inn," she said. "Slavica told me about this place. She stayed here. It's a bed and breakfast."

Ché gave her that I-don't-get-your-slang look. "It's an inn," she explained. "A place to spend the night."

"Ah." He looked toward the beach, and Ilana wondered what he was thinking. Then he turned back to her and said, "We've always returned to your home after all our excursions. Is there a reason we cannot stay here tonight?"

She swallowed her surprise. She'd thought he didn't want to sleep with her. "Well, a lot of reasons, all given by you."

He appeared clueless as to her meaning. "You do not want to stay?"

"I'd love to stay." But flying and sex with Ché all in one day? It seemed too good to be true, but she decided to go with the flow.

He opened his door. Ilana grabbed her purse and slung it over her shoulder. Slipping on her dark glasses—bought in the initial surge of paparazzi interest—she sat in continued puzzlement as Ché walked around the front of the car and opened her door. He seemed so composed, so "whatever," that she was sure he didn't understand the signal that sharing a room like this sent.

He was a world-class expert in sex. And yet he was so obtuse when it came to the more mundane social aspects of dating, sex, and relationships. Of course, he never was supposed to have had a social life in the normal sense. He'd expected to follow the path laid out for him at birth. Only that path had taken a wild detour.

239

A *temporary* detour, she reminded herself. He'd be getting married—and soon.

Ché took her hand and helped her out. She'd gotten used to and appreciated his chivalry. "I hope they have rooms," she said awkwardly.

"We only need one."

Okay. That answered that question. They'd be sharing. But, they'd been roommates for weeks. Why would he think this time was any different just because she did?

Ché opened the door to the huge cottage-style inn and let her walk inside first. It took a moment for her eyes to adjust to the dimmer interior. They stood in a wood-floored foyer decorated with antiques. The place smelled like cinnamon and lemon oil. No one was around, but there was muffled conversation. They walked in further. A sitting room led to a dining room that opened onto a wide porch overlooking the ocean. "It's so pretty," Ilana said on a breath.

Guests sat in a few of the wicker chairs, sipping wine and playing backgammon. A fat ginger-colored cat slept in a sun patch on a mat by the back door. It was peaceful, serene, leaving Ilana with no doubts as to where the inn had gotten its name.

Ché stood next to her, apparently as entranced by the inn as she was. She hadn't realized until now how crazy her life had been lately, wrapping up the Holt film, getting it ready for festivals and Sundance, working with her partners on the possibility of making SILF a galactic venture. And, of course, Ché's presence in her life. Walking into the inn was like stepping off a speeding treadmill. Life had simply stopped. No wonder Slavica had raved about the place.

As they stood there, taking in the gorgeous view, Ché's royal, top-secret, high-tech personal comm device made a sharp little chirp. They both jumped. "So much for real life not intruding," she said.

His expression told her that he felt as she did. He pulled the comm out of his pants pocket. The comm call was a direct and secure communication computer that Ché used to stay in contact with his advisor. But she'd never heard the thing call Ché, although she knew he checked in periodically to soothe the nerves of the bevy of people who fretted over his safety.

His thumb brushed over a blinking green LED and the unit went silent. The last she saw of it was a plaintive little light glowing steady amber as he shoved it back in his pocket. "There," he said. "Real life gone."

"What if it's an emergency?"

"It is not," he said with certainty.

"And if they need you for something?" *Like a wedding? Oy.*

"I will call them later."

"Hello!" A cheerful woman with arms full of grocery bags bounced toward them. She wore baggy khaki pants and a sweatshirt decorated with tiny cats. "Do you have a reservation?"

"No. If you have available accommodations, we would like to purchase a room."

One room. Ilana couldn't help grinning.

Ché took the bags from the woman and set them on a nearby table. "Why, thank you," she chirped. She wiped her hands on her pants, clearly taken with his good looks, good manners, and unusual accent. She smiled at Ilana. "Just the two of you?"

"Yes," Ilana answered before Ché could change his mind or realize what he was doing.

The proprietor went to a small antique desk and unlocked it, producing a ledger. Everything was so blissfully old-fashioned. No computers in sight. No digital clocks. "We have the Spring Room available.

It's our smallest, but you can have it until Friday. The Seagull Suite is available, but until tomorrow morning only. I have honeymooners coming, I'm afraid. But if you can do one night, it has a king bed, a balcony, a fireplace, and a hot tub. It's quite lovely."

Ilana gave Ché an eager look. She'd rather have paradise for one night than lesser accommodations for more days. Ché took one look in her eyes, apparently agreeing with what he saw there, and told the woman, "We would like the suite."

Ilana felt somewhat dazed as they went through the check-in process. They had no extra clothing, no toothbrushes; they were just doing this with total spontaneity, and she still wasn't sure what Ché had in mind. He'd been so adamant about not wanting casual sex with her that she couldn't see him changing his mind so suddenly, and without a formal request. She had visions of him getting down on one knee and asking for permission to get in her pants.

"Mr. French," Ché said, giving his name when asked.

"I'm Mrs. French," Ilana added. Ché threw her an amused glance and paid for the suite in cash.

They climbed the stairs to a hallway of rooms. The door on the end had a piece of driftwood etched with letters that read *Seagull*.

Ché unlocked the door and let them in. It caused an immediate cross breeze. The balcony's French doors were wide open. Gauzy white curtains billowed inward. An earthenware vase of cut sunflowers stood in the middle of a square antique table set with a bowl of fresh fruit, a bottle of champagne, two glasses, plates, and a knife.

When Ché locked the door behind them, the breeze stopped. Ilana couldn't contain her happiness and did a little pirouette. "This was the best idea."

She lifted her arms and wriggled her fingers at him. "A hug." He stepped into her open arms, and she pulled his warm, hard body close. Pressing her cheek to his chest, she inhaled his smell. A hug was okay, wasn't it? But, God, she wanted more. She thought of what Linda said, about not letting him go, and then shoved the thought out of her mind. It wasn't that simple. The whole idea of her and Ché together— well, it was too complicated for words. "Thanks," she said, softer. "Thanks for today. I mean it."

He moved her back to look down at her. "You were the one who decided it was time," he reminded her. Then he grinned. "And what a time it was!"

She laughed. "You're just as happy about this as I am."

"And why wouldn't I be? After tearing your leaden feet off this Earth—finally."

"Leaden!"

"Not only that, Ilana. I lived to tell about it. Warriors have come home from battle with lesser tales of courage than that."

She laughed. "Well, now you'll have a good story to tell the family when you get home."

"I'm afraid they wouldn't believe it."

"Neither family would." She sobered for a moment, searching his equally serious face. The subject of their families was always intrusive, because they both knew that news of their friendship and intimate living arrangements would raise eyebrows on both sides. Everyone's eyebrows except Ian's, she thought.

"But they're not here," she said. "Only we are. Let's open that champagne."

He lifted the bottle. "It is warm."

She breezed into the kitchenette and opened the freezer. "Voilà! Ice cubes." She carried over the plastic tray. She started plopping the cubes one by one

243

into the flutes and then stopped. "Unless you want to ruin the mood by making me wait until you chill the bottle."

"Nothing will ruin our moods today, Ilana." He popped the cork while she added more ice to the glasses.

When the flutes were filled and foaming over with champagne, they lifted them. "To taking chances," she said, and gave him a meaningful gaze. If he didn't start getting the hint that she wanted him tonight, wanted to sleep with him, then she was going to have to be more proactive.

He dipped his head in that grave and charming *Vash* way of his, and gave no hint that he'd caught on to her desires. "To the rogue."

Her flute paused halfway to her mouth. "Rogue?"

"I have admitted this to no one." His mouth tipped slightly. "A rogue lives inside me. Always has. It is he who urges me to take risks, to go against advice, to be impractical when conformity is expected—or even required. But when I think back over my life, the moments instigated by the rogue are the ones which stand out as the times when I felt truly alive."

Her throat closed. It took a few tries before she could breathe again. She tapped her flute to his. "To the hijacked garden carts of life, Ché."

"Indeed." Their flutes made a musical chime as they connected.

"Drink up," she coaxed. *Whatever it takes to loosen you up.* Closing her eyes, she took a healthy sip of champagne. It was dry, crisp, and perfect.

Giddy, and not entirely from the champagne, she came up on her toes and kissed Ché lightly on the lips, then pulled away slowly. He appeared more pleased than surprised. "See? There are lots of ways to celebrate," she said.

She put down her glass. Her heart was beating faster now. The role of seductress was one in which she felt comfortable—usually. But not only had Ché rejected her once before, she wanted him. Badly.

She stepped closer and combed her fingers through his hair. The sun had bleached out the short ends, contrasting with his tan that had deepened during the weeks spent in L.A.

Her pulse was flat-out racing now. Making love with Ché would either get him out of her system or make matters worse than they already were.

Probably get him out of her system, she decided. That was the way it had always worked in the past with men.

He stood very still as she took her time exploring the rugged curves of his face, and his eyes closed as she brushed her thumb over his lips. He was fighting her, she realized, trying to pretend she wasn't touching him like this, that it didn't feel as good as she knew it did. "Resistance is futile," she whispered without a trace of threat in her voice.

He kissed her thumb, reached for her wrist, turned her hand over, and pressed his lips to her palm. She almost groaned aloud, aching from temptation. Until now, the only thing that had kept them from each other was total physical abstinence. They'd just blown that sky high.

She wasn't sure who started it, but the next thing she knew they were kissing; it was that natural. At first, their lips skimmed and touched, small, sipping kisses, tender and affectionate. She couldn't help sighing, couldn't help thinking about how so few men had made her genuinely sigh. Warm fingertips lingered. Hands caressed. Only the sounds of their lips touching and of their breathing interrupted the absolute silence in the room.

Then Ché's fingers skimmed across Ilana's throat and collarbone. She ached for them to reach lower. But he made no move to cross the invisible line he'd drawn all those weeks ago when he said he didn't want casual sex with her. So the kiss stayed tame, however much she wanted more.

How could he not want more? The attraction was there. The hunger was there. The time was right.

She sighed again and arched against him. Ché kissed his way to the hollow under her earlobe, nuzzling her there. She laughed softly and shivered, hunching her shoulders. His voice was a deep murmur in her ear. "Are you ticklish, Ilana?"

"Not ticklish. Sensitive. You know all my sensitive spots."

"Not all," he confessed.

If he weren't wearing those damned gray contact lenses, the gold would have taken her breath away. She cleared her throat because it felt suddenly dry. "Why don't we start from the top, then, and work down?

"Show me the rogue, Ché." Holding his gaze, she took his hand and placed it on her breast. Her top had a thin shelf bra for support, and that was all. She could tell by the tightening of his mouth that he could feel every contour covered by the stretchy fabric.

One convulsive flex of his hand, and her nipple contracted. Her chest rose and fell with her breaths. Her arms hung at her sides, her hands in fists. She couldn't look away from his eyes, though it was so intensely intimate to watch him as he touched her. She'd gone up in an airplane today, a tiny little rickety plane. She could do this; she could let him look into her soul.

"Ilana . . ." His voice sounded thick, huskier than ever. His gaze dropped away from her face, to his hand covering her left breast. His thumb rubbed across her tight nipple, and it was as if the sensation were hardwired to a place between her legs, each stroke of his thumb setting off tiny explosions in her nerve endings.

Her knees became disturbingly weak. She placed her hand over his. Breathing hard, she said, "We probably shouldn't take this any further unless it's going to go somewhere."

His breaths were just as uneven as hers. She recognized the sharp hunger in his face. To her, he looked suddenly very male. Not quite a stranger, not quite frightening, but a man who could enthrall her with sheer sexual magnetism.

She took the chance and moved closer until their stomachs touched. He had a choice: He could put his arms around her or push her away.

He put his arms around her.

She pressed her cheek to his chest and smiled. His hands were flat on her back, keeping her close. His heartbeat was like thunder. He wanted more. She wanted more. What was stopping them other than some irrelevant *Vash* honor code? Or was he as scared of taking the relationship to the next level as she was?

She reached for his T-shirt and tugged it from the waistband of his jeans. "Now, where are you hiding that tattoo of yours?" She tried to keep her voice light. "Can I see? I'll still respect you in the morning. I promise."

He grabbed her wrists. He was so damned strong.

"Easy, Ché," she crooned. "You're doing great. Just great. There's no need to worry." She tried to reach the top button on his jeans, but he wouldn't let her. It was equally difficult to keep her smile from showing. "Look, I know how to do this. Just hang in there and you'll be okay. I know how to fly, if you know what I mean."

Suddenly he tipped his head back and laughed. With shocked satisfaction, she saw amusement, surprise, and wry delight light up his eyes. "That is precisely what I said to you in the airplane."

She grinned and nodded. "When you thought I was going to panic. And it worked."

He released her wrists so he could wipe his eyes of laughter-induced tears. "And you think because you ask to see my tattoo that I will panic, too?"

"No. But if I ask you to make love with me, I think you might." She brought her hands to his waistband again. Raised her brows. "I flew today. You gave me the confidence to do it. My decision was spontaneous, maybe impulsive. And I don't regret it for a minute." With a jerk of her wrist, she opened the top button of his fly. For the first time she noticed the sizable bulge there—not the faint beginnings of interest, but a full-fledged erection. "I don't think you will either, Ché."

"Ilana . . ."

"Look where we are. It's so romantic. It'd be so special here. Isn't that how you wanted it? I thought your people considered sex something beautiful, a holy act between consenting adults."

"It is."

"But you act like there's something wrong with lovemaking."

"I certainly do not think there is anything wrong with lovemaking!"

She was almost glad to have made him angry. Some emotion, any emotion, was better than that tight control, his warrior's resolve. "Then it has to be me. You think sleeping with me will be a mistake. And what if it is? I think we're both mature enough not to ruin our friendship over it." To her shock, her throat tightened. "Okay, just forget I brought it up." It had suddenly become painfully humiliating, having to convince him to make love to her.

Ilana Hamilton begged no man. This was the last time she asked Ché . . . for anything! She spun away to hide the embarrassment and emotion she felt welling up in her eyes, grabbed her glass of champagne. "I'm going to get drunk and celebrate. You can do what you want. In fact, return that phone call from your papa. You can't seem to break the umbilical cord anyway—"

He hauled her to him with a strangled sound of fury. This time his kiss was hot, hard with passion. A groan rumbled in his chest as he expertly maneuvered her backward. The edge of the table butted up against the small of her back. Water sloshed in the vase of sunflowers as he pushed her backward. The room spun and tilted, and she was flat on her back, Ché's powerful body pressed to hers, his muscular thighs holding her in place.

His hands landed on the table, to either side of her head. In a sort of pushup, he lowered himself and kissed her—hard at first, but then the intensity eased a little, as if the kiss blinded him to everything else. His tongue was velvet, stroking hers in an expert, never-ending, carnal caress. After all this, she found she wanted that kiss, a simple kiss, to go on and on and on. . . .

Ché made a muffled, drawn-out, rumbling groan. There was something so indescribably intimate and satisfying about that sound. Honeyed warmth spread through Ilana, and the rest of her body quickly caught up to what her lips already knew.

Suddenly a shudder ran through Ché's body and he wrenched his mouth from hers. Breathing hard, he swore in a language she didn't recognize. Her eyes opened wide. He gave her little time to ponder the raw expression on his hard, noble face before he lowered his head and tugged off her jeans.

He kept his face down, as if on purpose, so she couldn't read his eyes. His broad shoulders blocked the light flooding through the French doors as his fingers slipped under the elastic of her panties and yanked off her thong. The wetness on her upper inner thighs cooled in the rush of air.

She felt him shift his weight, bump against the table. It creaked. The sunflowers sloshed in their vase. There was the pop of releasing buttons overlaid with Ché's ragged breaths. He lowered his pants while she lay sprawled on top of a table designed for cozy romantic dinners, not the round of disturbingly detached coupling into which this had turned.

He wasn't going to make love to her at all; he was going to steal himself a round of brain-numbing sex. Steal? Ha! Hardly. Not when she was there, right along with him.

Sex for her was no different from a long jog or a hard swim, but with a bonus at the end. Physical exertion with a sweet prize waiting at the finish line. Why should she expect any different with Ché? She'd wanted casual sex all along, and now he was going to give it to her. Only she couldn't quite convince herself that this was her reward and not a punishment for her persistence.

His strong fingers glided up her to where his leg had wedged her thighs apart. It was a cold, self-assured offensive, and yet he kindled in her a breathless carnal urgency. Her mind might be confused, but her body knew exactly what it wanted. She raised her knees, squeezing his hips. But he pushed her legs down.

Knowing fingers slid though her engorged folds.
He'd learned about her in the shower, knew where
she was the most sensitive; pushing aside the covering of flesh, he exposed that spot to his practiced
fingertips. He'd done this to women, to the courtesans at his disposal many times before. Yet a choked
cry exploded from Ilana, and her hips writhed. As if
she were his little puppet.

"Goddamn you, Ché." She grabbed the collar of his
shirt. Wrapping the fabric in her knuckles, she used
the leverage to lift her shoulders off the table. Her
voice sounded strange to her own ears: guttural, tight
with unrequited need. "You'd better not leave me this
time. You'd better stay until we're through."

He pushed her back onto the table. An emotion
she couldn't read contorted his features. Grabbing
her bottom, he lifted her hips and thrust his pelvis
forward. There was no fumbling; he knew where to
go. With a harsh grunt, he pushed into her and sank
himself home.

Her body jerked in shock at the sudden, thick in-
trusion. She burned, but the burn turned quickly to
sharp pleasure.

Dragging her upper body off the table, Ché seized
her mouth in a breathless, punishing kiss, angling his
firm lips to force hers apart with the pressure. He
made a deep growl in his throat, his fingers sinking
into the skin of her thighs as he ground her against
him, ramming deeper each time, his breaths harsh.
Ilana clutched at his shoulders, riding the tidal wave
that was her response to him. She was ready; hell,
she was more than ready, but he'd surprised her. She
hadn't thought he'd do it; hadn't thought he'd take
her like this. Where was the *Vash Nadah* finesse she'd
heard so much about?

The comm in his jeans pocket started chiming

again. They froze. It was his family, she thought.

"Ah—Great Mother . . ." Gasping, he held fast to her upper arms. So many emotions flickered in his face. And then, when he opened his eyes, the Ché she'd come to know was back.

"No," he said. His expression was gentler now, almost regretful. "Not this way, Ilana. Not with us, love."

Love. Relief pierced her.

And then he withdrew from her, his entire body shuddering as he pulled out. Still rigid, his sex sagged damp and heavy against her belly. She throbbed inside where he had been.

It had cost him, that retreat. His voice was so rough that he almost whispered. "May I . . . try again?"

She swallowed, nodding, too emotionally unsettled to reply. But he must have seen what he'd needed to in her eyes, because he lowered his head and kissed her—a tender, loving caress. She wrapped her arms over his shoulders and kissed him back, tears pressing behind her eyes, her throat aching from emotion.

He scooped her off the table, supporting her weight in his muscled arms. She kept her own wrapped tightly around his neck as he carried her into the bedroom they hadn't yet seen. It was cool and shaded, smelling of lavender and freshly laundered sheets. A thick red and gold comforter lay over the bed, folded back partway to reveal lavish red satin sheets.

Almost tenderly, Ché laid her on her back on the sinfully plush bed. Foil-wrapped chocolates were scattered, ignored.

They stripped off the rest of their clothes, rolling over the big, soft feather bed, savoring the feel of warm bare skin and cool satin sheets. Passion rose, but Ché took time to move his hands and lips over

Ilana's breasts, her throat, her face, as if he wanted to memorize her, the kind of caresses that should have preceded their initial attempt at lovemaking but hadn't.

He'd said he wanted to start from scratch. If he was willing, then so was she.

Chapter Eighteen

Only after Ilana was breathless from their foreplay, nearly begging him to take her, did Ché seek to complete the act. He rolled her beneath him so he could better watch her sweet face as he made love to her.

Her eyes closed. "Look at me," he whispered. "Ilana . . ."

Her lovely eyes opened. At first, desire glazed them, but she blinked, focusing on his face, poised so close to hers. And then those eyes became so clear and blue that looking into them made Ché's chest tighten with emotions he couldn't name, because he had no experience with anything so intense.

Propping his weight on his elbows, he lifted his hips. Ilana's hands rested lightly on his shoulders. When he pressed at her opening, she raised her hips to meet him. With a swift inhalation, watching her face contort with the pleasure only he could give her, he pushed deep inside her body. This was no feverish plunge; he savored every contour of her wet inner

walls, every contraction of her muscles. He kept up
the slow, steady, erotic push until he was sure it
would kill him unless he let loose and thrust into her.
But he called on every ounce of discipline he had,
finally reaping the reward for his patience when she
sheathed him fully, gloriously. There, he held himself
still, his breaths uneven as he watched her. Her eye-
lids lowered as she tipped her head back and
moaned. She would lose herself in the pleasure unless he called her back.

"Ilana," he whispered sharply. Her eyes flew open.
"I want you here with me." He needed her with him.

She nodded, and then her breath hitched as he
began to move inside her. She lifted her knees, pressing them to his swaying hips to hold him close. He
held her face in his hands, gazing down at her as she
looked up at him, their eyes locked.

Take me. To Ilana, he gave more than his body and
years of experience, far more. He began to sweat, his
loins clenching with the heavy, potent pleasure-pain
he knew preceded release. He gritted his teeth, his
breaths hissing, wanting first to open himself to her,
to let her see inside him as he devoted his entire being to this exquisite, strangely poignant lovemaking,
giving her what he'd never given any other, gifting
her with what he knew in his heart he would never
bestow on anyone else, no matter what the ancient
laws of his people demanded he do.

Always before, he'd sought the goal of maximum
physical release. But this time it was different. This
time he wanted the woman he was with to hold him
close. He craved that connection, a taut thread between them that seemed to rise above the joy of physical sex, turning it into something far more
transcendent.

Groaning, he fought to hold off the explosion he

knew was coming. But with each one of his fierce, reckless strokes, Ilana's body responded, clutching him, her inner muscles convulsing wetly. She cried out then, a throaty plea.

His reaction to her coming peak overwhelmed him. His lower belly tightened; exquisite, excruciating heat clutched at his loins. Frenzied, he squeezed the muscles in his buttocks to hold back, just a few moments more. Where was his self-control?

But to his mortification, he knew he'd have to go completely still if he wanted to last. "Ah, Ilana," he said sorrowfully on a ragged breath, lowering his head to her throat. To his shock, Ilana arched her back, climaxing almost immediately, her nails digging into the flesh of his shoulders.

That was all it took. He could hold back no longer. His acute embarrassment went up in a blaze of pleasure the likes of which he'd never known. He pushed up on rigid arms, his back arching. One, two jerks of his buttocks and he exploded deep inside her. He had no more power to hold back on his release than he did to stop his heart.

He collapsed on top of her. Somehow he managed to support his dead weight with his elbows and knees. She felt just as limp. Murmuring to her in Eireyan—it was the only way he knew to express his shock and pleasure at what he'd discovered in her arms—he kissed and stroked and nuzzled her, holding her close until her spent body and his stopped quivering.

"I guess I couldn't wait," he heard her say after a long while.

"Hmm?" He lifted his head. Her cheeks were flushed pink, and her lips were puffy. Damp curls framed her face. Her eyes were so blue that it almost hurt to gaze directly into them.

"Nor could I," he said. Great Mother, it pained him to say it. "Heaven knows I tried. I am embarrassed, Ilana."

"No, you're not," she scolded. She smiled up at him, a soft, wondering smile, and combed her fingers through his damp hair. "You're incredible."

His chest tightened, and an odd feeling of lightness swept through him. "As are you, my sweet Earth girl." Their mouths came together in a kiss. It was wet, deep, languorous . . .

. . . and it went on, it seemed, for hours, that kiss, Ilana thought.

It didn't take much for the heat between them to build from simmering to a slow boil. "That was but the first orgasm," he promised, rolling her atop him.

"But the first?" She laughed. "Okay. I'm game."

His hands stroked up and down her back. "Now I will give you another, and it will be far better."

Ilana smiled at his utter confidence, a smile she knew faded when he lifted her over him and plunged deep inside her. She threw her head back and gasped. Each roll of his hips sent a shockwave of pleasure coursing through her.

Sweat beaded on his forehead. His body heat radiated his scent, musky and male. She clutched his broad shoulders, her breath hissing. He was an athletic lover, tireless, but it was his tenderness that made her ache with longing. More than wanting him, she needed him.

It scared her to death. But the fear felt conquerable this time, as her fear of flying did the minute that little airplane rolled onto the runway.

They tumbled across the big feather bed. Ché pinned her beneath him, pressing her into the soft, red sheets. Lifting one of her legs high over his back,

257

he rocked his hips, gradually deepening his strokes. "Ilana . . . my sweet," he whispered, his breath hot against her ear. His English melted into a language she didn't know. Eireyan? It was a lyrical and sexy litany of words. While she had no clue what he said, the eroticism of his tone wasn't lost on her.

"Feel me," he whispered harshly. "Feel me as I love you." Stroking her hair back with his palm, he watched her face as he had before. In its incredible intimacy, the gesture rivaled the powerfully erotic way he moved inside her.

This is what it's supposed to be like, she thought dazedly. This was why her mother had remarried, and why Ian couldn't wait to make Tee'ah his wife. This was why people fell in love and took a gamble on spending a lifetime together. No, not only for the sex. For this exchange of feelings, to be able to open oneself to another.

Trust, reciprocated.

She pulled him down to her, whispered breathlessly in his ear. "Do you know what Linda once told me? That if I ever opened up, if I ever let a man inside this stubborn, smart-ass head of mine, I might be surprised and like it."

He lifted his head. As he gazed down at her, his lashes only partly shielded the satisfaction glowing in his gold eyes. "And do you?"

She laughed softly, disbelievingly. "Yeah."

Taking full breaths became a lost cause as he brought her closer and closer to the second peak he'd promised. And when that climax and then a surprise third shattered Ilana, her personal epiphany and searing pleasure was only intensified by Ché's powerful, almost violent release.

*   *   *

After a long afternoon and evening making love and napping, Ilana woke, sated and drowsy, tucked into and spooned by Ché's body. He'd fallen asleep holding her. He'd insisted on it, in fact; all but demanding that she stay next to him.

She didn't mind. Maybe she'd wanted the closeness as much as he did. It wasn't just physical; it was something else. Something more.

She'd never been a fan of cuddling after sex, let alone actually spending the night with someone. But with Ché, the compulsion to distance herself hadn't kicked in. It felt natural, wanting to cuddle close to him. It felt good, and right somehow.

Or was she overanalyzing everything, as usual?

Smiling at herself and her racing thoughts, she made herself relax. Judging by the sound of Ché's slow, even breaths, he was still sleeping. Carefully she turned in his arms to face him. But he came half awake and drew her to his chest. "Stay with me," he murmured into her messy hair.

"I will," she whispered back, and wondered if in reality she'd promised more than what those few words would indicate.

You're thinking too hard, Ilana.

Right, she thought.

First she turned off her brain, and that was hard. Her body soon followed in relaxation. Finally, lulled by the sound of Ché's heart beating, she fell back asleep.

When she woke again, Ché was up. He walked out of the bathroom, naked, scrubbing a towel over his hair. It stood up in short spikes all over his head. She came up on her elbows. "Hey, lover boy."

His mouth tipped in that crooked smile he gave no one else but her. "Blue-eyes," he said with affection.

"Blue-eyes?" Her breasts bounced as she rolled onto her belly. She ached all over, but she wasn't about to complain.

He nodded, smiling. "Or I can call you luscious bottom."

"Luscious bottom!" She supposed it beat *fat cheeks*. "I had no idea the word luscious was in your vocabulary."

It was clear Ché was trying hard not to smile. "I looked it up one day when I was feeling particularly . . . inspired."

"I knew those shorts were too tight," she muttered.

His gaze traveled down to her bare butt, lingering there. "Choose whichever endearment you prefer. Now is the time to state your preference, lest I become too used to one or the other."

"I'll take blue-eyes in public." She winked. "Luscious in private."

Lounging on her stomach, she hugged her arms to her chest. The swell of her breasts peeked over her forearms as she watched him dry off. His Greek-god physique was the result of discipline, exercise, and, yeah, genetics. On a superficial level, his appearance attracted her, fascinated her, and made her blood run hot. But the man inside that body was what drew her to him more than anything.

To his people, he was a peacemaker, an open-minded leader who just happened to be from the most conservative of families. A prince wise beyond his years. She'd witnessed all that when his unexpected public support of Ian—at the cost of his brother Klark's disgrace—did more to keep the Federation stable and intact than any other action could have.

But to her, Ché Vedla was fun, patient, easy to talk to, generous, intelligent, and heroic. More importantly, she admired, and respected him. Deep down, she'd always known that she'd never be able to love a man for whom she felt neither of those things. "So. How long have you been up?"

"A half of one of your hours, no more. I ordered room service."

"You know how to do that?"

He gave her a dry look. "It is not that difficult."

Ché dropped his towel into a hamper and reached for a robe hanging on a hook on the bathroom door. That was when she noticed his tattoo, on the very lowest part of his flat abdomen, just above his groin. She pushed off the bed. "Ah, there it is. The famous tattoo. I want to take a better look. The last time I was close enough to see it . . . ah, my attention was focused a little lower."

His heated gaze told her that he hadn't forgotten the feel of her mouth. "Indeed."

She bent down to study the tattoo. It was small and finely made, crisper in detail than Earth tattoos, a gold, gray, and black bird, depicted head-on with spread wings.

The fascinated attention she paid to the area so close to his privates embarrassed Ché not at all. He was as comfortable in the buff as he was clothed. "It is a sea-raptor," he explained, looking downward. "An ancient aerial predator. It lives only on Eireya, and feeds only on creatures born in our seas. It is the symbol of my family."

"Do all the Vedla men have these tattoos?"

He shook his head. "Firstborn sons only. You may have noticed that the other clans, like you B'kahs, use signet rings to identify the heirs. We don't. This is why. We are marked at puberty like this, instead."

While she'd been playing girls' soccer and suffering through braces, Ché was enduring eons-old coming-of-age rituals. It was at times like these that she realized how different their upbringings were.

Ilana bent forward, touching her fingertip to the sea-raptor. Ché's stomach muscles contracted, and his penis gave an interested twitch. "Oops," she said, smiling.

He took her by the shoulders and pulled her close. Her stomach pressed against his damp, freshly washed skin. "Not 'oops,' " he corrected.

Heat pooled in her lower belly, carnal anticipation of what was to come, as he lowered his mouth to hers and—

Beep, beep, beep. Ché's damn comm call chimed from somewhere in the other room.

They groaned and moved apart. "Haven't you called them back yet?" she asked.

"No." He sighed. "I was going to wait. But they are persistent."

Her heart skipped a beat. "Maybe something's wrong. Your family. Someone might be sick."

He shook his head as he searched out the comm device he'd thrown out of the way earlier. "Ian would have relayed the message, if that were the case, and he would have at least tried to call your cell phone. Any illness or death, or birth or marriage for that matter, in any of the eight families is immediately reported to the Great Council, and then forwarded to the B'kahs. Trust me, whatever this is will be something that could have waited. And should have," he added irritably.

"I hope so," Ilana said under her breath, noting the reluctance with which he drew on his underwear and jeans.

He opened the comm. His face formed immediately into a frown. "Yes, Hoe."

Ilana backed up. "I'll be in the shower." She had

the feeling that while he wouldn't demand it, he'd rather have his privacy. Taking her clothes with her, she ducked into the bathroom.

One long, luxurious, steamy shower later, she emerged dressed in a fresh robe, a thick towel wrapped around her hair.

The room-service attendant had come and gone, apparently. Ché sat in one of the chairs at the dining table, the one with the vase of sunflowers they'd almost toppled. He was the picture of laid-back sophistication as he sipped from a glass of red wine, staring into space.

Her glass waited, full. She took it, sat in the chair next to him, and sniffed the fragrant air. "Mmm. Smells like steak."

"Filet," he confirmed. "With baby asper . . . aspar—" He sighed. "Those little green stalks with the odd tops."

"Asparagus," she supplied.

"Yes." He seemed preoccupied. "It was the meal they were serving the guests in the dining room tonight. It was all they would serve."

"Then we lucked out. I love steak, and I love asparagus." She lifted the lids off the plates. Delicious smells made her mouth water. "Ooh. The chef has a hollandaise sauce fetish. I love him." She began to serve the food as Ché watched absently.

She put down the utensils, folded her arms, and leaned forward. "It's the comm call, isn't it? Your advisor. What did he want?"

"He asked me to come home." Ché lifted his half-full glass of wine to the overhead light, studying the color. Then he downed what remained in two deep swallows before he turned back to her. "It seems they have found me a wife."

Chapter Nineteen

"Ché refused to return home?" Klark demanded when Hoe burst into his chambers the next day with the news. "He wishes to remain on Earth?" As hard as he tried, Klark couldn't imagine Ché abandoning Eireya for good, his tolerance toward the frontier barbarians notwithstanding. Klark knew his older brother better than that.

"Banish the thought, sir." Hoe rubbed his hand over his face. "But he wants to delay his return journey. He wouldn't tell me how long he wants to remain . . . there. 'We have plenty of time left,' he told me." Hoe dropped his hand and added, "I was afraid of this, my lord."

"I have to say that I anticipated it, too."

"It's all because of the Earth princess."

"Of course it is." Klark rolled his eyes. "Did you think that he went there for the coffee?"

"My lord?"

"Never mind." Stroking his chin, Klark regarded

Ché's agitated advisor. "We must not let emotion overcome us. The Treatise of Trade tells us that the unexpected brings opportunity. Let us discern the opportunity in this, and take advantage."

At Klark's admonition, Hoe visibly forced himself to relax. "Prince Ché is like a son to me. I want only the best for him."

"And that is what we will win for him." Klark clasped his hands behind his back. Confidence swelled inside him as a plan unfolded—in detail. It seemed his brother had unwittingly simplified his task. "First, Hoe, we let our heartsick Prince Haj continue to divert everyone's attention in the Great Council while we think this through."

"Yes! While everyone's attention is elsewhere, we will act. You need not do this alone. We share a common goal, do we not, my lord? As Prince Ché's advisor, I have much to offer. Tell me your plans. I . . . I can help."

Hoe sounded both eager and nervous, as if he didn't fully trust Klark. Which was too bad. But Klark didn't quite trust Hoe either. "All right, then. Let us take time to think. Return here tonight, and we will discuss what options our meditations have illuminated." Then, with a wave of his hand, Klark dismissed him.

Something about Ché's advisor made Klark's senses prickle. It was the feeling he might have in Bajha with an opponent who didn't parry as predicted. It told Klark that, as yet, he shouldn't be certain on which side of the line the advisor fell when it came to ensuring that Ché's future took its proper course. Was Hoe his ally or enemy? Before Klark divulged his true intentions regarding the Earth princess, he'd have to be sure.

* * *

"A wife." Ilana let her back sag into the wicker chair. The meal didn't look as yummy as it had a minute ago. "So, what does that mean?"

Ché steepled his fingers on top of the table, gazing at them as he spoke. "It means we must talk."

"Ah, the big talk," she said flatly. It had always been she who gave the kiss-off speech when ending a relationship. It was weirdly nauseating to finally end up on the other side. She tried to sound light and cheery, but she felt about as buoyant as an old brick. "I mean, we knew this was coming. We knew you'd have to marry."

"Yes, but—"

"Then we're done. We've talked. Now, let's eat." She chose the bigger of the two filets and speared it with a fork. "Hand me your plate." At the dangerous look in his eyes, she lowered the fork. "What is there to talk about? Nothing's changed."

"You are right. The feelings I have for you have not changed. Nor have yours. I know—you have given me the proof. If what happened in that bedchamber, the lovemaking, had been a lie, you would not be trying to change the subject."

"Yeah . . . well." Sheepishly she stuck her hands in her lap. "Why do I suddenly feel like the kid caught with her hand in the cookie jar?"

Ché shook his head. "Cookie . . . jar?"

"It means you're right. I was trying to avoid this talk." She braced herself. "So do it. Say it. They found you a wife, and now they want you to come home." She forced herself to ask, "When are you leaving?"

"I did not say. I merely accepted the information as it was passed to me and left matters vague as to when I would return to Eireya."

"Vague? I bet your advisor had a cow." Before Ché

could call her on her slang, she said, "Isn't your advisor upset?"

Ché jerked his hands in the air. "Let him be! For all the good it will do him." Ché's outward emotion surprised her. He wasn't one to let show what he felt inside. "I did not say I would refuse to marry. I only declined to scurry home at their command. I did that to give us time, Ilana. Time to think."

Think. Ugh! She already analyzed everything to death. Ché was as bad as she was. "Everything was fine until you got involved with me, and now you don't know what to do. Right?"

"I know one thing: I do not want to marry Princess Jienn."

"Ah. The lucky girl who won the lottery." The bitterness underlying her light tone surprised her. She had never been the possessive type, but the idea of giving Ché over to another woman lit the fire of jealousy in Ilana's stomach.

"I will wed her if I must. But if I have a choice—if you allow me a choice . . . and the honor—I would rather marry you."

Whoa. Her ears started ringing. The pulse pounding in her throat built to a crescendo. A future. With Ché Vedla, lord of the *Vash Nadah*. Gah. She tried to remember to breathe.

Frantically she reached for a glass of wine and gulped down half of it. Their cooling dinner lay on plates all around them. "Gah," she choked out, putting down the glass. "We need more time to think about this."

"We do not have the luxury of more time." Ché spread his hands on the table. Those hands were sinewy and strong. On the middle finger of the right one, a scar marred his knuckle. Childhood pranks or swordplay? Ilana wondered. Those same hands had so passionately excited her, and afterward, tenderly held her. In a way, those hands represented how much she knew about him, and how much she didn't. "It is why we must talk with nothing between us. No ulterior motives, no feints, no false sentiments. It must be as it was when we made love. Do you remember that, Ilana? Do you remember how it was with us, only a few hours ago?"

How could she forget? "Of course I do, babe," she whispered.

Babe. It had just slipped out. Tender, unexpected.

Ché's answering expression melted her heart. He hadn't put back his contacts. His eyes were pale gold and totally open. She could see straight through him. She, on the other hand, was desperately trying to hold a screen in front of her feelings. It was getting flimsier by the minute, but she was afraid to take it down completely. "You have feelings for me," he said, gauging her reaction.

She fidgeted in her chair. "I have so many feelings that I don't know what they all are yet."

He spoke soothingly. "I am not asking you to sort them out now."

But she knew she wasn't going to get off easy in this conversation. And she wasn't sure she wanted to. This wasn't like the other "are we going to get serious or not?" talks from her past. With Ché, she wanted him to know how she felt . . . if she could express it; sometimes she was better with cameras than she was with words. "I do know this," she offered. "You're the first man I've ever imagined wanting to be with in a permanent . . . you know, a permanent comm—" She licked her dry lips. "Commit—"

Ché smiled. "Commitment."

"Yeah. That."

"It is not so hard a word to say once you practice, Ilana."

"Commitment," she mumbled.

He put his hand to his ear.

"Commitment!" she said, louder.

"Better."

She sat back, smirking as she shook her head in amazement. "You are amazing. You can take me when I'm this serious, when I'm this tense and obsessive, and still make me smile." She grew more serious. "You balance me, Ché. You steady me. For that reason alone, I could fall in love with you, given a little more time."

"Thank you," he murmured.

She forced herself to meet his eyes. "For what?"

"For not turning me down outright." Unexpectedly, the ends of his mouth curved. "You give me hope."

She snorted. Then she squeezed her eyes shut. "Stop it. You're making me laugh again. I don't feel like laughing. I feel like having a panic attack. You want to talk? Then let's talk. Before I pass out from nerves"—she eyed her nearly empty glass of wine— "or the Merlot."

"Ilana, I know and admire your ambition. But I also know that you desire something more than your career. You want a mate and, someday, children. In that, as in many other ways, we are the same. We want to achieve our professional goals, but we want a satisfactory private life, too."

Stubbornly she shook her head. "Satisfactory isn't good enough, Ché. I want more than that. I want real happiness. I know it's out there. Look at my mother and Rom. They didn't settle. Seven years and counting and they're still happy—blissfully, over-the-moon happy. I want to have what they have. I want the person I'm with to feel that way about me, too. Yes, happiness cycles. There has to be trust, also, to keep it going. Trust is what makes for a stable home life. It's what keeps you from worrying that it'll all disappear the minute you turn your back. I want a man who won't betray me, who won't lie, who will want to protect me, to keep me safe. But one who won't be threatened by my independence and, if it comes, my success. I . . . I want everything I didn't have when I was growing up."

Ché's eyes were molten gold. "I can give you that. I can give you what you want, Ilana."

Her throat thickened. "Your culture can give me that. But can you, Ché? Think about it. It's not the trust—that's not the issue. I never would have gone up in that airplane otherwise, and I sure as hell wouldn't be having this conversation, either, if I didn't trust you. To be blunt, I don't know which is scarier, the flying or this." Under her robe, she felt suddenly chilled. She hugged her arms to her ribs. "Everyone knows me as a party girl. Even my family. I love to have a good time; I love socializing. You've seen it firsthand."

He smiled. "Indeed."

"But I'm too much of a striver to be just a party girl. It's too frivolous a life, and I'm too goal-oriented. For as long as I can remember, I've wanted to craft original films and to be successful at it. Ever since we talked about bringing Hollywood-type entertainment to the *Vash,* I've known that'll be my life's work. It comes down to this, Ché. I'm ambitious, and so are you. On top of that, I'm creative, and that complicates it more. It's not unusual for me be totally distracted by a script, or to stay up all night developing an idea. Do you really, truly want a wife who has interests outside the nursery?"

Ilana saw his strong hands give a tiny quiver. It was

so brief that she wondered if she'd imagined it. Was the relentlessly composed Ché Vedla actually nervous? She didn't dare meet his eyes. It was bad enough that she was spilling her guts. She gulped down some more wine. A wave of dizziness passed quickly. "I adore children, Ché. When the time comes to have them, I'll be home with them. I'll be a mother to them in every way." She heard the sudden tenderness that had crept into her voice, and she smiled. "But to be able to devote myself that completely, in that phase of my life, I have to be ready. It's going to be a while before I'm ready . . . ready to nest. Maybe a long while, Ché. If you're serious about marrying me, you have to take a hard look at that fact."

"How long?" he asked.

"Several years, at least."

He nodded, absorbing what she told him.

"Are you willing to wait that long, Ché? Be honest. Your situation is different from most men. That's why your family is going through all this trouble to find you the right woman. I . . . I don't know if I am that woman."

She winced. It hurt to say that, more than she ever thought it would. It hurt even more to see Ché lower his brooding gaze to his hands.

Outside the billowing curtains, the waves crashed. The seagulls had long since stopped crying and had settled down for the night. A chorus line of strident crickets in the hydrangea bushes below the window had taken their place. Ilana listened to the sounds, inhaling the fragrances drifting into the suite, trying to pretend that Ché wasn't having a tough time trying to decide whether her value as a breeder could take second place to her importance as a companion and lover.

It was even tougher trying to pretend that she

271

wouldn't suffer a broken heart if he were to agree with her and admit that she wasn't right for him.

He startled her by getting up. In all his golden, bare-chested magnificence, he walked around the table to where she sat shivering in her plump white robe, wet hair, and bare feet.

The lean and noble prince knelt in front of her, took the hands she'd balled in her lap, and covered them with his. They felt warm, dry. Strong. "You are chilled," he murmured, rubbing her hands.

"I get cold when I'm nervous."

His expression softened. She thought he'd pull her into his arms, but something held him back. Maybe he sensed what she did, that if they started touching, embracing, kissing, the attraction smoldering between them would flare up all over again and this conversation would be over.

This conversation was one they needed to finish.

Ché rubbed his palm over her knuckles. "I believe the events of the past year have unfolded as they have for a reason. Your brother, and mine, and Princess Tee'ah—all their actions brought about events that led me to you. It never would have happened otherwise."

She laughed softly in agreement. "If any two people weren't supposed to meet, it was us."

"The heavens had a hand in it, Ilana."

Awash in sudden tingles, she kept her eyes on their clasped hands, his bronzed and strong, hers paler and more delicate. Two people from very different worlds, brought together, only to find out they were more alike than either would have dreamed. "I think so, too," she whispered.

"That is why I will not walk away from this—from us, Ilana. I will not turn my back on our future. I am willing to wait before having a family."

Her heart did a cartwheel, and her gaze jumped to his.

"Marriage, however, cannot be put off. If I wait to marry, I will have betrayed my people. I gave them my word I would do as they asked." His mouth thinned. "It seemed a small gesture at the time, because it was all so . . ."

"Inevitable?"

"Yes." He chuckled to himself.

"What's so funny?"

"At the time, I was not certain what qualities I wanted in a wife," he said, shaking his head. "All I knew was that she should not be anything like you. Wild . . . undisciplined . . . willful . . ."

"Nothing like me, huh?" Grinning, she pushed at him. "Thanks a lot."

He laughed, pulling her toward him. Their lips met playfully, tasting, nibbling. "Great Mother," he said against her parted lips. "I was such a fool. You are exactly what I want. What *I need*." His lips were soft, tugging on hers, his fingers tangling in her hair. "You make me laugh. You make me feel alive," he murmured, kissing her lightheartedly. "You bring out the rogue in me."

"The garden-cart rogue," she agreed against his mouth.

"The rogue, except for a few forays, was buried for many years."

"Not anymore."

"No," he said.

She lifted one hand to his jaw. His skin was hot; the stubble of his beard pricked the tender pads of her fingers. A breath passed, and then another, during which she was sure the kiss would continue to deepen. But it didn't. She ached for more, but she

273

knew he intended to finish this, and she couldn't blame him.

"Ilana." He moved her back so he could look at her. "When I am with you, I feel as if I can do anything. I can, and I will, if I know that you are mine." He reached up and framed her face with his hands, his eyes shining. "I feel it, Ilana. Our future. I can see it spread out before me, all the days to come."

His eyes took on a faraway look, as if he were truly channeling the future. His voice grew deeper, hushed. "I see greatness, for your people and mine. Another golden age will come upon us, and it will be our doing—our generation's. Me, you. Tee'ah and your brother. The other princes, the princesses, too. The galaxy is ours. Our actions now will ensure peace for generations to come."

When he stopped talking suddenly, the silence in the room swelled. Ilana didn't know what to say. Ché's impromptu, emotional speech had left her stunned. She worried about making a commitment. He worried about making history.

But maybe, just maybe, the two were intertwined . . .

In her mind's eye, she imagined Ché years from now striding down the grand halls of his palace, his capes swirling behind him. He'd be a powerful and respected political leader, not the disgruntled, aging king ground down by bitterness and years of sacrifice that he might have become had he not risked listening to the "rogue." His charisma would impress, intimidate, and inspire, a passion generated by an inner fire that would never burn out, because those who loved him fueled that fire.

Those who meant more to him than anything else.

In that one strange and wonderful and totally out-of-character moment, Ilana knew, beyond a doubt, that if she took the risk, took this once-in-a-lifetime chance, she'd come to love this prince, that theirs would be a lifelong devotion far different and vastly better than the instant, giddy gratification of infatuation and lust.

It took some doing to compose herself. The only way she could keep her eyes from tearing was to bite her lip. "I had the strangest daydream," she whispered shakily.

Ché met her statement with eerie aplomb. "It was a vision. I saw it in your eyes."

"You're *Vash*. You're used to these kinds of things. I'm not." Between Ché's speech, her daydream—vision, whatever—and the strange, zealot's glow lingering in his eyes, she felt faint.

"Do not fear it, Ilana. It means we are on the right path. I know it is sudden for you to make such a decision. You are not used to the idea of arranged marriages, and to a degree, that is what our joining would be. To the outside, it would appear to be the ideal solution to an embarrassing problem. Me, the spurned prince, marrying before the upstart Earth-dweller crown prince does. And not only that, taking his very sister as my bride, thus uniting the B'kahs and the Vedlas."

Ilana gaped at him. "Do you have any idea how scary you sound? You make us sound like pawns in some giant game of chess."

"We are!" He laughed so hard at her bemusement that she began to wonder how pervasive madness was in the Vedla family (Klark was a Vedla, after all) and what symptoms Ché might have shown all along that she'd missed.

"We will have fooled the entire Federation, Ilana!" He grabbed her hands. Her fingers throbbed in his grip. "They sought to manage the marriages, and the joke ended up being on them! You see, they will view our union as the ultimate solution to a terrible predicament, and we will have our love match." He lowered his voice. "Or, at least the beginning of what I am confident will grow into one."

If she let him go, she might never find another man with whom she was as compatible, whom she could trust like him, or respect as much. The pragmatic part of her told her to grab hold of the one guy she'd met that she felt she could actually make a life with. That she should go after him the way she'd gone after the other, more concrete goals and dreams in her life.

That same realistic part of her also said that she'd better damned well have an escape route ready, should the love story not have a fairy-tale ending.

She leaned forward. "And if the love isn't enough? What then? What if we get into this and find out it was a huge mistake? You can't get divorced in your culture."

The dent in Ché's cheek appeared, just as she thought it would. "We do have *asser'ak*. It is equivalent to an annulment, I believe, in your Catholic church."

Ilana was raised Catholic. She was familiar with annulment because her mother had sought one from her father sometime after marrying Rom. "I don't remember reading anything about this in the Treatise of Trade."

"It is there. In the passages relating to forms of exile."

"Oh." It gave her a good indication as to how the Ché's people viewed marriage breakups. Her chin came up a few notches. "Would you grant me *asser'ak*, an annulment, if I asked?"

His throat moved. "I would."

At his obvious pain, her stomach began to hurt. "What would be the consequences, for you if you ended your marriage?"

"My culture would see it as a failing on my part. As a husband, a mate—a protector, which is our ancient term—I would not have fulfilled my duty to you."

"You'd be disgraced, then."

"Well, yes," he replied, almost too matter-of-factly.

"Oh, Ché." Her voice grew husky. "You'd be willing to do that for me?"

His expression was mournfully frank. "I would pray it never came to that."

"Me, too," she whispered.

Ché stroked one knuckle over her cheek, making her shiver. "But if you asked to be set free, Ilana, I would let you go."

Unwilling to trust her emotions, she pressed her lips together and focused on the floor. All the men in her life had allowed her total control over the relationship, had watched her walk out of their lives when she'd decided it was time. But deep down she knew Ché would fight hard to keep her, as he was doing now. No man had been this way with her. Secretly, she'd always wished she'd find one that would be. "Okay," she whispered. "I accept your proposal." *Oh, my God, oh, my God!* But at his expression of abject confusion, she blushed. "You did propose, didn't you? I mean, I got to thinking that we belonged together, and that we had better do this before one of us changes our mind—"

Laughing, he swept her off the chair and into his arms, carrying her to the bed, where he sat at the edge with her balanced crosswise in his lap. "Yes, Ilana. That I did. I asked you to be my mate, my wife. Excuse my Vash manners. We draw up papers and sign them, you see. The arrangements are made when the future mates are but small children. This proposing, as you put it, is new to me."

Smiling, she wrapped her arms around his shoulders. "We have the guy get down on one knee. But you can wait until you buy an engagement ring." At his puzzlement, she informed him. "You know I'm not leaving my Earth traditions behind. This is going to be a mixed-culture marriage."

He bent his head to her neck and nuzzled the side of her throat. "As long as I can have my tock in the morning."

"And I can have my coffee."

She let her head fall back as Ché nibbled her ear. "Klark's going to love having me as a sister-in-law. Does your family employ a food taster? We'd better. I'll brush up on antidotes to common poisons—"

Ché nipped at her earlobe.

"Ouch!"

"Klark will commend me on my clever maneuvering in winning your hand."

She had her doubts about that. But Klark so passionately supported his brother, maybe he'd approve of her if he thought she'd be good for Ché. Then again, maybe not.

Her elation faded into looming reality. "You have to call them. Your family."

"Not tonight," he assured her with a sexy glint in his eye. "Tomorrow. I will have them send the closest starspeeder. Then I will fly to the Wheel. My father is there. I will speak to him first."

The Wheel was a majestic, five-thousand-year-old space station, home to the Great Council, the governing body of the Trade Federation. Kings, like Ché's father, traveled there periodically when the council was in session to keep abreast of politics. Or when they needed to arrange marriages for jilted sons, which the man was likely doing now.

"Once my father knows, we will discuss the details with my advisor and close council members."

"What about your mother and sisters?"

"Oh, yes." He grinned. "I can feel their wedding fever from here." Then his smiled faded. "In the meantime, we tell no one."

"Not even my mother? Or Rom? What about Ian?"

"Not until I am sure it is safe."

"Safe! I thought you said this marriage was the perfect solution. If it's so perfect, then why are we sneaking around?"

The little hollow in his jaw was back. "I am confident all will be in favor of our joining. But there are always those who cannot see beyond their own views."

"Like Klark?"

Ché turned somber as he played with a curling lock of her hair.

"Sheesh," she muttered when he didn't reply. "Does everything you *Vash* do have to be so complicated?"

He pressed his lips to the pulse on the side of her throat. "No, Ilana. Not everything."

"Mmm." She hunched her shoulders as his lips tasted their way to her temple and hairline. At the same time, his hot, dry hand found its way inside her robe, parting the fabric. Cool air hit her bare breasts. Her nipples tightened with the change in temperature and with anticipation instantly quenched when his wet mouth found one and his magical fingers the other. Toes curling in delight, Ilana arched her neck and bit back a sigh, twisting restless fingers into his thick, mink-soft hair.

Someone knocked on the door. Paused. Then

knocked again. Ché lifted his head, and they exchanged a dismayed glance. "Did you order anything else from room service?" she asked.

He shook his head. "They may have arrived to collect the trays, as we have been remiss in eating our meal."

"Very remiss," she murmured, trying to pull him back to her. "They'll come back."

The knocking became pounding. Ché sighed, setting her on the bed and wrapping a towel low around his hips. "I will have them return later."

Ilana clutched her robe closed and followed him into the living room area of the suite. Before she could warn him otherwise, Ché flung open the door without checking the peephole.

The bright light of a camera like Ilana's Canon blinded them momentarily. When her eyes adjusted, she saw a pert, familiar woman standing in the hallway, dressed sharply in a lemon yellow suit. The woman held a microphone to her ice-pink mouth. "This week our focus on the summer's hottest couples continues. Today we find our *formerly* reluctant Cinderella and her very yummy Prince Charming snug as bugs in the famed-for-secret-getaways Serenity Inn. Let's meet the B'kah heiress Ilana Hamilton and her very eligible *Vash* beau, Prince Ché." She winked at them. "Rose knows!"

Clutching a bath towel around his hips, Ché swung his disbelieving eyes to Ilana.

"She's Rose Brungard, the talk show host," Ilana hissed under her breath as resignation leaked out of every pore.

Everyone knows what Rose knows. Right. So much for keeping their relationship secret from the Vedlas.

Chapter Twenty

Muffin drove his car down the road fronting the building where Ilana Hamilton lived. Or used to live, he thought dismally. It was late on a weeknight, and no lights brightened her condo windows. He'd taken Copper out to dinner in Santa Monica on purpose, so he'd be able to see that Ché's ground car had returned before he went home to his apartment at the end of the night. But the couple still hadn't shown up. The lights were still off. "Blast," he mumbled, and turned off the music playing in the car to see if he could catch a broadcast of the news.

Copper protested. "Hey, I like that song."

"One moment." Muffin concentrated on the announcer's voice. No airplane crashes, thank the Great Mother. Then where were they? Ché had to fly in the morning. Ilana had to work. Or had they taken the night off, like Muffin had, turning his back on his charges when they may have needed him most?

"This is the third time we've driven past this building. You're starting to creep me out, John."

He winced every time she called him by that name.

"I'm beginning to think your old girlfriend lives here, and you want to see if she's home."

"So I can show off my new one." He showed his teeth in a grin.

Copper preened. Then she frowned, her eyes shooting sparks. "I knew it."

"Copper—I joked. I have no woman living here, there, or anywhere." That much was true. But the more time he spent with her, the less he wanted to lie to her about anything else. "But the woman I'm observing has not arrived home, and I am worried about her."

Her green eyes grew wide. "Are you a private investigator?"

He hesitated. "Yes."

"What did she do? Is she dealing drugs? Is she having an affair?"

"No! No drugs. An affair? If you mean a relationship with another's man, no." He wondered what Copper would think if she were to find out the heir to the galaxy had all but dropped a man in Ilana's lap, hoping he'd bounce into her bed. "She is a fine, upstanding young woman, the sister of . . . a good friend. But the man she is seeing, he worries me."

"Why? Is he abusive?"

"Blazes, no. But I don't trust his family."

"They don't approve of her."

He'd been so starved for someone to talk to, so hungry for a woman like Copper, that he gave in to the temptation to share what had been troubling him. To his chagrin and shock, his words tumbled out. "Whether they do or don't, they live too far away to interfere. But still I worry. I feel . . . uneasy. I should have watched her today. I should have done my job instead of . . ." He stopped himself.

"Instead of having dinner with me," Copper finished.

"And lunch, and the walk on the beach, and the bowling—"

"The bowling was fun," she said with a smile. Then she turned to look at him with those penetrating eyes of hers. "This is the couple you were watching at the airport, right?" She didn't wait for him to answer. "Are you a private investigator, really? Or are you snooping for the tabloids? I like a man with principles." Her voice softened. "And I really, really want you to have them, John. Because I'd really, really like to keep on seeing you. But I won't if you don't. When you're on your own, like I am, with no family, you tend to be picky." She lifted her chin. "I'd rather be alone than be with a guy I didn't respect."

Taken aback, Muffin gripped the steering wheel. He pulled over to the curb and stopped the car two blocks from Ilana's empty condo. "My name is Muffin."

"What?" She shook her head. "I don't understand."

None of the Earth-dwellers did, Muffin thought, but he felt he had half a chance with this one, with her own unusual name. And if he wanted half a chance of continuing to "see" Copper Kaminski, as she'd put it, he'd blasted well tell her as much of the truth as he could.

"My given name is Muffin. It is not John. John Black is an alias, one I use in my work, as an investigator for . . . a private and very wealthy man." There, that was close enough to the truth without risking his cover. "I thought you should know my real name."

"Muffin. Like blueberry muffin?"

He gave a silent sigh. "A sweet little breakfast cake,

yes. But on my home—where I am from—Muffin is a name of rugged masculinity. It is an old name, and comes from the word for a warrior's stamina."

"I bet you get hell for that name here."

He exchanged a glance of commiseration. "You may know a little of what that is like. You sounded surprised when I found your name such a lovely one."

Smiling, she nodded. "Black isn't your last name?"

That was a tougher question to answer, if he wanted her to believe he was from Earth. "Muffin of Thorme" was how one would introduce him. Everyone born on his homeworld Thorme had that surname, the entire population, few of whom ever left, unless recruited offworld, as Muffin was, to be someone's bodyguard. "Thorme," he said finally, figuring it would suffice.

"Muffin Thorme. Well, I think Muffin is adorable. I think you're adorable, too."

"Adorable!"

Her eyes twinkled. "Yeah. A big sweet man. That's what you are, on the inside. On the outside . . . well, no one in their right mind would mess with you."

"Except for copper-haired women named Trouble." He made a face. "No one has ever taken me down like that. What is your secret? I would like to know, so that it never happens again."

She lifted her hands in surrender, and he pretended to flinch. Giggling, she said, "I have no idea how I did it. And I don't know if I ever will. It just happened." Shyly she clasped her hands in her lap. "And I'm glad it did. We have the best 'how we met' story."

Muffin's hulking frame filled the small cab of the car. It didn't take much to move close enough to give Copper a kiss. He moved a fraction, waited a heartbeat or two to see if she'd run, but she stayed still, as if waiting to see what he'd do. And so he did: Closing his eyes, he moved his lips over hers, hovering there long enough to taste her sweetness before he moved back. His blood roared at that brief contact. But he made himself behave, content to brush his fingertip affectionately down her freckled nose and across her plump bottom lip. He felt her mouth quiver under the thick pad of his finger. But he crushed his hand into a fist before he demanded more than she wanted to give, more than he had the right to ask for this early in the courting game, and returned his big hands to the steering wheel. "We have to work in the morning," he said. "I had better get you home."

"What about the girl you're watching?"

"I think tonight I will let her enjoy the privacy that is her right." Why deny Ché and Ilana what he hadn't denied himself? Muffin smiled what he feared was a lovesick grin and pulled away from the curb.

Ilana took charge. If it were Ché's palace, he'd know what to do. But this was California, and her turf.

She grabbed her Canon off the counter in the kitchenette, swung it around and up to her eye, flicking on the power at the same time. Like a six-shooter facing down her nemesis in Dodge City, Ilana turned her full attention—and her camera—on Rose and her camerawoman. Years of practice made Ilana fast; she liked to think she'd never miss a shot. Quickly she checked the viewfinder, seeing Rose's startled expression on the other side. Good, plenty of battery life left, and enough time to shoot her way out of this mess.

"I'm no Cinderella," she told the talk show host as she panned around to the open door. "I may be Romlijhian B'kah's stepdaughter, but also I'm director of photography for SILF Filmworks. Our project with Hunter Holt has been received extremely well by the critics. Have you seen it?"

Rose's microphone wobbled. "I didn't know it had been released."

"It hasn't yet, but we've hosted several private screenings. Let's get you to one of those. Linda!" she shouted toward the bedroom, as if her assistant were in there, working away. "Put Rose Brungard on our VIP list for the next screening."

To Ilana's glee, Ché jumped into her hatching plan feet first. "I do not think Linda heard you, Ilana. She is on the phone with the studio." He turned to Rose and gave her one of his killer smiles. "*Back from the Brink* is a riveting work. Holt is magnificent, of course, but Miss Hamilton here, she is a creative genius."

Ilana tried not to laugh.

"You do not want to miss it, Miss . . . ?"

"Brungard," the woman supplied. "*Rose Knows*."

"That's the name of her show," Ilana explained to Ché, never letting Rose out of her viewfinder. "It's one of the top-rated personality news shows." Actually, she'd heard the show was struggling against heavy competition in its time slot, which would explain why Rose had gotten so aggressive in her pursuit of celebrities.

Ché spoke up before Rose did. "I am terribly sorry that I did not know sooner of your show, for in a few days I must return home, and will not have time to grant you an interview. Nor can I speak to you tonight, as we are behind schedule." He gestured apologetically to his state of undress. "As you can plainly see. Ilana, her partners, and I are so behind in our filming schedule that we often overlook modesty in the rush to finish on location. My apologies. I opened the door thinking you were the caterer. And you, it seems, were equally mistaken as to my presence in this room. Ilana and I, lovers? Heavens." He smirked at Ilana and then Rose, as if they all shared the world's biggest joke. Then, holding his towel around his hips, he nodded smoothly at Ilana and disappeared into the bedroom.

She almost cried with relief when the door closed behind him. His clothes were in there. His contacts, too, though it was obviously too late for disguises. More importantly, the phone was there. She was confident Ché was picking up the receiver now to call the front desk. The sooner someone came and showed Rose Brungard the door, the better.

Ilana kept filming. "As you might have understood from the prince, I'm doing a documentary on his visit to Hollywood, which, as he said, is almost over. He's making inquiries into the feasibility of mass distribution of Hollywood movies in the Federation. I find that so exciting." Ilana zoomed in for a close-up shot of Rose's face. "You're in the industry—what do you think? Is the Federation ready for Hollywood?"

Rose dropped her arm to her side. To Ilana's surprise and then filmmaker's delight, the woman launched into a long and passionate answer to Ilana's question. After a moment or two, in the corner of her eye Ilana saw the other camera turn off. Rose seemed to have made the transition from reporter to interviewee with little problem. And she had a lot to offer, with her thirty-something years in the business.

Miraculously, by the time someone from Serenity Inn's staff trotted down the hallway to get rid of Rose, Ilana had her proof: When it came to sending Earth's stars to the stars, most people on Earth would get as excited about it as she was.

"Watch out, galaxy, here comes Hollywood," Rose said with a thumbs-up as she waved goodbye.

Ilana lowered her camera and grinned. She'd even stopped shaking. Well, almost. She was still shaking a little, only now it was more from excitement than from fear that the news of her relationship with Ché would break wide open before they could do damage control and tell their families first.

She'd lied about making a documentary about SILF's and Ché's joint venture into the galactic market—lied in a desperate, knee-jerk reaction to protect her privacy, and Ché's. But if her gut was the indicator it usually was, that little fib had just turned into the hot new project she'd been looking for.

Prince Vedla, Hollywood's unlikely champion and patron-of-the-arts.

She'd been filming Ché in his various Earth adventures all along. As well as others' reactions to him, including those of her SILF partners. She had a wealth of fantastic footage already, more than enough for the beginnings of a good documentary. Now all she needed was the rest: Ché's navigating the holy halls of the Great Council to win them the support they needed to give the film industry its toehold in a future that no one on Earth dreamed of a decade ago.

Breathless, she put the Canon back on the counter and hurried into the bedroom to find Ché. He sat on the bed, his bare back to her, the towel barely clinging to hips. "I got rid of her, Ché. She believed me. She thinks we're doing a documentary feature on you—"

Ché waved her into silence. She stopped mid-breath and mid-step. He held his comm in his hand as he spoke in Basic, too rapidly for her to understand it all.

Her heart sank. His family. He'd said he wouldn't contact them tonight. But after seeing Rose, he probably felt he had to.

288

The clock was ticking, wasn't it? With a wife picked out and ready to go, and threat of news of their relationship beating Ché home, what choice did he have?

She hugged her bathrobe around her and sat lightly on the edge of the bed. Ché closed the comm. "That was my advisor."

"What did he say? How did he sound?"

"Quite surprised." He appeared to be puzzling something out. "I wished I could have given him the reason for my sudden change of heart. He has been with me since I was a boy. He deserves to know."

"I almost wish someone did," she admitted. "Then this engagement might feel real."

Ché walked around the bed and sat next to her. "It is real," he vowed, holding her close long enough to assure her that his feelings for her went beyond sexual. A man and a woman could tell each other anything they wanted, but unspoken communication like this said more about a relationship, about feelings, than words could.

After the cuddling had steadied them both, they moved apart. "You're worried about something," she accused. It amazed her how easily she could read his expressions now. "Klark?"

She saw his jaw stiffen. "Hoe did say a few things about my brother that disturbed me."

Her heart sped up. "Like what?"

"That Klark is acting agitated, that he is openly obsessed with the possibility of a relationship developing between us, and that he broods about it constantly. Hoe said nothing more, probably because he doesn't want to upset me, and seemed to be sorry he had said anything at all. Hoe overprotects me, he does. As for Klark, he has always intimidated Hoe, and I think rather enjoys it." Ché's mouth twisted. "It follows that I am used to Hoe exaggerating reports of my brother's behavior. In other words, I am not worried, and I don't want you to be, either, Ilana. Even if what Hoe says is true, and Klark wishes me to stay away from you, what more can he do about it but grumble and gnash his teeth as a prisoner in the palace?"

What more could he do? A lot. She kept that opinion to herself only because she felt caught between her feelings for Ché and the sociopath brother he loved. But the thought of Klark being "obsessed," even if it was an exaggeration, made her skin crawl. The last time Klark got fanatical about anyone—her brother—he'd almost killed him. If she were a brain surgeon instead of a filmmaker, she'd give Klark Vedla a preemptive lobotomy, free of charge. "How long before you have to leave?"

"My advisor tells me a starspeeder will arrive at Los Angeles Intergalactic in approximately four Earth days. That includes the usual half-day to clear ESPAC customs."

"Wow. That's fast."

"There were several Vedla craft, in fact, outside the solar system. Luck was on our side."

Or was it bad luck? A dreadful second sense nagged at her, a sick feeling that once Ché arrived within the sphere of influence of his family, he'd come to his senses and marry the woman they'd picked for him. A woman who didn't dream of making movies before she bred heirs.

A tap on the tip of her nose with a scolding finger startled her. "That is far too somber an expression for what I intend to do to you in this bed," he said in that sexy voice she felt right down to her toes.

She tried to make light of the cold, sick feeling of helplessness in the pit of her stomach. "Oh, I was just thinking how much I don't want to go back to dating the Coles of the world and storing their dog bowls in my kitchen."

"We will not be apart for long."

"No. Take me with you." She pressed her fingertips to his mouth before he could argue. "Hear me out. I have the perfect plan."

His mouth turned down with that familiar here-we-go-again exasperation.

"Come on, Ché. You know I'm not the waiting type. It'd drive me crazy, sitting here for who knows how long, waiting to see what your family decides."

"*I* have decided," he mumbled past her fingers.

"I know. But if our marriage is really the perfect union, then why didn't your father or anyone else in the Vedla family figure it out a long time ago, hmm? I think they're going to try to change your mind."

He tried to talk, but she wouldn't let him.

"Oh, you'll protest at first," she went on. "You'll try to explain what you have to me already, how we'll unite the B'kahs and the Vedlas, beat Ian to the altar, blah, blah, blah. But if they really, truly protest your choice in wives, what then? Are you going to look your father in the eye and tell him you're choosing an Arizona-born Air Force brat over eleven thousand years of tradition?" Ché mumbled something unintelligible past her fingers. "Maybe you would. But I won't let you. I won't cause that kind of rift in your family. That's why I'm coming. Not to interfere, but to be nearby. If it comes down to 'Hasta la vista, baby, sorry it didn't work out,' you're damn well going to say it in person."

While Ché puzzled over her move reference, she grumbled, "Now, would you please hush up a minute so I can finish telling you about my plan?"

Amusement glinted in his eyes. She heard a weary sigh of resignation rumble in his chest.

"Rose Brungard gave us the perfect excuse to travel together. I'm making a feature documentary on Hollywood's efforts to woo the Vash Federation, right? I'm a frontier filmmaker sympathetic to the *Vash*, and you, Ché, are known for your progressive thinking. Naturally, you invited me to go along with you to the Wheel—in a gesture of goodwill and out of your desire to further unite the frontier with central, settled space."

She felt the muscles tugging at his mouth change from irritation to surprise. All those conversations with Ian had paid off, she thought. "I'll be going as an official guest of the Vedlas. Not a fiancée, not a threat, but a filmmaker. That part's real, Ché. I really do intend to chronicle the film industry's efforts to reach the Federation audience, two different cultures, clashing and also connecting." She traced the outline of his lips. "Like us, babe."

Many emotions crossed his face—exasperation, admiration, tenderness, and something deeper, something that made her heart give a little hitch. He grasped her hand and lowered it. "I am beginning to think that in your past, you must have had a Vedla ancestor."

She smiled. "I can scheme with the best of you, can't I?"

"Not only does your plan allow me to keep you close by, it ensures against family embarrassment. Should Rose Brungard release any information to the media about seeing us here, we will have a ready excuse. Will you be able to get prepared in the time we have left?"

"I'll make it happen. Tomorrow I'll meet with everyone at SILF and work out the production schedule.

Linda will come with me, if she can go. And I'll need to bring extra equipment, too. . . . Will there be room in the speeder?" Her stomach wobbled. "I don't want to overload the thing."

"Speeders have room for a goodly number of passengers and cargo, depending on the model, although they are much smaller than the type of craft in which you traveled to your mother's wedding."

"Oh, good." She let out a breath. "Size matters. In this case, the smaller the better. I hate flying in huge ships and airliners. It's like lying in bed in a big house all by yourself at night—you're trying not to think too hard about what's lurking in the shadows *waaay* downstairs and out of sight."

He tucked a curl behind her ear. "You think too much, Ilana."

"I know. Distract me."

Ché's mouth slowly curved in a very male, totally self-assured smile. His gaze dipped to the cleavage revealed by her loosely tied robe, and then returned to her eyes. His voice deepened. "Come here," he said.

She scooted closer. Cupping the back of her head, he pulled her to him in a heated kiss. One warm, dry hand slid up her leg and under the terrycloth fabric covering her thigh. Almost immediately, her body was ready for him.

But even as Ché lowered her to the silken sheets, her thoughts returned to the Vedla ships lurking so opportunely at the perimeter of Earth space. Safeguarding their prized prince from afar? Probably. But it made for a convenient on-call taxi service, and their best chance at getting to the Wheel quickly enough to derail Ché's marriage to the handpicked princess. For the first time, Ilana found herself blessing, not cursing, the almost frightening efficiency of Ché Vedla's family.

Klark reached the end of the balcony and turned on his heel, beginning the long walk back to the opposite side.

Unfortunately, his restlessness would see no release in a woman's body tonight. By the terms of his sentence, he could not partake of the services of the pleasure servers while in custody. So his unrelenting impatience kept him pacing long after the third moon had risen.

Ché was on his way at last. At first, Klark expected he'd remain on Earth until the last possible moment, but Ché had suddenly reversed that decision. Why, though? Was he not enamored of the Earth princess? Had he not fallen for her charms? What was going through his brother's mind? The questions consumed Klark, and he had summoned Hoe to discuss them. While he waited for the advisor to arrive, he paced.

By coming home, was Ché giving in to the vow he'd made regarding his upcoming nuptials? Or did he have something else up his sleeve? What if he came home and did not listen to Klark's advice?

Klark drained the glass of ale he carried and threw it over the edge of the balcony. The invisible shield bowed outward like a soap bubble, then burst in a sparkle of lavender, allowing the heavy drinking glass the freedom to sail downward. It was night, and the beach was too far below for Klark to hear the glass shatter. The shield repaired itself instantly. Almost as fast, three guards burst into the chamber. "Lord Klark!"

Klark leaned lazily against the railing, observing them through slitted eyes. "I dropped a glass, gentlemen. That is all."

"Yes, my lord."

He could tell by their troubled expressions that they thought it was he who had taken the suicide plunge over the edge.

Fools, he thought as they retreated from his view. Why did they always mistake his ambition for madness? He was not ready to end his life in any form or fashion. Especially when he had an older brother whose activities so plainly begged for his input.

When Hoe arrived at last, Klark somehow refrained from rushing to the door. He detested being isolated from the goings-on of the council, having to rely on Hoe for every morsel of news. In the past, Ché had kept him informed, but his holiday had left Klark dangling. "When will he arrive?"

"Lord Ché is traveling directly to the Wheel to see your father." Hoe took a breath. "He is bringing Princess Ilana with him."

The force of the news hit Klark like the incoming tide. But he kept his face carefully blank, a skill the Vedla men had inherited from their resilient ancestors. He took a seat at the table of petrified amber. "Go on."

"Sir, it seems the princess is traveling with another woman—someone from her staff, I believe, who of course will need Federation approval to disembark at the Wheel. In such cases, a background check is required, and these things take time. That is the reason I'm tardy in meeting with you tonight, sir. Lord Ché asked me to see where the woman's request is in the system, and then to speed it along, if I could."

"Do it. I don't want an unplanned-for outsider complicating matters. Or, better yet, Hoe, make alternate travel arrangements for the staffer."

"I have."

"Ah. Good." The man, irritating as he was, was a master of efficiency.

"The princess and her staffer will travel separately. I have just now informed the prince. Let us sing praises to the heavens that Lord Ché agreed, for he didn't want the princess to travel on her own." Hoe was aglow with self-congratulation. "It took some doing, but he saw the necessity after I reiterated the importance of his swift return."

"What did you tell the poor man—that the Lesok princess was already being fitted for her ceremonial gown?"

Hoe's smile curved smugly. "More or less."

Klark shook his head. At times like these, he was glad he wasn't the Vedla heir. As second-born son, he'd never have to marry if he didn't care to.

"Ah, but this is all falling into place so well. Bringing Ché home separately from the princess will work out for the best. It will give me the chance to deal with him outside the princess's influence. I often wondered whether the Great Mother had abandoned me," he admitted in a rare air of generosity toward the advisor. "Particularly after the Hamilton fiasco in the frontier and its aftermath. But this—*this* proves She has not. Our quarry has all but jumped into our hands. I fretted for nothing. Now everything will appear to have happened naturally."

"Or rather, accidentally," Hoe added with a conspiratorial smile.

"Accidentally?" Klark raised his brows. "I suppose that is one way of putting it," he agreed lightly.

"But what are semantics when the results are the same?"

He wanted to believe Hoe felt as he did. But the man was speaking in riddles and half-finished thoughts as if he hoped Klark would finish them. But

Klark would not fall into that trap. "You have given this much thought, Hoe—that much is obvious." Klark waved at the empty chair across from him. "Tell me what that resourceful little mind of yours has conjured up."

Bright with excitement, Hoe took a seat across from him at the table of petrified tree sap. As the man unveiled the arrangements he had made, Klark held his tongue—at first, out of the belief drilled into him by his father that the best tacticians did not discount input from their subordinates, and then out of sheer awe.

He had seriously underestimated Hoe.

Long after the advisor had left him alone, Klark remained sitting at the table with its fossilized menagerie. With their mouths pulled back in grins of rigor mortis, the creatures imprisoned within the amber table appeared to smirk at Klark's glaring miscalculation.

Hoe's tactics went far beyond anything Klark had considered, even in his darkest, most inspired moments. Who would have thought that this cherubic and efficient counselor to a future king would possess such a gloriously cruel mind, and the capacity to devise such macabre ideas?

No matter. With Hoe's plan under way, Klark was going to tweak it just enough to put control back into his hands, and he would do it by making sure he got to the princess before Hoe did.

He and Hoe had agreed that victory or defeat hinged on having only the two of them being involved in this game of political Bajha. The Vedlas had suffered much humiliation recently, and Klark would give his life to repair his family's reputation. That was why no others must know of the plan, even if they would agree with it, which Klark suspected they would not. But no matter how this coldheartedly brilliant game played out, someone would have to die.

Chapter Twenty-one

Mission accomplished, Muffin thought as he observed Ilana Hamilton and Prince Ché from his parked car across the street.

Ché and Ilana walked up the stairs to her home, arm in arm, as if they no longer cared about paparazzi. On the landing by her front door, unaware that he was being watched, the once-reserved prince drew Ian's sister close for a kiss before the pair disappeared inside for what Muffin speculated would be more of the same. It had been this way ever since they'd returned from their night away.

Starting up his ground car, Muffin looked for an opening in traffic. If he stayed much longer, Copper would wonder where he was, and he didn't want to be late for their dinner out.

As he drove into the road, one thought clung like a thorn-toed hissock: As soon as Muffin reported that Ilana and Ché were most definitely a couple, Ian Hamilton would likely call him back to Sienna. But maybe he'd wait a little longer before relaying his news. He had a few loose ends to wrap up first, namely those tied to a certain redhead known as "Trouble."

In the hour before the Eireyan sun peeked over the endless sea, droplets of bright crimson spattered into a sink the color of midnight.

Sweat broke out on Klark's brow as he dug a small blade into his flesh. Pain blossomed from the cut, raw and white-hot. Only the discipline forged by Bajha kept him from making a sound. That, and the knowledge that what he was about to do would save his family from shame.

He had to take charge. He couldn't and wouldn't let a mere counselor take the reins of something so critical to the future. Klark and not Hoe would act as the angel of death.

A red haze of pain blurred his vision as the blade hunted. Then he heard and felt a faint metallic click, muffled by blood and sinew. He didn't need to see his reflection in the mirror to know that he'd located his treasure.

With steady fingers, he reached into the incision he'd made near his skull, behind his right ear. Scooping out the tiny locator device implanted there when his imprisonment had commenced, he let out the ragged breath he'd been holding.

The locator dropped into the sink with a drizzle of blood. Klark let the tiny computer sit there as he tended to his wound, sterilizing the cut, cauterizing it, and then hiding what he had done with a bandage. The sharp, throbbing pain was distracting, yes, but he could afford no more than the topical anesthetic he'd applied. Pain pills would blunt his ability to think, and everything he'd ever desired hinged on his mind being razor-sharp.

He cleaned himself and the work area, then wrapped the locator in a swatch of cloth, brought it to his bed, and placed it under the head cushions. "Sleep well, Prince Klark." Then, dressed humbly in the manner of a palace servant, he slipped past the guards and off to freedom.

He and Ché had suffered much scolding for their sins of hijacking garden carts when they were boys. But from those innocent antics, Klark had learned invaluable skills. Tonight, and in the days to come, he would finally put them to the test. This time he would not fail.

With his long legs bent at the knee, Ché sank deep into Ilana's bathtub, his eyes closed in pleasure. Droplets glistened on his shoulders and chest. A water buff, he needed at least one bath a day, even if he showered, which never seemed to satisfy him the way it did her.

Hot mist carried the scents of the bath oils she'd poured in for him. Dressed in a bra and thong, she leaned toward the bathroom mirror to apply a couple of coats of mascara. Waterproof mascara. When Ché launched into space in a few hours, her eyes weren't going to stay dry.

All over again, the pressure of tears built behind her eyes and made her throat close. The wand pinched between her fingers shook. "Bite me," she muttered under her breath, grabbing a tissue to clean the smudge she'd made. She couldn't start crying, not yet.

Ché opened an eye. "Bite me?" he queried.

"It's an expression. Slang for being pissed, which is lingo for being scared, mad, sad, and frustrated."

She shoved the wand into the tube of mascara. "But," she said with a sigh, "I'll get over it."

Turning, she intended to exchange the bathroom for the quiet solitude of her bedroom, at least until she could get a better grip on her emotions. But there was a tremendous sloshing from the tub. Ché grabbed her wrist and pulled.

She shrieked. "Ché!" She landed on her butt in the bath with a splash, her legs splayed awkwardly. Ché pulled her backward until her shoulder blades impacted solidly with his chest. His arms came around her, his hard thighs corralling her hips. Water spilled onto the bathroom floor. "What are you doing!"

"When I first arrived here, you called me a beast." He nipped her on the side of the neck. "I would not want you to think I had changed."

At the side of her throat, his mouth was warm and wet, his beard prickling. She sighed and tipped her head back, closing her eyes as his hands smoothed over her stomach and around her ribcage, and up to where they slipped under her bra to caress her slippery breasts. "Mmm," she said and arched her back. "You haven't changed. You're still the same arrogant, spoiled, incredibly sexy charmer as when you got here."

"And you are just as wild, just as willful as when I first saw you," he said low in her ear.

"Then what happened?" she whispered. "How the hell did we fall in love?"

Ché went still. Ilana blushed as she realized what she'd said. He shifted her as she turned her head to look at him. His voice was quiet. Calm. "*Do* you love me, Ilana?"

Her chest felt suddenly tight. "I'm getting pretty darned close," she whispered.

He touched his fingertips to her face, as if in wonder. His eyes were more midnight than gold. She held her breath.

Running his hands over her face, he kissed her. And then again, groaning softly. Breathless, she turned, angling her head to deepen the kiss. His mouth tasted salty in contrast to the sweet-scented bathwater that wet his face. His tongue stroked hers. Desire scorched through her, and she slid her arms over his shoulders as the kiss went on and on.

What if this was their last time? She squeezed her eyes shut. Heartache and desire twisted sharply together until she couldn't separate them. The embrace intensified, and she wondered if Ché knew what she was thinking.

She came up on her knees, tugging off her panties. Blinded by tears, she reached desperately for Ché, straddling him. His rigid sex slid through her soft folds. Quivering, she took him in fully, welcoming the thrust that plunged deep inside her.

Ilana let out a low, guttural cry of pleasure. Ché grasped her hips, his fingers sinking deep into the pliant skin there as he moved inside her, rubbing her most sensitive point against him with each upward stroke.

Tightening her arms around his neck, she held him close as her oiled body moved slickly against his. The bathtub was small; there wasn't a lot of room to move. Knees banged, elbows skidded off the tub walls. But cramped quarters weren't the only reason they stayed pressed close together.

As if by mutual consent, they couldn't bear even an inch of physical separation. They gripped each other. Their mouths never parted, though she rode him hard, sloshing water over the edge and onto the floor. It was fierce, their coupling. Intense. A breathless kind of lovemaking. She had never felt anything like it, this storm of sensations: the feverishness of the emotional bond she felt with Ché, coupled with an almost overwhelming physical demand for satiation that shattered the last shreds of control.

The pressure deep inside her built. Her head tipped back, and she couldn't keep from crying out. But Ché brought her back to him, crushed her hard to his chest, his mouth searching for hers, feverishly, even as he groaned, his entire body taut as he fought against his own release.

They seemed to hover there forever, at the peak of pleasure. She wasn't sure if either of them breathed.

Then, his muscles going rigid, Ché shoved into her, deep and hard, his body shuddering. She wasn't sure who came before the other, or if it was at the same time. Ilana's inner muscles clamped down, pulsing with each contraction. She felt it in her womb. She felt it clear to her breasts and down to her curled toes, a physical and emotional upheaval that shook her to the core and plunged them both into stunned exhaustion.

By the time she became aware of her surroundings again, the bathwater was noticeably cooler. Ilana lifted her hips and turned, sagging weakly against Ché's chest. "Wow."

He chuckled deeply. Sated, affectionate, they kissed, smiling as they did so, tender, after-the-loving kisses. He stroked her hair, her face, and she smoothed her hands over his jaw, his strong neck, the back of his head.

Only the knowledge that they had to get to the airport sometime that afternoon ruined the mood. "God, Ché. You seem so relaxed, like you're not nervous about the flight at all."

"I am not."

"I'd give anything to be that calm when I leave with

Linda." And she'd give anything to have Ché traveling with her, but she left that part out. It wouldn't take much to convince him to remain behind until they could leave together. But his family was champing at the bit to get him home, and she didn't want to delay him, though she prayed Ché's marriage wasn't as imminent as Hoe made him believe.

But, if irritating, the advisor's position was understandable. He was under tremendous pressure to get Ché home, while dealing with the volatile Klark. "At least I'll have Linda with me—if she ever gets her clearance. Damn bureaucracy. I don't know who's to blame, yours or mine."

Ché pressed his mouth to her wet and tangled hair. Then, with his hand, he pushed aside her damp curls and took her earlobe in his teeth. "Ours," he reminded her with a playful tug.

She snorted. "Fine. Ours. I'll blame both governments for losing Linda's passport."

"Hoe said he would track down who made the error."

"No offense, but didn't it seem to you that things got even more bogged down after he got involved? I think we should leave it up to Ian, but I sure wish I knew who to throttle for screwing this up. It's the only reason we can't travel together."

"Do as I suggested—sit near the pilot when you are nervous, close enough to see everything he will see. It will give you the same sense of control as when we flew together." Ché took her arms by the wrists, raising her hands out of the water. "The flight controls in a starspeeder are somewhat different from our Cessna."

"I figured that." She laughed, but quieted as he maneuvered her hands, aware that he'd become very serious about familiarizing her with the steering of a starcraft. She remembered he'd told her that he empowered himself with knowledge. "The more skills you have," she whispered, paraphrasing him, "the less likely you are to find yourself helpless in any situation, right?"

His fingers clenched around her wrists. *Yes*, the movement told her, and she felt a rush of gratitude at his desire to ensure that she didn't panic when she got on that speeder with Linda.

"There is a stick, not a yoke," he went on. "And the onboard computer controls much of what we did today in the Cessna . . ."

The flying lesson went on for a long while, long enough for her to replace the initial butterflies in her stomach with genuine interest. Then, from her bedroom, she could hear her comm box chiming, the one connected directly to her family on Sienna. She splashed upright. "That's Ian."

They exchanged a questioning glance. Without her having to ask, he said quietly, "I know you feel quite alone in this. But I ask that you refrain from telling your brother about our plans to marry until I speak to my father. I have played this game of political Bajha all my life. Trust me when I say it is for the best that we take one step at a time. In case there are any complications."

"Like, when your dad says I'm the wrong girl."

"He will not."

"Okay. Sure."

Ché's mouth flattened. "Ilana. Give me some credit for knowing my family."

"What about Klark? Do you know him?" she challenged. "I know my father's true colors—I think we both do. But I wonder sometimes if you really know your brother. I have this bad feeling—"

The comm chimed again. Ilana hesitated before

leaving the bathroom. Ché had fallen into his brooding again, and she watched helplessly. Klark was going to be an issue in their marriage—that was a fact. Marrying Ché would bind her to Klark in a lopsided triangle of feelings. She'd love Ché, he'd love both her and his brother, and Klark would love Ché. That was where the breakdown occurred. She had a tough time imagining any feelings besides resentment between herself and Klark. Her upbringing and her faith told her that she should forgive Klark. But the possibility of forgiving the man whose fanaticism remained a real threat to her family seemed beyond her at the moment. There was enough other crap to deal with, and she pushed the issue to the back of her mind, knowing they'd have to address it once they were reunited at the Wheel.

"I'll give your regards to Ian," she said, wrapping her robe over her drenched underwear.

At that, a strange sort of masculine admiration replaced the gloom in Ché's eyes. He lifted his arms, linking his fingers behind his head. Water dripped from his triceps and ran down his slick, bronzed chest. "You and I talk of Klark and his schemes, but your brother's are even more admirable."

She stopped in the doorway, scrubbing a towel over her hair. "Huh?"

"Ever since you admitted to your role in distracting me from my wedding plans, I have been suspicious of the man."

"It was Ian's idea, the bet we made."

"He wanted this all along—us, together. Everything points to it. His not announcing my arrival, so that I would surprise you. His goading you into a wager, where you would tempt me with your female friends, knowing I never would take the bait. He knew from the start I wanted you, I think. And he has done every-

307

thing in his power to make it happen. He knew that we suited."

Ilana's voice gentled. "Before we knew it ourselves."

"Or wanted to admit it." Ché's voice was equally tender. It made her want to believe that love could overcome the monumental obstacles they faced.

The chime sounded again. She left Ché soaking in the tub. In her bedroom, she opened the comm. A tiny projection of Ian beamed to an invisible midpoint between the unit and where she stood. She knew he saw a similar projection of her, on a planet light-years away. Every time she pondered the eons and eons-old technology that made the communication possible, her brain froze. It was easier on the mind if she thought of lag-free comm as simply another modern miracle, like steaming-hot showers, microwaves, and Advil.

With her suspicions and Ché's fresh in her mind, she greeted Ian with a sassy smile. "I'd say good morning, Ian, but it must be the middle of the night there."

In fact, Ian did look tired. He had an enormous responsibility in his role as crown prince. Coupled with his upcoming wedding and her pestering him like this, no wonder he looked as if he could use eighteen straight hours of sleep. That, and a cold bottle of beer. "It'll be morning in five hours, so I guess that's close enough." His brown hair looked finger-combed, giving him that self-effacing, boyish charm that had always snared him women. And now that he was so buff from working out and playing Bajha, the contrast would make him even more irresistible, she thought with sisterly pride. But he had eyes only for his sweetie-pie of a fiancée, Tee'ah, and she was glad for that.

"I got your message. Congratulations on the new project, Ilana. Mom, Rom, Tee'ah—we're all excited about it."

"Yeah, well . . . thanks. So am I." She shrugged. "I bet none of you expected I'd turn out to be such a good ambassador."

"An ambassador of culture. I'll have to see about creating a position. Ilana Hamilton, Minister of Federation and Hollywood Affairs."

Normally, she'd give him hell over such a presumption, that she'd actually involve herself in politics, but if she were going to be living on Eireya and commuting to Earth, an official Trade Federation title might make her having a career more palatable to the traditionalist Vedlas. And it might give her more power to wield in her campaign to bring movies to the galactic masses.

"And Ché is willing to cooperate?" Ian asked pleasantly.

"Very much so." She tried to keep a straight face as she changed the subject. Gah, she wished she could tell him. Her secret was tearing her up. "About Linda's clearance . . ." She lowered her voice so Ché wouldn't hear. "The Vedlas' staff mucked it up. I'm particularly pissed at Ché's advisor. Now Linda and I have to travel separately."

"I got Linda an expedited diplomatic passport," Ian said. "She's all set. It'll be available for download at the embassy on Friday. The error did come from the Vedlas' end. Her passport information wasn't lost, Ilana. It was deleted from the galactic database."

Ilana's throat felt suddenly dry. She imagined Klark typing away at a remote computer no one knew he had, using it to hack into the galactic database and cause chaos with her plans. "Deleted? Entirely? How did that happen?"

"I'm looking into it."

She sensed grimness in Ian's tone. But she swallowed, nodding. "They did much better arranging the transportation. Both speeders are already here, at LA Galactic. Ché's going to inspect them both before he leaves. Linda and I will go on the other as soon as we get her passport. I'll call you from the Wheel." She let out a breath. "And don't be too hard on Ché's advisor. He might be bureaucratically challenged, but he helped us out, getting those speeders here so fast." She considered revealing her suspicions about Klark, but decided to keep her paranoia to herself. Klark was locked up. There was nowhere for him to go. And even if he did leave, by the time he got to Earth, she'd be gone, and by the time he reached the Wheel, she'd already be there, under Ché's protection.

Instead, she used the remaining minutes of the call to tease her brother. "By the way, you haven't said a thing about me losing that bet we made."

"He hasn't married yet. We'll settle the wager when he does." Ian acted almost smug. It was nothing she could put her finger on, just a twin's instinct.

That was when she knew Ché was right. It was what she'd suspected all along. Ian wanted this, wanted them together, wanted to give the interest that was there from the day they first met the chance to grow into something more. If only Ché's brother Klark felt the same way. But then she'd already have her fairy-tale ending when her gut told her that she was still far from the end of the book.

Ché hired a private anti-terrorist security firm to scour both starspeeders from top to bottom. While he questioned the starpilots—both skilled, reliable men he had seen before—the security team crawled through every crevice onboard the speeders. They even tore into several sealed containers of food and water. When he was sure both the pilots and the ships were worthy of transporting his wife-to-be, he returned to Ilana, who was waiting patiently and none too happily on the tarmac. "Which one would you like?"

Her eyes lit up. "I get to pick?"

"I will always give you a choice."

Her eyes became a smokier blue, the way they looked when something he said particularly touched her. But he meant it as truth, not as a frivolous lover's comment. As long as the circumstances were normal, and her safety was not at risk, he would never try to control her. For him the joy of their relationship was its unpredictable nature, and the mental challenge her spirit presented him. If he'd wanted a meek and compliant wife, he'd have done as his family asked.

Ilana slid an arm around his waist. "I'll take the one named Patience, if that's how it translates."

"It does."

"Good. I'll need it. And you've got Arrogance of Eireya." She squeezed him. "How could I in good faith take that from you?"

He laughed. "It translates to *Pride* of Eireya, not arrogance."

"If you say they're distinct and separate qualities, I guess I will, too," she teased.

Ché pulled her hard against him. Outside the gleaming silver speeders, the starpilots waited at attention, discreetly off to the side, allowing Ché his private goodbye. He brought his hands to her face, framing it. Shaking his head, he held her gaze. "Somehow I have fallen hopelessly and irreparably in love with you."

She made a small sound of surprise, and her blue

311

eyes turned the color of the mist-strewn sky above. "Me, too."

He dragged her into another fierce hug. No matter the ups and downs of their relationship, he thought, he would always know where he stood with her. No guessing. He did not like to guess.

Ilana cleared her throat, as if struggling against powerful emotion. She spoke against his chest. "Go," she whispered. "Do what you have to do. I'll be there, at the Wheel, waiting."

"I thought you were 'not the waiting type,' " he said with gentle humor.

"I'm not." She lifted her head. Her eyes sparkled with love and tears. "You got a one-time good deal. Don't blow it."

"Slang," he complained, stroking his thumbs over her cheeks. As their smiles faded, their gazes held. He willed her the strength to do what he knew was difficult for her: waiting, believing, *trusting* that he would follow through on his promises.

Once more he drew her close, and she hugged him back with all her might, laying her head against his shoulder. Whispering to her, he circled his hand on her back. "Only you can give up hope. No one can take it from you, if you do not let go. It is what my ancestors learned when all seemed lost. Through the darkest times, they never lost their faith."

He could feel her trembling, this strong woman, and that endeared her to him even more. He kissed her, drawing away slowly.

Tears glinted in her eyes as she dragged her fingertips along his cheek. The caress raised tiny bumps on his skin. "I'll keep the faith, Ché. And you—be the diplomat you were born to be, and make the entire Federation bow to your will."

His fingers were slow in leaving hers, dragging over

her warm palm as he stepped away. "They may have taken my title of crown prince, but they will not take the woman I love."

He turned away, walking slowly at first, expressing his reluctance at leaving her behind. But as he commenced the climb up the boarding ramp, his strides lengthened. Bow to his will the Federation would. Devotion and determination were what made a man a *Vash Nadah*, and Ché, Prince of the Vedlas, was *Vash Nadah* to the very core.

Klark sat close behind the starpilot on the sea-raptor class starfighter he'd commandeered, a surprisingly easy feat. The Vedla hangars were guarded lightly. After all, who would dare steal from a Vedla?

Klark chuckled. Leaning forward, he spoke quietly into the young man's ear. "Keep your hands on the steering yoke, and do not remove them."

The blade he pressed into the pilot's throat rode the bob of a swallow. "Yes, my lord."

Klark didn't care to abuse a loyal Vedla soldier in such a way, but even his hostage starpilot would understand why he'd had to do it soon enough. Now, with the blade at the starpilot's neck and the ion pistol he'd wrested from the startled man at the ready, Klark made certain he'd be light-years away by the time someone entered his quarters and discovered that he was gone.

The alert had not yet gone out about his escape—or if it had, it was being handled as a private, internal crisis. He would hear the transmissions when and if a Federation-wide search commenced. But no matter how the Vedlas chose to handle his escape, Klark was on his way. His throbbing neck-wound pounded out a staccato beat of anticipation.

Soon the starfighter would leave the sprawling domain of Eireyan space. Klark watched his home star shrink to a pinpoint of light. "Now," he murmured.

With a blade pressed to his throat, the starpilot made transmissions that gained the ship clearance beyond the commercial space lanes, and into interstellar space where it could accelerate to greater-than-light speeds, arguably the greatest gift of technology left to the galaxy's modern humans from the lost civilization that predated history and spawned them all. But to Klark, the incredible speed was a gift of a more personal nature. It would allow him to rendezvous with the Earth princess before Hoe or anyone else stole from him that long-awaited, singular satisfaction.

Only two men knew the identity of the second speeder, the one that would carry the Earth princess, the one Klark would snare as soon as it left Earth space, stealing that victory from Hoe. How could he fail? With the speeder's identification entered into his starfighter's computer, the commandeered war craft would track her down like a hungry night-shark.

Klark whispered to himself, and to the starpilot's consternation—it seemed he frightened the poor fellow, as he did most everyone else: "Soon, my little princess, soon. And then I will arrive to escort you to your destiny."

At that, Klark began to laugh. He'd always had the most delightful way of phrasing things.

Chapter Twenty-two

Muffin whistled as he trimmed the hedge along the walkway at Coast Municipal Airport. Ché was no longer on Earth; there was no need for Muffin to report to work. He could have quit, but somehow he didn't. What kind of signal would that send to Copper? He wanted her to see in him a man of responsibility, a man with a good work ethic, a man whom a woman could trust to be a good provider, not one who abandoned an agreement he had made with an employer, regardless of the situation. Certainly, he had no intention of keeping his job at the airport, but it anchored his waning time on Earth with a feeling of "normal life." A life he'd once scoffed at, but that now had become more and more enticing. He would put in his notice to quit, just like any other employee, once he decided what he wanted to do. He was working up the courage to ask Copper if she wanted to continue seeing him. She might not, once he told her who he really was. But he would not do that until his charge, Princess Ilana, was safely offworld.

"Hey, Big Boy," he heard Copper call out. "I brought us lunch."

Muffin turned to find her, dressed in a water-and-soap-splattered jumpsuit that told him she'd been working hard all morning washing airplanes. In her hands was a plastic cooler. Copper, he discovered, made lunches from the heavens. He wheeled his cart into the tool shed and locked it. Then they sat at one of the "picnic tables," as Copper called them, to eat their meal. The buzz of light planes filled the background. The sun was bright and warm. It turned Copper's round checks pink, and Muffin could count a few new freckles. She looked happy.

Eating silently, he enjoyed watching her. She simply smiled, already used to his quiet nature. "Have another." She passed him a roast beef sandwich. She'd layered the meat with a tongue-searing sauce that he found delicious. He ate hungrily, his stomach nowhere near full. But luckily, there was more. Copper had brought boiled eggs, apples, grapes, a block of cheese, a variety of cold drinks, and a confection called "brownies" for dessert. Copper always served dessert. And when he took her out to eat, she always ordered it. It indicated a sweet and generous nature, his mother, had always insisted, a lover of desserts herself. Muffin would have to tell his mother, next time he called home to Thorme, just how right she was.

When they'd eaten their fill, they sat drowsily at the table. "It's such a pretty day. I don't want to go back to work," Copper complained.

He wished she didn't have to. He'd rather spend the day in her company. But reluctantly they cleaned up after themselves and trudged back to their jobs, planning to meet after work, as was their routine. She had just left when Muffin's private comm chimed—a rare and rapid ring that was a signal for an emergency.

Adrenaline rushed to his muscles. He whipped out the comm and fled with it to the tool shed, slamming the door closed and locking it. It was dark, and the air was thick with the odor of grass clippings. But he was alone.

"Where is my sister?" he heard Ian bellow through the tiny communicator.

"Ahh . . ." Muffin wasn't sure. "Packing her bags?"

"You aren't watching her?"

"But, sir, Prince Ché has departed. I thought—"

"So did I. I apologize, Muffin, but we have a problem. Ché Vedla's advisor Hoe put a call in to the Vedla king, who then passed on the information to Rom and me. It doesn't get any more official than that."

"Wh-what?" Muffin stammered uncharacteristically.

"Klark Vedla escaped. They found his locator, but no Klark. No one's sure how long he's been missing. Worst case, it's long enough to interfere with Ilana's flight, and *I can't reach her.* Klark, or the rest of the Vedlas, I don't know, may suspect that any relationship Ché has with Ilana could interfere with the Vedla wedding plans. For God's sake, even I'm reduced to speculating. I have no facts. All I know is that Ilana is filming Ché. But if I believe it's probably more than that, you can bet the Vedlas do, too. And that includes Klark."

Muffin felt Ian's fear as if it were his own. "I'll find her."

"I've tried her cell phone and her home phone, and she didn't pick up. I left messages there and at SILF, and with Linda. All I got were answering services.

317

Doesn't anyone work in their offices anymore?" Muffin could see Ian taking a steadying breath. "She leaves tomorrow. I hope to God she's out running last-minute errands. Find her, Muffin. Keep her safe until I figure out how to handle this. It's a very delicate situation, as well as an urgent one. I can't screw this up, and I can't let my sister get hurt."

Muffin came to attention, a warrior in a tool shed. "I'll find her. I'll protect her." And by the Great Mother, he would.

Muffin made a round trip to Ilana's apartment before Copper got off work. Ilana wasn't there—or anywhere. He searched the vicinity, including the small grocery store Ilana frequented and the beach where she jogged. He'd watched her long enough to know her habits. But she was gone. And so was her car, missing from its parking space.

His neck prickled to the point of distraction. He swung his ground car into the employee parking lot and saw Copper walking to her motorcycle, her helmet and backpack hanging from one hand. Even from this distance, he could tell that she was forlorn. He'd been in the habit of meeting her, and then walking her to her car. She'd probably looked for him and found him gone.

"Copper!"

Her head lifted, and her smile broke like sunshine from behind a cloud. "I looked for you—"

He got out of his car and walked to her. "You once told me that you volunteered for overtime washing planes at Los Angeles Intergalactic." He didn't bother with the usual niceties. He couldn't waste any time.

She eyed him curiously. "The company does business there, and also at Long Beach."

"Can your ID get us onto the ramp at Galactic?"

"The tarmac, you mean? Well, yeah. It's standard airport employee issue."

"Will it get us onto the space pad?"

She shrugged. "I don't see why not. I never tried, though. The spaceships never need much washing," she added with a grin, sobering when she read his anxiety, worry he knew must be flying off him in waves. She narrowed her eyes. "Why?"

"The woman I'm hired to watch may be in danger. I think she might have gone to the airport. If she's there, I have to warn her before she takes off."

"Can you call the airport? Or the police?"

He shook his massive head. "My boss wants to keep it quiet. The risk to her isn't here. It's what lies in wait at her destination that worries us." Now he was speaking for Ian, but he was sure the crown prince would agree. Klark would not have had time to make it to Earth and be a threat to Ilana. But he was out there, somewhere, and Muffin had to protect her from him. He'd seen firsthand what Klark Vedla could do. He'd seen firsthand the man's hatred. *Blast it all!* The Great Council should have executed him while they had the chance.

He didn't need to explain further to Copper. She read his concern on his face. "We have to take my Honda," she said. "It has the stickers we need to get on. That, and our airport IDs around our necks will get us a wave through the employee gate."

Muffin eyed her two-wheeled vehicle with dismay. It suddenly looked very small. "I do not know how to drive this."

Copper winked at him. "I do, Big Guy." She tugged on her helmet and slung her leg over the seat. Lowering her visor, she glanced at him over her shoulder. "Trouble," the letters stamped on her helmet practically shouted at him. Something told him this expedition was going to lead to nothing but.

"There's an extra helmet in the saddlebag," she instructed. "Put it on and get on."

Muffin smiled. Copper could be as sweet as could be. But he never minded when she took charge.

The small black helmet was too snug. It made his skull throb. But as long as it didn't cut off the blood supply to his brain altogether, he would not complain.

He settled his bulk behind Copper. The motorcycle sagged under his weight. Copper laughed. "There you go again, making me feel like I weigh nothing. We almost did a wheelie!" But Muffin was in no mood to smile. Copper started the noisy engine and they were off.

Ilana climbed into the luxurious starspeeder. Linda followed her into the cockpit, which had room for a dozen people in a semicircle of seats against the rounded wall well behind the starpilot's station. Ilana's stomach was flipping, and her hands were sweating. She'd taken a Valium, and that seemed to be holding her steady—relative calmness that she owed to Linda's reassuring presence and to Ché's flying lessons.

God, she wished he were here. Not only for the support, but because she missed the guy. Rarely if ever had she missed a man she was dating. But as soon as Ché had left, she felt as if half of her were missing. Wait a second—dating? They were more than dating. Way more. They were engaged.

If his family approved, they were going to get married!

For a few uneven heartbeats, her anxiety over the impetuous decision she'd made regarding Ché was worse than her nervousness over flying. But it soon faded into mellow warmth that told her she'd made the right choice.

Her heart wrenched at the thought of her absent lover. He'd be arriving at the Wheel tomorrow. But with an earlier-than-planned departure and a willing pilot, she'd be right behind him.

When they'd gotten the word that Linda's passport had arrived at the Federation embassy, Ilana and Linda had agreed: Why sit around waiting now that they had her travel papers in hand?

No one knew about the change in plans, not even Ian. And the starpilot had agreed to play along with her and not radio ahead. Ché would be so surprised!

"Let me make sure you're buckled up nice and tight," Linda said, fussing with Ilana's seat harness.

Ilana smiled at her. "You're such a mom. You should have had kids instead of dogs."

"Don't tell my babies that!" Linda buckled into her own seat next to Ilana's. "They're going to miss me as it is."

The starpilot was a middle-aged man with friendly eyes and a cool, confident aviator's manner. His light gold-brown eyes hinted at some *Vash* ancestry mixed in with his common blood. He checked that they were safe in their seats before giving them a briefing in curt Basic. "I'll tell you when you can get up, my ladies," he finished. "Remain seated until then." Linda looked to Ilana for a translation.

"He wants us to sit down and shut up," Ilana said out of the corner of her mouth when the starpilot returned to his station.

"At least some things are universal among pilots."

Smiling, Ilana found Linda's hand with her shaking sweaty one. "Keep making me laugh. I'm nervous."

Linda's hand squeezed hers back. "You used to

laugh every time I brought up the idea of marriage and commitment. Any plans to keep in touch with that Vedla boy now that he's gone home . . . I hope?"

Ilana's heart skipped a beat. She wished she could tell her friend, but she'd promised she'd wait. "Yeah," she replied with a private smile. "I guess you could say that we've decided to keep in touch."

The spaceport held anything but a place of honor at one of Earth's busiest airports. The pad was far from the commercial terminal, and far from any crowds. At this stage in Earth's development, the spaceport didn't see much traffic. In the years to come, as Earth's culture caught up to the technology brought by its new association with the Trade Federation, that would change. Technology would drive tourism, and vice versa, and would eventually make the idea of space travel attractive to Earth's billions, Ian had told Muffin. But, suiting Muffin's needs perfectly, the nearly vacant space pad hosted but one craft, ejecting jets of steam. Muffin had seen a lifetime's worth of starships poised for departure, and this was one of them.

Muffin squeezed Copper's thigh, causing her to swerve the motorcycle. "There! That is the one!"

Copper stopped at a painted yellow line on the tarmac. The motorcycle's engine idled, letting them speak without shouting. "Take me to it quickly."

"Why? What are you going to do?"

Copper's integrity was what originally attracted him to the girl. But, Great Mother, it made his bodyguard duties very difficult. Ahead, the spacecraft let go of another fountain of steam. Muffin growled. He'd run for the ship himself, but instinct—and his prickling neck—told him that on foot he wouldn't make it in time.

"The woman I'm trying to save is on that spacecraft. We can't let it launch."

"No, we can't." His nervousness had finally rubbed off on her. "We'll tell the space tower. They'll stop the launch. Here, I've got their phone number." She twisted around as if to open the saddlebag. "Somewhere in my backpack . . ."

A rumbling penetrated Muffin's too-tight helmet. The crew of the ship hadn't raised the cargo ramp, but they'd started up their auxiliary ground engine, the prelude to starting the far more powerful thrusters needed to push the ship out of Earth's atmosphere. They were minutes from leaving, maybe less.

Blast Ilana Hamilton for leaving early and not telling her brother! "Not enough time!" he yelled at Copper. "Go! Ride around to the nose and I'll get the pilot's attention."

He saw those green eyes studying him, trying to ascertain whether to trust him. "If I say no, you're going to go anyway," she said, swallowing.

He hated to admit it. "Yes. I have to. It's . . . my duty."

"Duty," she said. "That word gets to me every time." She gunned the engine and they were off, speeding across the tarmac to the spacecraft. "Let's help that woman!"

Laser-bright lights above the lowered cargo ramp began to blink in warning. As soon as the crew raised that ramp, launch would be imminent.

Copper leaned forward, strands of bright red hair rippling behind her as they gained speed. She didn't veer around to the front of the ship. Instead, she aimed for the ramp.

"Great Mother!" Muffin blurted out. She couldn't be intending what he feared she was. "The ramp!" he shouted, warning her.

"I know!"

The ship's lights blinked. Steam hissed. Then he heard the scrape of metal on asphalt as the ramp shuddered and began to retract.

"Hold on, Big Boy!" Copper cried. "We're going in."

"Copper, no!"

They bounced over the ramp's threshold. "Here we go!" she sang out.

He didn't know this woman. This wasn't the sweet girl he'd been dating. But she was the woman who'd thrown him onto his back the day they met, meaning the two were one and the same.

They roared up the huge ramp. Muffin was too surprised to do anything else but clamp his big hands to her hips. Just as their acceleration gave out, the ramp lifted past the horizontal, sending them careening down the other side and into the huge cargo bay.

The shiny silver floor was slippery, and the lighting in the bay was dim. Copper lost control of the motorcycle, and they spun, skidding sideways. Sheer luck kept them from slamming into the boxes of freight piled high within. By the time the Honda fell onto its side, it was nearly stopped. They went over easy, but went down nonetheless.

He heard Copper's helmet bang against the metal flooring. In an instant, he dragged her from under the fallen motorcycle and tugged off her helmet before tossing aside his own. Her eyes glowed with the thrill of what she'd just done. "I got us in! Now go, save her!" Her hair fell all around her sweet, round face as she pushed at him. "I'm not hurt."

"You're beautiful." Muffin took her head in his hands, brought her mouth to his, and kissed her. Then the ship rumbled under his knees. His blood surged. "They will launch unless we tell them we're here."

They scrambled to their feet. Not wanting to leave her alone, he took her hand. They sprinted through a cargo bay filled with crates of coffee, chocolate, and beer. Odd. He thought the Vedlas shunned Earth products, and here the bay was full of Earth's bounty. It looked more like the haul of an independent frontier trader than what one would expect to find in the bowels of an Eireyan starship.

The ship tipped forward, and then to the side, keeping in the bank angle as acceleration shoved them to the floor. Muffin's hands and knees clanged against the flooring. He tried to catch Copper, but she'd managed to keep her footing. No one would be able to tell that he was the one with decades of space-travel experience.

He stumbled after her. She waited for him at the base of a ladder, her hands wrapped around the bottom rung. "Did we launch?"

"Not yet," he said as he led the way up. "We're hovering above the airport, getting into position. There's still time."

The thruster's rumble built to a roar. The echo was especially loud in the cargo bay, as it was with any starship. The shaking increased until it was nearly impossible to hang on to the ladder. He and Copper spilled over the top and into a crawlway. Her eyes were huge. "That was the launch. It had to be."

He could hardly bear to tell her the truth. "We'll have them return to the airport."

Copper's mouth spread into a huge smile. "I'm an astronaut."

She was also a stowaway, but there wasn't time to get into that part now. "Come." Again he reached for her hand.

Atmospheric penetration was always the bumpiest part of any space flight. Not being strapped into a comfortable seat magnified the experience. The bumping seemed to reach a crescendo when they burst, breathless, into the cockpit. Bright sunshine flooded the compartment, a startling contrast to the dimly lit lower part of the ship.

Muffin blinked, impatient for his eyes to adjust. When he could finally see, two very astonished star-pilots dressed in tan and gray cargo gear stared back at him. Sure, his size had something to do with their open-mouthed stares—and the pretty woman pressed to his back—but having anyone stumble into a cockpit in mid-launch would unbalance even the most jaded of space crews. "Princess Ilana," he said. "Where is she?"

The two pilots glanced at each other. Then the one who wasn't flying found his tongue. "Princess?" he asked in Basic. "What princess?"

Muffin was less confident now. He could feel Copper's eyes boring into his back. Basic was a language few Earth-dwellers had bothered to learn; she'd want to know why he knew it. The list of explanations he owed her was getting longer by the minute. "The Earth princess Ilana," he told the pilot. "Are you not escorting her off planet?"

"The woman you were watching is Ilana Hamilton?" Copper asked in surprised awe.

"I'll explain later," he assured her, switching to English.

"You gosh darn better, Muffin."

The vibration began to ease. Outside, the sky had turned from pale blue to dark indigo dotted with stars. The flying starpilot was now able to give Muffin his full attention. "Is your princess a stowaway, too?" the pilot asked mockingly.

Muffin stumbled into speech. "She is not on this ship?"

The pilot turned to his friend and said, "Looks like we got more cargo than we bargained for, Jal."

At that, Muffin swore. By the heavens, he'd boarded the wrong ship!

Chapter Twenty-three

From the speeder's forward view window, Ché could see his destination. Lit from within, the tiny disk rotated slowly, like a bejeweled finger ring lost amongst the stars. But as the speeder neared the Wheel, gradually matching its rotation in order to dock, the space station grew into the grand city it was. With a million winking lights and spokes wider and taller than most city buildings, the Wheel was still a marvel of engineering five thousand years after it was built.

This was the seat of the Federation government. Much history had transpired here, Ché thought as they docked. And he couldn't help but wonder if the conversation he was about to have with his father would someday fall into that category.

Or would his father refuse his request to choose Ilana as his mate? By the heavens, he prayed that would not be the case.

He had never wished that he'd been born a commoner, and he didn't now, but he couldn't help thinking how much less complicated his quest to marry the woman of his choice would be if he were not a royal.

Ché waited with weary patience until the speeder docked in one of the Wheel's thousands of bays. His father would meet him there. From Eireya, Hoe had communicated with both Ché and his father. Now the king awaited his son at the dock.

As the speeder settled into its berth, Ché spied a group of men standing in the arrival bay: the king, Councilman Toren, and several others of high rank within the Vedla council.

Dressed in typical Eireyan travel clothing—dark trousers, overshirt, and boots, and a heavy black cloak draped over his shoulders—Ché disembarked from the speeder. After weeks of living in casual Earthwear, it felt both odd and welcome to be wearing the mode of dress he'd worn all his life.

King Vedla embraced him. With his smooth amber skin and coppery-blond hair that was becoming silver at his temples, he was tall and had the incisive pale gold eyes typical of his class. His face was leaner than Ché's—and meaner some said, like Klark's. But despite his aristocratic appearance, his welcome for his son was as warm as the one Ché gave him back.

Ché's father had a fearsome reputation as a taskmaster of the Treatise of Trade, a man whose traditionalist values drove his actions within the Federation. But Ché had often wondered of late if Klark's misadventures in the frontier had changed him, as they'd changed Ché, himself; he'd wondered if the king's core conservatism had softened somewhat in the new era of change that was so obviously upon them. Ché could only hope. He planned to appeal to both his father's desire for Vedla superiority and the

spark of broadmindedness the family's recent humiliation may have initiated.

The king gripped Ché's shoulders and moved him
back. "It is good to see you. I hear you have had
adventures of late."

Darkly, Ché thought of Hoe. So much for his advisor keeping a secret. When had he told the king?
Today? Or weeks ago? Fool was he for thinking he
could enjoy a holiday in peace and privacy. "It is
good for a man to have them."

"Indeed." His father smiled. Perhaps, Ché thought,
the king had known all along, and chose to let him
continue his holiday without interference. Before
Ché's gratitude could take root, his father's expression chilled. "Your timing is impeccable, Ché. We
have a crisis. Klark escaped. Hoe believes he left the
palace as early as the day you departed Earth."

"Are we certain it's an escape? Abduction can be
made to look like an escape. Klark's base of support
has eroded, perhaps—"

"The palace staff found his locator under his pillow," his father broke in. "The one he'd worn implanted in his neck."

"Great Mother," Ché breathed. Klark had dug out
his locator like an Earth wolf gnawed its leg off to
escape a steel trap. But had he escaped in order to
survive, or was the act merely one of defiance? Why
hadn't Ché sensed that desire in Klark? Usually Bajha
was ideal for discerning a man's dark secrets, and
they'd played much of it before he'd left.

"Hoe confirmed all this," his father stated, looking
grim.

Hoe again. The man was probably delighted. There
was no love lost between Klark and Hoe. "Sir, Klark
appeared quite accepting of his incarceration. He
didn't enjoy it, mind you, but he seemed to under-

stand the reasoning behind it. I truly didn't expect anything like this of him."

Toren spoke up. "Nor did we. We must tell no one. It would make the Vedlas the butt of jokes, that we are incapable of holding on to a prisoner, and that he escaped without Security's knowledge. The B'kah king and crown prince agreed to let us track down and punish Klark on our own."

Ché's father nodded. "My second son has brought the family enough scandal; We don't need more."

Ché winced at that. Some might interpret his marriage to Ilana as a scandal. Did he dare add another when his family was battling one already? As his father said, his timing was impeccable.

A somber, gravely worried group, for myriad related reasons, they moved from the corridor to the more secure Vedla private chambers. Thick silk carpeting cushioned their steps. Ancient Eireyan art graced the walls, reminding Ché of his heritage, and of the significance of what he'd come here to do.

A small, lifelike image of Hoe waited for them on the communication table. A reassuring presence, that, Ché thought. His dependable advisor.

The king spoke to Ché as Hoe and the councilmen looked on. "Hoe believes that your association with the Earthwoman may have spurred Klark's disappearance."

Ché faced the semicircle of men loyal to his family. Not one face revealed what they thought of Hoe's insinuation. But then, they were Vedlas. You weren't supposed to be able to read a Vedla, even if you were one.

Before he could consider telling his father of his plans to marry Ilana, he had to make sure she was safe. Ché clenched and unclenched his fists behind his back. "Are you saying that you believe Klark would try to harm the princess?" For all the mistakes Klark had made, Ché couldn't fathom him doing something so evil while leaving such obvious tracks. But then, emotions drove Klark and made anything possible.

Hoe's reply sounded bleak. "Prince Klark made many comments along those lines over the past weeks. I dismissed them as his usual ramblings, my lord. And that was my mistake."

Ché began to pace, something he did only rarely, and only when at a loss, which was equally rare. "We have no proof of my brother's ill intent."

"I am afraid we do," Councilman Toren said, producing a computer.

Ché stopped, took it from him. "Hoe found this," Toren informed Ché as he read the text. It was a directive from a palace computer that had ordered the cancellation of Ilana's assistant's passport.

The order had come from Klark.

Ché felt as if the floor had fallen away from beneath his boots.

"We believe that Klark delayed the travel documents to ensure you traveled separately from the princess, so he could prevent her ship from reaching the Wheel without harming you," the councilman said. "And if he made it look like an accident, you would not blame him for the act."

It took all the discipline Ché had not to rush from the chamber, jump in the fastest ship he could find, and go after Ilana. He plunged his fingers through his hair and turned to his father. "She has no protection on Earth. Klark will have unimpeded access to her. We must move quickly to keep her out of danger, and provide her with a starfighter escort for her journey here. I will see to the arrangements myself. I will move heaven and Eireya to ensure Ilana's safety."

His father caught Ché's gaze. "She is traveling here in an official capacity, to make inquiries as to her entertainment business." Faint distaste marred his father's restating of the facts Ché had passed along to him a day ago. But there was nothing more than that hint of disapproval. It gave Ché hope that his family would come to accept Ilana and her career.

Time was short. He had to leave the Wheel, go after her, and keep Klark from harming her, if that was indeed his brother's intent. "There is more to her journey here, sir," Ché confessed. "We have little time, so I'll be blunt." So much for the carefully worded, tactful speech that he'd rehearsed. "Klark has reason to be worried."

Something passed between them then, father to son. He knew what Ché was about to tell him; he'd sensed Ché's feelings for Ilana. Councilman Toren stood behind King Vedla, overseeing their nonverbal interaction like a goth-hawk perched on the king's shoulder.

Ché's father flicked his hand. "Excuse us for a moment, gentlemen." The councilmen scattered dutifully for other parts of the chamber.

"Worried?" the king queried. "Why?"

Ché's stance didn't waver, reflecting his staunch determination to have Ilana as his wife. He would not accept the first "no," he decided. Nor all the subsequent refusals. He'd keep fighting, as his ancestors had eons ago in the Dark Years. And if it came to an all-out failure to convince his father of the benefit of a marriage to Ilana, as a last resort he'd rally his mother and sisters. If they agreed with him, that was.

Ché shook his head, banishing his doubts. Defeat, he decided, trying to boost his optimism, was a long way off. "Father, the humiliation our family suffered when the Dar princess ran off with the crown prince

333

lingers. To repair our reputation, we decided that I must marry before Ian Hamilton."

His father listened intently. "Yes, go on."

"I agreed with that solution. But I have taken it a step further. I, the spurned prince, will marry first, and I will take the crown prince's very sister as my bride, thus uniting the Vedlas and the B'kahs, and proving that no one should ever underestimate a Vedla."

Ché felt oddly lighter for having said it. When he and Klark were boys, they used to believe that when you said a wish aloud, it would come to pass.

The king said nothing for a moment, a moment that stretched into an eternity. Then he laughed. Laughed! "Ah! You make me proud, my boy."

The king's statement hit Ché like a fully charged Bajha sens-sword. His mouth longed to form the words *Say again?* but he was too shocked to speak.

King Vedla lowered his voice. "Here I thought you had gone to Earth for a frivolous holiday. All along, you were busy plotting, like a true Vedla." He waved Toren over. "None of us had ever considered bringing the only available B'kah female into our family. But you did, Ché. Ah, but I expected nothing less of you. In uniting the Vedlas and the B'kahs, and in such an overt way, we would bring our family back to its rightful position of glory."

"Can you stop the current plans?" Ché asked hoarsely.

"The Lesok promise? Yes. Yes, indeed. Prince Haj will be glad to hear it. He has been protesting here, at the sacrifice of his family's good name, but, clearly, he doesn't care. He's in love." His father shook his head with exasperation. "Now we must face the thorny problem of convincing the Princess Ilana to marry you in the limited time we have left. If she were a traditional *Vash* princess, I would not bring this up.

334

But she is of a different culture, and may choose to refuse you." His father's eyes twinkled. "You will need to work that Vedla charm on her. Convince her of the benefits of having you as a mate, Ché. Do it in barbarian—er, the Earth-dweller fashion if you must. And I will discuss the matter with Romlijhian B'kah."

Ché finally found his voice. "No worries, sir." His mouth slid into a smile. "She wants to marry me."

"Ah, the Vedla charm triumphs again! As soon as the lucky girl arrives, we will sign promise papers."

Klark's escape came crashing back into Ché's thoughts, and he swore. Here he was, gloating with his father over snaring the woman of his dreams and his father's ambitions, while Ilana sat innocently in her little condo, at risk. "I will contact her now, warn her of Klark's escape. I will arrange for safer transport than the speeder."

"Embassy personnel will guard her and escort her to her craft when it arrives," the king assured him, but it didn't keep the dread from creeping up Ché's spine.

Then every comm in the Vedla quarters began bleating. All present drew out their ringing units, reading, Ché assumed, the same thing he was: a text message from Vedla security hovering in three-dimensional urgency above the small screen.

A starfighter was missing . . . It had not returned to its berth . . . Without a scheduled mission, it should have never left. . . .

Alone, the news wouldn't have been so startling—Ché expected that Klark would commandeer transportation off-planet if he had the chance. But what followed spurred Ché into action. "The family B'kah received an emergency call from a bodyguard they'd apparently had in place on Earth," Ché read, looking up. "It contains confirmation that Princess Ilana has launched. One Earth day early."

Adrenaline rushed through Ché. "If Klark truly intends to harm Ilana, he can find her easily now that she's left the protection of Earth space."

The king held up one hand. "If our family issues a galaxywide alert, the embarrassment will be many times worse than what Klark brought us last year. We will find the princess, but we will do so without anyone else finding out—the B'kah king excluded, of course."

Ché's jaw tensed. "Understood. But if this endangers her, I will intervene. Her welfare comes first, Father."

Ché stormed the comm table where the flickering image of Hoe hovered. He'd felt the compulsion to protect Ilana before, but never so acutely. He vowed he would keep the woman he loved out of danger at the cost of family pride, his own life . . . and that of a beloved brother. "Get me the location of Princess Ilana's speeder."

"Er . . . how, my lord?"

Hoe was usually resourceful. Such helplessness was not what Ché would expect from him. "You arranged for the speeders. Give me the transponder identification code for the princess's craft, and I'll do it."

"Shouldn't you go after Prince Klark instead?"

Ché balled his hands into fists. "Do as I ask, Hoe." While Hoe anxiously complied, Ché turned to the grim men surrounding him. "Arrange for a battlecruiser—the fastest we have," he told the councilmen. Then he told his father, "I'm going after her."

To his shock, his father, king of the Vedlas, waved to the group. "All in this chamber will come. No one who knows of this will remain behind."

Except Hoe, Ché thought. Good. Tucked securely away on Eireya, the man would serve as a source of outside information, should any more news come in to help them. "Pass on any new data that you see," he told his advisor. "Do not screen it first. Send me everything."

"Yes, my lord. I won't fail you."

Ché gave a curt nod, then strode with the determined group of Vedlas to the docks.

For Ilana, cruising in hyperspace was always tougher on the mind than the body. The concept of how it was accomplished was nerve-wracking, though the flight itself was as smooth as glass.

They'd been traveling for about a half-day. After they ate, Linda put her seat back all the way and fell asleep. Ilana draped her with a blanket, so that all that showed of her friend was a tousled fluff of bright red hair. But Ilana herself couldn't relax. She could breathe, which was good—it helped to breathe, kept you conscious, though sometimes she wondered if she'd be better out cold—but actual relaxation remained for her the Holy Grail of flying.

She gripped the armrests, her fingers throbbing. Periodically, she'd let go to flex her cramped fingers. That helped her mark the passage of time, which seemed to crawl.

She wished Linda would wake up. They'd brought a deck of cards. And they could talk. But Linda slept on. Finally, Ilana took out her palmtop and tried to write more notes for the documentary.

Every few minutes, she glanced at the pilot. Ché had mentioned that starpilots used "go-pills" to avoid getting sleepy on longer flights like this one. Since they were traveling with only one pilot, there would be times when he'd have to sleep. The idea of that was unsettling, as the sleep period would take place in his chair, a high-tech bucket seat crisscrossed with spidery extensions, some of which disappeared into various places in the pilot's uniform. She hoped one of those wires shot out a wake-up shock triggered by unscheduled sleep.

Gripping the armrests, she sat up straighter, staring at the pilot: the girl watching the starpilot watching the computer that was watching the ship . . .

The pilot's body gave a couple of sharp twitches. *Ah-ha.* Caught in the act. He *was* falling asleep. She waited to see if any of the connectors attached to his uniform would set off an alarm. But his head slowly fell forward, and no alarm that she could see or hear went off.

Ilana sat in disbelief as the man's upper torso followed his falling head like a freshly chopped redwood. Not only had the pilot fallen asleep, he'd turned his worktable into a pillow.

"Hello!" she called, but he didn't answer.

Maybe he was just exhausted. She remembered her father returning home from airline trips that way, entirely out of energy. But this pilot had enjoyed at least a week off before having to fly today. There was no excuse for such exhaustion . . . unless he'd been out at the Earth clubs all night. Her heart began to pound. Had he been drinking? Could he still be drunk?

Stop it. She squeezed her eyes shut and tried to work moisture into her dry mouth. Eyes open again, she told herself in Ché's voice that the speeder would fly just fine with a sleeping pilot at the helm. But it didn't seem right; it didn't seem like professional behavior on the pilot's part. She'd have thought anyone working for the Vedlas would have more discipline than . . . this.

A shudder ran thorough the ship. In an instant, Ilana's heart was in her mouth. They were traveling in hyperspace and many times the speed of light—there shouldn't be any bumps. Her gaze swung to the forward view window. The stars, stretched into streamers of light in hyperspace, were shrinking back to normal size. Shit! They'd dropped out of light speed. "Wake up!" she shouted in Basic. "Something is wrong."

Linda threw off her blanket and rooted around for her glasses. She slipped them over puffy eyes. "Wrong? What's wrong?"

"We've slowed down, and I don't know why. The pilot's asleep!" Ilana squeezed the armrest so tightly that she could no longer feel her fingers. The blood had gone out of them. *Keep calm, keep calm.* "Those sensors in his uniform, they might detect . . . incapacitation. The ship might be designed to stop if the pilot—"—she took a couple of deep breaths—"dies."

Linda snorted. "You and your worst-case scenarios, Ilana. He's asleep."

"He's lying on his face!" She was shouting now, and the pilot still didn't move. "Isn't that uncomfortable? And look at his arms; they're hanging straight down. I nap all the time like that, don't you?"

Linda pressed her lips together. "Now you're scaring me."

"We have reason to be scared." She yelled to the pilot, "Hey! Wake up, damn it!"

The pilot didn't stir. Ilana licked her dry lips. "That's it. He's getting a kick in the ass." She forced her stiff hands to unbuckle her harnesses.

She crossed the cockpit—a miracle in its own right. Trying to keep her temper in check, she shook the sleeping pilot by the shoulder. He remained slumped over. His body was strangely rigid, as if every muscle were pulled tight. "Open eyes!" she shouted in Basic. "Big sleep is not good."

But there was no response. Holding her breath, she

felt for a pulse in his neck. Nothing. "Linda," she whispered hoarsely. All her worst fears were realized. "He's dead."

Linda brought her hand to her mouth.

A trickle of blood and spittle glistened on the dead pilot's lips. "He bit his tongue. I think he had a seizure," Ilana guessed.

Her heart pounded in her head. "Shit, shit, shit," she squeezed out. A dead pilot. She wanted to scream almost as much as she wanted to laugh hysterically. If she were alone, if she were here without the recentness of her experience in the Cessna to steady her, she would have panicked. Instead, she turned to Linda. "We've got to get him out of the seat."

Linda joined her. She undid the harnesses as Ilana pulled out the cables connecting the pilot to the ship. Then they pushed his bulk off the seat. He wasn't a small man, and fell heavily.

Ilana jumped into the seat. Linda dragged the body away, into the back. Breathless, she joined Ilana at the controls. "What do we do now?"

How the hell do I know? Ilana wanted to say. The control panel was just as Ché had described it. But talking about flying while naked in a bathtub and doing it for real were two different things.

Ilana stared straight ahead. If she looked at Linda's face and saw fear there, she'd lose it. "Ché told me a pilot always has to think several steps ahead. That includes knowing what airfields are nearby in case an emergency requires an unexpected landing. But I have no idea what stars have planets." She held tight to her unraveling composure. "Or even how far away they are."

"Let's look for some kind of button that calls for help."

"Good idea." The Cessna had been so simple. This starship's control panel was a kaleidoscope of readings, and all in Basic, which made it even more difficult to know what she was seeing.

A klaxon interrupted them. Both Ilana and Linda shrieked. Above their heads a screen flashed. In Basic. Ilana squinted up at it. Half the navigation panel was blinking like Christmas-tree lights. "It's warning us of a collision."

"With what?"

"With *that*!"

Linda's gaze jerked outside. "Oh, my . . ."

A starship filled the center of the forward viewscreen.

In the back of her mind, Ilana wondered if the ship's computer would help them avoid the collision. But what if it didn't? What if she was wrong?

The ship closed on them. From where she sat, it looked as if the other guys wanted to play a game of galactic chicken.

"Damn it! I can't just sit here and die." Ilana pulled the control stick hard to the left. And lost sight of the oncoming ship as the speeder rolled away, wing over wing. The stars whirled counterclockwise so fast that vertigo almost overwhelmed her senses and made her pass out.

The other way, she thought. She had no clue what she was doing, but she clenched her teeth and shoved the stick clockwise to counter the roll of the ship.

Too hard. The movement threw them the opposite way. Ilana jerked sideways in her seat, transverse whiplash. The speeder groaned, metal straining as it switched from spinning in one direction to the other. Dizziness she could handle, but the thought of the speeder breaking apart in space made her want to puke.

Crying out in frustration, she countered the new spin. This time she moved the stick less abruptly and they leveled out. She and Linda bounced in their seats as the speeder reacted like a bucking bronco. But determination overpowered Ilana's panic. Concentration erased her nausea and cold sweats. And then the flight smoothed out.

"I think we're straight and level now," she said, looking out at the trillions of stars all around them.

Linda glanced over at her. The woman's face was chalky.

"Though who's to say what's up and what's down?" Ilana added.

"Ilana. Don't do that to yourself." Linda smiled weakly. "And don't do that to me."

Ilana scanned the stars ahead. "Where did that ship go?" Boy, she sounded calm. What a joke.

"Let's hope he's not coming back for round two."

Ilana snorted. "It's just my luck, isn't it? In the infinity of space, I almost have a head-on collision with what has to be the only other ship for miles—I mean light-years—around."

Incredibly, they both began to laugh. If Ilana stopped to analyze why she was laughing while tears streamed down her cheeks, she'd go crazy. So she didn't. Didn't stop to think, for once in her life. She was barely hanging on to sanity as it was. When her crazed giggles subsided, she wiped her eyes. "We're alive because of Ché, Linda."

"No. We're alive because of you."

"Well, then he gave me the means to do it. The means to save myself. To save us." Emotion threatened to steal her words but she tamped it down somehow. "His culture is so paternalistic, so old-fashioned. His family is the worst of them all. But, somewhere along the line, something went right with Ché. He's like them, Linda, but he's not. He's . . . an evolutionary step in the right direction." She smiled. She could imagine what Ché would say to that. But it was true—he'd taken what his culture demanded of him and turned it into something better. And in doing so, he'd given her the ultimate gift: control.

Of course, Linda brought her back to reality. "What do you think happened to the pilot?"

"A seizure? Epilepsy, maybe? I'm no medical expert." She heaved a weary sigh. "But then I'm no pilot, either."

"Tumors can cause seizures out of the blue. But you'd think a starpilot would be checked all the time."

Ilana pondered the cables hanging from the seat, the ones that had been connected to receptacles in the pilot's suit. "Where do those wires lead once under his suit? Do they penetrate the skin? Or make contact?"

Linda went pale again. "Are you saying that something entered his body from the ship and hurt him?"

"I don't know," Ilana said quietly. "Everyone knew how I was—how I am—about flying. His death could be some kind of sabotage. Kill the pilot, kill the chick, you know?"

"Why would someone want to kill you?"

There was no use keeping the secret now. "Ché asked me to marry him." She smiled. "And I said yes."

The parade of emotions on Linda's face would have been comical had Ilana not been so shaken. She reached across the space between the seats and gave Ilana's hand a joyful squeeze.

"Do not turn your craft," boomed a voice in Basic over the cockpit speakers. "I will retry docking."

Both women jumped apart. Outside, off the nose, floated the ship they'd swerved to avoid.

Chapter Twenty-four

Onboard the battleship, Ché paced in front of the forward viewscreen. He kept alive the hope that the coordinates Hoe supplied would bring him to Ilana before Klark got to her. By the heavens! Would his brother do such a thing? Hadn't he learned from his mistake in the frontier? Hoe had evidence to the contrary. Computer records. Data trails. Hard proof—all of it obvious and indisputable. Ah, Klark, why?

Frustration vibrated inside him. Love had made him forgive Klark for things he should not have tolerated. But if his brother did anything to hurt Ilana, an innocent in all this, Ché would kill him with his own hands.

Was Klark unspeakably evil? Or had his fanaticism pushed him to insanity? Regardless, if he harmed Ilana in any way, he was a dead man.

Ché tried to ignore the twisting in his chest, the sense of betrayal that Klark's actions conjured. Reaching deep, he silently summoned Chéya, the ancient warrior-prince whose blood he shared. *Help me to see . . .* To see the truth.

Before his confidence faltered, he turned to the lead pilot. "How much longer?"

"Two standard hours, my lord. No more . . ." The pilot stopped speaking in mid-sentence. He and his co-pilot peered at their screens, and then at each other.

"What—what is it?" Ché demanded.

The lead pilot looked up slowly, meeting the king's eyes first before turning his gaze to Ché. "The princess's speeder has merged with another target."

Ché's father pushed forward. "What target?"

"One that matches the identity of the missing star-fighter."

"It's a starfighter," Ilana said. "It has weapons. But he wants to dock?"

Linda tried to sound hopeful. "At least we know he didn't mean to hit us on purpose."

"Yeah. But I don't know if I like the idea of strangers boarding us, either. Then again, we're in the middle of nowhere and I don't know how to get anywhere." She squinted at the approaching fighter. "It's a Vedla ship. I can tell by the lettering."

"Rescue!"

"That, or they're here to kill me."

Linda groaned. "If they really wanted you out of the picture, Ilana, we'd be bits and pieces of metal already. This speeder slowed down by itself—it probably sends out an SOS by itself, too."

Everything Linda said made sense. Ilana worked at trying to believe it.

The speeder jolted. Ilana grabbed for her armrests. "What the hell was that?"

As if he had heard her, the starfighter pilot transmitted, "We have your craft under control. Tow to docking . . . commencing on my count . . . three, two, one."

The speeder shuddered and began moving toward the larger craft. Ilana's heart thumped, and she tried to keep her breathing steady. It would be so easy to hyperventilate.

The fighter's fuselage filled the entire forward window now. Sweat prickled Ilana's skin. Neither she nor Linda spoke. Then a metallic clanging noise signaled contact. A dull thump confirmed it. Something pinched her eardrums, and was gone as soon as the sensation registered. A pressure change, she thought. The connection between the ships must have been made. Not that she knew anything about docking spaceships, but making intelligent guesses worked wonders at keeping her calm.

Ilana unstrapped. "I'll go answer the door."

"I'm coming with you." Linda bounced out of her seat and followed Ilana to an airlock.

There was a knocking from the other side. "Oh, so *we* have to open it?" Ilana asked. "So much for automated doors. But I guess you can't have everything."

"We're being rescued and you're complaining?"

"Linda, I'm in a very, very bad mood." She put her hands on the handle. "Okay—together."

Linda grabbed hold with her and they pulled. The door swung inward, revealing a tall, amber-skinned man with pale gold eyes. Klark Vedla. Ché's fanatical brother. Ilana would know him anywhere.

Muffin practically breathed down the necks of the cargo pilots. "Can't you go any faster?"

"If we go any faster, our skin will ignite." The older

of the two pilots turned around. "Not our flesh, the ship's," he clarified.

"I know that," Muffin growled.

"And if the fuselage combusts, guess what follows?" The two pilots scowled at each other.

Muffin considered himself an easy soul with whom to get along. But ever since Romlijhian B'kah had ordered the two cargo pilots to pursue Ilana Hamilton's speeder, the pressure to reach her before Klark did had eroded his patience to nothing.

"I will check back soon," he grumbled and lumbered back to the seats where he'd left Copper sleeping. The pilots were right, of course. They were traveling as fast as they could. Ian had given them the speeder's identification. That was all they'd needed to track it. At first, they'd merely kept pace with the princess's craft. But in the past few hours, they'd eaten up the distance between them like a plate full of Copper's brownies. Muffin feared the worst: that the speeder was no longer flying but was floating, marooned in space. He prayed that when he finally caught up to Ilana, he would find her alive.

Ilana raised her fists in the sparring stance she remembered from childhood Tae Kwon Do lessons. Her nostrils flared with each breath, and her heart felt as if it would jump out of her chest. "So, you wanted to do it in person, you bastard."

Klark raised both hands in a move that so resembled Ché's gesture when she used too much slang that her offensive stance faltered. Then she caught herself and lifted her fists, her feet apart. "Basic, please," he said. "I don't know English."

"Yeah, I bet you don't. You probably think it's beneath you." But wasn't her own prejudice toward the

Vash the reason she hadn't perfected her Basic over the years?

She gritted her teeth. "I will speak Basic." If only to keep Linda from getting hurt. And maybe to avoid answering her own inner question. "Why you here?"

"You are in danger."

"Well, duh." And Klark was supposed to be the cunning brother.

"I have come to take you aboard my starfighter and bring you to the Wheel, where my brother awaits you."

"You rescue me?" *Was he for real?* "You try to hurt my brother," she said in a low voice. "Why I trust you now?"

His sharp golden gaze softened almost imperceptibly. "Because Ché is in love with you."

Her mouth fell open. She snapped it shut. That he'd rendered her speechless was an understatement.

The expression in her face must have confirmed Klark's hypothesis. He appeared almost amused by her discomposure. "It wasn't difficult to guess his feelings for you. I saw how he looked at you that day on Earth—I read what was in his eyes. That is how I knew, knew the real reason he went to Earth . . . before, it seems, he knew it himself." Klark took a breath.

"I want superiority for my family first and foremost. We Vedlas deserve it," he said simply. "We have earned it. But, too, perhaps equally, I want contentment for my brother. He, too, deserves it." Regret flared briefly in the man's pale eyes. "In the past, I tried to win him that contentment in ways that displeased him. Through this, I hope to regain his favor and secure my family's reputation. I am escorting you to Chéya's Fist, an impenetrable outpost at the border of Eireyan space. I have summoned my family to meet us there—if they respond to my message." His mouth spread thin. "I am not the most liked, or the most trusted man in my family at the moment. But I cannot yet risk announcing that I have you safe. The news may force your would-be assassin to take desperate measures to counter my move. He . . . is a desperate man. The battleship will follow us there. My father is aboard," he said with confidence. "As is your future protector."

Protector. It was the ancient term for husband or spouse. He meant Ché. Her pulse quickened, and a thousand unnamed emotions whirled like seagulls in a storm. Love, longing, anxiousness, doubt. And the sense that in marrying him, she was doing something right. She'd had a similar rush of rightness the day she decided to apply to UCLA, only this was much more powerful. She was, as Klark put it, about to accept Ché as her "protector." And she was none the weaker for it.

Klark pushed past her and crouched by the dead starpilot, checking him for vital signs as Ilana quickly translated for Linda.

Ilana wasn't sure, but she thought she'd detected a bit of guilt under all that arrogant posturing and noble, holier-than-thou attitude. Guilt for what? For trying to hurt Ian and Tee'ah? Could it be possible? She could have sworn that when he appeared in the airlock that she was dead for the sin of wanting to marry Ché.

Ilana remembered the night Ché had come to her house, how sure she'd been that he was a killer. She prayed she was wrong again.

Klark stood and wiped his hands. His face was lean, almost as if the bronze skin was stretched too tightly over the bones beneath. He had no dent in his jaw—like Ché's tense-ometer, a useful little tool for determining worry. Nonetheless, a sense of urgency flowed off him in waves. A rock could have picked up on his apprehension. Why was he scared? Not knowing frightened her. "Someone hurt the pilot," she said, swallowing.

"On solo missions, a ship's computer monitors star-pilots' brainwaves and heartbeats. Through these sensors that touch the skin, it is possible to disrupt a body's nervous system."

"This disrupt"—damn, if she lived through this, she was becoming fluent in Basic—"it go from ship to man?"

"Yes, it is meant to restart a heart, correct a seizure."

"But not kill."

His gaze was grim. "No. Obviously not. But one can program the computer to administer a deadly shock, through nefarious means." Klark drew himself up to his full height. He was a little shorter than Ché, but there was a brutal sleekness to him, as if he were skin, sinew, and muscle and nothing else. A deadly weapon on legs. "I know who did this."

Ilana's stomach sank. *Crap.* Someone *did* want her dead.

"Come quickly. We must leave this speeder." Klark's mouth twisted. "The little worm despises me. He would be no sadder to see me dead than he would you." Ché's brother glanced at Linda. "And you simply because you were fool enough to come on this journey."

"Oh, boy." Getting a grip on herself, just barely— now was not the time to puddle to the floor in a quivering, sniffling mass, as much as the thought appealed—Ilana translated for Linda.

Linda grabbed her arm. "We're going with him, Ilana," the woman said in a no-arguments tone that

Ilana knew all too well. "Pardon my French, but screw the history between you two, honey. He's making nice. Take it!"

"I'm with you, Linda. I don't know what's happening, or what's going to happen, but . . . I believe him." Klark. The nut job jailed for trying to knock off her brother. Well, the *Vash* made everything complicated, and this was proof.

The women grabbed their gear and abandoned the speeder. Ilana was startled to see a pilot in the seat when they entered the starfighter. The man looked worn-out and apprehensive. "Prince Klark," he said, "we are being called by one of our battleships. A flagship."

Klark lifted a brow. "My father. And brother."

Ilana's pulse surged. *Ché.*

"They moved quickly," Klark told her, as if she understood the intricacies of this unfolding plot. "Don't open communication with them. We'll leave for Chéya's Fist, as planned."

When the pilot hesitated, Klark barked, "Now, Ensign!"

"But—but they have our coordinates. They'll follow."

Klark groaned, glancing at Ilana as if looking for support in his irritation with subordinates. "Of course they'll follow. That's the point." He pointed a determined finger at the stars ahead. "Now go! We will lead them onward in a merry chase."

Linda, hugging her purse to her lap, took one of the empty seats in the fighter and buckled her seatbelt. The woman was a trouper, but Ilana had no doubt she'd be hearing about this for years. Maybe the rest of her life. Speaking of which, it'd been at least an hour since Linda had harassed her for her worst-case-scenario neuroticism. Too many far-fetched things had happened in too short a period of time for Linda to argue that philosophy. *Hah.*

Klark stayed by Ilana's side. The urgency he radiated was making her twitch. He could use one of her Valiums. He turned to her and said: "When we reach Chéya's Fist, you must marry without delay."

"What?" she blurted out in English. "Today?" *Marry? Help!* She wasn't quite ready for this.

Klark's face contorted with hatred. "Yes. Before the man who wishes to prevent the union does so. Do you understand? The longer we wait, the more likely those who wish to stop the union will do so. Your family will not be able to attend in person, but you will see their images on the comm—though we do need a B'kah witness, according to the Treatise of Trade, and I am hoping via two-way comm is sufficient." Klark looked positively frazzled. *Wedding fever.* "My family will be there, whether they realize the reason or not. The attire, the documents, the ceremonial oils—it is all in place."

"You make my wedding? You invite the guests? Choose place?" Klark Vedla, wedding planner. She had to be dreaming.

He tried to make light of her amazement. "The ceremony, if done properly, would last seven days. We don't have that luxury, I'm afraid."

"I happy, Klark," she assured him. "Very happy! I not want a week of ceremony." Shoving curls away from her forehead, she pressed one hand to her brow as she regarded the man she saw in a new light: a troubled soul, maybe, but one loyal to his brother—out of love, not obligation. "No trick?" she asked quietly.

Fluidly he brought his fist to his chest and dipped his head in the traditional show of *Vash* fealty. "You have my word, Princess."

Princess. He'd actually called her princess, a title she'd never thought she'd hear from this racist's lips. *Who's held on to more prejudice?* her conscience demanded. *You or him?* The fact that she couldn't answer the question quickly and without reservation gave her the answer. She'd been wrong on a lot of things about Ché's people. She nodded back. "Let's go to the wedding."

As the battleship approached Chéya's Fist at top speed, Ché's doubts threatened to overwhelm him. Hoe had produced proof that incriminated Klark. And yet Klark had brought the woman Hoe accused him of trying to kill . . . to Chéya's Fist. And, as if bringing Ilana to a highly guarded outpost wasn't inexplicable enough, Klark had apparently invited Ché's mother, Queen Isiqir, and his sisters, Tajha and Katjian, to join them there—and had contacted the B'kahs, inviting them, too! Security had documented all the transmissions from Klark's fighter. Ché could see their cruiser now, docked at the Fist along with Klark's stolen starfighter.

Ché's father stood beside him. "Has Hoe arrived?"

"No. I expect to hear from him soon."

"It is good, to want him here." Approval shone in his father's gaze. "I will let you handle the situation as you wish. I will intervene only if necessary."

Ché nodded. "I hope it will not come to that." If he was wrong about Hoe . . . He gave his head a curt shake. He did not want to ponder any further the lifelong loyalty and almost fatherly devotion of his advisor—and what it may have led the man to do. Patience. He must say nothing to Hoe yet. He must not give the man the motivation to flee, should he have reason to do so. Better to lure him into the net

Ché had cast. Then, if Hoe had helpers, he'd snare them as well.

And then he'd obliterate all of them.

For all its immense size, the battleship slid gracefully into its docking bay. Chéya's Fist was a military space station on the border of Eireyan space and what was once considered the "uncivilized" wasteland. The space station was rugged and spare, and filled with those who would give their lives to defend Eireya, even though the galaxy had been at peace, except for a few short periods, for over eleven thousand years. The Vedlas had learned the hard way never to let their guard down. And, yet, that was exactly what he had done, Ché thought, reflecting on the man who had deceived him.

As his father prepared for deboarding along with the councilmen, Ché's comm chimed, telling him of a private message. "Greetings, Hoe."

Hoe appeared weary. As well he should, Ché thought. "My estimated time of arrival at the Fist is point-five standard hours," the advisor said without Ché having to ask. The man then sighed deeply, and with great sadness. "Again, I am sorry for the tragedy today. Princess Ilana, she was so young. Too young to lose her life."

Ché's lip curled with malice. "I . . . find it difficult to converse on the matter." Thickness in Ché's voice came from horror, not the grief it seemed to mimic.

"Understood, my lord. We will find Prince Klark, and we will handle the matter quietly and decisively. I spoke to your father, and he agrees."

Ché sensed his father and Councilman Toren standing somewhere behind him, glaring darkly at the small comm screen. They'd approved of the trap Ché had laid for Hoe by inviting him to meet them at Chéya's Fist, and choosing not to tell him that Ilana had made it off the speeder alive. Soon they'd be able to tell by the emotions of both men, Klark and Hoe, who was the one who'd meant to murder Ilana.

Ché knew. It seemed obvious. But to prove it to all, he needed this game to play out to its utter conclusion.

Ché closed the comm and shoved it into his pocket. His mouth lifted in a snarl. "Betrayal," he muttered. "It does not taste pleasant."

His father nodded in quiet empathy. "The pain is unlike any other."

Ché glowered as he tromped down the airlock and into the outpost. Ahead in the crowd of greeters, he saw a flash of wildly curly blond hair looking so vibrantly out of place. "Ilana," he murmured. In that moment, all that mattered was to touch her again, to hold her. His relief at finding her unharmed pierced him like the sharpest blade. He strode off the battleship and into the arrivals hall, where Ilana saw him striding toward her.

"Ché!" He glimpsed blue eyes that were moist with tears of joy as she ran into his arms. He hugged her back in a most un-Vedlalike fashion, gripping her close, his eyes shut, until he had breathed in her essence, pulled her into his very soul, and come alive once more.

He moved her away, his chest tight. They seemed to soak up each other's features, to the apparent delight of the surrounding Vedlas and staff. To them, his "possession" of Ilana Hamilton was quite a coup. To see her respond so favorably to him only increased family pride. And then Ché saw Klark.

Klark stood still, surrounded by guards, but without shock cuffs or any other indication that he was an escaped prisoner. Unarmed, in a space station full of loyal Vedla soldiers, there wasn't anywhere he could go. He had to have known that before coming.

Klark turned his gaze to the floor. It was as if he couldn't bring himself to look at the brother he had so disappointed.

Ché took a step toward him. "Wait." Ilana grabbed his forearms. "Remember the garden carts," she whispered desperately. "How you and Klark used to hijack them from under the gardeners' noses. You always took the blame. Even when it was Klark's idea."

"I was the older," Ché replied.

"You felt responsible."

"Why, yes."

"That's what he feels. Your brother. He's ready to take the blame for the sabotage to my speeder because he feels responsible for what he did to Ian and Tee'ah."

Great Mother. Ilana must have thought he was about to berate Klark, and felt compelled to defend him. Ché pressed his lips together to keep the love and relief he felt from showing in his face. That the woman he wanted to marry had somehow made peace with his brother, a man she had every right to despise, gave him the personal proof he needed: Hoe was the traitor. Hoe was the one who didn't want him to marry Ilana. And had tried to murder her to prevent it.

A commotion in the big hall announced another arrival. Ché thought—and hoped—it was his advisor, but a hulking man tramped inside with a copper-haired Earthwoman.

"I don't believe it." Ilana squinted at the pair. "It's my father's bodyguard. Muffin!" She waved.

The big man whirled in her direction and closed the distance between them in a few long strides. He shook his head in incredulity. "I chased you here all the way from Earth," he said in English.

"He did," said his companion, rolling her eyes.

"Earth?" Ilana demanded. "Nobody told me. Why were you there?"

"To guard you from Prince Ché."

Ché and Ilana glanced at each other in surprise. "I would say that your mission was a failure, then," Ché said with good humor.

Muffin grinned. "I think not."

Ilana extended her hand to the bodyguard's companion. "Hi. I'm Ilana."

The woman smiled. "Yeah. I know. Copper Kaminski," she said, and then the women shook hands in Earth-dweller fashion.

Councilman Toren came forward. "Can you act as witness?" he asked Muffin. "We need a representative from the B'kahs here in person to make the binding legal. As it is, we're pushing all the rules. That one we cannot break."

Muffin squared his enormous shoulders. "I will act as the representative of the B'kahs," he proclaimed. Copper gazed up at him with admiration.

Ooh, Ilana thought. *Was this budding love?*

She heard grumbling in the crowd, and Hoe, Ché's advisor, entered the room.

Hoe looked as if he'd seen a ghost. The room went silent. He was not as adept as Ché at hiding his emotions. The advisor stopped abruptly, almost tripping over his feet as he stared at Ilana. Revulsion and shock fought for dominance over terror. "She is alive," he managed hoarsely.

The expression she saw in Ché's face broke her heart. Ché flicked a hand at the guards standing near Klark. "Arrest him."

"Yes—arrest Prince Klark," Hoe cried out. "He tried to kill the Earth princess. He—"

But the guards left Klark and swarmed around Hoe. Ché moved Ilana away from the struggle. "We picked you a princess. A *Vash* princess," Hoe yelled.

Ché walked closer to the fray. "Ilana of the B'kahs *is* a princess. To see her otherwise is an insult to our people . . . and to my judgment as your future king."

Hoe continued to spew a lifetime's worth of misogynistic, racist crap, while the stoic Vedlas encircled him, their pale eyes cold. "Take him away," Ché told the guards.

Ilana watched the scene unfold, her heart in her mouth. So, Ché's advisor had been behind what had happened. He'd been the one that had mucked up Linda's passport. As the guards led Hoe away, amazingly, the sourness of hate didn't fill her, as it had after Ian's attack. There was only a deep calm, a confidence that this time justice would be done. Gah. Maybe she was more *Vash* than she thought. Was stoicism contagious?

Ché took her arm. "He may not have acted alone. We will not know for certain until after investigation. Your safety is in jeopardy until our union is official."

Official. Union. Her heart flipped. She was getting married, here and now. She gulped, smiled. "Can I at least shower and change first?"

"I was going to ask the same of you." Ché grinned as two women approached. They were younger than Ché, and beautiful as only highborn *Vash* princesses could be. Ché's sisters, Ilana thought.

"Tajha and Katjian," Ché said with an older brother's affection. "They will help prepare you."

In the princesses' eyes, Ilana read curiosity and happiness. Yeah, they were going to be all right, she thought, wondering if they'd ever consider trading their long dresses for shorts and spikes and helping her organize a *Vash* women's soccer league.

"Come," Tajha said, smiling.

"You, too," Ilana told Linda.

"Don't worry," her assistant said. "I wouldn't miss this for the world."

One phrase kept repeating itself in Ilana's mind as the two silent, exotic women lead her from the room. *What the hell am I doing?*

Chapter Twenty-five

Ilana caught sight of herself in a mirror, and her breath caught. She looked nervous . . . and pretty. Like a bride. She gulped.

Her hair was a pile of ornate braids woven by Ché's sisters. The gown they'd brought for her was made of white silk, or something like it, and shot through with opalescent threads of every color in the rainbow. Tinted nano-computers created a three-dimensional prism effect, shimmering as she moved. The bodice was snug and modestly cut. Sleeves hugged Ilana's arms to the wrist, where they ended in a point that reminded her of the dresses she'd seen at Renaissance fairs. *Vash* modesty kept a running theme all the way to the hem of the lushly flowing skirt that swept the floor.

She'd always loved dressing up, but this was the pinnacle of primping.

She did her best to glide into the room where she would bind herself to Prince Ché Vedla for a lifetime.

Princesses glided, didn't they? But she felt like a fake trying, and so she simply walked slowly. Ilana's family was there, too—life-sized glowing images. Her father, Jock Hamilton, returned her smile, his eyes deep blue as he nodded. Uncharacteristic emotion tugged at his features. To his right stood Rom, Ian and Tee'ah, and her mother. "Mom," Ilana mouthed, with a little girl's look-at-me excitement.

Jas was dry-eyed until her gaze met Ilana's. Then her eyes filled with tears. "Love you," she mouthed back.

Copper clung to Muffin's arm, and Ilana winked at her. Then Ilana moved forward, her hands at her sides. *Vash* brides didn't carry flowers, and she missed having something in her nervous hands. But there'd been no time to ask for any of the few traditions she might have wanted.

Ian smiled at her. She quirked her mouth right back at him and formed the words: *I won*.

And he shot back: *Wrong*.

The bet, it seemed, was in dispute.

Then she saw Ché. He moved to the center of a small dais. Dressed in *Vash* royal ceremonial regalia, he looked like a stranger. His severe uniform was midnight-black with dark silver trim, with a tight, high collar, accentuating his sculpted features and making him appear merciless and cold.

Was she crazy? What was she doing?

Maybe this was a trick, and Klark was in on it. Get the B'kah princess into the Vedla family. Lock her away and make heirs with her to increase Vedla influence. She could almost imagine the maniacal laughter following Ché's pronouncement of that scheme.

Her heart thumped harder. Her palms sweated,

and she grasped the fabric of her skirt to keep her hands from shaking.

Ché extended his hand to help her step up to the dais. His hand was cool, this stranger's. He led her to a small altar where bowls of oil sat, heated by flames to release their scents into the air.

She wondered if the castle tower that would become her virtual prison would be comfortable. She wondered also how long it would take to grow her hair long enough to play Rapunzel and escape—

"Ilana," Ché admonished under his breath. "Thought warp."

Busted. She winced sheepishly.

Ché pulled the top of his pocket away from his hip just far enough for her to peek inside. A smell reached her nose.

It was the unmistakable odor of nacho cheese.

"Corn Nuts?" she whispered back.

He looked smug. "I thought we might need them for this."

Their backs were to the guests, who thus couldn't see her struggling not to giggle and cry at the same time. "Yeah. I could use one."

He pressed one into her palm, took one for himself, and they furtively crunched as the *Vash* priest conferred with the Vedla elders. Then, as Ilana wiped salt from her palms, Ché reached behind the altar. Another surprise, she thought, falling in love with him all over again as they stood there, stood before the guests in a room with fortified alloy walls that resembled a bunker more than it did a church.

He produced a bouquet of flowers. Fresh flowers. Her throat squeezed so tight that saying anything would be hopeless. But she had no doubt that Ché could read the astonished gratitude in her eyes. She grasped the bouquet. "They look like little bells," she whispered, inhaling the delicate, unfamiliar scent. The blooms reminded her of diaphanous lilies of the valley. "Eireyan?"

"They grow in the shaded hollows of the hills above the palace."

"Take me there," she said huskily. "First thing."

"That is where I will marry you in Earth fashion," he promised.

He grasped her hand in his, and they turned to the waiting Vedlas and B'kahs who had assembled to watch a mighty and much-hoped-for alliance form between their two families. Their meddling and advice echoed in the heads of the bride and groom:

—*Now you won't have to attend the B'kah wedding, looking . . . so alone, Ché. You'll arrive with your new queen on your arm, the most eligible of all the princesses, and the B'kah wedding will be a much happier occasion for all.*

—*Ilana, I think if you ever opened up, let a man inside that stubborn, smart-ass head of yours, you might be surprised and like it.*

—*To the outside, it would appear to be the ideal solution to an embarrassing problem. Me, the spurned prince, marrying before the upstart Earth-dweller crown prince does. And not only that, taking his very sister as my bride, thus uniting the B'kahs and the Vedlas.*

As the abbreviated wedding ceremony began, Ché and Ilana looked at each other and smiled. *Us, pawns of the Federation?* she thought, gazing up at her prince. *I don't think so.*

As if knowing her thoughts, Ché bent his head to murmur in her ear, "The joke, my love, is on them."

Epilogue

Prince Ché Vedla strode down the center of the wide hallway, his capes swirling behind him. His black boots thumped solidly on a gleaming floor—polished stone that threw his looming reflection back to him. He regarded the image a curious detachment, thinking that this was how he'd always pictured himself as a man: powerful, respected. A political leader. Ché was not yet at the top of his game, but he was well on his way. In only a few standard years, his generation had taken the Great Council by storm with ideas that would pull the *Vash Nadah* into the future—many of them kicking and screaming.

"Suck it up or leave." Ché cracked a smile and imagined the expressions that would have appeared on the faces of the dour, elderly councilmen he'd met with tonight if he had followed Ilana's advice. A chuckle escaped him and he shook his head. That was precisely why *he* was the one in the family who handled political mediation, and Ilana . . . well, she

tackled diplomacy of a different sort. But however unconventional, Ilana's contributions to their society were no less important.

It was for that reason that he did not wish to be late. He increased his pace. No, not tonight of all nights when the future wobbled in a delicate balance. What was about to transpire might very well determine its course.

His personal future.

He, one of the richest men alive, heir to the longest known unbroken line of kings, did not wish to spend the eve of his third wedding anniversary—a celebration that was so very important to his Earth-born bride—in the "dog house."

Ché turned the corner and headed into the buzz of activity outside the Grand Parlor. A red carpet sliced across the expanse of pure white stone. It formed a path for hundreds of invited guests, many of them celebrities from Earth, funneling them into the theater for the premiere of SILF Filmwork's first Federation film.

Ché halted, scanning the vast room. Some guests he recognized as studio heads, actors, and directors from past meetings arranged by Ilana. Others were *Vash* dignitaries. Ah, and there were Ilana's colleagues: Linda, Flash, Slavica, Leslie. Yes, and his brother Klark, too, who like the guests themselves, was a study in contrasts, dressed in the traditional Vedla way as he sipped from a glass filled with an Earth concoction called a "martini."

In the sea of faces, Ché found Ilana's immediately. He nodded, pleased, as she smiled back, extending one arm, her fingers wriggling. A flush of pure pleasure warmed him, and he began to stride toward her. They hadn't lost that special ability to find each other in a crowd, or that spark of recognition on an elemental level when their gazes met, a spark that had flared from the moment they first saw each other. It had not dimmed, that fire. And it only confirmed that he'd done the right thing when he'd listened to the rogue in him and decided on a trip to Earth rather than an arranged marriage.

Ché disappeared into the crowd, moving past strangers and associates, staff and Earth celebrities, shaking those hands extended toward him, returning myriad greetings and niceties, smiling for photos and holo-images and news cameras with none of the impatience he felt trying to reach his wife. As he closed on her, his chest clenched at her beauty. Ilana's long black dress hugged her curves. Her hair and eyes and the sea-hued jewels he'd bought her for this special night, which she now wore around her neck, glowed in contrast. This was her night, he thought. He would make it one to remember.

Before she had the chance to greet him, he swept one hand behind her head, pulling her into a kiss. Pleased murmurs rumbled all around them; cameras illuminated the scene. Ché pretended nothing existed but the two of them, as he often did in a life that demanded incalculable amounts of his time.

As he moved away, he let his fingertips drag down her throat. "Luscious . . ." he whispered huskily into her ear, noting smugly that she reacted with a shiver of delight. She might be his independent, ambitious, activist wife, but he could still turn her into putty.

They moved apart but remained close. "Congratulations," he told her as they posed for photos. "You have assembled an impressively eclectic crowd."

Ilana grinned. "Yeah, well. Who would have thought I'd be such a good ambassador?"

"A talent needed by a Minister of Federation and Hollywood Affairs."

For once, Ilana didn't scoff at her official title. She slipped her hand into his and gave his fingers a squeeze, smiling at those gathering around them. Ché heard the laughter of children, and he turned to find the source of the sound. "We even have a contingent from Thorme in attendance," he noted. A large, gregarious group from a planet so few ever left included Muffin, the former B'kah bodyguard, his Earth-born wife Copper and their young family. "How they created so many children in such a short a time, I can't help but wonder," Ché commented.

"How?" Ilana laughed, glancing up at him. "I think you know." Her cheeks were aglow and her eyes mischievous. She looked as if she were about to say something more but changed her mind.

He watched her warily—he knew her too well to believe everything she left unsaid was insignificant. But she diverted his attention by tugging on his hand. The crowd was filing into the brand-new Vedla Theater. "Come on," she said, leading him toward the red carpet. "It's showtime."

Ché woke in his royal bedchamber with the warm, nude body of his lover held in his arms. They'd slept as one, limbs twined, hearts beating in unison.

A breeze fresh off the sea flooded the room. Ché pulled sheets of red Nandan silk higher to shield bare skin from damp, almost chilly air. As he did so, a suntanned, long-fingered hand slid up his thigh to his waist. "Good morning, luscious," he murmured into a mop of fragrant, bleached-blond hair tousled from a blistering round of late-night lovemaking.

Something between a grunt and a sigh met his greeting. Though they'd been exhausted upon returning to their bedchamber after the successful premiere, their celebratory mood had given them energy they didn't think they'd have. "It's not every day that you live your dream," Ilana had reasoned, eagerly coaxing him to the limits of his sexual stamina.

Now, Ché watched with amused interest as she scratched her fingernails down his chest and over the muscles on his abdomen. The teasing touches brought an aching, sweet heat to his loins, and a need for completion that he satisfied immediately by rolling Ilana beneath him and thrusting deep. "Wait," she protested breathlessly. "I have a present for you."

"Ah, but you have already given me your greatest gift. The gift of your woman's body."

Ilana snorted and then laughed. "Once a Vash, always a Vash. . . ."

Ché plunged deeper and remained there, drawing from Ilana a soft cry of pleasure. "Yes," he said roughly. "Always a Vash." He gripped her buttocks, pressing her close. "Always a Vedla."

He moved inside her, just how he knew she liked it, watching with pleasure when his wife's head fell back onto the pillow, her fingers gripping his shoulders. Then she inhaled on a hiss. "You're making this more difficult than it has to be."

He lifted his head. "Difficult?" It seemed anything but that to him.

Ilana gave him a you'll-see sigh, reached behind her head and withdrew a small silken bag from under the pillow. "I meant to give this to you last night, but we got . . . sidetracked. Before it happens again, open it."

Ché held himself still. Her knees pressed firmly against his hips as she handed him the little sack. "Here."

Supporting his weight with one elbow, still buried inside his wife's body, he took the bag. "Open it," she cajoled, tugging on the ribbon.

369

Watching her expression, he did as she asked, wondering what she had in mind. He was the one who most often gave spontaneous little gifts, not Ilana. From the silken sack, he pulled a woven object. "It is . . . a sea finch nest?" Ché glanced from the creation of straw and twigs in his palm to the smiling face of his wife.

"If only you could see your expression," she said, love shining in her eyes. At his silence, she covered his hand with hers and said, "Yes, Ché, it's a *nest.*" She waggled her brows.

The significance of the little gift exploded inside him. Nesting. She'd always called it that, the desire to have children that she'd put aside while she concentrated on her career.

She wanted to start a family. She was ready to bear his children. Joy flared inside him, chased by a sharp rush of desire. He throbbed, deep inside her body, and bit back a groan.

"I think we should start a family, Ché."

"Now?"

Ilana laughed huskily. Her warm hands cupped his buttocks as her pelvis tipped up. "Unless you want to wait. . . ."

"Wait? Hell no," he half-growled, taking her with renewed passion.

By traditional Vedla standards, this woman was totally unsuitable. An uncultured frontierswoman. Undisciplined and willful. A woman he now knew was the shining example of everything he'd ever wanted in a mate. Under an ever-changing three-dimensional holographic image of clouds drifting across a windswept sky, he made love to her, his wife, both of them intent on creating the first of a new generation of Vedlas, a brood that would bring them both joy for the rest of their lives and who, Ché suspected, would someday rock the very foundation of the *Vash Nadah*.

Of course. Ilana Hamilton B'kah Vedla always insisted on a happy ending.

☐ **YES!**

Sign me up for the Love Spell Book Club and send my
FREE BOOKS! If I choose to stay in the club, I will pay
only $8.50* each month, a savings of $6.48!

NAME: _____

ADDRESS: _____

TELEPHONE: _____

EMAIL: _____

☐ I want to pay by credit card.

☐ **VISA**   ☐ **MasterCard**   ☐ **DISCOVER**

ACCOUNT #: _____

EXPIRATION DATE: _____

SIGNATURE: _____

Mail this page along with $2.00 shipping and handling to:
Love Spell Book Club
PO Box 6640
Wayne, PA 19087
Or fax (must include credit card information) to:
610-995-9274
You can also sign up online at **www.dorchesterpub.com**.
*Plus $2.00 for shipping. Offer open to residents of the U.S. and Canada only.
Canadian residents please call 1-800-481-9191 for pricing information.
If under 18, a parent or guardian must sign. Terms, prices and conditions subject to
change. Subscription subject to acceptance. Dorchester Publishing reserves the right
to reject any order or cancel any subscription.